Sept. 1986

To my precious
friend, Rita,
from Patti Welles

The dedication in
this book is the
most and possibly
only interesting
thing in it ! !

THE GHOST
OF S.W. 1

ALSO BY PATRICIA WELLES

THE GHOST OF S.W.1

by Patricia Welles

DONALD I. FINE, INC. NEW YORK

ACKNOWLEDGMENTS

I would like to thank the many people who gave me first-hand ghost stories, in particular Joan Langdale, Berthe Alton, Mrs. Barkhat-Ram, John Stevenson, Anne Wolley Dod, Charles Robinson and grateful thanks to Mary Saunders Burton, who lent me the flat from which the ghost sprang. I dedicate this novel to Gita Raymer.

—Patricia Welles
London, 1985

"The particular thing to learn is how to get into the crack between the worlds and how to enter the other world . . . there is a place where the two worlds overlap. The crack is there."

—The Teachings of Don Juan

Chapter 1

"WHEN I CAME HERE IN 1946 FROM LAHORE, I HAD a small house in Deanery Mews by the Dorchester Hotel. During the war the American army used the house to entertain girls. There were still beds all over the place. A Scots girl was living with me then as a kind of housekeeper-companion. One evening I was going up the stairs. As I turned at the landing, I felt something pass me. A few nights later I told the Scots girl I thought there was a ghost in the house. Oh, yes, she said, she had felt the same presence. It was a woman. We both knew it without questioning."

Mrs. Patel-Ram sighed, remembering. She put her delicately veined hand to her silver hair and smiled at Lavinia Cross, who was fiddling with the tape recorder.

Glancing up, Lavinia returned the smile. Although Lavinia herself didn't believe in ghosts or the supernatural, she found the subject fascinating. Still, one didn't expect to sit in an opulently appointed flat on Morpeth Terrace and listen to a woman of breeding discuss ghost stories. Never would she have thought that this elegant woman not only believed in ghosts but actually claimed to have seen them.

Well, Lavinia thought, this was what she was here for, and she was determined to maintain her objectivity about the subject.

"The gas man came to the house one day and said, 'My, how things change...,'" Mrs. Patel-Ram continued in her cultivated

Dublin accent, a charming contrast to the turquoise sari she wore. "Then he told me that a young girl had burned to death in there." "How awful," Lavinia said, "but true to form. Ghosts are usually associated with tragedy. Did this one try to get your attention?" "Oh, no," Mrs. Patel-Ram said quickly, almost as if she were defending the ghost's appearance. "She was no problem at all."

Lavinia liked the older woman very much. She had first met Mrs. Patel-Ram years ago through Mary Saunders, an English girl she'd made friends with when she'd spent her junior year studying in Paris. Although in her early seventies, Mrs. Patel-Ram had hardly changed, and Lavinia thought it a nice coincidence that they should meet again. Mrs. Patel-Ram was of Irish descent but had married a Pakistani, and subsequently lived for many years in Lahore. She had a son, Marcus, whom Lavinia had met when he had been in New York on business. Now, Mrs. Patel-Ram lived only a few minutes away from Mary's flat, where Lavinia was staying during her assignment.

"I do like the way you look now," Mrs. Patel-Ram said, changing the subject. "Your hair used to be long, but this is much prettier."

Lavinia smiled, shaking her short, blond, curly hair, which she'd had cut just before leaving New York. She had wanted to make some changes in her life, and a different hairstyle seemed a good beginning. She had quite unintentionally fallen into a solitary life, not keeping up with old friends, going out only occasionally. She had even stopped eating and lost a lot of weight. She knew, of course, it was all a result of the end of her affair with the Hungarian, as she called him, a relationship that had gone on for far too long and then ended abruptly.

Finally she had pulled herself together—more by sheer willpower than anything else—and landed a plum assignment as a researcher for an ABC documentary on ghosts and the supernatural. Now, at thirty-four, she felt her career as a television researcher was back on track. And if the producer liked her work, there was the possibility of a regular staff position with the network. Although freelancing gave her a certain amount of freedom in determining her work schedule, it didn't offer much security or the chance to move up the career ladder. She had a lot at stake, but she felt more than ready to take on the challenge of this assignment.

And to be in England! For the first time in a very long time she felt happy with her life.

"In fact," Mrs. Patel-Ram said, refilling Lavinia's tea cup, "you are looking rather lovely, my dear. Marcus will be so pleased to see you when he's back from the Continent at the end of the month."

"Thank you," Lavinia said, pleased with the compliment. "I'm looking forward to seeing him again." Although still thin for her five-foot-six frame, she had more than recovered her appetite and she was taking good care of herself, doing Yoga each morning, stretching, bending and meditating to keep fit. Lavinia Cross had a kind of twenties, silent-screen beauty with a lovely, gentle face, clear blue eyes surrounded by a dark fringe of lashes, and full lips. The cleft in her chin hinted at a certain determination, or stubbornness. She was used to men deciding they were in love with her and wooing her with flowers and dinner invitations. Somehow she always fell for the rogues—the ones whose escapades and schemes took up so much of her time that she inevitably neglected her own life. After this last disastrous affair with the Hungarian, she had decided to focus on herself and her work for a while.

Now, anxious to continue with the interview, Lavinia re-checked the tape recorder, then moved closer to Mrs. Patel-Ram, whose voice tended to soften as the afternoon wore on.

"Are you ready for another story? And perhaps more of these nice French biscuits?"

"As many stories as you wish to tell," Lavinia said. The more Mrs. Patel-Ram talked, the more certain Lavinia was that she would look fabulous on television. She hoped she could convince Mrs. Patel-Ram to agree to a filmed interview.

"I'll tell you a story from India, about a Nepalese princess. She was a great friend of mine, a child-widow who was drinking herself to death at twenty-eight, poor woman. She had become very ill and was near the end. According to Indian custom, they must not die downstairs. They will do anything to prevent that from happening. I had to go to Jaipur with my husband, but before I left, the princess asked me to speak to her brothers. For some reason she was worried that they wouldn't respect the custom. I went to them and begged them, please, to let her die upstairs. They promised me they would."

Mrs. Patel-Ram paused and shifted her weight in the chair, seeming a bit disturbed at the memory.

"I went to Jaipur," she continued, "and that night I could not sleep. At twelve o'clock I woke up. The princess was standing at the end of my bed. We just looked at each other. The next morning my husband and I went camel riding; when I got back to the hotel there was a telegram which read, 'Sister died at midnight last night.'"

"That is what you would call an astral visitation, correct?" Lavinia asked. "If, in fact, she were still alive when she came to you. I've read many accounts of the bereaved seeing someone immediately after death, too."

"Yes, it is rather commonplace," Mrs. Patel-Ram said. She smoothed the sari around her. "And she continued to visit me, my dear. I was very distressed. Clearly her soul was not at peace. Finally I discussed the matter with the maharishi, who offered to take me to his guru. The guru spoke with me at some length about the princess and our friendship. He assured me she would never come again. She never did. I later learned that her brothers had brought her downstairs to die. I never knew why. But she had come to me because her funeral rites had not been done properly. We cannot always explain human behavior, you know. Sometimes it's easier to understand ghosts. The princess's brothers broke their promise to me and to their own Hindu tradition."

"She was a purposeful ghost, the kind who goes about her business, like the girl who was burned," said Lavinia, impressed by the sincerity of the older woman's story. "She didn't need to directly attract your attention. I've also read of instances where ghosts are quite insistent in making contact with this side."

"I don't know," Mrs. Patel-Ram said, "but it was very distressing." She stopped, lost in her thoughts for a moment, then gazed affectionately at Lavinia.

"Are you comfortable in Mary Saunders's flat? You could always stay here."

"Oh, thank you," Lavinia said. "But I'm very comfortable there. It's charming."

They chatted for a while as they sipped tea and ate the biscuits, then Lavinia excused herself and left. She was eager to keep to her schedule. She wanted to transcribe the tape and type up her notes from her visit with Mrs. Patel-Ram, and she had several leads to follow up for other interviews. And she still had not quite unpacked one suitcase. . . .

Walking along Vauxhall Bridge Road, Lavinia decided to do some quick grocery shopping on her way back to Mary's flat on Belgrave Road. Belgrave Road stretched from St. George's Square to Buckingham Palace Road, and Mary's flat was closer to St. George's Square. Once an elegant, cobblestoned street, it was now dotted with cheap hotels and had a slightly shabby look to it. Lavinia knew that on a similar street in New York she might be worried about her safety. But this was London, and her surroundings seemed picturesque and benign. The attractive façades of the old Georgian buildings had been preserved, and Mary's flat was well out of sight of the hotels.

Her apartment was one of fourteen in the building, formerly the private home of a well-to-do family. The place was small but cozy, with two terraces and a lovely spiral staircase that led up to the bedroom.

As she had expected during the summer months, the small market closest to the flat was crowded with tourists. Squeezing her way down the aisles, she overheard conversations in Italian, French, Spanish and several other languages she couldn't identify. Without realizing it, she smiled happily, feeling less like a foreigner. She wasn't here merely to see the sights and move on. She belonged here.

"Good afternoon. It's Lavinia, isn't it?"

Startled, Lavinia looked up to see Paul Chamberlain, her upstairs neighbor.

"Hi," she said, smiling. Paul was the typically polite, reserved Englishman, but she had nevertheless learned from their first meeting over drinks shortly after she'd moved into Mary's flat that he was forty and divorced. A graduate of Oxford, he was a lawyer whose obvious breeding and background were complemented by

15

his charm and intelligence. Although he was not conventionally handsome—"interesting looking" had been Lavinia's first thought—he had wonderfully expressive, penetrating brown eyes that seemed to convey much more than he actually said. She saw in them an intensity that his personality belied.

Although Lavinia had liked him immediately and felt that the attraction was mutual, she had warned herself against anything more than friendship. She had a deadline to meet, not to mention her self-imposed caution about men. She certainly didn't want a repeat of her protracted—and ultimately painful—relationship with the mad Hungarian.

"I haven't seen you in a while," Lavinia said. "And now we meet in the aisles of Tesco Market, of all places."

"I see you're stocking up on provisions," said Paul, glancing at the jumble of canned goods, chicken and fresh fruits and vegetables in her wire basket. "Mmm, those Cadbury chocolate biscuits are my favorites." He smiled.

"You'll have to come share them with me at tea some afternoon after I've settled in." The words were out of her mouth before she could think about them. Well, he seemed to be a very sweet man, and there was no harm in having him as a friend.

"I'd love to," Paul said immediately. "How is your research going? Met up with any fascinating ghosts?"

Lavinia couldn't tell whether he was mocking the subject or just being humorous. "My work's coming along fine," she replied, ignoring his slightly cynical tone. "I've just come from interviewing someone who gave me a couple of really terrific ghost stories."

Paul followed her down the narrow aisle. "Surely you don't believe in all that," he said. "To be frank, I don't go in for all that supernatural nonsense."

"Then I guess I won't be getting any ghost stories from you."

"No, none from me." He looked slightly embarrassed as she glanced over her shoulder at him.

"Lavinia..." he began, then stopped.

"Yes, what is it?" Maybe, she thought, he was covering up something. She knew from experience that some people, more often men than women, were reluctant to talk about their encounters with ghosts. They were usually the same people who thought that you had to be crazy to see one. But she also knew from her research that it was the eminently sane, rational folk who most frequently had experiences with seeing ghosts.

"My mother," Paul said. "Well . . . she's been involved somewhat with ghosts, that sort of thing."

He grinned suddenly, revealing straight, white teeth. Perhaps he'd been teased about his mother and her involvement with the supernatural, whatever it might be.

"You could meet her, if you like," he said slowly, as if coming to a decision. "I wasn't going to get into this with you but I'm sure she would have plenty to tell you. She's deeply involved with the paranormal. Personally I think it's absurd."

"Do you?"

"Oh, yes, definitely," Paul said, choosing a loaf of whole-meal bread from the bread rack.

"I see. I'll have to remember that." Was he implying that he thought her research was silly? If he did, he could consider any possibility of a friendship ended, right now.

Lavinia could not have guessed how reluctant Paul was to discuss the subject of the occult or how dismayed he'd been to learn of the assignment that had brought her to London.

He was sick of anything to do with the occult, having had it foisted on him since childhood. But ever since she had knocked on his door to introduce herself, Paul had found himself fascinated by this very attractive, obviously intelligent and independent woman.

"Does your mother live in a haunted house?" Lavinia said, teasing him.

"Certainly not." Paul wasn't the least bit amused by any of his mother's beliefs or, worse, by the thought that what Lavinia was suggesting probably wasn't far from the truth. Lady Chamberlain lived in a large manor house near Seven Oaks, Kent. While Paul thought the notion of a "haunted" house ridiculous, he had to admit there was a curious aura about the place that he could never quite explain.

"Too bad," Lavinia said, wondering why he sounded so offended. "I would love to find someone who actually lives in a house they believe to be haunted and who would be willing to have a television crew come in."

"You'll have to find someone else, I'm afraid." Perhaps he should not have suggested a meeting with his mother.

They took their places in the checkout line, where they waited for a few minutes without speaking. As they walked out onto Denbigh High Street, Paul insisted on carrying her bag of groceries despite her protests that she could manage. He was intrigued by her assertiveness and open manner. Was that typically American, he wondered, or just her way?

"You're staring at me," she said.

"Oh, sorry."

Paul had been lost in a fantasy in which he'd thrown down the grocery bags, wrapped his arms around her and was kissing her passionately. Lavinia was so bloody attractive. He thought she liked him, but she was oddly elusive, as if she were reluctant to be as friendly and warm as she normally might be. Paul found this puzzling, since women generally responded to him.

Since his divorce several years earlier, Paul had had his choice of women. He was a likeable, bright, appealing man whose self-assured manner reflected his success as a criminal lawyer in the Treasury Counsel. He enjoyed sports (he was still tops at cricket and squash), the theater, good food and wine. But he was never as intrigued with the women he dated as they were with him. Maybe he was still smarting from the fact that his wife had left him for another man. Or perhaps he was reacting to having grown up with a mother who, for all her weird ideas about the occult, had an unusually lively, open mind about people and ideas.

He'd been thinking about Lavinia since the day they'd met, had intended to call and invite her to dinner and was delighted to have bumped into her at the grocery shop. Perhaps what he was sensing was shyness. It was so hard to tell with Americans, especially American women. He hoped he hadn't insulted her by not taking her work more seriously.

"What makes you so interested in parapsychology, anyway?" His words came out more harshly than he had wanted, but he couldn't help wondering why this woman couldn't be interested in art history, politics, fashion . . . anything but the supernatural.

"I told you that it's a job assignment," Lavinia said, "but I *am* finding it intriguing. I have always been fascinated by those things that can't be explained. But I've never seen a ghost myself, if that's what you're wondering."

"Of course not," Paul said. If only, he thought, he could say the same about his mother. She loved Ouija boards, seances, anything that wasn't scientific. She could put herself into a trance in five seconds and claimed she could contact spirits of the departed. She adored the idea of someone's sending her a memo from the great beyond. . . .

"Still, I think it's important to keep an open mind," Lavinia said. "Although I must admit, I probably wouldn't take it all quite so seriously if I hadn't been assigned to this subject. I've done enough research now to wonder if there isn't something to it."

"I'm sure you're right," Paul said, "in keeping an open mind. Anyway, you and my mother would get along just fine. She's a medium, you know."

"Why didn't you tell me that before?" Surely he should have realized she would be interested in that sort of information.

"I try to forget," he said, laughing. "Actually I meant to, the next time I saw you."

"Does your mother see into the future?"

"I suppose that's part of what mediums do, isn't it?" Was it destiny that he meet a woman who was involved with this sort of thing? He wasn't even sure if he believed in destiny. . . . "I'll take you to visit her, if you like. It's not far. A half-hour from Victoria by train. When would you like to go?"

Lavinia paused and thought for a moment. "Sunday," she said.

As they turned up Belgrave Road, Lavinia was momentarily blinded by the sun, which shone directly into her eyes. She felt dizzy all of a sudden and reached for Paul's arm to steady herself.

"What's the matter?" he asked, noticing how pale she'd become.

Lavinia shielded her eyes with her hand. A cloud seemed to be hanging in the street, blocking out the sun's rays. Rain seemed imminent. Gazing down the length of Belgrave Road, she saw a man on horseback approaching them at a fast gallop. She pulled Paul out of the way. As the man raced past them she noticed that he was wearing some sort of uniform that didn't look familiar.

"Are you all right?" Paul asked.

"Yes, of course," she said. The cloud had disappeared. The sky had returned to its original brilliance.

"I'm sorry," she said, "but I honestly thought he was going to plow into us."

"You thought *who* was going to plow into us?"

"The man on horseback. My God, he flew right past us."

How embarrassing. Paul had been so caught up in his daydreams about her that he had completely missed whatever she had seen.

"Didn't he look rather old-fashioned?" Lavinia asked. "Was that uniform what the guards wear at Buckingham Palace?"

"I'm sorry, I really wasn't looking."

They walked the rest of the way home, and Paul got out his key.

"Are you sure you're all right? It's such a warm day for June. Maybe what you could use is a good stiff drink."

"No, thanks. I'm okay, really. I just feel slightly queasy. It's nothing to worry about."

"Let me take your shopping up for you," Paul offered. He had been looking forward to continuing their conversation over a cool drink.

Lavinia smiled as if she were reading his mind.

"Really, I can manage. But you must come for a drink soon."

Paul waited at the door to Mary's flat as Lavinia got out her key and turned the Chubb lock.

"What did you mean about the man looking old-fashioned?" he asked, hoping to prolong the conversation.

"He looked out of place on Belgrave Road. Now that I think about it," she said with a laugh, "he looked Victorian. But then, so much of London looks Victorian to me."

Paul nodded politely. Since he hadn't seen the man, there was nothing more he could say.

"Don't forget Sunday," Lavinia said. "Around two?"

"Oh, yes, absolutely. I'll ring up my mother. We'll have tea with her. She'll be delighted."

"See you then," Lavinia said, closing the door.

She put the groceries away, hoping the dizziness would go away. But still not feeling quite herself, she decided to lie down before she got to the tape recorder and the work that awaited her. Just as she closed her eyes and was beginning to relax, she heard a noise coming from the direction of the terrace. She glanced outside. Nobody was there, of course. She closed her eyes again, but now the room seemed stuffy. Lavinia got up and opened the terrace door so that a light breeze wafted through the living room. She lay down again on the couch, trying to relax. Not even her meditation technique would work. She thought she heard a noise coming from the terrace.... Footsteps? Impossible.

Reluctantly, she got up and walked outside. The terrace was empty, as she expected. Could she be hearing things? And why hadn't Paul seen the man on horseback? It was hardly the sort of thing one could miss. Maybe he was right... all she needed was a good, stiff drink.

Lady Chamberlain's manor house was set on fourteen acres of beautifully landscaped gardens. The manor house itself was two hundred years old and was filled with priceless antique furniture.

"My dear girl," Lady Chamberlain said warmly, rising to greet Lavinia as her butler, Derek, ushered them into the music room. In one corner was a harpsichord she regularly played in the evening. Next to it was a handmade virginal that she played in the afternoon.

"Paul has said delightful things about you," Lady Chamberlain said. "I'm so glad to meet you." She clasped Lavinia's hands between her two.

Lavinia wondered if she were dressed properly for Sunday tea with a Lady. Although titles did not impress her, Lady Chamberlain did. It was not every day she got the chance to meet a medium.

In contrast to the room's elegance, Lady Chamberlain was wearing seersucker slacks, a blue silk blouse that was torn at the collar and gym shoes, or plimsolls, as the English called them. Several gold bangle bracelets covered each of her wrists, and she wore antique-looking gold hoop earrings.

A true eccentric, Lavinia thought as she sat down in a magnificent tapestried chair and accepted a small glass of sherry from Lady Chamberlain.

"I understand you are interested in ghosts," Lady Chamberlain said somewhat breathlessly. "Of course I am, too. We have this in common, Paul told me."

She smiled up at Lady Chamberlain who, like her son, was short. She wore her burnished auburn hair on top of her head in a bun, probably the way she had worn it for the last forty years.

"I've got some stories for you. I have many, actually, but we'll start with Grannie—all right, darling?" She looked at Paul but didn't wait for an answer. "There have always been unusual happenings in my family," Lady Chamberlain added.

"I thought we would have tea first, Mother," Paul said. His nervous manner made Lavinia feel awkward. She didn't want to be a source of conflict. But then Paul smiled at his mother, dispelling her misgivings.

"Yes, darling," Lady Chamberlain said, immediately ringing for the butler. "We, or rather I, can talk while you munch." She laughed merrily.

The butler offered Lavinia a large silver tray of delicious-looking little sandwiches. "Cucumber, marmite and watercress," explained Lady Chamberlain. She poured tea for her guests and herself, then settled herself comfortably.

"To my knowledge, everything I'm going to tell you is true," Lady Chamberlain began. "Did you bring your tape recorder?" she interrupted herself.

Lavinia nodded and switched on the machine.

"I know you're doing some research for the telly, so go ahead, it's all right to tape me. I sound a little like the queen when I'm recorded but don't hold it against me." Her booming laugh filled the elegant sitting room. Lady Chamberlain certainly wasn't what Lavinia had expected.

"This poor, unfortunate boy," Lady Chamberlain said, shaking her head at her son. "He has heard my stories over and over. But you haven't. I'm not certain of all the details, because a lot happened so long ago. My maternal grandmother was a religious woman who often had vivid dreams that she would describe to us. In 1907 my Aunt Hilda, my father's sister, was seriously ill. We didn't expect her to live. One afternoon my grandmother suddenly said, 'I think I see Hilda walking across the room.' Then she added, 'She must have died.' Then my mother came down-stairs and said to Grannie, 'Who was that who just went across the hall?' But none of us had moved. Later we learned that was just when Aunt Hilda died."

"Amazing," Lavinia said. "I recently heard a very similar story from a friend of mine, Mrs. Patel-Ram. Do you know her? She lives in London."

"No," Lady Chamberlain said, "is she a medium?"

"No," Lavinia answered, "but she believes strongly in the pos-sibility of spirits."

"Unlike my skeptical son," said Lady Chamberlain, patting Paul's hand fondly. "Paul is so terribly bright, but so terribly stubborn and close-minded."

"Mother . . ." Paul protested.

"How long have you been associated with the occult?" Lavinia asked, seeing Paul's discomfort.

"I knew I had some sort of unusual power when I was a toddler. I remember my family moved to Kent, and my nanny took me out in my pram for a first look around. She walked down the road that stretched in front of the house, and when we came to the turning I said, 'No, no, go on, white gate, white gate.'"

She looked at Lavinia.

"Mind you, I was a toddler, just a wee girl, maybe two years old. I had no way of really knowing what was ahead, did I? Nanny proceeded, and there was a white gate. So you see I began quite early seeing things other people simply did not perceive."

"Maybe they weren't there," Paul said quietly. His mother ignored this comment, as if she were used to his disbelieving attitude.

"If you ever need any help," Lady Chamberlain said abruptly, focusing her dark eyes on Lavinia, "just come to me. You need never explain."

"Thank you," said Lavinia. Paul's mother was certainly odd, but she was obviously sincere in her beliefs. And Lavinia admired how outspoken and confident she was.

"Why would she need your help?" Paul asked, sounding more than a little exasperated.

His mother had the unfortunate habit of telling people what she divined about them, although she invariably said she could not help herself. She believed each human being had an aura, which communicated itself to her and into which her psychic powers became inextricably locked. Furthermore, she felt compelled to tell the person what she perceived about him or her, in particular those things about the personality that were hidden. Sometimes, she tuned in to something negative, and she had that expression on her face at the moment.

"I believe we need more sandwiches," Paul said, attempting to wrest attention away from his mother. "I'm still hungry, and I think Lavinia liked the marmite. Let's have more, shall we?"

Lady Chamberlain ignored her son.

"I just had a strange feeling," she said, looking at Lavinia. "Something very curious is going to happen to you—and soon. Do you feel it?"

"No, I don't." Lavinia suddenly felt frightened. What could Lady Chamberlain know about Lavinia that Lavinia did not know about herself?

"Oh, Mummy, do be quiet," Paul said, "and let's get on with tea. We don't have to be so serious, do we?"

"Stop trying to censor me, darling," Lady Chamberlain said crisply. "I feel I must tell this lovely girl that something extraordinary is about to happen to her. But it needn't be dreadful. I can see you are looking worried. Please, don't."

"I'll try not to," Lavinia said, trying to match Lady Chamberlain's amused tone of voice.

"What do you think is going to happen? Could you be more specific?

"No, it's simply a feeling. But I am almost always correct. Wait!"

She closed her eyes and went into what seemed to be a trance. In a matter of seconds her eyes were open again and she was smiling at Lavinia.

"It's about love. Yes, definitely love."

"Then it's something good?" Lavinia probed.

Lady Chamberlain closed her eyes again.

"Something good, something bad. But I don't know what precisely. It's something that will shake the very foundations of your existence."

Paul reached across to his mother and gently shook her plump arm. She was upsetting Lavinia. He could tell from the look on her face that she was much more frightened than she was letting on.

"I suppose it's just another one of your ghosts, out for revenge. Isn't that it, Mum? If you believe it."

"Believe it?" she said accusingly, "of course I believe it! It's documented, as Lavinia herself knows. We have proof. And besides, some are rather friendly creatures. Paul is exaggerating."

For a moment Lady Chamberlain and Paul exchanged angry looks, but then Paul patted his mother's arm affectionately.

"There's no need to get het up over this," he said, "even if I don't believe any of it."

"No, darling," his mother agreed. "And there's no need for you to believe it. You practice law, and that does not involve itself with the paranormal. But how dull to have it all so cut and dried."

"That's precisely why I chose it," he said, winking at Lavinia.

"Mmm, yes," Lady Chamberlain said, rising from her chair. "Now I think I would like to show Lavinia the gardens."

Lady Chamberlain guided them around the lavish grounds, showing Lavinia the stables and the four horses she kept.

"I ride every day, summer or winter, regardless of the weather," she said proudly. "Paul is, of course, also an excellent horseman. And what about you, Lavinia? Do you ride?"

"I haven't in quite a while," Lavinia replied. "I'm not sure I'd remember what to do."

"Of course you would, my dear," said Lady Chamberlain, laughing heartily. "We don't have time today, but you come visit me again—with or without my doubting son—very soon. Whether or not you want to explore the spirit world with me further, I insist that you tour our lovely Kentish countryside on horseback."

Lavinia suddenly remembered the man she'd seen riding his horse down Belgrave Road and thought briefly of telling Lady Chamberlain about him. But what was the point? What would she say to her? That it had been very hot, and that she'd been stunned when the rider had appeared out of nowhere?

"I'd love to come again, Lady Chamberlain," she said, realizing she meant it.

Paul's mother was delightful. She and her son were very similar—unpretentious, intelligent and extremely hospitable. Lavinia could see that despite their differences of opinion about ghosts and the occult, they loved each other very much. She felt very fortunate to have met two such interesting people.

Paul and Lavinia stayed for another hour chatting about the difference between English ghost encounters and American ones.

"The past is still a visible part of our present," Lady Chamberlain said, "and maybe this accounts for the abundance of ghost encounters here."

She smiled but then became serious as she launched into a short lecture on parapsychological events.

"We need more scientific evidence, I believe, to support our experiences, yet we should not fall into the trap of always trying to explain everything in the terms we know."

She looked deliberately at her son as if she were sending him a message.

"The real question," she said, turning to Lavinia, "is are ghosts proof of an afterlife? Isn't that what we all want to know?" Lady Chamberlain patted Lavinia's arm, her clinking gold bracelets breaking the silence. "Maybe you will find some answers."

"Lavinia isn't looking for answers," Paul said quickly. "She's simply conducting interviews, doing research. Isn't that right?"

"Well, I would like to know about your mother's idea of disengaging from the body."

"It's not just my idea," Lady Chamberlain said. "It's a fairly common theory. After you've read more and talked to enough people engaged in this area, you'll see what I mean. Some people think that there is an energy of some sort, an etheric body, so to speak, which can disengage itself from the physical body. Maybe we all leave our physical selves when we die. But where does the physical self go? Perhaps some of us disintegrate, but others don't. It's possible, yes?"

"Piffle," Paul said, not unkindly. "Rubbish and nonsense. And it's time to go to the train."

"Don't forget my invitation," Lady Chamberlain called, waving goodbye to them from her doorway.

On the train back to London they nibbled more of the tiny sandwiches that Paul had filched from the kitchen, and chocolate bars that his mother had handed them as they left.

"She didn't tell you the story about my cousin, Simon, did she?"

"Perhaps she wanted to save one for when I come back."

"Never fear, Lavinia," said Paul with a wry grin. "She has many, many more to tell you. And she'll take it as a promising sign that I'm becoming a believer if I tell you this story."

He looked so mischievous that Lavinia couldn't help giggling.

"You're a wonderful audience, Lavinia," said Paul. Despite his misgivings, the afternoon had been very enjoyable. He was pleased that Lavinia and his mother had gotten on so well.

"All right, let's hear about your cousin."

"When Simon was about twelve or thirteen, Mother, Simon, my aunt and some friends went to visit a historic house in Gloucestershire. It was the house where Guy Fawkes was reputed to have hatched his famous plot to blow up Parliament."

He looked at Lavinia, as if to ask whether she had heard of Guy Fawkes, the sixteenth-century English rebel.

Lavinia nodded at him to continue.

"There was an elderly caretaker-guide who escorted them around. The rooms were all empty, the windows boarded up. Simon had run ahead of the others, and then they heard him screaming that he'd seen a ghost. When they questioned him, he described a man in a Cavalier costume, complete with armor and helmet. He insisted that the man had disappeared into a wall. The caretaker said that lots of people had seen the ghost, but he was quite sure it wasn't Guy Fawkes. So there you have a mistaken identity ghost story!"

"You think it's all nonsense, don't you?" Lavinia asked. She had to admit that the green garden countryside of Kent, which she glimpsed through the train window, seemed entirely idyllic and quite removed from ghosts or even the possibility of ghosts.

"I have never found the least shred of evidence to substantiate the existence of ghosts," Paul said. "All this silliness about psychic research doesn't appear to me to be even vaguely scientific. I cannot accept that just because people claim they see ghosts, they do. Anyway, I see little point in worrying about death or an afterlife or what happens when we die. Why should I? I would rather enjoy life. Besides, if one does exist after death, then the word 'death' has no meaning."

They argued spiritedly until the train pulled into Charing Cross Station, and continued as they rode the subway to Green Park station and on to Pimlico. Paul was impressed by Lavinia's defense of the possibility that supernatural forces, beyond our cognitive understanding, could exist. As a lawyer who had often acted as prosecutor, he respected a coherent, well-spoken argument, particularly since he knew that Lavinia herself had many questions about ghosts and the occult.

"I think we should explore this over a bottle of wine and dinner," he suggested as they approached their building. "We should take some spirits to raise some spirits."

Lavinia made a face.

"Sorry, a bad pun. But let me show you that I do have some real wit," Paul said. He imagined a candlelight dinner, Lavinia's eyes sparkling at him, her beautiful soft smile. What was it about this woman? The truth was, he knew the answer. He was quite taken with the contrast between her soft, sensuous looks and her intellectual rigor and curiosity.

"I know some of the most interesting restaurants in London," he said with a smile, trying to persuade her. "Places you'd never find without an adventurous Englishman as your guide."

Lavinia was tempted to say yes, but she thought she recognized the look in Paul's eyes—the look of a man who was interested in much more than dinner and a good-night kiss. Not that she wasn't tempted by this very attractive, attentive Englishman. But somehow, she wasn't quite ready for what he had in mind—if he had in mind what she did. She laughed aloud.

"What's the joke?"

"I was just imagining what my women friends in New York would say if they knew I was turning down a dinner invitation from a very charming, straight, single man." She didn't add that she was also amused by her realization that she was very attracted to him and was doing everything she could to deny that fact. "But I really should get some work done tonight. I want to transcribe the tape of your mother."

"How unflattering. You'd rather spend the evening with my mother than with me. But I thank you for the 'very charming.' Well, perhaps some other night," Paul said, kissing her lightly on the cheek and heading upstairs.

"Great, I'd love that," Lavinia called after him. *Am I crazy?* she thought, letting herself into her apartment. *That is a very nice man. I could have left the tape for tomorrow.* She shook her head and ran her fingers through her curls. No, she decided, remembering her promise to concentrate on her work. Besides, she comforted herself as she sat down at the typewriter, she would be in London all summer. As far as she knew, Paul wasn't going anywhere. They had plenty of time to get to know each other better. She laughed again, imagining her friends' reactions to her logic, then lost herself in Lady Chamberlain's stories and comments about ghostly apparitions.

Two hours later, Lavinia looked up and saw that the light was just beginning to fade. She wandered out onto the terrace, decided that the plants looked thirsty and made several trips with the watering can until she was satisfied that Mary's geraniums, marigolds and daffodils were feeling happier.

She realized that she was hungry, too. She'd eaten quite a few marmite and cucumber sandwiches, but they were so *tiny.* She had never been able to understand the English custom of dainty tea sandwiches.

Her dinner of mushroom paté, tomato salad and Fortnum and Mason crackers looked quite elegant on Mary's sky-blue enamel tray she'd brought back from China. Lavinia poured herself a glass of chianti and went into the living room to savor the meal. The sky, framed by the terrace doors, changed from deep blue to black.

Lavinia luxuriated in the peacefulness and quiet of the hour. Her New York apartment was on the fifth floor, but it faced University Place, which was heavily trafficked. Mary's flat, facing as it did onto the garden, was well protected from street noise. Her decor also contributed to the feeling of serenity. The Laura Ashley country print fabric on the couch, the Victorian rocker and lace doilies, the Tate Gallery posters, the working fireplace with its tall oak mantle covered with Mary's collection of Victorian bibelots, the low ceiling at one end of the room—all created a coziness and warmth that bespoke calmness.

Perhaps, Lavinia reflected, it was also her state of mind that made her feel so at peace with the world. Her work was going better than she could have hoped for and was even more fascinating than she had expected. Lavinia had dreamed for a long time of writing fiction, and she was aware, as she organized the material she was collecting, that someday she might be able to work some of it into a novel. "If I don't become an important producer," she said aloud, enjoying her fantasies about where this work could take her.

Yes, she thought, the summer would be well spent. In addition to her research, she planned to explore as much of London as possible. The London Tourist Board offered wonderful walks around the city, and she had heard there was marvelous outdoor theater and concerts in Regent's Park. It would be even nicer to attend all the events with an interesting companion... Paul Chamberlain. There was no question but that she liked him. Maybe it was time to make room again for someone in her life.

She tried to imagine herself in bed with Paul. And almost immediately stood up to break the spell she had created. She had no trouble envisioning Paul's arm around her, kissing her, caressing her tenderly. And Lady Chamberlain had said something about change... Was she truly being psychic or was she putting in a plug for her son?

A cool breeze was blowing in through the terrace door, and Lavinia suddenly felt chilly. She shut the door, switching on two of the lamps, and considered inviting Paul down for a drink. Dialing his number, she was almost relieved when there was no answer. Just as well. She didn't want to turn to him when she wasn't sure what she wanted. Besides, she was tired and not in the mood to even think about whether or not ghosts existed. If only he didn't get quite so irritated about the subject. Still, he must have had his fill of the supernatural as he was growing up. It couldn't have been easy for a proper, upper-class English boy whose mother was as offbeat as Lady Chamberlain.

Her Aunt Jane, who had raised Lavinia after her parents had died when she was four, had told her that although her mother and father no longer existed as living beings in this world, their spiritual presence remained. Aunt Jane had even tried to contact Lavinia's parents through a spirtualist friend of hers. But she had never attempted to persuade Lavinia of the possibility of a ghostly afterlife.

Suddenly tears filled Lavinia's eyes and came tumbling down her cheeks. She was overwhelmed by sadness. Yes, she thought, I am still grieving for my parents whom I don't even remember. Aunt Jane had shown her pictures. Her mother was a tall woman with dark hair and a big smile. In every photo she was smiling, holding her husband's hand or hugging him, or kissing her small baby, Lavinia. Aunt Jane said her father was a terrific raconteur who was always the last to leave parties. He was a generous man, never lacking in friends.

She seldom thought of her parents or how they died tragically in a car crash. But now the memories made her very tired. She was about to go upstairs for a bath and a good night's sleep when something attracted her attention to the low end of the living room. Reluctantly, she glanced over, feeling that she was somehow being forced to focus on something she did not wish to see.

There was a gray shadow. A shape. She looked harder. She

was not the sort of person who "saw things." And yet, there against the wall was the definite outline of a man—very tall, long-legged, broad-shouldered. The outline seemed to grow larger and larger until his arms, legs and head shook violently, like a person having a seizure.

"Oh, God," Lavinia said hoarsely, frozen with terror. She stood motionless, watching the bizarre gyrations. Abruptly the shape disappeared, and she was staring helplessly at a blank wall.

"I'm inventing my own ghost," she said aloud as she walked upstairs. Perhaps this was her way of forging a link to the paranormal. She wished she could tell Paul. He would be objective, could explain why she thought she'd seen a figure on the wall.

Drawing a hot bath, she was struck with the knowledge that she damned well had seen the outline of a man. She had not invented it.

She mused on it as she bathed, not knowing quite what to make of the experience. Then, as the immediacy of the experience faded, she was less and less convinced that she had really seen something. She climbed into bed to watch the late News, until she finally fell into a dreamless sleep.

Chapter 2

I N THE MORNING LAVINIA USUALLY HAD HER BREAKFAST of café au lait, toast and marmalade on the downstairs terrace. As she ate, she would go through her mail, read the London Times and figure out her schedule for the day. But the morning after she saw the figure on the wall, she breakfasted at McDonald's instead.

Eating fast food made her feel guilty. Eggburgers were not the most nutritious fare. McDonald's on Victoria Street, an English copy of the American ones, was not the most charming establishment. It was near Westminister Cathedral, where drunks liked to congregate.

Nevertheless, for several days she went out for breakfast, all the while feeling a little silly. What was she avoiding? Her own imagination? By Wednesday her thoughts returned to her work. Thursday morning found her on the terrace again drinking her coffee.

In the first mail delivery, she received a four-page letter from Lady Chamberlain filled with ghost stories, one of which involved a ghost pet. Lavinia was greatly amused by the idea of a pet ghost pet.

Although clearly a modern woman, Lady Chamberlain was old-fashioned enough to write a long letter in her own fancy boarding-school handwriting on expensive flowered notepaper. Lavinia would have to write back to thank her for the lovely tea and for the additional material. She certainly could include the ghost pet story in the weekly tapes she was sending to her producer. He might want her to explore the story further.

She had read about a famous phantom dog at Peel Castle on the Isle of Man. Supposedly, the dog appeared from time to time in the basement of the guardroom. His high-pitched howl was often heard by visitors. She could just imagine Paul's reaction to the notion that dogs, too, had an afterlife.

As she finished her coffee, she jotted down her goals for the day, one of which was to type up Lady Chamberlain's fascinating stories, then edit and record them. Her producer expected weekly reports as well as the cassettes. On the basis of her progress he would decide whether to have a crew shoot some of the people she had interviewed.

She worked steadily for two hours at her typewriter, at the top of the landing of the spiral staircase. When her legs began to ache she got up to stretch. The day seemed unduly hot and close, almost like New York in August.

Needing a breath of fresh air, she opened the doors to the upstairs terrace and went outside. Mary's flower tubs smelled wonderfully earthy. The sky was overcast.

Suddenly she felt dizzy. Perhaps she should walk over to Dolphin Square to the indoor swimming pool. She definitely needed to clear her head and cool off.

Lavinia pulled on a pair of jeans and a tee-shirt and tied her sweatshirt around her waist. Some days the pool was empty but other days it was filled with children and tourists and the residents of the Dolphin Square Hotel. Still, it was convenient—just a four-minute walk from the flat—and luxurious. A pleasant restaurant with a long curving bar overlooked the pool. She might even go up there for a lemonade after she swam.

She stuck on her dark glasses and checked her swimming gear in her white leather holdall. Fluffing up her blond curly hair, she walked outside. She glanced up at Paul's windows, wondering whether he was at work. She hadn't seen or heard from him since Sunday, and she hoped that didn't mean he was annoyed with her.

No one was carrying an umbrella, she noticed, which meant that it would rain. Just another typical English summer's day.

She should possibly go back to the flat for her umbrella, but she was lazy. Besides, her hair would already be wet from swimming.

The Georgian buildings on St. George's Square had retained their original façades. The tall, sometimes ornate buildings with the porticos that reminded her of Italy were like opera sets, remnants of an epoch of grace and elegance. She imagined the lives that had been conducted behind the façades a century ago. Social life then had been so different in terms of manners and the way in which people behaved toward their peers. Or was she being fanciful? There had been hideous poverty, she knew. Yet people had a sense of themselves, a sense of who they were and a feeling about where they belonged. How wonderful it must have been, she thought, as she passed the Thomas-Cubbit-designed houses, to have been born into the upper class in the nineteenth century.

Although the pool was crowded, Lavinia did her twenty laps. She swam methodically and well, having been a member of the YWCA in New York. Afterward she sat at the edge of the pool, dangling her feet in the water and observing the other swimmers, who were mostly tourists like herself.

Two young children, a boy and a girl, were playing in the pool. They were Scots and had cheerful accents. She bet they had some great ghost stories, but she imagined their mother might be put off if she asked them.

The children splashed at each other, laughing and screaming with delight. After a while their mother intervened, dragging them out of the pool and away into the changing rooms. Now the pool was almost empty. Only two people were left, both doing laps.

Glancing upward at the restaurant, Lavinia saw a lone man sitting at a table, drinking a glass of wine. She couldn't see him clearly through the glass, but there was something familiar about him. Had she seen him walking around Pimlico? Maybe she had seen him before at the pool.

She rose to leave and, looking up again, she saw that the man was staring down at her. Who was he? Why did his gaze provoke an unaccountably unpleasant sensation, as if someone had scraped chalk across a blackboard?

And then she recognized him. He was the man on the horse,

the one who had almost knocked her over. Yes, he had the same dark, thick hair. At that moment, he stood up. He was very tall, perhaps six feet three or four, broad-shouldered, a large man with large hands and feet. But he carried his size gracefully.

Lavinia felt a momentary urge to communicate with him, to raise her hand in a wave. But that was ridiculous. He would misinterpret, think she was trying to pick him up. What would be the point?

She turned away, feeling his eyes upon her. Although she walked casually toward the shower room, telling herself that nothing had happened that was out of the ordinary, she was unaccountably frightened.

By the time she reached the door to the shower room, the man was gone.

Outside, the street was empty and it was beginning to rain. Lavinia realized that she half expected the man to be waiting for her.

She was being silly again. Why would that man be waiting for *her?* She put him out of her mind altogether.

The gentle summer rain was a nice way to end the swim, which had cleared her head and invigorated her, the way exercise always did. I'll work a few hours and then break for lunch, she decided. Breaking up the day with short trips outside made her work better.

The job assignment in London meant she had a built-in vacation as well. London was divine in the summer.

Tomorrow she was going on an early evening ghost walk that ended in a pub and was certainly as much a social occasion as anything else. She knew it would be interesting and fun—even if all the ghosts were invented by the London Tourist Board for the foreigners who flocked to the city in June—and during the day she had various people to interview, including a young couple who had lived in a flat that had been invaded by a poltergeist. The poltergeist had beaten up the husband and terrorized them so that they had to move out.

The only problem with all these horrible, sometimes tragic stories of vicious ghosts, attacking apparitions and macabre astral visitations was that they did not make for real peace of mind.

Recently, she had more than once waked at night with terrifying thoughts and the recollection of some ghastly nightmare. She had to keep reminding herself that a strong sense of humor and a little emotional distance were required. After all, this was only a job, and a temporary one at that.

Paul was getting out of a taxi just as Lavinia arrived home. He was clearly delighted to have met up with her.

"Your hair is wet," he said, smiling and gesturing for her to join him under his large Burberry umbrella.

"I've just been swimming, and then I walked home in the rain. It feels terrific."

"How about a before-lunch drink?" Paul asked. Lavinia looked extremely fetching in her bright yellow tee-shirt and jeans, with her curls all damp and tousled. "It's a very English custom," he added. "And you owe it to yourself to investigate not just our ghosts but our mores."

Lavinia was very pleased to see him. She grinned and nodded her head in assent. "What are you doing home at this hour?"

"The judge chucked my case, so I gave myself a mini-holiday and brought my brief home instead of staying in chambers. You know, you must let me show you around Lincoln's Inn one of these days."

His apartment was an interesting blend of contemporary and antique pieces—which, Lavinia correctly guessed, he'd taken from his mother's home. She sat down on the couch.

"This is charming," she said, admiring his art, some of which she was sure were originals.

"Thank you. I must admit I had some help from a friend of mine. She's a decorator and gave me some good advice about how to combine the old with the new. I'm having vermouth with a twist of lemon. How about you?"

"That would be fine," said Lavinia. She caught herself wondering whether the decorator was really just a friend, or more.

"How's your work going?" Paul said, handing her the glass of vermouth.

"Very well, actually. I haven't had any trouble tracking down sources. What's hard is maintaining my objectivity. I find that I'm thinking about ghosts so much that I'm almost seeing them myself. She laughed nervously, not sure that she wanted to tell Paul anything more than that. He'd think she was crazy if she went on to describe the figure she'd seen—or thought she'd seen—on the living room wall.

Paul took a sip of his drink. "Perhaps your exposure to these tales has made you more accessible to the family ghosts," he said teasingly. "Have you any long dead relatives who might be knocking about, trying to communicate with you?"

"Actually," Lavinia said quietly, "my parents both died when I was very young."

"Lavinia, I'm so sorry. I didn't mean to be disrespectful. I promise, I'll try to stop teasing you. Of course, it makes sense that you should get so involved in your research. You obviously take your work very seriously. I think that's quite marvelous."

He looked so stricken that Lavinia put her hand on his to reassure him. "I know you're joking. It's just that. . ." she stopped, not sure what she wanted to say.

"Yes," he prompted her, but she simply shrugged her shoulders.

"Well, to make amends, I have another ghost story for you. I heard this one the other night at dinner. The woman who told it to me is perfectly sane, I assure you. She and a friend of hers went to stay at a cottage that's over a hundred years old. Their very first night, they'd gone up to bed when they heard footsteps downstairs. They went down to investigate and saw that the latch on the front door had been undone. Then, to their horror, they heard a noise at the front door. But there was no one there."

Paul paused for effect. Lavinia was gazing at him intently. He was momentarily distracted by her wide blue eyes and the dimple in her chin, which he longed to touch.

"Do go on. Don't leave me hanging," Lavinia said, sounding like a child whose storytelling had been interrupted.

"Oh, right." Paul caught himself blushing. "Well, they searched the entire cottage, turned on all the lights, even looked under the beds, but they couldn't find anything, not even a kitty cat who might have been scampering about. They hardly slept a wink that night, as you can imagine. But in the clear light of day they felt a bit foolish. Before they had a chance to broach the subject with the owner, he happened to mention to them, half-jokingly, that the house was supposed to be haunted. Many years before, two children had been murdered there by their father. He'd hidden them in a trunk in the attic. The local people believed that the children wandered through the house at night."

"How awful," Lavinia said. And in fact, the story had made her feel rather uneasy. "But for my purposes, it's also terrific. I should probably find out from your friend where the cottage is, and go talk to the people there. My producer would love it. I bet we could get some fabulous visual footage." She began to get very excited, imagining an American audience's reaction to shots of a rustic, old English cottage with a voiceover of Paul's friend describing her experience.

Her face was lit up with enthusiasm. Paul mentally thanked his friend, a former lover he'd remained chums with, for the anecdote. When Lavinia smiled, the room seemed to glow. If it took a ghost story to get her happy and excited, then so be it.

"You probably need to get to work, and so should I," said Lavinia, finishing her drink. She checked her watch. "Oh, no," she said in mock horror. "Already twelve-thirty. I'm way behind schedule. You're a bad influence, Paul Chamberlain."

"I'd offer you lunch, but I'd much rather you joined me for dinner." Paul smiled. "Now, don't tell me no," he said, anticipating her refusal. "I can't take more than one rejection in a week."

Lavinia suspected his invitations were rarely refused. The truth was, he was delightful company and she had no other plans for this evening. Why should she say no? In order to prove a point to herself? That she could keep herself unentangled? Maybe the more important point was that she could meet and become involved with someone without giving up her own interests and life. And Paul might be just the man to practice with, since she'd be leaving at the end of the summer.

Paul mistook her silence for reluctance. How odd. If she had previous arrangements, she would have said so at once. And she clearly enjoyed him—unless his radar, well-tuned to the messages of women, was suddenly on the blink. Perhaps she was on a tight budget and wasn't sure she could afford an evening out. Yes, he decided. That must be it. And she's too polite to say so.

"Look," he said. "You'd be doing me the greatest kindness. I have many talents, as I hope you'll discover, but cooking is absolutely not among them. So...," he said, sighing deeply, "I'm forced to eat out almost every night, either at the local bistro or down at the pub." He pretended he'd just come up with a wonderful idea. "We could do a trade. Let me treat you tonight, and you can invite me in for dinner some evening. I never care what I'm served, so long as I don't have to prepare it."

"Fair enough." Lavinia laughed. The man was not only persuasive but also amusing. She stood up and realized she was slightly tipsy—the effect of vermouth on an empty stomach after a swim.

"Are you all right?" Paul asked, touching her lightly on the arm.

"Oh, yes, just not used to drinking at noon. I lead a very quiet life in New York," she said.

He walked her to the door.

"I meant to tell you," she said. "I saw that man again."

"What man?"

"The one on the horse who nearly rode into us when we were coming home from the grocery the other day. He had on that strange get-up."

"To be honest, I didn't see him. But I do remember your mentioning him. He quite startled you, didn't he?"

Lavinia looked at Paul sharply. He didn't think she was imagining things, did he? She'd had a drink, but she certainly wasn't drunk. And she had seen the man on horseback—and again today at the pool.

"Yes... well, I guess you'd be less likely than I to notice a good-looking man." Lavinia spoke more quickly than she'd meant to. "See you later, Paul."

"Looking forward to it," he said, hoping he hadn't offended her again.

Downstairs in Mary's flat, Lavinia fixed a cheese sandwich and poured a glass of orange juice. Then she settled herself at the typewriter on the landing and reread Lady Chamberlain's letter. One of her stories, about a headless ghost, was particularly gruesome. *But it's certainly caught my attention,* she thought. *It would make a great horror film or nightmare. Hope it won't be mine.*

She typed up the rest of the stories, editing them as she went. It was amazing how fast her research was proceeding. The stories were certainly fascinating, and some were even fun. The scariness of a horrible ghost story was like the thrill one experienced going through a fun-house and staring into a distorted mirror, or seeing a two-headed lady in a freak show. The shock and fear were exciting. People liked to visit haunted houses in hope that they would encounter a ghost, no matter how threatening or bizarre the ghost was reputed to be.

When she'd finished typing, Lavinia checked her watch. It was nearly six-thirty. She went downstairs and plugged in the electric kettle, one of England's most worthwhile inventions. Time for a cup of tea before she got dressed.

Then she remembered that she and Paul hadn't discussed what time to meet for dinner. She put the tea to steep on the kitchen counter, left her door ajar and ran upstairs. Paul answered her knock on his door immediately.

"Hi, when would you like to go?" she asked.

"Forty minutes? Does that suit you?"

"Yes, perfectly," she said, running down the stairs, "see you later."

Just enough time to drink her tea, shower and change.

She went straight to the kitchen. The cup of tea was gone.

Lavinia stared at the spot where she knew she had left the brown ceramic mug filled with hot tea. She surveyed the rest of the kitchen, opening the cupboard where Mary kept her glasses and mugs, thinking she might have stuck it in there absent-mindedly before she went up to Paul's. She opened the refrigerator and peered into the tin where the teabags were stored. This was ridiculous. She knew she'd made herself tea; the kettle was still hot.

Could she have taken it upstairs with her? she wondered. No, she very clearly remembered leaving the mug on the kitchen counter. Besides, she would feel too foolish—especially after their conversation about the rider Paul insisted he hadn't seen— if she called to ask about her mug and it wasn't there. So she made another cup, helped herself to a couple of tea biscuits and went into the living room. The brown mug was sitting on the oak end-table at the far end of the living room where the ceiling sloped. She knew she had not put it there. At least she had no memory of putting it there. She had gone straight from the kitchen to Paul's flat. Hadn't she?

The mug was empty except for a couple of shreds of tea leaves that had escaped through the strainer.

Tiny goosebumps rose on her arms. A stab of panic hit her. She had left her door open. Someone might have come in and moved the mug. But why?

And then she realized that whoever had come in might still be in the apartment, might have gone upstairs. She started toward the stairs, then changed her mind.

Mary had left a note with emergency phone numbers, in-cluding Paul's, on the wall next to the telephone in the kitchen.

Lavinia dialed Paul's number, but the line was busy. She waited a couple of minutes then redialed, but it was still busy. By then she felt quite calm. She put down the receiver.

There were no sounds coming from upstairs. Certainly no footsteps, no indication that anyone else was in the flat. She would just go up there and have a look around and stop being so silly. Maybe she *had* brought the tea into the living room, drunk it and left it there. It was possible. Anything seemed pos-sible these days.

Lavinia reached the landing and looked at the desk where she knew for certain she had left her notes. They were still exactly where she left them. Nothing on her desk seemed to be disturbed. She opened the door to the bedroom and glanced inside. Nothing seemed to have been touched. A pile of clothes were folded over one chair—the ironing she had planned to do sometime that day. Her hairbrush and combs were lying on the dresser exactly as she had left them. She checked her wallet, which was in her bag. The credit cards and money were all there.

She looked at the dressing table. Had she left her jewlery box open? She really could not remember. She looked carefully through her jewelry, the rings and earrings, the silver and gold chains. She had brought with her only a few pieces, thinking she might buy some old jewelry at one of the antique markets. Anyway, when she traveled she liked to take the minimum.

Something inside her jewelry box caught her eye. It was a ring with a bright red stone. A ring that did not belong to her. How in the world had it found its way in there? she wondered, slipping it on her finger. Could it be Mary's? It was exactly the sort of Victorian jewelry her friend liked.

The ring fit perfectly. Lavinia examined it closely. The stone was medium-size and surrounded by a ring of diamonds, each set independently. The stone might have been a ruby, or a garnet perhaps. No, she decided, it was a ruby, and a beautiful one at that. She would have to remember to ask Mary when she wrote or called her.

Then she remembered why she had come into the bedroom and a momentary feeling of anxiety swept over her. She sat down on the edge of the bed.

There was no escaping from the truth. Someone had been in the flat and moved a few things around. And whoever it was might have left the ring.

This was altogether insane. The fact that she had no explanation made it far worse. She debated going to see Mrs. Patel-Ram the next day, to talk to her. The woman would be open to such a story, having no resistance to the unexplainable. But Lavinia felt uncomfortable. She liked Mrs. Patel-Ram but had only met her a couple of times. She hardly knew her. Mrs. Patel-Ram might even think Lavinia was inventing the story to amuse her.

Damn. She would simply tell Paul and hope that he would be at least sympathetic. He was certainly levelheaded, and that in itself might prove a help. She imagined him saying, "Oh, yes, kids from the neighborhood. Didn't Mary warn you? They do more mischief than harm."

As she considered that scenario, twirling the ring around her finger unconsciously, she began to be aware that someone was out on the terrace. She got up, wondering if it might be her next-door neighbor, whose upstairs terrace adjoined hers. She went outside and got a cursory glimpse of a tall man in a dark suit disappearing into Carol's flat. Carol's boyfriend, she decided, and went inside to get dressed for dinner.

Should she wear Mary's ring? She had to admit that it was beautiful. The stone had a brilliance and fire within it, a magical quality about it. Maybe she should regard it as a talisman. She would wear it. There would be no harm done. Perhaps it would shield her from harm.

Suddenly Lavinia felt slightly absurd. She scolded herself for being superstitious. She had never believed in omens. Her work was definitely getting to her. Or was she uncovering something in herself that had been there all along? Although she had always regarded herself a skeptic, she did realize that Aunt Jane had brought her up, and Aunt Jane must have had an influence somewhere along the line.

She selected a red cotton dress with long sleeves and a low neckline, which she wore with a wide black patent belt. She took out Aunt Jane's jet beads and earrings and wondered about tying a black scarf in a bow through her blond curls. It struck her as odd when she realized she was coordinating her outfit with the ring, but she brushed away her misgivings.

Gold eye shadow, a little dark blue mascara and a dash of lipstick completed her preparations. She examined herself criti-cally in the full-length mirror. And liked what she saw—a beau-tiful, sexy woman with spunk enough to take on any challenge.

It had been quite a while since she had gone to such trouble getting dressed and putting on make-up. She smiled, imagining Paul's reaction. She realized how much she was looking forward to spending the evening with him. She wanted to find out more about him, and not just how he felt about ghosts. Tonight she was not going to worry about keeping up her guard. Paul was nothing like the mad Hungarian, she decided. Devotion to her work was all very well, but not to the point that it had her hearing strange noises and seeing shadows in the dark.

Glancing at the dresser to make sure she hadn't forgotten any-thing, she noticed Mary's bottle of bright orange nail polish. How typical of her friend to decorate her apartment with Victorian furniture and do her nails in Day-Glo orange. One of the things Lavinia had immediately appreciated in Mary was that she was so quirky and unpredictable.

Should she borrow some of Mary's polish? She held out her hands. No, the color would be too jarring a contrast next to the red stone. And it was inexplicably very important to her that the ring should shine as brightly as possible.

She opened her front door just as Paul was about to knock. He was wearing light gray summer pants, a dark blue blazer and a blue shirt with a dark tie.

"You look lovely," he said admiringly, "more like the south of France than Belgrave Road."

"Well, thank you," Lavinia said, laughing. In fact, she felt very summery and sophisticated, and was pleased that Paul had noticed. She was slightly overwhelmed by how distinguished he looked. The men she dated in New York, most notably the mad Hungarian, were mainly artists and writers who scorned navy blue and gray almost on principle.

"Where are we going?" she asked.

"I thought we'd go to Chimes. It's nearby, just on Churton Street. I think you'll like it. They go in for wooden tables, lovely veggies and classical music."

"Sounds terrific," said Lavinia. She was very glad she'd accepted the invitation. She'd forgotten how marvelous it felt to be out on a balmy summer evening, dressed up in the company of an appreciative man, on her way to a pleasant restaurant. "How did your work go this afternoon?"

"Very efficiently, actually," replied Paul. "I had to make a couple of phone calls, but otherwise there were no distractions. There's a lot to be said for working at home. But I suppose you know that far better than I."

"It has its pluses and minuses," Lavinia said. *Like sometimes you begin imagining things*, she added silently.

They rounded the corner and headed down Churton Street, toward the restaurant.

"Paul," Lavinia said abruptly, "have you ever seen this ring before?" She held her left hand up so he could look at it properly.

Paul held her hand in his for a moment, his brown eyes moving from the ring to her face. Then he dropped his hand, as if reluctant to let go.

"It's very beautiful," he said, gazing deeply into her eyes. "But no, I haven't. Should I have?"

"I just thought you might have noticed it sometime when Mary was wearing it."

"I don't know Mary all that well. We only rarely cross paths. She always seems to be rushing off to the library, and I'm out so often myself. Besides, I don't usually notice jewlery, unless I'm particularly intrigued with the woman who's wearing it. But why do you ask?"

Lavinia shrugged. "Just wondering. Somehow it got misplaced with my things, so I took that as a sign that I should borrow it for this evening." She changed the subject, asking him whether he enjoyed theater. In fact, Paul was an avid theatergoer and enthusiastically described a new play he'd seen the other evening in the West End. He was gratified by Lavinia's intelligent questions. She wasn't just asking to be polite or keep the conversation going. It was a pleasure to talk to her.

"Here we are," he said, interrupting himself.

He held open the door to the restaurant, which was small and crowded and well lit. It had a lively mood to it, just the kind of place Lavinia had hoped for. The perfect antidote to whatever had been spooking her this afternoon. They were quickly seated, and a waitress appeared almost instantly to take their drink order.

"May I make a suggestion?" Paul said. "Try the cider. It's a house specialty, but I should warn you, the alcohol in it tends to sneak up on you."

"Thanks for the warning," said Lavinia. "And what do you recommend for the main course? I'd like a very English dinner."

"Are you very hungry?"

"Starving," Lavinia said cheerfully. She felt relaxed and happy. The aromas in the restaurant were both tempting and comforting.

Paul ordered steak and kidney pie, boiled potatoes and steamed cauliflower, as well as two more large glasses of cider.

"Mmmm," said Lavinia appreciatively. The food was delicious, the cider as intoxicating as wine. She was on the verge of telling him about the disappearing tea and the fright she'd had earlier in the day, when he said, "My children will be here soon. They're going to spend some time with me in London before I take them to Turkey on holidays,. We usually do a bit of exploring in town, and I was wondering whether you might want to join us."

"That sounds lovely."

"I should warn you, though, they're both hell-raisers, constantly in trouble and at each other's throats. It's a punishment to be with them together, but sometimes I can't avoid it."

He looked so woeful that Lavinia couldn't help laughing.

"In that case, maybe I should decline the offer with thanks. Doesn't sound like much fun."

"It helps sometimes when there's a fourth person around. Emily actually behaves like a human being around my mother." He looked up at her hopefully, almost like a little boy pleading for a second piece of cake. "I suppose it's my own fault—mine and my ex-wife's, that is. Our divorce has probably been difficult for them. The tension and upheaval, you know."

She wondered whether he would take the conversation any further and tell her more about his marriage and why it broke up. But he seemed reluctant to discuss it.

"How old are the little darlings?" she asked.

"Emily is fourteen, and Christopher is eighteen months older. He's really worn everyone's patience thin. Even my mother won't have him for the weekend. Perhaps I'll lose him somewhere in Istanbul." He laughed delightedly at the thought. Then he continued. "I'm sorry. You must think me heartless."

"No, not at all," protested Lavinia. "Just honest."

The waitress reappeared to clear their plates and ask if they wanted dessert.

"We'll have apple crumble with hot custard cream," Paul decided, not bothering to consult Lavinia. "And," he said with a wicked grin, "two more rounds of your cider. Make it small glasses this time."

"Are you trying to get me drunk?" The question was moot. Lavinia knew she was well past the point of sober.

"Now why should I want to do that?" he asked, his eyes twinkling.

Lavinia felt wonderful. Again she considered telling him about the strange events of the afternoon, then decided not to. He might understand, perhaps even have an explanation, but she was having much too good a time to think or talk about anything unpleasant. Besides, seated in Chimes across from Paul, full of delicious food and drink, she was almost prepared to convince herself that she had imagined all of it, that nothing had happened out of the ordinary.

"Do you believe in God?" Paul asked her suddenly.

"Why do you ask?" She took another sip of cider, wishing she were a little more clearheaded if they were about to have a heavy philosophical discussion.

"I was just thinking," Paul replied slowly, "that a belief in ghosts and the afterlife presumes a belief in God. I mean, if ghosts exist, then we have proof positive of an afterlife."

"I'd have to call myself a fence-sitter about whether or not there is a God. My Aunt Jane thinks I'm begging the question, and perhaps I am, swinging back and forth about whether or not I believe. But more to the point, Paul, I don't have to believe in ghosts in order to do a good job on my research. I simply have to scare up"—she smiled at her choice of words—"enough stories to provide my producer with a choice of material for the documentary."

"Now that's an interesting word, 'documentary.' Doesn't that imply a program about news events, or facts or social conditions? An exploration of something that actually exists?"

Lavinia smiled broadly. She admired the way Paul argued, with animation and conviction. He was probably terrific in the courtroom. She liked men who had ideas. And she liked men who disagreed with her ideas. Not to be challenged was boring. Paul was definitely not boring.

Paul smiled back, staring directly into her blue eyes as if he were trying to mesmerize her. She found herself looking away, unable to respond to his directness. Although they were chatting about philosophical positions, she felt his look was sexual, and she suddenly felt inexplicably shy.

"Let's get down to the real business," he said. She was suddenly very conscious of her low-cut neckline that showed off her cleavage. Was he about to proposition her? And what would she say if he did?

All of a sudden the room seemed to be spinning around her. She felt foolish for having got so drunk. She looked up, tried to focus on Paul and pick up the thread of the conversation.

"I'm not a philosopher," she said, still feeling a bit dizzy. "I don't know about things that can't be seen or proven. I'm just collecting material for a television series. The public will have to make up its own mind."

She reached across the table and touched his arm lightly. "Why don't you come with me tomorrow night on a Tourist Board ghost walk? Perhaps that will answer some of your questions."

Paul laughed. "I doubt it, but I'll be happy to join you."

Just then something at the front of the restaurant caught her eye. A tall, broad-shouldered man stood uncertainly in the entrance. Even at this distance Lavinia could see he was looking toward her.

"There's that man again," she said excitedly. It was the same man she'd seen at Dolphin Square, riding the horse down Belgrave Road.

"Who?" Paul turned to see whom she was looking at. Her cheeks were flushed, and she appeared to be very excited. She was staring at the group of people clustered around the bar in the front.

"Which one?" Paul asked.

"He's wearing that same uniform. Look."

The man was frowning and looked intensely unhappy. Something was wrong, but what? She felt a strange urge to get up and go over to him.

"It looks like some kind of army uniform, Paul."

"There's no one in a uniform," Paul said. "They're all wearing just plain ordinary clothes."

"You're teasing me," she said.

The man suddenly turned around and left the restaurant.

"It looked like some kind of army uniform. But he was wearing his riding boots."

"I think you're confused," Paul said soothingly, "you're tired. Too much work. Too much reading. Too much typing. Too much of people like my mother. And I probably shouldn't have ordered that last glass of cider."

"I may be drunk but I'm not hallucinating," Lavinia said. "You really didn't see him?"

"I really did not."

Lavinia finished her cider. Paul's perceptions might be different from hers, she decided, but that didn't mean she was crazy. And she could trust her own perceptions enough to know the cider had nothing to do with it.

She knew beyond the shadow of a doubt that she had seen him at Dolphin Square, and he was the same man who was on the horse. He was a very handsome man, and now that she had seen him twice, she felt certain that she would recognize him again. Maybe he lived in the neighborhood. Maybe he lived at Dolphin Square. He was certainly a gentleman, a man of affluence. That was obvious.

He was a rich man and an unhappy one. In fact, she had sensed something extremely disquieting about him, possibly even violent. Her research into psychic phenomenon was creating a new sensitivity that she had not known she possessed. If Paul could not see what she did, it was because he didn't want to allow himself.

"Are you all right, Lavinia?"

"Of course. Just a bit sleepy."

She looked again toward the front of the restaurant. The man stood outside, looking through the window, directly at her.

When she reflected later on her behavior, she could not explain it. She found herself rising from the chair. "I've got to help him," she said to Paul, who stared at her open-mouthed. She hurried through the crowded restaurant. Her only thought was that he needed her.

She hurriedly flung open the door and stepped outside. The street was empty.

"What are you doing?" Paul asked, running up behind her and grabbing her shoulders. "Stop!"

Lavinia turned and stared at him.

"He was bleeding," she said. "I saw it. His arm was gushing blood."

"I don't know what you're talking about," Paul said. "Let me pay the bill and I'll take you home."

He guided her back into the restaurant and she waited numbly while he paid the bill.

"Are you all right?" he asked, taking her hand and leading her outside again. "You look pale. I could ring my doctor. He'd be around in a trice."

"No, I'm fine."

"Apparently you saw something or someone I didn't, Lavinia, but no one else saw him, either."

"Either I just saw a ghost," she said calmly, "or I'm going crazy."

"Must it be one or the other?" Paul said, putting his hand around her waist, trying to joke her out of her mood.

"Discarnate people who appear as solid, ordinary living people," Lavinia said nervously, remembering a line she had read only this morning. The author had meant that the person was dead but had not passed into the other world of the dead. It also meant that anyone could be a ghost, and who might know the difference? How could one tell a ghost from a real person? Since a ghost looked just like anyone else, one would not really know if the person was alive in the usual sense.

The air felt cool. She looked up into the black sky, wishing for a star or two, and shivered.

"I don't believe he lives in the neighborhood," she said, "not really. He may have lived here once."

"Are you talking about the man who was not there?" Paul asked. He wanted desperately to talk her out of it, make her admit that she had not actually seen what she said she had, that she was inventing the whole thing because she knew it bothered him. He did not wish to believe that basically she was unstable, or a nutter. She was a levelheaded, intelligent, rational woman. But here she was, all but insisting she'd seen a ghost.

"He was there," Lavinia said firmly, insisting she'd seen a ghost, her tone telling him that she believed in her own perception even if he did not.

He moved his arm from her waist to her shoulder and gave her a protective squeeze. He wished he could pull her out of this interest in the occult right now, tonight!

"Don't get so enmeshed that you can't extricate yourself," he warned. "You said yourself that a researcher must be objective."

"Yes," she agreed.

"The cider is powerful stuff," Paul said.

"Yes, powerful," she said, in a voice that he recognized to be quite sober.

He glanced at her with trepidation.

"I didn't see anyone, Lavinia, but maybe you did. And if you did, I believe you. But it doesn't mean that just because I didn't see him, you saw a ghost. He may very well live around here."

"No," she said stubbornly. And then she smiled. He was being kind and she liked him for it.

In the light of day Lavinia decided that Paul was right, she *had* had too many glasses of cider. The idea that the man was a ghost, or did not exist, no longer seemed right to her. He was obviously someone who lived in the area. Paul probably had just looked in the wrong direction. Or he might have been pretending not to see him out of jealousy.

She had no memory of seeing the man bleeding.

She looked for the man around the streets of Pimlico. She even returned to Dolphin Square and went into the restaurant to see if he was there. But she didn't bump into him again.

The next evening she and Paul went on their Tourist Board ghost walk. Neither of them even mentioned the incident at the restaurant. Paul thought it better to keep off the subject. And Lavinia had no desire to get into the matter. The walk, which ended in a smoky pub, was fun but silly. The guide was out to show the tourists a good time and a bit of London. The ghosts were almost incidental.

On the way back to Belgrave Road, Paul took Lavinia for a cappucino at the Europa Café in Victoria. He wanted to prolong the evening and sensed that she did, too. They'd kissed good-night the previous evening, but she was clearly upset so he hadn't pressed further. He wondered how tonight would end. They stayed as long as possible in the Europa, until the waiters made it obvious that they were waiting for them to leave so they could go home themselves."

At about midnight they turned down Belgrave Road, arm in arm.

As they approached their building, Lavinia suddenly tugged on his arm.

"Look," she said, "there he is. He's going into the building."

The man was up ahead. He was dressed in the uniform and riding boots. She instinctively glanced around to find his horse but didn't see it.

"Where?"

"Up there, right there, Paul."

Paul strained to see what she was looking at, but he saw nothing. The front of the building was deserted.

"Lavinia, I wish I could tell you I see a man standing there, but I don't."

Lavinia was ready to cry with frustration. "I swear to you, Paul, he's there, right in front of the building," she whispered urgently. "I'm not making this up."

Paul took both of her hands and looked at her squarely. "I know you're not. I know you *think* you're not. But perhaps the cumulative effect of what you've been researching... it's pretty overpowering stuff, I realize, especially if you've never dealt with it before..."

Lavinia wrenched her hands away. "So I'm seeing things, is that it?" she cried. She rubbed her eyes with one hand. "Oh, I don't know, maybe I am. I just don't know."

She turned back toward her apartment. The man was gone.

"Paul, I'm exhausted. Perhaps you're right. I just need a good night's sleep and a day off from ghosts. I think I'll declare a holiday tomorrow and take it easy."

"Excellent idea. Why don't you come visit me at my law office? I'll show you around Lincoln's Inn and we could have a lunch."

"I don't know, maybe," Lavinia said distractedly.

"Good. I'll call you in the morning. Are you all right?"

"Yes, fine," Lavinia said. "Thank you, Paul."

"For what?" he asked.

"I don't know, moral support, I guess." She closed the door gently in his face.

As she flicked on the light switch in the hallway, her head was filled with questions. Did the man live in her building? Had she seen him here and not paid attention? She felt more determined than ever to find out who he was, without getting Paul involved. She was a researcher, after all.

She would go to the Westminster Library first thing in the morning and look up photographs or drawings of current army and navy uniforms. His uniform looked military, but it was not the uniform of the Buckingham Palace Guards or any uniform she had seen on other men around London.

She would try the Navy Museum, if necessary, or the Army Museum in Chelsea. Maybe she would find a librarian with a firsthand ghost story as well. She did not want to subvert her interest. She could simply combine things, possibly—take out some books on the occult while she was at the library. She might even take her notes along and work at the library.

She double-locked the door, rechecked it and walked into the living room. At once she noticed that the room felt chilly and damp, as if she had left all the windows open, which she had not.

And then she took in the terrifying fact that the living room looked as if it had been turned upside down. All of Mary's little silver animals, her collection of glass boxes and bottles, her paintings that had been so carefully hung, were now strewn across the room. The furniture had been pushed around haphazardly. The drawers of the credenza were overturned. The lace cloths and silverware that had been stored in the credenza were scattered about the room. Lavinia stood rooted to the spot, unable to move. She stared at the jumble of objects, her mind unable to function.

"I've been robbed," she said out loud. Robbed. In England, Mary had warned her, no one is mugged or murdered. But you might be robbed.

She thought she ought to go into the kitchen and call the

police. The number was up on the wall, but she just stood there thinking.

An icy cold wind was blowing from the terrace, but the door was closed. *I should call the police,* she thought. And then she thought, *the robber could still be in here.* He must have come in and checked the place out when she was at Paul's the other day. Yes, that was it. He was the one who had moved the cup of tea.

Lavinia dashed to the door and ran upstairs to Paul's flat. She banged on his door, shouting, "Paul, Paul, hurry up."

Paul came to the door in his robe, surprised to see Lavinia breathless and flushed.

"What's wrong?"

"I've been robbed. God, the flat's a mess. Everything's topsy-turvy."

"I'll get the police," Paul said, going to the telephone and lifting the receiver.

"No, no! Don't call them! No!"

Paul put down the receiver.

"Why not?"

"I don't know," she said, shaking her head. "But I'd like you to come back with me."

"What for?"

"Just to have a look. I don't know."

"Have you gone round the bend, Lavinia?" Paul said crossly, "if you've been burgled, we better ring the police."

"No," she insisted, "definitely not. If you call the police I won't speak to you again."

She seemed to be almost hysterical. "What do you want me to do?" he asked her.

Lavinia shrugged. She felt disoriented and frightened but somehow she knew this was not a matter for the police.

They stared at each other while Paul waited for her to say something. After a couple of moments he went to pour her a brandy.

"Just a small one," he warned. "This will calm you."

"Thanks," Lavinia said, sitting down on the edge of his couch.

"I'll go down with you and check it out," Paul offered. "Whoever was there is sure to be gone by now, I suspect."

The door to her flat was still open. Lavinia had not thought to close it when she fled.

Paul walked ahead of her into the living room. Lavinia followed him, then stopped and gasped. How was it possible? Everything that had been so obscenely thrown around was now back in its original place. The paintings were on the wall, the drawers to the credenza were shut, the objects were exactly as they had been when she had left the apartment hours earlier.

"It can't be," she mumbled.

"No?"

"Believe me," she said, "the place was a complete mess. The furniture was all over the place. The contents of the drawers were dumped out."

She opened the top drawer of the credenza and looked in. Everything was in its place.

"You do believe me, don't you?" she said, staring into Paul's scrutinizing eyes.

"Maybe the person came back and put everything back for you," he said facetiously.

"Please," Lavinia begged, "please, believe me. Why would I make it up?"

"You, or we, had better look upstairs," Paul said, feeling that perhaps he ought to indulge her. Was she trying to tell him something? Maybe Lavinia was extremely interested in him but so shy that this was her way of inviting him to spend the night. As ludicrous as that seemed, it was the most plausible explanation he could come up with.

Lavinia walked timorously up the spiral staircase.

The desk on the landing was orderly. The bedroom was the same. She opened the wardrobe and looked inside. Everything appeared to be as she had left it. She opened her jewelry box.

"Anything missing?"

"No, I don't think so," she said to Paul, who was behind her, looking over her shoulder.

"I feel ridiculous," she said when they had returned to the living room. Paul had insisted on making them both a cup of tea. He didn't know what to say. If she were feeling amorous, she was certainly keeping it well hidden.

"The place was turned upside down. You do believe that, don't you? I'm not going crazy."

"Of course, I believe you."

"Maybe it's a poltergeist," Lavinia said, searching her mind for a credible explanation.

"They don't rearrange, to my knowledge," Paul said, attempting to be serious. "They only mix up, create confusion, throw things around. I don't know of any poltergeist who cleans up after himself."

Lavinia suddenly laughed, glad for the comic relief.

Paul laughed with her, wondering if he ought to put his arms around her and kiss her. Was that what she really wanted?

He moved closer to her on the couch. When she stopped laughing he put his arms around her and pulled her close to him, his lips brushing hers.

"No," she said, pushing him away. "No, don't." Her eyes suddenly filled with tears. "What are you doing?" she said. "I'm upset and you've got other things on your mind, obviously. My God, there's a time and a place for romance..." Her voice trailed off and she sniffled back the tears.

Paul stood up. He felt terrible, like an insensitive cad who had misread her totally. He had upset her further and probably ruined his chances with her forever.

"I'm sorry," he said. "I am truly sorry, Lavinia. Would you like to stay in my flat tonight?"

His well-meaning suggestion made the situation worse.

"Oh, please, go," she said. "I'll be all right here. I'm not scared any more. We've checked everywhere. No one's here."

But then a frightening thought crept into her mind.

"We didn't look on the terraces," she said, getting up, running to the door to the terrace. "Would you check the upstairs terrace?"

Paul ran up the spiral staircase, onto the landing and out onto the terrace. It was empty. When he came downstairs again, Lavinia was bolting shut the terrace door.

"It's all right," she said, "but I'm utterly exhausted. I'll speak to you tomorrow. Paul, thank you for your help. I mean it."

He edged toward the front door.

"If you need me, I'm up there. Ring me, or just come up.

Not to worry, you're perfectly safe." He grinned reluctantly. "Even from me."

Lavinia sat down to think about the series of events, none of which had any rational explanation. She concluded that they must all be linked together, but how and why?

The mess in her living room was no practical joke. Why would anyone bother? And the door had been locked, double-locked with the Chubb lock key. So whoever had entered the flat came from one of the terraces. Even more puzzling was how anyone could have straightened it out in so short a period of time.

Someone was trying to communicate something to her. But what? So many questions and no answers, she thought as she went upstairs, feeling a sense of trepidation at each step. Whoever had entered the flat from one of the terraces could do it again. The prospect did not thrill her.

Her head was beginning to ache, and then a comforting thought emerged from the pain. Psychokinesis. The ability to influence objects through thought processes.

A few weeks before she would never have imagined that the idea of psychokinesis could cheer her, but now she could use it to look at this puzzling event in a new light. According to what she had read, extrasensory perception was within reach of anybody who had an open mind. Perhaps her mind had been opened through exposure to these new ideas.

It was all a matter of seeing reality differently from the way she usually viewed it.

Yes, she could have, simply by thinking about it, moved everything in the living room and then returned it to normal. Except, of course, that it was not simple. But she could be operating on an unconscious level so deep that she was totally unaware of it. She knew that the mind could interact with matter in powerful and dramatic ways; she just had never thought of herself as having this ability.

But then, what was the point of it? If she herself had been responsible for throwing everything around, what had been her motive?

To convince herself that she was no longer frightened, she

went out onto the upstairs terrace. She reconsidered the idea of herself having special powers. No. It was impossible. She was just an ordinary person. There was no magic in her subconscious. Someone else must have moved everything into a heap and then moved it back again. Was the person looking for something? Could the incident have had something to do with that ring she found?

The dog in the courtyard opposite barked loudly. She leaned over the balcony and called out to him. "Be quiet!"

The dog continued to bark. There. Nothing magical about her. She felt relieved to be just a normal woman.

She rummaged in the medicine cabinet and found some Panadol. She was definitely not imagining a headache. She lay down on her bed, waiting for the Panadol to take effect. A headache was as much the product of the mind, the psyche, as an apparition. Everything began and ended with the mind. She might have hallucinated the robbery, or whatever it was, in the same way as she was now hallucinating a headache. On the other hand, was this some indication of precognition? Imagining a robbery might be a prediction? Maybe she would actually be robbed shortly.

Her head was throbbing. She could not deny this—and whether it was imagined or not, it hurt. She wished she could imagine it away. She closed her eyes to try and concentrate on something peaceful. If only she could blot out some of the thoughts that were now assailing her, she knew the pain would disappear.

For a moment she felt sorry and even resentful that she had taken this job assignment. Her ambition to go up the ladder in television, to reach an executive level, perhaps to become a producer, had been in the back of her mind when she accepted the research job. It would be an excellent stepping stone, she believed, if the research was first-rate. But she had not bargained on having her mind play tricks on her.

She breathed in and out slowly, using the Yoga technique that had helped her before in times of stress. She was acutely aware of her breathing, the dog barking outside and the creaking floorboards.

She opened her eyes and sat upright to listen.

Were those footsteps? Was somebody coming up the stairs? She jumped off the bed.

"Paul?"

But it couldn't be Paul. She had locked the door to the flat. He couldn't have gotten in.

Terrified, she had to come to a quick decision. Either slam shut the bedroom door or confront whoever it was. She went out to the landing, leaned over the staircase and peered into the darkened living room. Damn! Why hadn't she left a light on.

"Hello?" she called, her voice tremulous.

She was not going to panic. If somebody was down there, she would confront him. She walked down the steps and switched on the lamp. The living room was empty but she felt someone was there. She looked at the wall in the corner, expecting to see the outline of the man. The wall looked the way it always did.

Maybe she *was* going around the bend. If so, she would like to be the first to realize it.

Lavinia turned to go back upstairs, then she saw him. Just the merest glimpse, but enough for her to know it was the man in the uniform. He was moving quickly up the spiral staircase.

And then he disappeared through the wall.

She stared after him, her mind whirling, her thoughts as confused as Mary's jumbled objects. She did not feel frightened, only perplexed.

Lavinia quickly came to a decision. She was going to stop trying to make sense out of this, but she *was* going to do some more research.

She went to the kitchen phone and dialed the international operator, then waited anxiously while she was connected to Athens.

"Hello," Mary said. Her voice sounded remote, but it was Mary all right.

"Darling," Lavinia said, "it's me."

"Oh, Lavinia," Mary said. "How are you? How's the flat?"

"Mary, I have something important to ask you." She worried that Mary would think she had gone out of her mind. "Mary, is there something about the flat you didn't tell me?"

"Like where are the cutting shears for the roses on the upstairs terrace?"

"No," Lavinia said, "it's something else. Something odd."

"Oh, you mean the footsteps."

"Well, it's more than footsteps."

"Lots of people live with footsteps," Mary said. "There's no harm in it. You could think it's the floorboards."

"You're not bothered because you're a Celt," Lavinia said, "but I'm nervous, let me tell you. Tell me the truth now, Mary. Am I living with a ghost?"

"Darling, we're all living with ghosts," Mary said and for an instant the line went dead. "If you see anyone," she said, coming back on the line, "let me know. We'll charge him half the rent. Lavinia, love, I'm quite late for meeting up with some people, so let's say adieu."

Her voice faded in and out, and after a moment she was gone, leaving a frustrated Lavinia staring at the receiver. Perhaps Mary knew more than she was saying, but perhaps not. Mary always was enigmatic and she liked to make a wry joke out of everything. This was part of her charm, but at the moment it didn't give Lavinia much comfort.

If this were some sort of a daydream, it was turning into a nightmare. She might be sharing the flat with a ghost in uniform, a uniform that did not appear to be very modern. Who was this man and was he going to harm her? According to her research, some ghosts played mischievous pranks and some actually caused bodily harm.

Still, if Mary knew something important, if she knew that the ghost was harmful, she certainly would have told her. That meant, by deduction, that if there were a ghost in the flat he was harmless.

She went into the living room and looked around, making certain she was alone. Most ghosts dated back two or three hundred years. She glanced anxiously up the staircase to where she had seen the man. He had not come through the front door, nor the windows, nor the terrace. He did not need a key or ladder.

The ghost was haunting the premises. Yes, if she really got down to it, he was haunting. The very word made her want to weep in fear. He could be haunting the whole building, moving from flat to flat. He could have appeared elsewhere in the building. Maybe others had seen him. She would have to ask around.

Or it could be that this section of the building had some special significance to him. This could have been where the tragedy happened. There had to have been a tragedy; otherwise he would not be hanging around.

The haunting, she knew, was a plea for help from the living. All a ghost wanted was to be able to pass into the world of the spirits. Such a passage was not possible until the ghost was set free, vindicated by someone alive.

Lavinia remembered that sometimes clerics, a priest, a nun, a minister or a very religious person could set a ghost free. Occasionally a medium could help a ghost by simply telling the ghost that it was all right to join the spirit world. This message had to be conveyed with the greatest love and compassion, or the ghost would not stop haunting. The soul of the ghost had to be loved by the person setting it free.

"Damn," Lavinia said. "Why me? Couldn't you have waited until I left? Why choose me?" She felt like screaming but held back for fear that a scream would bring the ghost back to the flat.

She felt intensely frustrated and angry at the same time. She was not the sort of person who could ignore the ghost, as Mary suggested. She would sit up and take notice as she did with all things and she would feel impelled to find out who he was, or used to be. It was another confounded research project to vie for her attention.

She didn't relish the notion of sharing the flat with a ghost, particularly a ghost who seemed so eager to be in touch with her. Otherwise, he would have behaved like a purposeful ghost, the kind that went about its business, ignoring the living beings who happened by.

She could not help wondering about him, despite her terror. What did he want from her? Who was he? Had he been murdered, or was he a murderer? Had he committed suicide? Had he died in some ghastly way?

Why had she been chosen to help him? Would she be the person to conduct him out of his state of limbo into the world where spirits dwelled in peace? And if so, how? Why would a fence-sitting skeptic such as herself be selected for this job? Or was this random? Had he appeared to her just because she was in the flat or was there some special connection between them?

So many questions, and with it all she could not shake off her panic.

She closed her eyes. She knew full well that she could not conjure up a ghost, yet she wished she could. Perhaps if he appeared to her in some calm, sensible way, and they could communicate normally, she would know what to do. She wished she knew more about him. As a practical matter the idea of finding out about him through his uniform seemed a good beginning. If she knew the kind of uniform he was wearing, she might be able to establish him in the right time period.

This was all she needed! A ghost, a real ghost, to muck up her work, to distract her from the research, to interfere with the job she was trying to accomplish in London. In some ways a ghost would be far worse than being involved with a living man. Whatever faults a living man might have, at least she knew he existed. And with her kind of sensitivity and her thorough, methodical research techniques, she might become so obsessed that her real work would suffer.

This was absurd. The whole idea was absurd. She would exorcise the ghost from her mind, because that was obviously where he existed. But her mind was already racing ahead, searching for pieces to this puzzle.

If the man were haunting the flat, it probably meant that he had lived in this house. She could go to the library archives and look up the previous owners. There wouldn't be that many. English families tended to keep their houses for many years and bequeath them to relatives.

She had to find out who had sold the house to be redivided. Most of the London property was owned by charitable trusts or the Crown Estate. The buildings usually reverted back to the original owners when the leasehold ran its course.

Lavinia went upstairs, ran a hot bath, pouring in some of her Caswell-Massey apricot bubble bath. As she soaked, she tried to analyze her situation. She tried to fight her sense of despair. She was used to tracking down bits of information, to discerning the total picture from lots of tiny details. But this was something altogether different. Something in a very gray area.

She dried herself off, put on her nightie and got into bed. She pulled the comforter up to her chin. English summer evenings often felt like autumn evenings in New York. Cold.

She wanted badly to sleep, needed the sleep, but it did not come immediately. Her mind was fixed on the image of the man she had seen.

He was extremely handsome. He had a shock of dark hair and what seemed to be chiseled features. He was the kind of man to whom women were invariably attracted. In a way he was too handsome, almost overwhelmingly so, as if he had no physical flaws. Although he appeared to be strong, he seemed to be unhappy, brooding. Finally Lavinia drifted off to sleep, imagining she felt him nearby.

Sometime later she opened her eyes. She had left on the light on the landing. Although the bedroom was almost dark, she could see quite clearly that she was alone in the room. Nevertheless, she felt a presence that made her gasp for breath.

Lavinia sat up and pushed away the comforter, feeling suddenly too warm. She waited for the ghost to appear. When he did not, she lay down and tried to think about something else. If she were to continue to stay in Mary's flat, she would most definitely have to adopt some other attitude about the ghost. It was a mistake to wait for him. If she let that happen, her whole life would be controlled by the appearance of the ghost.

Her thoughts began to wander as she drifted toward sleep, yet her mind kept coming back to the apparition. She saw him in uniform riding down Belgrave Road, charging toward her as if he would plow into her. She saw him as he sat alone at the table, looking down at her in the pool. He seemed unhappy, deeply unhappy. He was reaching out to her.

And then she thought she felt his arms around her, holding her gently, his hand on the back of her neck. She looked up into his face and saw his green eyes, intense and sad. He stared at her with a hurt look, and she wanted to kiss him the way a mother would kiss a child. But she held herself back. They looked into each other's eyes as if they had known each other for a long time.

But then he cried out and as he did so, she realized that she had never heard him say anything before. He pushed her from him and moved away. She felt as if she were watching herself interacting with him, as if she were looking through a camera, taking pictures of something happening to someone else.

He was no longer there. Had it merely been a dream? She found herself feeling increasingly disoriented. She did not know where she was. Was she in her apartment in New York in Greenwich Village on West Tenth Street? It all seemed familiar, but she knew she wasn't there. . . .

As her mind focused, it seemed she was in her Aunt Jane's apartment, where she had lived for so many years. She remembered standing in the kitchen looking at Aunt Jane's flowered dish collection, which was carefully wedged onto shelves. She picked up one of the plates to examine it more closely and dropped it. The plate broke, the pieces of fine china scattering in various directions.

She felt so sad and confused. The center was not holding. Everything seemed to be falling apart.

Her thoughts were completely muddled. *What is happening to me?* She sat up in bed and reached for the bedside light as if that might shed some light on what was happening.

Chapter 3

LAVINIA AWOKE THE NEXT MORNING WITH ONLY THE vaguest recollection of what she had seen the night before. As soon as she had breakfasted on the terrace, she walked over to Buckingham Palace. She had been right. Their uniforms were nothing like what the man had been wearing. He must have had on some kind of military uniform from the past. Her next stop, therefore, was the Westminster Library to see what she could find on military uniforms. They had drawings, prints and photographs of uniforms of the last one hundred years, and she might be able to pinpoint his if she recognized it.

The Westminster archivist, who was enthusiastic about helping the library patrons, dragged out every book, drawing, photo and print she could think of that was related to the modern British army and navy. When a disappointed Lavinia found nothing that resembled the man's outfit, the archivist suggested she go to the Army Museum in Chelsea to see if they had drawings of uniforms that dated back past a hundred years ago.

The librarian also helped her look up the leases of property owners in the Westminster area. Lavinia was able to locate the building on Belgrave Road—which, she discovered, had been planned by the master builder Thomas Cubitt.

Cubitt's famous mansions in Belgravia, a more fashionable section in Westminster, or S. W. 1, had found buyers with remarkable speed. Then he went on to build Pimlico, where Mary's flat was located; Belgrave Road, to be exact. Apparently, this section of Westminster had been difficult to lease at first. Even though the houses were beautiful, in 1863 the aristocrats did not immediately flock there. In a few years, however, respectability was bestowed on the area by the three lovely squares in Pimlico and the solid churches that overlooked them. The upper classes began to move in. Belgrave Road was situated at the end of one of the squares, and one of the first to own a house there was a Major Walter Melton.

When Lavinia saw the word "Major" her heart beat more quickly. She must be on the right track. Perhaps there would be no need to go to the Chelsea Army Museum. She might find all she needed right here, right now.

She called over the librarian.

"Look," she said, "this is terrific. And a Colonel Wheatley-Croft owned the building I'm living in."

"Maybe the army held the head lease."

"There could be a connection, you mean? It isn't random that two army families lived in the building?" Lavinia said.

"No, it was commonplace for the army to own the head lease on a property. They still may."

"Eighteen seventy-three," Lavinia said, staring at the page. "It looks as if he owned the house for many years."

"I have a suggestion," the librarian said. "If you want to find out more about him, try looking him up on *Who's Who*."

Of course, She hadn't thought of that.

"I'm sure we have the volume for that decade," the librarian went on. "If any of these people were really important, he would be mentioned there. And it is quite possible they were. Remember, this was the period of the Raj in India, and some of those army officers were exceedingly rich and important to the Crown."

Lavinia pulled out the *Who's Who* for 1873 and found a half-page entry on Colonel Wheatley-Croft. He had, indeed, served during the Raj in India. He had been a distinguished officer and an author of two books of poetry, which had been popular at the time. Lavinia's eye flitted down the page until she read:

Colonel Wheatley-Croft died of a heart attack shortly after the bizarre murder of his brother, Christian, who himself was a major in the army. Christian Wheatley-Croft, the author of the book *New American Psychics*, was found stabbed to death in his brother's home. The colonel died in 1886.

Lavinia closed the book. Here was the connection. It was staring her right in the face. This could not be a mere coincidence. Major Wheatley-Croft was perceptible to her because they shared a common bond—the occult.

She knew that near the end of the nineteenth century, a few aristocrats, mainly men, had been involved to various degrees with the paranormal, but most people looked askance at it. A group of women writers, all upper-class, used to spend their evenings writing stories about ghosts, apparitions and poltergeists.

The Society for Psychical Research had been formed in 1882. This group, which still existed with its offices at Number One Adam and Eve Mews, in Kensington, were skeptics who hoped that a scientific investigation of the occult would lead to a debunking. Curiously, some of them had been converted into believers. Perhaps the major had been part of their society.

Lavinia thanked the librarian, photostated the page on the colonel and his murdered brother and walked slowly back toward Belgrave Road.

She could see Major Wheatley-Croft quite clearly. He had an odd expression on his face, a look somewhere between astonishment and fear. She imagined that was what he looked like as his attacker came at him with the knife.

Then she saw the blood gushing from his arm. It was ugly, horrible, she thought, trying to push the image away. All the way back to Belgrave Road, she imagined she could hear him screaming, crying out for help. *Why can't I stop thinking about him?* she asked herself frantically.

And then she realized that she was—somehow, inexplicably—seeing the past. The images that had been flashing through her mind were of the past, a past she would have no way of knowing about in any conventional way. Her "siting" of the ghost now seemed to include backdrops of the time he had lived in. Even worse, Lavinia knew that these episodes of seeing the major and the past were beyond her control.

Who could she discuss this with? Lady Chamberlain! She must go down to Kent and talk to Lady Chamberlain about what was happening. Paul's mother had said something extraordinary was going to happen to Lavinia, and this certainly was. . . .

The phone was ringing when Lavinia walked into the flat.

"Hello, Lavinia, it seems ages since we've spoken."

It was Mrs. Patel-Ram. Lavinia immediately cheered up, hearing the woman's warm, kindly voice.

"I do hope your research is going splendidly and that you're finding time as well to enjoy our wonderful summer weather."

Lavinia debated confiding in Mrs. Patel-Ram. But her story didn't seem the kind one told over the telephone, and for some reason, she felt that Lady Chamberlain might be the better person to share it with.

"I wonder whether you might like to meet Janet Grier, a young friend of mine," Mrs. Patel-Ram want on. "She has a fascinating ghost story. Authentic, of course. She could be over in ten minutes if that's convenient for you."

Lavinia did not protest. She needed a break from her own ghost story. Perhaps Janet Grier's stories would divert her. She hung up after promising Mrs. Patel-Ram to come visit her soon.

Janet Grier rang the buzzer in exactly ten minutes. She was a beautiful, dark-haired English woman whose manner was friendly and charming.

"I don't really believe in ghosts, or anything like that," she said after she had admired Mary's decor.

"Oh, I don't either," Lavinia said, thinking that just a week before she would have felt more sincere in her comment.

"Well, I'll get right to it, shall I? Although I must admit the subject makes me rather nervous."

"By all means," Lavinia said, thinking that were she to tell this woman about the recent goings-on here, she would jump up and run away. She turned on her tape recorder and Janet began.

"It was after we moved into our new house. I became aware of the thing in the living room. The room was at the back of the house, facing the garden. There were French windows leading to the garden. That part of the room was different. It was lower."

"Oh, like this room," Lavinia said, pointing to the other end where she had first seen the outline of the man whom she now took to be the major. As she listened to Janet Grier, she wondered about the reason for the major's appearance. It had to be something more than the fact that she was a researcher for a television special on the paranormal. How would he know that she might be friendly toward him? In fact, she had the same reaction as most people do when confronted with a ghost. She was terribly frightened. She hoped the major would not return. She really did want to be left in peace, to get on with her work.

"Like this room?" Janet said. "I suppose so. But there was something funny about it. The front door had been moved to the side. And the house next door, which was supposed to be architecturally identical, should have had a fireplace in the hall. I went over there to see if there was any sign of a fireplace like ours, but there wasn't. I felt a definite evil presence. I could have lived with a friendly presence, maybe, but not an evil one."

Lavinia sighed. Another horror story.

"Shall I go on?" Janet asked, noticing Lavinia's discomfort.

"Yes, certainly," Lavinia said, a knot in her stomach.

Was the major evil? And what did he want from her? Did he want her to help him in some way? Ghosts did want to return to the world of the spirits. He might want her to help him leave Belgrave Road. But how could she do that for him?

"The previous owner had been separated from her husband, and he had gotten himself involved in a shady deal. One night he came home to find three men waiting for him. They attacked him with an ax."

"An ax? Did he die?"

Janet shrugged.

"That's just it. No one really knows. Oddly enough, his body was never found. I think he must have been haunting the house. In the end I couldn't tolerate it, so we moved."

"How awful," Lavinia said, wondering if she ought to move

out of Mary's flat. She would go to a hotel if she could find one. This was tourist season and everything was fully booked. Or she could stay with Mrs. Patel-Ram, who had already invited her. She did have a choice, after all.

On the other hand, she had to admit she was extremely curious, and that alone might keep her in the flat. She wanted to find out more about Major Christian Wheatley-Croft, who had died in tragic circumstances.

"My daughter said things used to move, too," Janet said, startling Lavinia. "A balloon had floated from her bedroom all the way downstairs into the living room. We hated that house. Maybe something awful happened there aside from what we already knew. I think we got out just in time," she said, laughing. "I've got to rush home to the children, but I really hope I've helped in some way. Mrs. Patel-Ram has been a friend of my mother's for donkey's years. She said you wanted some firsthand stories."

"You were very helpful," Lavinia said. "Thank you for stopping by."

After Janet left, Lavinia remembered she needed a new typewriter ribbon, and she needed to do some grocery shopping. She walked over to the Upper Tachbrook Street open market where she enjoyed browsing among the stalls of appetizing fruits and vegetables, flowers and clothes.

She picked out a bouquet of purple heather, bought her groceries and two cassettes for her typewriter and decided to head back to the flat, making a mental note to call Paul. She had forgotten about his lunch invitation. It was too late now, anyway.

As she walked along, a curious feeling of déjà vu came over her, as if she had made this exact trip before, possibly many times before. And, briefly, an image flashed into her mind. A woman with blond hair piled up on her head was walking along in front of her, holding a bunch of purple flowers.

The woman stopped, turned and went down Belgrave Road, hesitating at 112.

There was something strangely familiar about the scene, Lavinia thought. And, then, the woman turned and looked her way. Lavinia saw herself. The woman looked exactly like Lavinia, except that her hair was much longer and she was wearing a

Victorian dress. Was this clairvoyance, the ability to see by unusual mental power events taking place at a distance?

Then the image faded away. Lavinia was standing outside the flat at 112 Belgrave Road. No one else was in sight. She sniffed the heather. The aroma was reassuringly strong and real.

Evidently, she thought, she was discovering mental capabilities she'd never been aware of, even though her education and sense of logic told her that was nonsense.

After she had unpacked and put away the groceries, she went upstairs to get Paul's office telephone number.

I should have called him earlier, she chided herself as she came down the spiral staircase. And then she saw the major. He was sitting at Mary's Victorian card table, eyes half closed, a pained expression on his face. In his right hand, which had long, tapering fingers, he was holding the ring with the red stone that he must have taken from her jewelry box.

He began to weep, the tears rolling down his cheeks.

Lavinia impulsively rushed forward to comfort him.

"Don't cry," she said. "It's all right. I'll help you."

She reached out to touch him. Her hand went right through the uniform, through his shoulder, so that she could see it protruding on the other side. She gasped, withdrawing her hand, aware that she could not feel any flesh. It were as if nothing were there.

The major disappeared. She was alone in the room.

Lavinia sat down, staring about her, hardly aware of her surroundings.

He had not seemed to be aware of her. She could see him, but could he see her? She looked down. The ring lay on the carpet. She picked it up and slid in onto her finger. Was he frightened? Was that why he had gone away so quickly. She could neither conjure him up nor could she communicate with him when he did appear.

Was there any way to make him materialize again? Or would she have to wait for him to appear? And how long would that be?

Lavinia got up slowly. She felt as if she were waking from a trance or a dream. She had no appetite for lunch, but she did remember to call and leave a message for Paul, apologizing for not having called him earlier. Then she went up to the landing and sat down at her typewriter.

She would write to Lady Chamberlain and describe all the odd, frightening occurrences. She wanted to explain to her, event by event, what had happened. The situation was too complicated to convey over the phone. She would begin with the major's first appearance on horseback, riding down Belgrave Road, and tell her about his tearful behavior this morning. Lady Chamberlain would understand and might have some helpful advice for her.

When she got to the part about how her hand had moved right through his body, she shivered. She was frightened by the fact that when she touched him she had felt nothing solid. It was a unique—and disconcerting—sensation.

Abruptly, this brought to mind another encounter she had had with the major when he came to her in her bedroom. She had wanted to kiss him, had wanted to feel his mouth on hers, his arms around her. Had she kissed him? Had he been flesh?

Lavinia stood up from the typewriter and went out onto the terrace. The dog opposite was barking as usual. She turned and leaned against the railing, looking up at the back of the building. She could see Paul's windows, which gave her a sense of security.

She must have dreamed of the major. She had embraced Christian Wheatley-Croft in her mind. . . . But why would she have such a fantasy about a ghost? The question sent her back to her typewriter to finish her letter to Lady Chamberlain.

There was no reason to hide anything, including her dream about the ghost.

There, it was done. Would Lady Chamberlain be put off by a three-page letter from someone she'd met only once? No, Lavinia thought not. She glanced at her watch. There was still time for her to make the late mail collection, so that the letter might get to Kent tomorrow.

After she had deposited the envelope in the mailbox, she decided to go for a walk. Instead of her usual route around Dolphin Square and up and down the streets of Pimlico, she would explore the other way, toward St. Vincent's Square. Perhaps she'd walk over to the Tate Gallery, which was on the Embankment, not far away.

The late afternoon air was warm and lots of people were out. St. Vincent's Square was up ahead. She turned the corner and there it was, slightly run down. It had probably once been a beautiful square, but she always felt there was something gloomy about it. It looked like a set from a movie about a haunted house.

She laughed at herself for invoking such an image. Children were playing in the square, and several nannies strolled through, gossiping and pushing prams. A couple of people rode past on horseback.

Lavinia stared after them. They were either wearing costumes or had, indeed, come from a movie set. The woman sat sidesaddle and was wearing a long dress, the kind Lavinia had seen in movies or in photos of the nineteenth century. She looked grand. So did the man. He was wearing hunting gear, a black hat and a red coat. They trotted out of sight.

Lavinia sat down on a bench. What was next? She glanced at the three children playing with a ball. There were two boys and a girl, all about seven or eight. They, too, were wearing old-fashioned clothes. Then she noticed that the nanny, who had on a long dress and a straw bonnet, called out to them sharply in a country accent that Lavinia could not identify.

Was she seeing things? She closed her eyes briefly. When she opened them a man stood in front of her. He was shabbily dressed in a pair of cotton trousers, a white shirt, the cuffs rolled up to the elbows. His hands were covered with dirt.

"Sara, Sara," he said crossly, looking at her, his cheeks flushed, perspiration on his upper lip. "You said you'd be back by four and it's five now, girl. We'll get the sack yet."

He grabbed her arm roughly and pulled her to her feet. She was about to say he was mistaken, that she was not Sara, when she glanced down and saw she was wearing a long dress of a coarse fabric that was gathered at the waist. She reached up and touched her hair. It was coiled tightly on top of her head, tucked beneath a straw bonnet. She could feel the smooth material wound around the bonnet.

"Come in straightaway," he said, "and stop staring at me as if I'm a stranger."

"Yes, Rob," she answered. Obediently, she followed him around to the side of the house.

And, then, she was sitting on the bench. She was alone. She was wearing her ordinary Lavinia clothes, not a Victorian dress. She glanced around, remembering the address of the house in Vincent Square. 92 Vincent Gardens. Lord Evans's house. But how did she know that? Where was this information coming from?

Now the square was empty. There were no children, no riders on horses, no nannies. A few people walked by on the perimeter, all wearing contemporary clothes as she was.

Lavinia walked to the other end of the square to retrace her route and to look for 92 Vincent Gardens. She knew she had been there, just as she knew that Sara was the woman she had seen with the purple flowers, the one who looked just like her. Sara Standard, a kitchen maid, married to Rob, a gardener. She had somehow crossed the time barrier to visit a world that had existed over a hundred years before.

Lavinia made her way to Vauxhall Bridge Road in a state of utter confusion. As she walked along, knowing she had been this other woman in a previous life, she was still aware of herself as Lavinia. But once again, it was as if she were looking through a camera.

She stopped at the corner, thinking that she must have been given time off. She was supposed to go to the fabric shop to order curtains for the reception room. She might even have time enough to go to the lace shop that had agreed to sell some of the lace she had brought to London from Devonshire.

Dressed in her Sunday best, Sara might even have a chance for a fleeting look at Pimlico, possibly a quick stop at the sweets shop to buy a bit of chocolate and imagine herself someone else.

Sara Standard needed to imagine herself someone else because of the misery of her life. After her latest argument with her husband, who was jealous of everything she did and anyone she knew, she felt even more disturbed.

Rob had noticed that she wore her best clothes to do the errands for Lord Evans. She had chosen her cream voile dress with peacock-blue ribbons and lace at the neck and sleeves. She wore her best hat, which was decorated with the same peacock ribbons. It was the sort of outfit she would wear to a wedding or for a special occasion.

"Going to meet your lover, are you?" Rob shouted. But he could not prevent her from leaving as Lord Evans himself had asked her to fetch the material.

Rob was wrong. Sara had no lover. But she believed that in spite of his jealousy, he did not love her. She was sure he despised her for being barren. He placed her in the same category as his plants and flowers, over which he had total control. He wanted her to bear fruit, just as his garden did. She knew he was intimidated by her, however. He was put off by her occasional flashes of temper, by the fact that she was better educated than he was.

In 1885 the average Victorian woman liked to be protected by her menfolk from all the disturbing aspects of life; from the poverty, the filth, the unfairness. Sara was supposed to be content with her life, such as it was. She was supposed to be grateful to Rob for having taken her away from her village and bringing her to London, even if it meant she had to work as a lowly kitchen maid.

But Sara was not in the least thankful.

"Women go to universities now," she would say to him when he shouted at her to be docile.

"But not women like you," he thundered.

"This is eighteen eighty-five," Sara replied defiantly, "and life is changing."

But it had not really changed so far as Rob was concerned. He felt hoodwinked. She was not a delicate maiden, the way she had presented herself to him when he met her in Devonshire. She had woven a spell around him, entrapping him, a bachelor of many years, into marriage. He was dumbfounded to find that she was three years his senior.

After they were married, he brought Sara back with him to the house of Lord Evans. Lord Evans took one look at the beautiful blond girl, whose waist-length hair sent shudders through the men in the household, and gave her the job of kitchen maid. They lived in rooms at the top of the house along with seven other servants.

The other women soon began to defer to her; her looks gave her an elite position among them. When the rumors of her witchlike proclivities got out, some of the women were afraid of her. It could only have been Rob who was spreading the rumors. He was the only one who knew anything about it.

After only two months in the city, Sara had lost her country accent. She wanted to sound as posh as the people whom Lord Evans entertained in his elegant mansion. Rob was infuriated with her efforts to better herself. He firmly believed in having a sense of place and a sense of who you were. He didn't trust her and began to hate her for using him as her escape route. He knew he could not control her but he would not give up. He would neither throw her out nor would he ever let her leave.

They were trapped together, he informed her. Whether she liked it or not, she was obliged to stay with him. Forever.

She had no place to go, in any case. There were no alternatives for working-class women.

On this summer's day in 1885 Sara felt restless and dissatisfied. If only something would happen to her to help her get over the argument with Rob. If only there were another person to whom she might speak, to whom she could confide her innermost thoughts.

She glanced in the window of the fabric shop, noticing that the material was piled up helter-skelter as if somebody had just thrown it there. They needed some new shop assistants, she thought, imagining herself inside, waiting on customers. It would be more interesting than working in a kitchen. But she could not even hope to work in a shop. If she lived in Lord Evans's house, she would have to be content with working for him as well.

She longed to share her feelings about her position in life with her husband, but he was always disturbed by what he called her revolutionary ideas, ideas that did not suit a woman. She had images of a different future, too, which he did not understand.

She had heard that in America there were people, women like herself, who could predict the future. They could tell you what you were about and where you had been. She had heard they conjured up voices of the dead. Spirits came through them to contact the living.

As she walked toward the sweet shop to buy her penny's worth of chocolate, she was aware that men were looking at her. Even the aristocrats, or particularly the aristocrats, glanced her way, their eyes swooping over her like hungry animals.

If only she knew how to use her womanhood to advantage. Surely, God had given her good looks for a reason.

She smiled to herself. She might not be an assistant in a fabric shop but she had the feeling that something else might happen to help her change her life. And her feelings had often come true in the past.

Her marriage to Rob had rescued her from the tiny village she was born and raised in. And now here she was in London. She was just a kitchen maid, but she could be promoted upstairs. Her talents for sewing and lacemaking would not go unnoticed. Nor her good looks. And Rob was not going to get in her way.

"Good morning," a low, masculine voice said.

She looked up to find Major Wheatley-Croft looking at her, his green eyes twinkling.

Her hands flew up to straighten her hat. She was not used to being addressed on the street by a gentleman. And so handsome a gentleman. He was perhaps the most attractive man she had ever seen in her life. He was very tall, broad-shouldered and trim. In his dapper clothes he was enough to make any lady swoon.

"Good morning, sir," she replied.

"You may not know who I am, Madam," he said, his voice warm, "but do not fret. I have seen you numerous times. In my dreams, of course."

His green eyes penetrated hers. She hoped she was not blushing and making a fool of herself. Since she did not know what to say in response to this, she said nothing.

"I do not expect that you would notice me, however," he said, making her wonder if he were teasing her. His eyes remained fixed on her.

"A woman of your appearance would of course catch *my* eye," he went on. "It's the hair, perhaps."

"Are you making fun of me, sir?"

He laughed unrestrainedly.

Sara had tried hard to overcome her working-class accent. But now, to her consternation, her Devonshire accent had emerged. She wondered it her cheeks were vermillion.

"I know you work for Lord Evans," he said. "I have seen you there."

Sara remembered the gossip she had heard about the major. He was about fifty, unmarried, rich and considered eccentric. He had retired from the army, but no one knew why. It was rumored that he was writing a book of some kind.

"Would you like some sweets?" he asked, taking her arm and pushing open the door to the sweet shop. Sara quickly looked to the right and to the left to make certain no one had seen them entering the shop, arm in arm.

"You may have whatever you want," he said, ushering her up to the counter.

As nervous as she was, Sara enjoyed the touch of his hand on her arm. She felt very shy and, at the same time, excited. But she was not entirely surprised that they had met each other. She'd had a feeling that something was about to happen.

She selected five pence's worth of chocolate, more chocolate than she had ever bought before. Major Wheatley-Croft paid for the candy, took the bag and guided her outside.

"I realize that it is unwise for a married lady to be seen with an unmarried man of my sort," he said, "but I would like to invite you for tea."

"And my husband, too?" she said, chancing that her sharp tongue would not annoy him. It did not.

"It's you I want, not the gardener."

His blunt announcement of his intentions made her blush in spite of her resolve not to. She gazed at him, wondering whether he was teasing her again. But his voice and tone were as serious as the expression in his eyes, and she felt a swift, intense yearning shoot through her body.

"I live nearby," he said. Before she could demur, he grasped her arm and pulled her toward a waiting horse-drawn carriage that she had not previously observed.

Lavinia opened her eyes. She was standing on the pavement in front of her house on Belgrave Road. She had no idea how she had got there.

She knew, just as certainly as she knew anything, that she had been this other woman. And she was not going mad. She was the same sane Lavinia who had walked off the plane at Heathrow with the sole intention of doing a damned good job uncovering tales of ghosts and spirits.

But she also knew she had entered the sweet shop in the person of Sara Standard, long dead.

She suddenly wanted badly to share this knowledge with Paul. She let herself into the building and rushed up to his flat, praying he would be home. For a person who was a fence-sitter about believing in God, she had been doing quite a bit of praying recently.

She knocked on his door. The moment he opened the door, a smile crossed his face.

"Paul, I got your message but I . . . I suspect that I have some strange powers," Lavinia blurted out before he could even greet her.

"Do come in," he said, trying to cover the worry in his voice. Lavinia was flushed and breathless.

"Would you like something to drink? Tea, or something stronger?"

"No," she said, trying to compose herself. "Look, Paul, I wonder if I could go and see your mother? I need her help."

"Of course, Lavinia. Sit down and tell me what's going on, and I'll ring her."

Despite his reassuring tone, Paul was concerned for Lavinia.

He watched her gnawing at her bottom lip as she prepared to tell him about her "strange powers." He realized he very much cared about this lovely American woman and would do what he could to help her. But he almost dreaded hearing what she had to say. And he was even more reluctant to have his mother get involved with whatever Lavinia was experiencing. He knew his mother would only push Lavinia further along the path, the path of the unknown. And yet he also knew that her voyage was almost inevitable.

Chapter 4

LADY CHAMBERLAIN HAD NOT YET RECEIVED LAVINIA'S letter. But after listening to Lavinia's story for several minutes, she invited both of them down to Kent for a few days to discuss the matter face to face, and to see whether she could help Lavinia sort it out.

She suggested that they have a seance to authenticate Lavinia's claim. It was not that she did not believe her. But she wanted to see how far her medium abilities went. Would she be able to cross the time barrier at will? Could her abilities be demonstrated in front of others, the way most mediums could?

Besides, Lady Chamberlain was herself interested in the people Lavinia so carefully described to her. The notion that Lavinia had previously lived the life of a working-class English girl from Devonshire amused Lady Chamberlain. It fascinated her, as well.

Lady Chamberlain looked fondly at an apprehensive Lavinia, who was seated in the music room, Paul at her side. "Seeing a ghost is a perfectly natural phenomenon," Lady Chamberlain said. "I assure you, my dear, you are not going mad."

"I really wonder, Mother, whether Lavinia should be subjected to all of this," Paul said, "Maybe she does not *want* to prove she is a medium."

"Oh, I do, I do," Lavinia said firmly. She had had twenty-four hours, after her phone conversation with Lady Chamberlain, to reflect on the entire matter. Although she felt some trepidation, she knew she wanted to participate in the seance, if only to prove to herself that she had not invented everything.

Lady Chamberlain smiled like a mother hen and took Lavinia's arm to guide her through the music room into what she called "my seance room."

It was a perfectly ordinary room, as exquisitely decorated as the other rooms in the manor house. The only difference was its size. Small and cozy.

In the center of the room was a small round wooden table, surrounded by five chairs. Lady Chamberlain noticed Lavinia's questioning look.

"We'll be five together," she said. "Myself, you and Paul, your friend Mrs. Patel-Ram and Dr. Hare, a good friend of mine. He's a psychic researcher who often attends seances. I think you'll find him most sympathetic."

"What my mother means," Paul said drily, "is that *she* finds Dr. Hare most sympathetic. He's a researcher who seems to have lost most of his objectivity." He stopped suddenly, realizing that the same could be said for Lavinia. "Actually," he continued, "I hadn't planned to be involved in the seance."

He didn't want to admit how uncomfortable he felt about the possibility that a spirit might speak through Lavinia. Although prepared to do whatever he could to help her, he felt reluctant to explore the spirit world—a world he refused to believe in— with this woman to whom he was so attracted.

Lavinia gazed at him pleadingly. "Oh, please, Paul," she begged. "I need you here for moral support." She blushed, wondering whether he understood how important it was to her that he stay in the room.

"In that case, of course I'll stay," Paul said.

"Darling," his mother said, "would you rearrange the chairs so that we'll all feel comfortable at the table? And Lavinia, would you like a small glass of sherry? You seem rather apprehensive."

"I am nervous, I must admit. But do you think I should drink alcohol? I don't want anything to cloud my mind or ruin my concentration."

Lady Chamberlain's loud, uninhibited laugh filled the small room. She waved her hands so that the large silver bangles dangling from her wrists clinked noisily. "Makes no difference, none at all! You have those qualities in spite of anything you might do. It has nothing to do with you as you know yourself in this world we call reality."

"This is all so confusing," said Lavinia. To read about spirits and mediums was one thing; to participate in a seance in which she herself might be the medium was a much more difficult and daunting idea.

Lady Chamberlain took her arm and brought her over to a small brocade sofa. "We are merely going to see whether you can get in touch with these controls, or communicators. These voices from another place. But remember, a control is considered distinct from a communicator. The control will speak through you but seem to be a part of your personality. The communicators could give you all sorts of information about those present. For example, a communicator might tell us through you all sorts of information about Dr. Hare or myself, or even Paul. I hope you understand that you have nothing to be afraid of."

Paul smiled reassuringly at Lavinia, at the same time ardently wishing that the communicator would *not* have anything to say about him.

Lady Chamberlain poured three glasses of sherry and handed one to Lavinia.

"Now, you said you dreamed of this major, this ghost, and that you saw him, too. You know when he lived and you know where. And you were the woman Sara? Is this all correct?"

"Yes. I know it all sounds very odd," Lavinia said.

"Not at all." Lady Chamberlain shook her head vigorously. "But you say you cannot materialize him," Lady Chamberlain glanced at her son. She was so used to his protestations that she was amused to see how interested he was in the proceedings. But she suspected his interest had more to do with Lavinia than with ghosts.

"No," Lavinia said in answer to Lady Chamberlain's question. "I've tried to get the major to appear, but I haven't been able to. I know that sounds strange," she said, turning to Paul, "but it's bad enough to see a ghost, let alone a ghost who comes and goes as he pleases."

She realized how badly she wanted to see the major, or Christian, as she had begun to think of him. She wanted to be able to establish contact with him. There was so much more to know about him and Sara.

"Perhaps we can contact him today and give him strict orders to get out of your life altogether," Paul said with faint humor.

Lavinia said nothing. She couldn't admit to Paul, who surely would think she was crazy, that in fact she didn't want the major to disappear permanently from her life. Quite the opposite, she realized. She wanted to be able to return to the past, to the time and place where Christian, an actual man of the flesh, lived. But how could she admit this, especially to the skeptical Paul, who might quickly lose interest in her?

"It's all a matter of concentration," Lady Chamberlain said, sipping the sherry. "It's not something you *will*, exactly. It simply happens to you if it's going to happen. If you really are a medium. Although I have no doubt about that, Lavinia. . . ." She paused and looked at her meaningfully. "We will see right here today and very soon."

Paul stood up. "Mother. . ."

"Darling," Lady Chamberlain said, "Lavinia has never performed in public, and she is frightened. Just look at her. Please do her this kindness and stay."

Lavinia swallowed nervously. The word "perform" had caused a knot to form in her stomach. She was frightened. She would be expected to go into a trance. She might fail to find the wedge, so to speak. It might all get away from her. She wanted desperately to be able to cross over again but she did not feel the least bit confident that she could.

All she knew for certain was that she had to find out more about Christian's last year of life. If she knew enough she might be able to link it to the present. And for some reason this now seemed terribly important.

Lady Chamberlain jingled her bracelets to get Lavinia's attention.

"Don't slip away, dear, not yet," she said.

Presently, Mrs. Patel-Ram was ushered in, resplendent in a dark blue sari with a blue and silver scarf around her shoulders. Lavinia introduced the two women. They clearly liked each other on sight. Several minutes later the butler ushered in Doctor Hare, who shook hands with everyone and squeezed Lavinia's palm as if he were giving her a secret message.

He was a middle-aged man with a round face, thinning hair and bright dark eyes. Lavinia liked him immediately. She could feel how sympathetic he was to her.

He kissed Mrs. Patel-Ram's hand, admired her sari and discovered that they knew several people in common from various psychic meetings.

"I wonder why you and I have never met before," Lady Chamberlain said, addressing Mrs. Patel-Ram.

"Perhaps we have," Mrs. Patel-Ram smiled serenely.

Dr. Hare then inspected the table and chairs.

"I think we should get on with it as soon as we can," he said in his sonorous voice. "We don't want to keep someone waiting."

Paul sat down next to Lavinia at the table. Mrs. Patel-Ram sat next to him, and Dr. Hare took the chair next to her. Lady Chamberlain sat at the head of the table.

The heavy drapes had been pulled shut to obliterate any light. They sat in darkness except for the glow of the gas fire.

"You're going into a trance," Lady Chamberlain said softly. "Everything is quiet, peaceful. It's all right. You may contact the other side whenever you're ready. Just relax and let your controls come through you. Let them do the work. Let them speak. They want to speak through you."

Lavinia closed her eyes and listened as Lady Chamberlain repeated the words. She tried to let her mind drift loose.

She opened her eyes.

"I don't think I can do it. I'm terribly nervous. I'm sorry."

"You can. You will, dear. It's happening already," Lady Chamberlain said.

Lavinia felt her eyes closing on their own. Lady Chamberlain was speaking again in that low, soft voice. She concentrated on what she was saying.

Then there was silence. Lavinia listened to the silence. She felt she was being carried away on a gentle wave. She became aware of a strange sound, like a dog panting.

It was Lavinia herself, breath coming in short little spurts.

"Is she all right?" Mrs. Patel-Ram asked with alarm.

"She is quite all right," Lady Chamberlain said firmly. "This will not last long. She is going into an unconscious state. Let us not disturb her."

Lavinia continued to breathe haltingly. Her head bobbed forward and she slumped into her chair.

"This is terrible," Paul said. "She looks ill. We have to bring her out of this."

"My goodness, darling, you've seen trance mediums before. This is no different," his mother whispered.

Paul felt torn. He knew his mother was right but nevertheless he couldn't bear Lavinia's agitation.

"I don't know why we should put her through this," he said.

"She's all right," Lady Chamberlain assured him. "You're all right, aren't you, Lavinia?"

Lavinia sat up and seemed to nod.

"You are going to speak to Christian. Can you see him?"

Lavinia nodded again.

All eyes were upon her.

"They're here, the two of them. Sara and Christian. Yes," she said in a low voice.

She lifted her head.

"I am Sara Standard," a barely audible voice said. Although Lavinia spoke, the voice sounded not at all like her.

"Christian," the voice said.

Lavinia knew she was not dreaming, although there was a dreamlike quality to what was happening. The feeling of déjà vu was there again. She had lived it all before. But the "before" was now. It was happening, and it was real.

Her mind and body were one with Sara's.

"What year is it?" Lady Chamberlain asked.

"Eighteen eighty-five. Summer. The major is taking me to tea. We have met many times before. We have made love."

"The major is called Christian?"

"Yes, Christian," the voice of Sara answered. "We are in love."

Lavinia suddenly made a low rasping sound from deep in her chest, then slumped forward.

"This seems painful to her," Paul said. "I think we'd better stop now. She's made her case."

"Shhh," his mother said dramatically. "Are you there, Christian?"

There was no audible reply. Lavinia was lost in a summer's day of 1885. She was sitting next to the major, in the back of the brougham. The taxi was driven by a man with a whip who sat high up outside the carriage. Sara could hear the crack of the whip, reminding her that she was doing something illicit and that one day she might be punished for it.

But nevertheless she was enjoying this time with Christian. She had not often ridden in a private cab, except with him. Normally she walked or rode an overcrowded omnibus. She had always longed to ride on one of the two seats next to the driver that were reserved for men. A handrail went around the front for the safety of the passengers. As there were no boards underneath, the women's legs and feet could be seen. Because of this, and the difficulty in getting up the ladder in a wide skirt, it was considered unsuitable, even unthinkable for a woman to ride on the top. But she felt she could do anything with Christian, that somehow he would support whatever she wanted to do. And this made her very happy and excited.

And here she was, seated next to this handsome gentleman, being transported somewhere mysterious for tea. Her sense of adventure, certainly not her sense of propriety, had propelled her into this wonderful relationship. And at every crack of the whip, she felt a sinful excitement pass through her in defiance of everything she'd been taught since childhood.

Sara looked at Christian as he stared out the window at the flow of traffic. They had been lovers since the third time they'd met. She had never before experienced the intense sexual desire she felt for him.

One day, when Christian had left her in his bed to buy her flowers, she had found a medical report in his bedroom. She had lain in his bed reading it again and again, trying to make sense of it. She learned that her lover had some strange disorder that might come upon him at any time, particularly if he cut himself or were in an accident. If he began to bleed, nothing could stop the bleeding. It had to stop by itself. His doctors had given all sorts of tests and experimented with different techniques. But so far they had not come up with a diagnosis or a cure. Their only advice was for him to be careful.

"A man named Benz is designing a wonderful machine, a car with a motor in it," the major said, making a sweeping gesture with his fine hands. He spoke to her as if they were equals.

She loved when he told her stories of his past life, his days during the Raj in India, his travels throughout Europe, his trip to the United States. He vowed that in his next life not only would he be a medium but a writer, too. He wanted to communicate to others his own experiences as well as the experiences of those he had never known who had died and crossed over to the spirit world. He admired mediums for being able to do this. They could enter the lives of others almost as if they had created them. And in this respect they were, in a sense, like writers.

Christian appreciated all of Sara's stories about how, as a child, she had been able to see into the future, to predict what was going to happen to her relatives and to the other people in her village. Of course, she had been chastised for her ability. The village people had been frightened of her, and even her family had begun to reject her. In the end she became a person apart from the others, disdained and castigated.

"Many exciting things are happening," he said, stroking her hand, "in every sphere."

He bent to gently kiss her smooth cheek. "You're lovely," he said. "You understand things of the spirit and the soul better than anyone I know. Better even than the mediums in Boston, but you are a naif, unaware of your power. You have been afraid for too long, afraid to use this power."

"Yes, I fear looking into the future right now," Sara admitted.

"We know this other world exists," Christian said. "Apparitions, ghosts, clairvoyance, communicating with those who have died. Why should it frighten you?"

"You are the first man who understands," Sara said, wishing she were as spiritual as he believed her to be. Perhaps she just took her abilities for granted. In any case she would have to get used to admitting them openly after having hidden them for so long.

The taxi came to a grinding halt, almost having collided with a penny-farthing, a front-wheeled bicycle that had recently come into fashion.

Sara stared enviously through the window. To ride a penny-farthing was another one of her ambitions. Such a vehicle was impossible for women in long skirts and crinolines. She would have to wear bloomers in order to ride a penny-farthing, but she could not imagine Rob's reaction to such a daring, almost scandalous outfit. Yet here she was, Rob's wife, drinking tea and spending long hours in bed with another man.

The near collision had pushed her almost onto Christian's lap. When the driver cracked the whip again and they took off, he put his arms around her and gave her shoulders a hard squeeze, sending shivers through her. She could smell his natural masculine aroma as she nestled in his arms. An overwhelming desire to be in his bed came upon her, pushing away any other thought.

Christian leaned closer, his green eyes locking with hers.

"Do you want me to make love to you?"

"If you wish, Christian," she said. She was afraid to seem unduly sexed. The truth was, she would have him at any time.

He put his hand down the top of her dress, touched her breast and squeezed her pink nipple gently. They kissed passionately until he broke away reluctantly.

"We cannot go to my house now," he said. "They're doing inventory. We will have to wait. I don't want to take you to a *maison de rendezvous.*"

"What's that?" Sara asked, feeling greatly disappointed. She longed to be naked in his arms.

"We would have to go to Paris for that. One day..."

He smiled at her and she smiled back.

"I am taking you instead to a private club for tea."

"I can't go to a club," Sara protested. "I must not be seen in public with you, Christian. You know that."

Christian nodded. He did not want her to feel guilty, nor did he want to do anything to further arouse Rob's suspicions. Her husband was already extremely jealous, questioning Sara closely whenever she took time off from the Evans household.

"No one I know will see us there," he promised.

The carriage swung down Cheyne Walk, where the metallic sound of the barrel-organ street music greeted their ears. The sounds of laughter and conversation arose from the stalls, where fruit cakes, pickled whelks, pigs' trotters, ginger beer, lemonade and sherbet were temptingly displayed.

A squealing knot of women, their straw hats and skirts flapping in the breeze, caught her eye, reminding her that she could easily be among them.

"There's a gaiety in the air," Christian commented, peering through the little window at the women. "But underneath lurks misery."

"Because they're poor?"

"Yes. There's too much human misery and poverty. These are the diseases that afflict the working class.

Just because they are having an hour off from the crudeness of their lives doesn't erase it all."

"Can you help change their lives?" *As you've changed mine,* Sara added silently.

"No."

Christian looked sad. In the next road they saw a crowd of poorly dressed people haggling over yesterday's cabbage and ends of meat. Urchins picked through the gutter looking for any tiny scraps they could find. Christian grasped Sara's shoulder, trying to turn her away from the scene outside the carriage.

"I don't want you to see it, my love," he said.

"I know it better than you, Christian." How often had she hurried past such people doing errands for Lord Evans?

"I only became aware of this side of mankind rather late in life. In India. Starvation and early death were more common than not. But in India I also discovered the other world, the world where magical things could happen."

How lucky he was, thought Sara. Being born an aristocrat allowed him the privilege of traveling widely. He had been in places she could only dream about.

"Every Indian child has a horoscope done at birth," he went on. He had returned from India with a profound interest in matters that had yet to be proved scientifically. India had opened his eyes to myriad possibilities.

"The heavens and the movement of the planets are as significant to Indians as is the dreaded hunger of this lifetime."

"Perhaps they must think of the heavens in order to escape their misery," Sara suggested. She remembered that as a child she herself had escaped into her dreams and fantasies to temporarily forget the disappointments and deprivations that surrounded her.

"I believe you are quite right, Sara," Christian acknowledged, "but it's also true that one day all that we once considered bizarre, of the other world, will be explainable. And even if in our lifetime it is not explained, surely man will one day find a way to cope with the occult. It's just another view, after all, isn't it, my darling?"

He stroked her hand reassuringly, happy that he could express these ideas to her.

She smiled at him with a smile that revealed her love. No man had ever spoken to her the way he did.

"Tell me about your trip to America," she said. He seemed to enjoy talking about it as much as he liked talking about his time in India.

"I had a dream during my ocean voyage. Perhaps it was a vision. I dreamt I met an old woman who had the power to see into the future. But Sara, I did not know until I got there that I would meet the people who would change my life."

Sara nodded, a feeling of jealousy stealing over her. He had met a number of women psychics in Boston, and their circle of devotees. Had he loved any of them?

"I went to a seance and there she was."

"Who?" Sara said, dreading the revelation that he had loved another woman before her.

"The old woman." He laughed teasingly, touching her face with his warm hand. She had to smile. He already knew her so well that he had correctly interpreted her tone of voice.

"She was the woman in the dream, you see. It was under her influence that I decided to write the book. She said, 'Christian, you will write a book about us and take it back to the old world.

Then all of Europe will know about the Boston psychics. And we will visit London and people will see that you did not make us up.'"

"And now you cannot find a publisher," Sara said sympathetically.

"Not to worry," Christian replied. "I shall publish it myself. I shall print a limited number, sign all the copies and sell them to my friends."

The taxi bumped along and they both fell silent. Sara sank into her own thoughts.

Loving Christian was not easy for her. She could not envision ever being with him on any permanent basis, although that was what she wanted more than anything else in the world. Her true nature was not to conceal, yet she was concealing this part of her life from her husband each day. And each day she lived only for Christian. Each morning she waked wondering when and where they would meet again.

It was difficult to keep in contact without being observed. She was forced to walk past his house in the hope he would come to the window and see her so they could arrange to meet. Sometimes he would pay a visit to Lord Evans. They would pass on the stairs, or she would bring lunch on a trolley for Lord Evans and his guests. She hated seeing him there at the parties when he often brought a woman with him. He was sensitive enough to apologize to her each time and assure her that the woman was merely a friend. He loved her, he said, nobody else. Nevertheless, the sight of an elegantly dressed woman laughing coquettishly at Sara's lover was extremely painful. Sara felt continuously frustrated, knowing that she was caught in a hopeless tangle.

"I don't think we should have tea today," she said suddenly, her voice hoarse with the deep emotion she felt. "Take me back to Vauxhall Bridge Road, Christian. I must go home."

Surprised, he looked at her. Her cheeks were flushed, her eyes filled with tears.

"But what is wrong, my darling?" he exclaimed, putting his arm around her and hugging her. "Are you ill?"

Indeed, she looked feverish, and he wondered why he had not noticed before.

"I suddenly feel so overwhelmed with a sense of sin," she murmured, burying her head in his shoulder. "I am not ill, but I am sick in my soul because this is so wrong."

Christian immediately called out instructions to the driver to turn around. Sara never said anything she did not mean, and he knew he must respect her wishes.

He held her in his arms as the brougham retraced the route. Sara's passionate nature was clearly etched in her expression, in her large blue eyes and her bee-stung lips that he so longed to kiss. He ran his fingers under her bonnet and pulled some blond tendrils of hair from beneath it. He stroked her hair and the nape of her neck, remembering the first time he had encountered her on Churton Street.

She had had the grace, the carriage of a woman of his class. She was well attired in a dress that he later learned was of her own design and making. She was so beautiful and proud. It was no surprise that he had been immediately attracted to her, wanting her before they had exchanged even one word.

"Wednesday, four o'clock," he said. "No one will be at home then. You'll come to me, won't you?"

Sara glanced up at him and nodded, grateful that he had immediately obeyed her wishes. She felt Rob waiting for her, pacing to and fro in front of Lord Evans's house. And if she did not appear soon, she knew he would go looking for her.

In a few minutes she would be standing alone on the pavement, her lover gone. This image saddened her. She eagerly raised her face to be kissed. Their lips came together hungrily.

Lavinia's head rolled back. She jerked convulsively. When she opened her eyes, Dr. Hare was bending over her.

"Are you all right?" he asked.

Lavinia looked around the table anxiously, wondering what she had said or done.

Paul was staring at her, but she could not read his expression.

Lady Chamberlain laughed in delight.

"That was splendid," she said.

"What happened?" Lavinia felt dizzy and headachy.

"You don't remember?" Paul asked.

"I vaguely remember what happened," Lavinia tried to explain, "but did the voices come through? Were there communicators? Did you hear Christian? The major? Did you hear him?"

"We could hear several voices, which sometimes seemed to be mixed up together," Dr. Hare said, turning off his tape recorder. "There was a woman named Sara and a military person. Shall I play the tape back?"

"Not now, not now," Paul said, hastily getting up from his chair. "I think she's had enough for one day."

Lavinia smiled her thanks. Paul was right. She was very tired and not emotionally prepared to hear herself on tape.

"There is no doubt that you are a medium, dear," Lady Chamberlain said in a congratulatory way. "Next time it will be all the better. It's never very clear in the beginning."

"It was all clear to me," Lavinia said tearfully.

"Yes," Paul said, pacing about the room. "We heard two distinct voices, a man speaking in a man's voice and a woman speaking in a woman's voice. There was another man, I think, although that was something of a muddle, I have to admit. One of them said something to Mother."

"I don't quite understand," Lavinia said, Her head was pounding, and tears unexpectedly sprang to her eyes.

"It was fascinating, my dear," Mrs. Patel-Ram said gently. "Now don't be getting into a state. Eventually, it will all become clear."

"But it was clear to me," Lavinia said, "I suppose I'm not much of a success as a medium." She tried to make a joke of it, but her voice faltered, betraying her confusion.

"I don't like this very much," Paul said. "Wherever these voices are coming from, they're very upsetting to you."

"It's London, obviously," his mother said. "Nineteenth century. I'd stake my life on it."

"I don't think Lavinia should do this again," Paul said, pulling back the drapes and flooding the room with light. "Lavinia, you look exhausted. Come upstairs and lie down and I'll bring you some tea and sandwiches."

"I want to hear the tape," Lavinia said hesitantly, brushing away the tears with the back of her hand.

"Lavinia, if you insist, of course you shall hear the tape," Lady Chamberlain said.

"But for once I agree with my son. You've just been through a difficult emotional time. You'll be fine, and you succeeded admirably. But why not leave the tapes for later?"

"I shall have to take the tapes home and analyze them," Dr. Hare said. "I'd be happy to ring you in a day or two, Lavinia, and arrange a meeting in London. I'm not sure how much the machine actually picked up."

Lavinia looked at Dr. Hare, who was gathering up his equipment.

"In other words, what was in my mind, back there in the past, was not really communicated through the voices you say you heard?"

"You were speaking quite quickly, and at times the voices weren't distinct from one another. But I will know more once I've listened to the tape again."

"Please, ladies and gentlemen," Lady Chamberlain said, "we can continue this discussion later. I do hope you will stay for dinner. It's calves' liver with walnuts and prunes, one of my cook's specialties." She smiled graciously, determined to turn their minds to more practical and mundane matters than ghosts and spirit voices.

"How kind of you, Lady Chamberlain, but my car is waiting. I'm so sorry to rush away, but I've a dinner in London this evening," said Mrs. Patel-Ram. "But it's been a pleasure to meet all of you. You must come visit me in London."

She kissed Lavinia and squeezed her hand encouragingly. "And you, sweet Lavinia, must not worry. I believe you, and I believe in you. Do come to tea soon."

Mrs. Patel-Ram said goodbye to Dr. Hare and Paul. Then Lady Chamberlain escorted her to her car, suggesting that they arrange to visit Lady Chamberlain's favorite medium sometime soon.

Paul and Lavinia followed Dr. Hare out of the room.

"Thank you for sitting through that, Paul," Lavinia said. "I know you must not have enjoyed it much."

"I stayed because you said it was important to you that I be there. But I wish I could persuade you not to get involved again in this sort of thing," Paul replied earnestly. She was touched by the look of concern on his face but wondered whether what he had seen had influenced his feelings about her in any way.

"Have you learned anything more about this Christian fellow?" Paul asked. "Do you feel there was any point at all to what you just put yourself through?"

Lavinia sensed in his questions a suppressed agitation and anger.

"I don't know, Paul, honestly, I don't. But I'm glad we held the seance. . . . I still feel there's more to be learned about these people. And I'm absolutely starving. That was hard work."

She changed the subject and deliberately kept the conversation light as he led her out of the room. The look on Paul's face was a warning to her that he, for one, was not eager to learn more about Christian and Sara.

As soon as Lavinia entered the guest room after dinner she felt a strange presence. The room was cool, but the shivery sensation she experienced was one she associated immediately with an encounter with Christian.

She searched through the free-standing antique wardrobes that contained Lady Chamberlain's costume collection, and then felt silly. Why would he be hiding?

She would have to be patient.

She changed out of her clothes into the nightdress and dressing gown that Lady Chamberlain had given her to wear. Paul's mother had invited her and Paul to remain in the country for a few days. She was eager to try and repeat the seance, to see what else would emerge.

"One successful effort at being a medium is not enough to

prove psychic abilities beyond a transitory accomplishment," Lady Chamberlain had said at dinner. She wanted further proof of Lavinia's newfound power. And so did Lavinia, only now she believed that the power had been there all along. She simply had never before needed to call upon this gift.

Lavinia looked at herself in the mirror, admiring the pale pink satin nightgown Lady Chamberlain had loaned her. It was soft and delicate and cut low at her breasts. She wondered how her hostess happened to own such a thing.

Sliding between the sheets of the canopied bed, she felt a thrill of excitement, convinced that Christian was going to materialize. But in spite of her resolve to stay awake she could feel herself drifting into sleep. She was roused by a pressure at the foot of the bed.

Christian was leaning against the bed as he bent to retrieve the ring with the red stone. He placed it carefully in his pocket. He was out of his uniform, wearing an open-necked white shirt and somber black trousers. He looked different, younger and more relaxed.

"Please," Lavinia said, "please look at me. I am here for you. I want to help you."

Her voice was strong and clear with an urgent tone. To her surprise he jerked his head around and looked directly at her.

"I am aware of you," he said, "but..." He stopped abruptly.

He seemed to be moving closer to her—yet as in a dream where inexplicable distortion occurs, he also seemed to be standing in one place. Lavinia sat up, and the sheet fell away. Christian's eyes glanced over the soft, rounded line of her shoulders and breasts. But his expression showed nothing.

Lavinia was aware that she was trying to woo him physically. He was a large, handsome man, a man with the look of power about him. His eyes, however, suggested an inner gentleness and sensitivity to which she was inordinately attracted.

She deliberately didn't cover herself with the sheet, although the room was chilly and she knew how revealing her nightgown was. She had tried so hard with a concentration of her will, with all her powers of thought, conscious and otherwise, to make Christian materialize. But now something else had occurred to her. If she could seduce him, then surely she could make him flesh. Or, if she could make him flesh, she could seduce him.

"How do you think you can help me?" he asked, a faint smile playing on his lips.

"I don't know yet. It's unchartered territory. It will be revealed to me in time," she stammered. She felt unexpectedly nervous. He was standing so close to her. "But at least now you can hear and see me. You didn't before. Anything could happen."

"Yes." Christian nodded agreement. "And I can even touch you." He leaned forward to touch her. His fingers were hot against her cold skin.

"I am not an incubus," he whispered. "Is that what you want?"

And then he was gone.

What had been the firm, definite shape of a man seemed to melt down to nothing before her eyes. He had simply floated away. She was staring into empty space.

She almost cried out with frustration and disappointment. He did not want her. He had read her thoughts and rejected her. Well, why shouldn't a ghost have psychic powers? He might know even before she did what her true intentions were.

Now a nagging doubt preoccupied her mind. Who was she? Was she Sara or Lavinia? She had felt his touch, a warm hand upon her skin. She had felt the vibrations that another person communicates. But was that really possible? She remembered her hand going through his body, but when he touched her his hand had remained for an instant on the surface of her skin. And she *knew* she felt his flesh. Did this mean that she was Sara?

Lavinia got out of bed feeling somewhat foolish at the thought. She went to the mirror above the dressing table and looked at herself. It was Lavinia looking back. Her hair was cut short and curly. She was wearing Lady Chamberlain's nightdress.

She went to the red leather-top desk and found a piece of blank paper. She always found it helpful when she was confused to write down some of her thoughts.

"Do I wish to make him flesh in order to seduce him? Am I sexually aroused by him? Is it because I haven't been with a man for so long? I yearn for a myth?"

She stared at the last question, trying to make sense of it. I yearn for a myth? She repeated the words out loud. Where did they come from?

She took off her nightdress and studied her naked body in the mirror. She was Lavinia Cross, but once she had lived in the body of Sara Standard. She had had a previous life.

The body is only a shell, she thought. *That is what the Buddhists believe.*

She went into the bathroom. A hot bath was always therapeutic for her. Lady Chamberlain had various bottles of French perfumed bath oil. The blue bottle with the flowers on it smelled deliciously of roses. She poured a capful into the hot water and climbed in, luxuriating in the bubbles.

If only she could analyze the incident with Christian in order to put it at a distance! But fragrant hot water heightened her aroused sensuality. This was very disturbing. She did not want to have an affair with a ghost. It was absurd. She wanted to help him, to vindicate him, set him free, and she resolved to push anything sexual from her mind.

She considered what she knew about Christian and Sara. She had been Sara, but she did not yet remember everything about her life. It would take Lavinia's medium powers to bring it back, or to bring *her* back to *it*. As Lady Chamberlain kept telling her, it had nothing to do with her will, but with whether she could slip into the trance state to go back in time. She had faith in Lavinia, Lady Chamberlain had told her before Lavinia had gone upstairs. She knew Lavinia could do it again, and each time the voices would be stronger and clearer.

Lavinia was already familiar with the historical backdrop against which the relationship between Christian and Sara had been formed. What struck her was the similarity between the nineteenth century and the present century, romantic illusions notwithstanding.

She had read that people of the nineteenth century had felt that frenetic changes in the society were engulfing them. Almost overnight the emphasis in England had shifted from an agrarian life style to an urban one. Industrialization, socialism, the Irish demand for Home Rule—all had threatened and confused the social order that previously had established Sara and Christian firmly in their separate worlds.

Lost in her thoughts of two nineteenth-century strangers who had become very real to her, Lavinia was unaware that the bath water had become tepid. She awoke from her reverie, shivering with cold. She wrapped herself in one of Lady Chamberlain's large, thick bath towels and hurried back into bed, snuggling under the comforter. Perhaps now at last she would have a peaceful sleep.

She closed her eyes. Instantly a horrible, grotesque image came to mind. Christian was grasping his arm, and blood was gushing everywhere. He was covered with his own blood, seemed almost to be drowning in it. Then he staggered and fell to the pavement in front of the restaurant where she had seen him.

Christian lay on the pavement. Although he seemed to be crying out for help, Lavinia could not hear his pleas. "This is not really happening," she told herself. "It happened over a hundred years ago. There is nothing I can do to help him."

The library book had said he was murdered. But by whom? Unless she was able to relive his last months, she would never know. But how was she to do that? Then his words came back to her. "I am not an incubus," he'd said. What had he meant?

She leaped from the bed and rummaged through her white leather holdall where she kept her notes and tape recorder, searching for the book on the supernatural, which was an alphabatized guide to everything that had to do with the subject. The entry to "incubus" read:

> According to many Church Fathers, an incubus is an angel who fell because of lust for women. Essentially, the incubus is a lewd demon, or goblin, who seeks sexual intercourse with women.
>
> The incubus can assume either a male or a female shape; sometimes it appears as a full-grown man, sometimes as a satyr. If it is a woman who has been received as a witch, she generally assumes the form of a rank goat.
>
> If we seek to learn from the authorities how it is pos-

sible that the devil, who has no body, can nevertheless perform actual coitus with man or woman, they unanimously answer that the devil assumes the corpse of another human being, male or female as the case may be, or that, from the mixture of other materials, he shapes for himself a body, endowed with motion, by means of which body he copulates with the human being.

Lavinia put on the dressing gown, feeling that she must, somehow, protect herself from what she was reading. But what did this have to do with Sara and Christian? She was sure she had not simply picked the book up out of idle, intellectual curiosity. Something had compelled her to read the entry now.

After her recent experiences with Christian, and with the newly discovered knowledge that she could trespass time, she no longer believed that events or actions occurred merely at random.

She continued turning the pages, picking out certain parts.

Devils do indeed collect human semen, by means of which they are able to produce bodily effects: but this cannot be done without some local movement; therefore, devils can transfer the semen that they have collected and inject it into the bodies of others.

"How awful!" She momentarily pushed away the book, as if to distance herself from the horror of the concept. How had she got involved with this? The idea that Christian had used such a strong word disturbed her deeply. She forced herself to continue reading.

By the time of Louis XV, his personal physician suggested that an incubus was partly the result of an overstimulated imagination, and partly an excuse for illicit relations. The incubus is most frequently a chimera, which has no more basis than a dream, a perverted imagination and very often the invention of a woman. . . .

On page after page that followed were detailed Spanish, French and Latin references. She searched the pages for anything she thought could be relevant. An incubus was a thoroughly disgusting creature. But the concept was fascinating. She felt compelled to read on, although her stomach was knotting in horror. Christian had protested that he was *not* an incubus. But she nevertheless trembled as she imagined herself, sitting up in bed, trying to tempt him to make love to her. She read the words over and over until she had almost memorized them. The French doctor's explanation for the concept provided her with some comfort. It was simply a matter of carnal lust, he seemed to be saying. That, at least, was of this world.

Lavinia closed the book and got back into bed, her thoughts tumbling around in her mind. Christian was not an incubus. But she had felt sexually attracted to him. She wanted to have sex with a ghost. Would that be considered "illicit relations"? The idea was terribly old-fashioned, but perhaps her attraction to Christian was illicit in terms of the past.

He loved Sara Standard, not Lavinia Cross, and for him there was a perceivable difference. Although Lavinia felt, even knew she had been this other woman, she *was* no longer Sara. In the present she was Lavinia only. It was almost like having multiple personalities. Lavinia had read that mediums often appear to need a sort of alibi, an extra personality that acted as a master of ceremonies, standing between them and the living and what they believed to be spirits.

Furthermore, the controls and communicators could be considered secondary personalities. And these personalities took on traits of their own. Sometimes a control could actually transmit through the medium information that the medium had never known about before.

And that was what was happening. Sara Standard was a control, certainly part of Lavinia's personality, and yet she was a communicator, too, someone distinctly different.

Lavinia sighed, wanting desperately to sleep but too keyed up by all her questions. Although she felt utterly exhausted, she was determined to try to solve the mystery. She would persist until Christian was set free.

Still, she was troubled by Christian's choice of words. *Incubus.*

Had he committed some unpardonable sin, a crime against nature or God? Was he some sort of demon? She felt suddenly ill. Where there was good, there was evil. Could Christian have been unwittingly evil? Did he in fact think of himself as an incubus?

A sharp knock on the door startled her.

She sat up.

"Yes? Who is it?"

"Lavinia, it's Paul. May I come in?"

"Yes, of course," she said, pulling the quilt up around her.

"Sorry to bother you," Paul said. "I wanted to make sure you were all right. My room's just on the other side of your bath. I heard the water running before and thought you might be having trouble sleeping."

Lavinia was glad he'd come by. She wanted him to put his arms around her and hold her but decided against pursuing the desire.

"Sit down," she said. "I'm having trouble getting to sleep. I guess I'm still too keyed up from this afternoon. I can't seem to relax."

"Would you like a brandy? It'll give you pleasant dreams," Paul said, sensing that she was holding something back. He felt the urge to reach out and touch her cheek, stroke her soft skin. He ached to kiss her, but unless she openly indicated that this was what she wanted, he was not going to persist. He didn't want her to feel uncomfortable and he was sure that the day would come when she would invite him of her own accord. He could wait.

"No," Lavinia said. "But thanks for the offer."

She was staring at him intensely, her light blue eyes appearing dark in the dim light of the bedroom.

"What is it?" he asked.

"Nothing," she said. She realized she felt very close to him. Paul was so sympathetic, so nurturing, even as he declared his mistrust of the paranormal.

It was then that she realized the physical attraction she felt for him. She was so terribly confused. Was this some residue from her feeling about Christian, or did the feeling have only to do with Paul? Whatever it was, she yearned for him—to be held in his arms, to feel his lips, to make love with him.

Lavinia felt her breath quicken and she licked her lips nervously, wondering whether Paul sensed her longing. And yet she felt that somehow the timing was inappropriate. She stifled a giggle. Surely she wasn't worried that Christian might be jealous if she slept with another man! Or was it that Paul was becoming too important to her, and that she first wanted to resolve all her questions about Christian and Sara and herself?

Paul abruptly reached over and took her hand. His fingers were warm. He squeezed her hand reassuringly, communicating his affection for her but also letting her know that he would wait until she was ready.

"Lavinia, you seem so distracted and disturbed. When I first met you, you had a much calmer air about you. I have to admit I don't at all understand what's driving you to communicate with these ghosts or spirits or whatever they are. But I want you to know, I'll do anything I can to help you."

"Thank you, Paul." Her eyes filled with tears.

His words did, somehow, soothe her. She'd been feeling so alone and helpless. But she wasn't. Paul was her friend, and so was his mother. She trusted both of them. She could feel Paul's warmth and energy. Just the fact that he was concerned about her was reassuring.

He stood up and said, as if she were a child, "Now it's time for you to get some rest, young lady. Lie down and let me tuck this quilt around you."

She obediently snuggled under the cover.

"Close your eyes," he whispered, bending down and kissing her gently on the cheek. "Lavinia, I think there's something special between us. Promise me we won't let it disappear."

"I promise," she said. "Paul, sit a minute until I get sleepy."

"Of course." He stroked her hair soothingly. "Lavinia, I hope you find your answers."

"I must," she murmured. "I will."

"Perhaps we'll both find answers. Life is filled with surprises."

Her breathing rose and fell quietly. She was asleep within a few minutes. Paul kissed her again, then stood watching her face for a moment until he left the room, closing the door behind him.

Surprises, he thought, climbing into his own bed. Normally Paul didn't care much for surprises, but one that included a happy ending for him and Lavinia might be jolly pleasant.

Chapter 5

"**W**HAT DO YOU SEE? WHAT DO YOU HEAR? ALLOW them to come through," Lady Chamberlain said to Lavinia. They were gathered again, two days later, in Lady Chamberlain's "seance room."

"I hear voices," Lavinia said slowly. "A woman. It's Sara. She's about my age. I want to go now."

She closed her eyes, obliterating the present as she crossed backward to 1885.

Sara Standard, dressed in her straw bonnet and Sunday finery, peeked into the kitchen to check that all of Christian's servants were gone. The house was empty except for herself and her lover.

Christian's house was large and grand with numerous landings and many airy rooms. There were nooks and crannies everywhere and at least four terraces. The building was five stories high, and the servants lived on the top floor. She and Christian had their own private kitchen and sitting room, which he had built when his brother had passed the house on to him.

Sara thought the house was too large for one man who lived alone. Christian needed a wife and family. And this knowledge hurt her, because she could not be his wife. She had had a curious presentiment one afternoon in which she saw herself living in this very house with Christian and a baby. But she had brushed away the vision as wishful thinking, rather than an example of her clairvoyance.

Christian stood waiting on the landing.

The scene shifted. Sara and Christian were riding in his carriage, their arms clasped about each other. And then Sara was alone in the country church, having gone down to Devon to visit her two cousins, who had been kind to her when she was a child. An elderly brother and sister, they lived together in a small house, raising chickens and breeding King Charles spaniels.

Sara knelt in the confessional booth of the country church.

"We have made love many times, Father. I know I have sinned, and I know I will sin again. The first time was the bank holiday. We went to Greenwich in his carriage. It was a misty, summer day and we ate crumpets with the finest roll butter. He bought me sachets of lavender, which I hid from my husband. We returned to his house and we drank wine. The room became so warm I thought I would swoon. Forgive me, Father. Forgive me my sins. I know I will go to hell. But I love him."

Sara had spent the weekend with Christian, having told her husband she was going to Devon to see her cousins. They had stayed in bed most of the weekend, making love for hours, utterly wrapped up in their feelings for each other. They had lain naked, whispering to each other their fantasies, their hopes and dreams.

"You are lovely," Christian said, stroking her breasts, gently touching her nipples. She had beautiful, large breasts that emphasized her flat belly and slim hips. He sensed her health and youthfulness through her eager sensuality.

Christian had intended to tell Sara about his illness, which was the reason he had retired early from his army career. But he had not yet had the heart to explain his ailment. He worried that their age difference was a barrier and that she might be frightened off if she were to know the potential gravity of his bleeding problem, which did not even have a name.

He had discovered in India that he must be very careful to avoid cutting himself or being cut because he would bleed interminably. This was always in the back of his mind—the need to be careful—but he would not let it impinge on his life. He was by nature an adventurer.

When he found that there was no treatment to his mysterious bleeding and that complications might bring on his early death, he had resigned from the army. Life was for living, and there were many places to see and things to be done before he went to his grave.

His trip to America had opened up to him a whole new world. It was as if his illness had helped him to change his life, so in this sense it was a blessing in disguise. The psychics that he had met in Boston whose experiences he had described in his book told him about the writers and artists who met in the homes of London aristocrats. No one cared about a person's background or social status. There was a true democratic spirit, as he had observed in Boston. He wanted to introduce Sara to his new friends and have them help her explore the now dormant psychic abilities that she had demonstrated again and again when she was younger.

Sara had told him that her family and neighbors had regarded her as demonic. Some had even whispered that she was a witch. She had been shunned by many because her ability to predict the future frightened them. Eventually, she had suppressed the tendency, not wanting to make enemies of the village folk. Christian sometimes ached with sadness for Sara when he imagined her isolated and condemned for her marvelous ability to see into the future. Still, he understood how fearful most people were of the unknown. He, at least, could understand this part of her. That she could tell him the truth seemed to relieve her of an enormous burden. He hoped that she would always feel free to tell him the truth and was glad to share with her this bond.

Lavinia seemed to be in a trance. She thrashed in the chair, and tears ran down her cheeks. She spoke in a low, masculine voice.

"Does Rob know?" Christian asked.

"I love you, Christian, but he knows."

Another male voice emerged.

"I'll kill him," Rob shouted angrily.

Sara began to undress, pulling the crinolines over the silk underwear that Christian had brought her and that she had had to conceal from Rob. Rob had followed her from St. Vincent's Square one day and had seen Christian's carriage. When she came home he beat her, cutting her lip and blackening her eyes. She saw murder in his face. The price of love was high.

Christian had no intention of giving her up. He was determined to find a way to be with her. She was part of his destiny even if she were not yet free. There were so many obstacles, so many. No one of his background married a servant girl, and a Roman Catholic one at that!

But his passion had overtaken reason and convention. Nothing could prevent him from being with Sara—not custom, not society, not the Church, not Rob.

Sara stood in front of the Venetian glass mirror, pinning up her long, blond hair. "When will I meet your psychic friends?" she said.

Christian came up behind her and pushed his lithe, muscular body against her. He squeezed her waist until she cried out. She twirled around and put her arms around Christian's neck, pulling him close to kiss her. She thanked the good Lord for sending her such a man.

"I will take you everywhere," Christian promised, "but first we will have to free you of Rob, won't we?"

Sara frowned. She looked up at him with her large, innocent blue eyes.

"How?"

"There are ways." Christian smiled, thinking that a person like Rob was expendable. He was a narrow-minded man who attempted to tyrannize Sara, who had beaten her because he knew he could not force her to obey him. Christian could have kicked him when he saw the marks on Sara's body.

"I want to take you riding on Rotten Row," Christian said as he bent to remove the crinolines that she had just put on. Sara giggled as he took them off one by one. He was down to the silk underwear that he had chosen for her. The top was a cream-colored camisole with rose-colored butterflies. The pants were of the same design and trimmed with cream lace. He rubbed his fingers along her thigh and kissed her just above the knee.

"I want society to see you, my darling," he said, kissing her knee. He knelt in front of her, his hand around her thigh. Sliding his hands upward, he touched her flat stomach. He stroked the soft skin, then caressed her buttocks, bringing her body forward so that he was able to bury his face in her soft, thick mound of hair.

"I love you, Sara," he murmured, kissing her belly.

He would take her everywhere. He would introduce her to the controversial Oscar Wilde, to the people who aroused fear in ordinary men because they seemed to have contemptuous attitudes or were thought to be corrupt. But these were the unusual people, the ones who would leave a mark on society. And Sara, he knew, would fit in. They would be able to share these experiences. He had never dreamt that he would meet a woman with whom he could share his feelings.

Sara gazed down at him in an ecstasy of excitement. But at the edges of her thoughts crept a shadow of anxiety. Christian was proposing a tempting idea of freedom, but how? How could she ever be free of Rob? There were too many rivers to cross, and no bridges.

"It's a dream," she whispered as he gripped her around the waist and pulled her down to kiss her on the mouth. He never wanted to let her go. He carried her to the bed where they had already spent much of the day.

"No, it's not a dream," he said, pulling her on top of him.

The clarity began to fade. The image of the room, of the two bodies intertwined, merged into the face of Rob standing at the window of the bedroom he shared with Sara at Lord Evans's home. He was staring out the window, and he was waiting.

Lavinia's body twitched. Only the faint sound of a penny-whistle beneath Christian's window could be heard, and then slowly that too faded.

"What else?" Lady Chamberlain said. "Let Christian come through. Don't keep him back, Lavinia."

"Please, Mother," Paul implored. He now understood that Lavinia was preoccupied with a story about star-crossed lovers who had lived in Victorian times. One of the pair was the ghost she insisted she saw. He strongly suspected that she had read of the couple while doing her research and had adopted them as her own invention. But he didn't dare suggest this to his mother or Lavinia.

Lavinia opened her eyes. She felt tired, as if she'd been struggling with someone or something.

Paul was staring at her with the strangest expression on his face. She remembered how kind and loving he'd been last night, how he'd helped her finally drop off to sleep. But now he was looking annoyed, as if he couldn't bear to be a witness to what she was doing.

Lady Chamberlain stood and pulled open the drapes. The late summer afternoon sun flooded the room, banishing the spirits.

"Just relax for a moment, my dear," she said to Lavinia. "That must have been a strain for you, but it was most exciting. We could more or less hear the voices."

"More or less?" asked Lavinia.

"Congratulations," boomed Dr. Hare. "You are most certainly an authentic medium."

Lavinia smiled but she was less concerned with her authenticity than with communicating with Christian so that she could rescue him from his all too apparent distress.

"I could go back right now," she said.

"Back?" Paul sounded alarmed. "To New York, do you mean? Or just to London?"

"Back to them," Lavinia replied. "To Sara and Christian. To *their* London."

She saw Christian on Churton Street, limping, his arm flopping at his side. Blood stained the cobblestones. Christian fell forward, his large body crashing against the pavement.

"No! cried Lavinia. "No!" But she had seen this all before.

Sara stood in Lord Evans's garden. She was staring down at the ring and weeping.

"The ring," Lavinia cried. "The ring with the red stone."

Paul put his arm around Lavinia. She looked as if she were going to have a fit of some kind.

"Leave her," Lady Chamberlain said. "She hasn't finished."

Paul shook her gently. When she did not immediately respond, he shook her again, harder. She was weeping uncontrollably and emitting peculiar, rasping sounds, which upset him.

"It's over, Lavinia," he said, grabbing her by the shoulders.

Her eyes popped open.

"You frightened me," Paul said. "You were going into another trance."

"She was crying," Lavinia said. "Sara was crying. And she had on the ring. Paul, I..."

"Now, listen here, Lavinia." Paul interrupted her, his face very pale and stern. "I told you last night I'd do anything I could to help you, and I meant it. But haven't you had enough for one day?"

"You needn't shout at Lavinia," said his mother. Dr. Hare glared at him.

"Well, the two of you seem so intent on discovering a new medium that you're ignoring what a toll this is taking on Lavinia. She could hardly fall asleep last night, could you, Lavinia?"

His words sounded almost like an accusation.

"Well, I was... overtired," Lavinia stammered.

Lady Chamberlain was suddenly contrite. "My dear, Paul's right. This is all so very new to you. I know how eager you are to unravel the whole story, but perhaps you should limit your visits to the other world."

"Yes," Lavinia said, grateful for their concern. She felt as if she'd been drifting in and out of a dream state. She wanted to clear her head, to *not* think about Christian, to escape from him, if only for a little while. "Yes," she repeated. "You're absolutely right."

"We should probably be getting back to London," Paul said, smiling now that Lavinia seemed more herself.

"But darling, how can you leave me now? Don't you remember that Emily is coming?"

"Damn," Paul said. "I'd forgotten."

"Yes, her mother rang up," Lady Chamberlain explained to Lavinia. "She begged me to have her this weekend. The child acts up with her mother. It's the usual struggle of wills between mothers and daughters. I never had any of that with Paul, of course." She smiled mischievously. "And, of course, she is so looking forward to seeing you, Paul."

"Would you like to stay?" Paul asked Lavinia. "You said you

wanted to meet my children. And Emily is much more likable away from Christopher. Do you think you're up to it?"

Lavinia looked at Paul. She felt protected in his presence, and she liked the feeling. She had never thought of herself as a person who needed help. She had always been very independent. Usually the men she went out with relied on her for help and support. Her only period of uncertainty had been recently when she had been so unhappy that she had dropped out of the job market.

There was no denying that her new experiences as a medium had shaken her up, and here was Paul making her feel that she was not to worry. And that was wonderful, indeed.

"Please," he said. "She's sure to be impressed that you're from New York, and then perhaps she won't be as beastly to me."

"Yes, I'll stay, that would be pleasant," Lavinia said. She had no particular reason to go back to London, and she did want to meet Paul's daughter. She had heard a lot about her. Furthermore, it made no difference if she were in Mary's flat or here, since the ghost was sure to follow. He was in her mind constantly, it seemed, and she didn't need a seance or a trance for him to come through. Even now she could see him at Lord Evans's. He was drinking heavily, surrounded by well-dressed, fashionable people, the members of the aristocracy. It was a party. Sara, promoted to upstairs maid, was standing by the dessert table, dressed in a white uniform. She was helping the guests to choose a pudding. Christian never even looked her way.

Then Lavinia saw him polishing his gun. He stared at it as if trying to make up his mind. Was he planning to shoot Rob? Christian did not strike Lavinia as a man who could kill another human being. What, then?

Christian and Sara were standing arm in arm at the Serpentine, watching the boaters. Torrents of rain seemed about to descend, and people were putting up their umbrellas and leaving Hyde Park. The rain began to fall gently, but Christian and Sara didn't move.

Now and again Sara glanced around her, worried about being seen. Christian was unconcerned. As far as anyone knew, Sara was just another pretty woman the major was squiring around

London. At a distance no one would suspect she was an upstair's maid— and a married woman.

Sara looked like a lady of distinction, and she knew it. Her stylish dress, which she had made herself, was a perfect copy of a dress she had seen on Lord Evans's niece. The pale blue fabric was nipped at the waist, and she had sewn lace onto the low-cut bosom. The effect was one of virginal innocence, a look that the upper-class women liked to cultivate even if the opposite were true.

Lavinia saw Christian go into a craftsman's shop on Victoria Street. He spent a long time looking at rings, then bought the ring with the red stone. The merchant told him the ruby was from India.

"Then it will bring luck to the woman I love," Christian said with a boyish grin.

The quick flashes of Christian and Sara appeared to Lavinia like snaps from a disarrayed photo album. They were not in sequence, but she was nevertheless learning about them.

"Lavinia," Paul said, noting that she was staring abstractedly into space. Her eyes seemed to be out of focus, as if she were somewhere else or thinking about something that did not include any of them.

"Yes," she said, trying to sound patient when all she wanted was to be alone for a while.

"Would you like to stay?"

"Yes," she said, "but I'd like to go upstairs and rest now if that's all right."

"Of course it is," Lady Chamberlain said soothingly. "Dr. Hare and I were planning to drop by the village pub, if no one minds. Would you like to go with us, Paul?"

"Will you be all right, Lavinia? The servants are always around. If you want anything, you can ring Jamey."

"Of course, go ahead, Paul."

She needed to relax and was glad that the others were going out.

"We'll see you later, then," Paul said.

Lavinia excused herself and went up to the guest room. The

window was open, and there was a warm breeze coming in. She lay down on the bed and let the breeze waft over her face, feeling its light touch on her skin. A lovely smell of jasmine pervaded the room. She felt lightheaded, almost intoxicated.

Immediately, her mind drifted to Christian and Sara, whom she saw walking down a path behind his house in Brighton. The house was a small but gracefully constructed Regency with bow windows. It had been built by Christian's father in 1830 and faced the sea.

For Sara such luxury and beauty were altogether of another world. For a short time, at least, she could forget that she had lied to Rob, that she had told him she was visiting Devon. Perhaps she could even pretend to herself that this interlude with Christian would last a lifetime.

They had driven down in a private carriage, lunching at the famous Mutton's on the corner of West Street, where Christian had ordered for them both turtle soup and a glass of sherry. Sara, too excited to eat very much, had been entranced with the decor: the double-glass door at the entrance, the domed skylight from which hung an enormous crystal chandelier. She had stared across the room at the large mirror that reflected her and Christian at her side. She had never seen so many fashionable people, not even in London.

After lunch they walked by the sea. Very few people were out enjoying the view, and fewer still had taken out rowboats or sailboats, although the day was glorious. Later, Christian showed Sara the center of Brighton: the charming shops filled with French chocolate and bonbons, delicious buns, exquisite lace, the antique shops filled with bric-a-brac, the wig store that made King George's wigs. Here was where the crowds of fashionable people gathered, strolling up and down the King's Road, shopping, chatting, promenading.

Brighton was a meeting-place for writers like Mary Braddon, one of the best-selling authors of the day, and Cuthbert Bede, who had written a famous novel about Brighton. And there was Richard Jeffries, a mystic and social critic.

There were the socialites who spent much of their time window-gazing. Twice a day they paraded up the King's Road, showing off their clothes. And there were the Sunday visitors, who rode down from London for a couple of shillings. They only stayed for a few hours, drinking in the gin shops and public houses. Many of them attended the races, always a great attraction in Brighton.

The true socialites, the elite of the aristocracy, deigned to come to Brighton only in November and December, when the pea-soup fogs of London drove them to the pure sea air. By January they were wintering in Rome.

During the summer months Christian would be less apt to meet people who knew him. He and Sara could go about openly, without fear that their idyll would be disturbed.

Sara had never been to Brighton before. The classical squares, the terraces, the small Regency houses with their charming bow windows and hooded balconies and the Downs rising behind the town added to the romance of her adventure. She was determined to enjoy every moment of their stay.

When Sara had seen enough and was beginning to weary of what she called the social scene, they returned to Christian's house—empty of the servants, who had been dismissed for the weekend. She and Christian made love until the sun set and the moon rose in the sky. Then Christian went off to make arrangements for dinner.

Sara sat alone in the bedroom, gazing out the window, looking for stars in the sky. A starry sky, she had decided, meant that the next day would be a good one. She felt a sudden shiver, as a premonition of the autumn days to come flashed before her eyes. By autumn everything that existed between them might vanish.

She wanted desperately to forge a permanent bond with Christian. But how could she, a married woman, do that? He could have so many other, beautiful women. And she could not have a child. She had never conceived. She could not believe he would love her for her soul alone. She did not feel worthy.

The fact that Christian was much older than herself worried her, too. He might in the end consider her a plaything, to be thrown away when he grew tired of her sexually. That was the way of men. The possibility loomed over their relationship. He was handsome, wealthy and socially important. Surely the educated, cultured women he knew found him desirable.

What Sara did not realize was the Christian worried equally about keeping her. To him, her marriage was an obstacle of significance. Rob was more than simply a nuisance. As he became more suspicious of her infidelity, he was becoming increasingly aggressive toward Sara. And at times Sara seemed to withdraw from Christian. He knew she was brooding about the situation.

Christian had even on occasion entertained the fantasy that Sara might use her psychic powers to hasten her husband's death. But Sara's ability to forecast the fate of others seemed if anything to be on the wane, or else she did not like to use it. Recently she had refused even to discuss her psychic powers, preferring, she said, to use them in the most constructive way—to see into herself. She wanted to find a solution to her own life.

Still, there was something else—divorce. Although it was absolutely unfashionable, to Christian a divorce was the most plausible solution. He knew that he desperately needed and wanted Sara all of the time. He envisioned their future together. But when he had broached the idea of divorce she had responded negatively. She was, after all, a Catholic and had been brought up as a believer. Nothing, she told him, would ever shake her faith in God, not even the painful memories of her childhood when God seemed absent from her life. She had been singled out and segregated from the other villagers for having what they thought were black magic powers. But she'd never had an evil intent. She could see into the future and predict tragedies, accidents, events that no one could foresee, and she had tried to warn people. Then, when those events actually took place, they had blamed her as if she had caused them.

Christian had not given up the idea of divorce, but he was biding his time. If he had to destroy her belief in God in order to have her, he was prepared to do so. He believed that, in the end, it would be to the good. Sara would survive the loss of her religion, but he could not survive the loss of her.

They dined at the Albion Hotel, well known for its fashionable visitors. The town band played nearby. Minstrels, shouting their wish to be in Dixie, performed alongside ponies, monkeys and canaries. Street-hawkers offered brandy balls and pincushions made from cow's hoofs. Brighton-hired ponies trotted by, carrying beautiful young women wearing the smallest of pork-pie hats.

They dined on lamb listed on the menu by a fancy French name that puzzled Sara, which made Christian laugh merrily. He ordered champagne, and they drank a bottle and a half. Sara's senses were so besotted when they rose to leave that she had to cling tightly to Christian's willing arm.

"And now, my darling, a visit to Brighton's famous aquarium," Christian announced, enjoying Sara's excitement about a world that was entirely new to her.

The aquarium was filled with wonderful fish of every variety. There were sea lions, giant sturgeon, seals and alligators. She hardly knew what she was looking at, except that they were all creatures from the sea.

"All God's creatures," she murmured.

"And you are the most beautiful of all God's creatures," Christian told her.

Sara looked up at him longingly. The day had been full and wondrous, perhaps the happiest of her life. Now she wanted to return to Christian's house, to lie with him again in bed.

"Are you tired?" Christian asked. "I have one more stop for us this evening, a visit with some friends of mine."

She hesitated to demur, still shy about expressing her needs and desires.

Christian sensed her hesitation. "They deal in magic," he said.

As he had hoped, Sara's interest was immediately piqued.

"In magic? Are they mediums, then?"

"Some are, although not all of them," he said vaguely.

"And why are you so mysterious?"

"Indeed, why?" Christian said teasingly. He wondered whether she would be shocked or intimidated by what she would see at Katherine Campbell's home. But he was reluctant to tell her too much ahead of time. Once she was there, he expected her curiosity to overcome her bashfulness.

Instead he recited:

> When we die is there nothing but space,
> Or is there something beyond?
> Is Heaven but a figure of speech
> Of which cushion-thumpers are fond?
> Or is it all a solid reward?
> John describes how they opened the seal
> But 'twas probably only a dream
> Is it palpable, actual, real?

Sara was greatly impressed. "You learned it by heart. . . . But I don't understand it. Would you repeat it?"

"It's a poem by a Brighton writer and yes, I will repeat it."

Sara's face clouded over as she listened intently.

"It's supposed to amuse you," Christian said.

"He's making fun of God."

"Perhaps, in a way."

"But you believe in God. You believe in spirits, and without spirits, without people who have crossed over to the other side, there is no God. Their existence proves there is an afterlife, a God."

"There may be an end to this world but not the next," Christian said.

"I don't pretend to know anything, Christian," Sara said humbly, wondering why he had recited the poem to her. Perhaps it had something to do with the rest of the evening, and the friends to whom he wanted to introduce her.

Christian smiled and took Sara's hand in his. He brought her hand to his warm lips and kissed each finger slowly and artfully.

"Brighton is a place of religion," he said. "You noticed the many churches, I am sure."

Sara nodded and looked up into his green eyes that seemed to be tinged with the turquoise blue of the sea. She loved him if only for his eyes.

"And Brighton is a place of love," Christian added, "and we shall mix the two."

122

On the way back to his house Sara attempted to pry more information out of him about the people they were to visit, and the kind of magic they possessed. But Christian insisted that he wanted to surprise her.

She wanted to change her clothes first, and Christian agreed. He liked seeing her in the elegant outfits he bought for her. She had selected the materials and the design, and he had found a seamstress to make them.

Sara chose a midnight blue two-piece dress made of the finest silk and a black hat with black feathers, which fit low over her forehead. Christian had sent to Whitby in Yorkshire for a double strand of jet beads, and she wore them around the high-necked top of the dress. She carried a puffy handbag, made of silk and heavily patterned to match the two rows of patterned fabric at the bottom of the dress. Her shoes had been dyed the exact color of the dress.

She was filled with trepidation as she examined herself in the long mirror. It was not her appearance that troubled her. She looked more beautiful than ever before. But she was frightened of the evening ahead. She had never met his friends although, of course, she had seen him among his peers at Lord Evans's parties.

Ready to leave for Katherine Campbell's, they walked carefully over the pebbles to the water's edge and, with arms around each other, looked out at the water. The exhilarating effects of the champagne had worn off, and Sara felt a little let down, a little diminished. As Christian helped her into the carriage, she gazed at the water in the distance beyond the road and contemplated the blackness of the water against the millions of stars that had emerged.

"You will find the rest of the evening interesting," Christian promised, noticing her melancholy mood.

She began to feel better in the carriage. He told her that there would be a lecture, which surprised her as she had imagined a party of the usual sort.

A lecture meant she could sit quietly, listening rather than speaking. She had discovered that the posh accent she had cultivated appeared to aristocrats to be just that—a posh accent she had cultivated. She had, to her utter humiliation, heard some of Lord Evans's guests laughing at her in the cloakroom one day. She lived in fear that Christian's friends would scoff at her and wonder what on earth he was doing with such a woman, that they would interpret his interest in her as purely sexual. She did not wish to be thought of as his whore, nor did she want to embarrass him in any way.

Christian knew of her anxiety and tried repeatedly to reassure her. He told her that the people he found most interesting— unconventional, unusual people—did not give a tinker's damn about her accent. They listened to the content of her words, not how she pronounced them. This was the way they did things in America, and Christian had appreciated their democratic approach. He had adopted it as his own.

Sara wanted to believe him but she felt self-conscious and uncomfortable.

The carriage pulled up in front of a large Victorian villa set back from the street. Although it had a view of the seafront from the first floor, it seemed strangely detached from its setting.

Gas lamps shone through the windows, and Sara heard the sound of many voices and much loud laughter. In fact, Sara thought, it sounded as if a very noisy party were taking place. Her anxiety increased as they approached the entrance. The house had an ugliness about it, strange for Brighton, which prided itself on its beautiful homes. Or could it be something else? Houses, like people, had specific characters, and Sara sensed something ugly inside the house that was reflected in its exterior.

A servant opened the door and ushered them into the drawing room, where at first glance a fashionable party seemed to be taking place. A beautiful young woman, elaborately dressed and bejewelled, appeared to be the center of it all. She was surrounded by a group of admiring men in evening dress. Sara noticed that the moment she saw Sara and Christian, she excused herself from the circle of men and came over to greet Christian, ignoring Sara. She was six feet tall with hair as black as pitch and dark eyes, as dark as the Brighton seafront at night. She had a pointed, thin nose, delicate rosy lips and a way of looking through her slanted, half-closed eyes that Sara found unnerving. In fact, she thought, she looked like a beautiful witch.

She greeted Christian warmly, gazing up at him with eyes that revealed more than a casual interest. Then she turned her dark-eyed gaze at Sara and asked in an accent that revealed her Scots origin, "And who may this be?"

"This is my darling Sara," Christian said. "I should have got you two together a long time ago. Katherine Campbell, this is Sara Standard, and now I leave the two of you alone as I want to have a word with that publisher over there."

"Now, don't be nervous of me," Katherine said in a surprisingly affectionate voice. "I know all about you."

"About me?" Sara asked.

"Christian told me you have psychic powers."

"I don't know if you can call them powers," Sara said slowly. "So far nothing good has come of them, only bad things."

Katherine put her hand on Sara's shoulder and gently stroked her silk dress.

"Do not judge yourself harshly," she said. "We are all very interested in such powers." Katherine looked at her through her half-closed eyes, a half-smile on her lips.

"Are you a medium?" asked Sara.

Katherine shrugged.

"You're interested in the other world, then?" Sara said, feeling unaccountably ill at ease with her hostess.

"Come," Katherine said, ignoring the question, "I'll introduce you to some of the others and then the lecture begins."

She led her across the room, her arm encircling Sara's shoulders.

"Who is giving this lecture?" Sara asked, beginning to relax, feeling that she was, indeed, among friends.

"Why, *I* am, of course, my dear," Katherine said, drawing Sara into a group of men and women and introducing her to them as "my new but soon to be dear friend, Sara Standard." Then Katherine excused herself to direct the servants arranging the chairs.

After a few minutes of confusion people began to sit down. A servant lit the wrought-iron candelabras and adjusted the gas lamps to a dim glow.

The room was cold. Sara and Christian moved as close as possible to the front to be near the warmth of the fireplace. Sara looked around. The room was vastly different from what she associated with Victorian houses. The colors were pale, and the few pieces of furniture were light, caned and unexpectedly graceful. The usual china dogs, glass objects, the silver spoons, the bits of lace, all the clutter of the Victorian rich were missing. The room was almost oriental in style with a unity that revealed it was furnished and cared for by someone with a great interest in appearances. The someone, she assumed, was Katherine Campbell.

Sara glanced up at Katherine, who was dressed in a magnificent French frock, made from net, embroidered with forget-me-nots, trimmed with cascades of velvet, roses and a sash of leaf green velvet. She wore long, dangling diamond earrings and a brilliant diamond diadem in her hair. Her outfit was in sharp contrast to her dark looks. She was obviously a woman who understood appearances.

The other women in the room, whether very young or old, were all dressed in what seemed to be expensive Paris gowns. One was more fashionable than the next. Many wore dresses of sheer fabrics with loose-cut square-necked bodices, even though the sea air felt more like autumn than summer.

"My friends, tonight I am giving a simple lecture on witchcraft," Katherine announced in her strong, resonant voice.

The announcement caused a slight stir in her audience.

"And afterward we will drink and eat.... Those who wish to stay for the mass may do so."

She glanced meaningfully around the room. "This may not be to everyone's taste," she said, "but if you are not inclined, or feel offended, you may of course leave, my friends. But I urge you to come back another time. Remember there is a mass here each night whether or not there is a lecture."

"Mass?" Sara whispered to Christian. "A mass here tonight?"

"Not a Roman Catholic mass," Christian said. "Katherine is

a kind of priestess. But I don't think we will stay."

"Is she a medium? Are these people mediums?"

"Yes," Christian replied, "some are mediums. I know some of these people, and the others I've seen at meetings for psychical research, but let's see what happens. I haven't actually been here at Katherine's church before."

"Please," Sara said, "don't dignify it by calling it a church."

Katherine clapped her hands together for attentions. She looked at Christian and smiled.

"What men and women fail to comprehend becomes either something to fear and hate, or something to love and worship. Thus it has been with witchcraft."

As she spoke, Katherine unconsciously played with her long hair, which curled softly over her forehead and fell beneath her shoulders, reaching nearly to her waist.

"Witchcraft," Sara repeated to herself, looking up at Katherine, who appeared to be the embodiment of the new, freethinking woman Sara had heard and read about. She felt instinctively that this beguiling person, with her air of enormous self-confidence, was competing with her. When Katherine looked at Christian she seemed to want to consume him.

Although only in her late twenties, Katherine had the confidence as well as the power of a much older, more experienced woman. She seemed to have been born sophisticated and worldly. The casual yet authoritative manner in which she spoke evoked respect from all who listened. Sara could see that the assembled group was almost ardent in its attention to her.

Sara felt intimidated by this uncommon woman, who was both beautiful and brilliant. At the same time, she felt deeply attracted to her person. She had an aura, as if she were royalty. As she talked Sara felt herself falling under her spell, almost as if Katherine were hypnotizing her.

"Witches were treated with relative gentleness in England, compared to the brutal treatment they received in Scotland," Katherine said. "Merely to be accused in Scotland meant torture for a woman or a child. They were burned at the stake, or strangled and then burned. A woman was not permitted even to protest in Scotland. To be accused was tantamount to being murdered. Imagine that!"

Katherine gazed around the room, staring at each person in turn until she felt her words had sufficiently affected them.

"Some think that witchcraft was actually invented by the Inquisition. It provided work for the inquisitors, who had been threatened with unemployment in the fourteenth century. They decided that those who performed evil deeds must be in league with the devil, and that constituted heresy. Having established that witchcraft was heretical, the Church declared that the reverse, the refusal to accept the existence of witchcraft as put forth by the Church, was equally heretical. So witchcraft was invented by the Catholic Church, my dear friends. Those poor women who confessed to being witches usually believed their own confessions."

A servant handed Katherine a glass of red wine, which she drank down almost in one gulp, as if it were water. Then she proceeded with the lecture.

"The persecution of witches in this lovely country was much kinder, of course, than in my native Scotland. The thumbscrew torture, iron boots, the rack and other mechanical devices were used here, but the poor accused were allowed to plead guilty and defend themselves."

Katherine talked for an hour about the history of witchcraft in Scotland and England. Her witty comments and lilting Scots accent obviously amused some of the guests.

Sara was fascinated. She knew that witches had disappeared from England in the seventeenth century, when the last trial took place. She did not like the idea that the Catholic Church was responsible for the torture of women and decided to try to find some books on the subject that might elaborate on what Katherine Campbell was now saying.

Katherine concluded her lecture, saying: "There are good witches, which we sometimes call white witches. Magic and witchcraft are not intrinsically evil, nor is worship of the devil. Worship of Satan is more a rejection of the Church and its ugliness, deceit and undying effort to preserve the status quo, thus preventing human beings from going forward in whatever direction they wish to go. I know that if you who are here for the first time will come again, I can convince you that ours is the right way."

She smiled seductively, flashing her slanted, dark eyes at Christian and Sara.

"For example," she said, still smiling, "there was the Scots witch, Isobel Gowdie. Perhaps you already know about her? She was arrested in sixteen sixty-two and confessed to being a witch, but she performed good deeds, which were documented. She said, 'When we wish to heal any sore or broken limb, we say three times—

> He put the blood to the blood, till
> all up stood
> The lith to the lith, till all took with:
> Our Lady charmed her darling son. With her
> tooth and her tongue and her ten fingers
> In the name of The Father, The Son
> and the Holy Ghost.'

You can read the whole story, if you like. She covenanted with what was called Evil. She admitted to this."

Suddenly, Katherine stopped speaking. She closed her eyes and began to rock from side to side. Her color rapidly changed from rosy to sallow, and her breathing grew loud and heavy.

"It's a trance," Christian whispered to Sara, holding her hand. "I've heard that she goes into them. I should have warned you, but not to worry."

Sara glanced at Christian. He was frowning as he watched Katherine.

In a moment Katherine began to speak again, but in a voice that was much deeper than her own and made her sound like an old woman.

"The devil marked me in the shoulder and sucked out my blood with his mouth at that place. He spat it into his hand and sprinkled it on my head. He baptized me therewith in his own name, Christian. He lay with me naked in bed and copulated with me and gave me money. He was big, hairy, very cold and his semen within me was as cold as spring well water."

Katherine fell silent and her breathing returned to normal. She opened her eyes. She appeared to be momentarily disoriented but quickly came to her senses. Looking out at her audience, some of whom appeared to be shocked and surprised, she smiled again in her beguiling way.

"For those of you who know me and my, let us say, abilities, I want to remind you that after we have had our share of the grape and some lovely food in the next room, we will adjourn to the large room on the first floor for the mass. Thank you."

She bowed slightly and left the room, her maidservant running after her with a silver tray upon which was another glass of wine.

"Did she shock you?" Christian asked, an expression of concern on his face. Sara examined him closely. She could see that he hoped she had not been disturbed by Katherine's performance. But the truth was that she found the experience unnerving, certainly disturbing. The voice that emanated form Katherine frightened her far more than her own inexplicable powers ever had.

Still, she wanted to stay for the mass, if only out of curiosity. What were they going to do? How could there be a mass without a priest?

"That was the witch Isobel," Christian said, taking her into the room where food and wine were being served. "And I'm delighted you're not shocked. But after we have a drink, let's leave."

"Oh, no, no," Sara protested, "I want to stay for the mass. Please, Christian."

"If you insist," Christian said, "but if you are unhappy with the service, we can leave any time."

He was secretly pleased that she wished to remain. This was part of his plan. He was confident that Sara would never fall under Katherine's spell, although he recognized that Katherine was a powerful female. She knew how to control other people. She appeared to be warm, nurturing, even motherly. But Sara would resist her influence. There would be no harm done. And he would have his way. She would agree to a divorce, and in the end she would be much happier for it.

About twenty people stood about drinking champagne and

awaiting the start of the mass. A servant appeared at the door and announced that the guests should follow him. He directed them to the first floor, to a large, plain room devoid of furniture. The walls were painted black. On the floor was an enormous Persian carpet of the finest design. Against the length of one wall was an altar of sorts. Sara had never seen anything quite as opulent. It was covered with golden objects: pyramid-shaped cones, bowls, candlesticks in which large black candles were slowly burning. The only light came from the candles, which flickered in the drafty room.

Katherine stood to one side, wearing a long, black velvet caftan, the kind Sara had seen in books about the Middle East. Her luxuriant, long black hair hung loosely about her face and shoulders. Her large breasts pushed against the caftan, revealing that she wore no underclothes.

Christian was not the only man in the room to be aroused by Katherine. Guiltily he reached for Sara's warm hand, taking it between his own large, cool ones and stroking her fingers. Katherine knew how to manipulate her audience, Christian observed. He watched her moving her eyes form one person to the next, as if she had a personal message for each one.

"We are the descendants of the Brothers and Sisters of the Free Spirit," she said. "They believed that they were the inheritors of the Holy Ghost and that through its power they could be exalted in a special way."

She paused and looked directly at Christian.

"We believe the same. We believe that we are immune from the guilt of sin, the sins of the flesh. We are able to live in a state of nakedness. We are not ashamed, and we are not ashamed to say we enjoy lovemaking. We have reached spiritual perfection."

Several people gasped at her words, and about half the audience left, expressions of shock on their faces. Sara wondered nervously exactly what Katherine was getting at but she did not wish to leave.

"We are innocent," Katherine proclaimed, "like children. I know those of you who have stayed will understand. You will see that we have something wonderful and magical and miraculous here. It does not matter whether or not you are married. We can all love each other. It is love that is the basis of all religion."

She glanced piercingly at the remaining few.

"And who would disagree?"

Katherine's voice rose dramatically as she continued.

"I have been chosen to represent this love. Sin does not exist in me. I will be immortal, and all those who follow me will be immortal. And all true believers will make the act of love in innocence, without worry or fear of sin. You are not sinning, because our love transcends the bonds of marriage."

Christian was squeezing Sara's fingers as if he were gripped by what Katherine was saying.

"You're hurting me," Sara whispered.

"Sorry," Christian said. He quickly dropped her hand.

"Let us pray," Katherine said suddenly. Turning her back on the group, she began to murmur inaudibly. Two women rose and came forward, stood by her side and began to chant quietly.

Then, almost as they had rehearsed it, the three of them turned and began to dance, at first slowly, then more freely. They moved around the room, encircling those who were sitting on the Persian carpet, increasing the tempo of the dance. Katherine's movements were both graceful and erotic. She communicated unselfconscious sensuality and a sense of freedom.

Sara could smell the incense from the altar, mixed with Katherine's exotic perfume and the earthy smell of the dancing women. There was something intoxicating about the odor, and she felt she wanted to dance with them. She could hear music, a drum beating and a horn. Wherever the music was coming from, she knew she must move to it.

As the beat of the music increased, Sara and the three other women moved more and more rapidly. Soon several of the men joined in. One held Katherine in his arms, and they danced frenetically together to the wild beat.

The room was becoming very warm. Katherine abruptly stopped dancing and whipped the velvet caftan over her head. Stark naked, she continued to dance and then to alternately sing and shout a strange lament.

Christian stared at her with disbelief. His inclination was to grab Sara and run away, but he resisted the urge, still intent on his plan to free her of Rob. He did not object to Katherine's naked body. She was an exquisite sculpture, almost unreal in her perfection. She had large breasts, a small waist and round high buttocks. Although clothed she appeared rather slim, undressed she was a superbly beautiful, voluptuous woman. Christian realized he desired her.

But he knew he would never love her, certainly never in the way he loved Sara. Katherine was like a wild animal. And she was a devil worshiper. She could be dangerous if provoked. He also knew that she desired him. Each time they met she openly flirted with him, but he was determined to keep his distance. He thought she might be mad, although her public persona was that of a lucid woman. Seeing her now, he felt more and more convinced that he was right.

And while he watched the dancers, the other women in the room began to remove their clothes, as if they were not aware of what they were doing. They seemed in a trance, seduced by her words and her frenzied movements. He suspected there might have been some sort of drug added to the champagne.

Christian watched bemusedly as the women tugged and pulled to remove their layers of undergarments. Then Sara, who had been standing in the corner, her eyes closed, a smile on her lips, began to slowly undress, swaying rhythmically. Her dance was very subtle, much less obvious than Katherine's, but it was undeniably sexual.

Now only Christian remained clothed. A pretty young woman with pale skin and hazel eyes danced next to him, smiling provocatively and trying to remove his jacket.

"I'm sorry," he said, pushing her away. She merely smiled again and danced off with someone else.

The priceless Persian carpet was littered with shoes, underclothes, jackets, dresses and trousers. Men were kissing women, stroking and petting them. Two men embraced each other. A woman suddenly fell prostrate in front of the altar, mumbling words about the devil. A large urn crashed from the altar, narrowly missing her head.

Christian looked about anxiously for Sara. She was dancing

in the center of the room, her naked body glinting in the candlelight. He took her arm and bent to kiss her neck. Sara opened her eyes. She looked drunk, her eyes wide and transfixed.

"Love me," she slurred. And then her eyes rolled back into her head, and she did not seem to know where she was. She was mumbling words he could not understand in a foreign language he could not place. Frightened, Christian lifted her up to carry her from the room.

"Don't go," Katherine cried, suddenly alert to his intention.

"Sara has fainted, I think."

"She's asleep," Katherine said. "I have cast a spell upon her. Put her here."

Christian glanced down as he lay her on a clear space on the carpet. She looked as if she were peacefully sleeping.

"You see my power," Katherine said.

"Next you'll be wanting her soul," Christian muttered. He looked into Katherine's tempestuous eyes. He would be able to control her, this witch, and manipulate her to his own ends. This he had to believe.

Katherine stared at him with obvious lust. She stood tall, her large breasts just inches away from his body. Her breath was hot and smelled of the sweet red wine she had drunk.

"What is it you want?" he asked calmly, knowing she desired him.

Katherine pitched her voice low. "I want you, but you do not want me. But you will take me, or something hideous will happen to you, Christian. I feel it within me."

She pushed her voluptuous body closer to him as if to overwhelm him with her nakedness. With no distance between them, he felt she had some strange energy that came from something sinister. For an instant he felt threatened. Involuntarily he stepped back, away from her hot breath.

"You are beautiful," she said, reaching out and stroking his face and hair. She thrust her hands under his shirt and pressed her nails across him, scratching him. He pushed her away, worried that she might break the skin.

"You want me," she hissed, brushing her hand between his legs and finding his erection.

134

"No," he said, "but I am a man. And you are tempting me."

"And I am the devil," she said, laughing wildly.

She continued to touch his hardness under the cloth of his pants. The intense pleasure that she aroused flowed through him like a dam about to burst. She was pushing against him, and he could feel her large breasts upon him. He saw in her wild, abandoned animal look that he could have her, do anything he wished. She was his for the taking.

He looked around, searching for Sara. A naked man stood over her, about to kiss her between the legs.

Without thinking, Christian pushed Katherine away and pulled the man away from the sleeping Sara. He punched him in the face. Blood spurted from the man's lips as he spun around and slumped to the floor.

"All is love," Katherine screamed hysterically, tears pouring down her face.

Christian was horrified. He had not meant to hurt the man, and because of his own illness, the mere sight of blood made him very anxious. He picked up someone's crinoline and ripped away a piece, which he applied to the man's swollen lip until the flow was stemmed. Sara remained in a deep slumber. Christian did not attempt to wake her but picked her up in his arms.

"Get her clothes together," he said to Katherine, who was now more composed. She had slipped back into her dress, as if to indicate that the mass was ended.

"Hurry, Katherine. I want to get her dressed and home."

He carried Sara from the room, worried about her but reluctant to alienate Katherine. Perhaps he would need her in the future.

Chapter 6

BY THE TIME LAVINIA GOT DOWN TO BREAKFAST THE next morning, Emily had already arrived and was seated at the breakfast table with her father, her grandmother and Dr. Hare.

"Good morning," Lavinia said. "Sorry I'm late. You should have awakened me, Paul."

"Don't be silly, my dear," said Lady Chamberlain. "You needed the rest. I've just been telling my granddaughter all about you—that you live in New York and work for a television company." She turned to Emily. "I'd like you to meet Lavinia Cross, our resident medium."

Lavinia blushed. "How do you do, Emily, but I'm just a researcher with an interest in the spirit world."

"Hmph," said Dr. Hare, helping himself to another portion of scrambled eggs. The sideboard was lined with dishes heaped with eggs, croissants, bread, jams and jellies, porridge and Emily's favorite, mushrooms on toast. "You're much too modest. I tell you, Lavinia, you are a medium, and I should be proud of my abilities if I were you."

"Never mind about all that," said Emily. She was an elfin creature with blazing red hair and enormous amber eyes. Lavinia noticed she was wearing ice-blue eyeliner on her lower eyelids and had smudged red blusher on her cheeks. Silver skeletons dangled from one earlobe, where she had had two holes pierced.

"What I want to know, Lavinia, is whether you really live in Greenwich Village."

"Emily, you've interrupted Dr. Hare," chided Paul.

"So..." Emily challenged him with a scowl.

Lavinia smiled at her rudeness. She surmised that Emily was a fairly typical fourteen-year-old, no different from her friends' teen-age children in New York. They talked whenever they pleased, they protested and argued and were utterly obnoxious when they weren't being charming. Somehow Lavinia never minded their behavior too much.

"Do you think I look as if I belong in the Village?" Emily asked Lavinia, standing up to show off her spiked hair, tight jeans and long, black, cotton tee-shirt, which reached to her knees. "Look," she said, pointing to the small, razor-shaped earring in the other ear.

"Perhaps Lavinia would like a chance to drink some coffee before you begin bombarding her with your questions," said Paul.

"That's quite all right," Lavinia said. She welcomed Emily's questions as a diversion from her preoccupation with Christian and Sara. She wanted to stay in the present rather than let herself drift back to them and their world.

Turning to Emily, she said, "Yes, you look very punk. You'd fit right in there."

Paul rolled his eyes. "Please, don't encourage her." But his tone was loving.

"Lavinia," said Lady Chamberlain, "do help yourself to breakfast, and then I'm going to tell you all the precognitive dream I heard recently. I've been saving it for when Emily was here, because I know she enjoys them—don't you, dear?"

She beamed at her granddaughter. She obviously adored Emily, despite the outfit and Paul's comments about how difficult she was.

"I'd rather hear about Humphrey," said Emily.

"Humphrey?" Lavinia asked.

"The poltergeist," said Lady Chamberlain. "Very well, if you don't care to hear this dream..."

Emily interrupted again. "No, no, Gran, I would like to hear it. And I can tell Lavinia about Humphrey later, all right?" She looked hopefully at Lavinia.

Lavinia nodded. She had scored a success with the child, and for some reason that pleased her. She sat down at the table with a plate of food. "I'd love to hear about the dream, Lady Chamberlain."

"Well, then. A friend of mine was on a film shoot in Zurich with three of his friends. They had to drive a long way to get to one of the film locations, and the four of them were taking turns driving and sleeping. When they got closer to the border, Nick, my friend, was driving. He suddenly felt quite exhausted, so he simply pulled over and went to sleep without waking any of the others. He awoke out of a hideous nightmare, calmed himself and started up the car again."

She looked around to heighten the drama of the story.

"Do go on, Gran," begged Emily.

Even Paul looked absorbed in her tale.

"Presently the other three men woke up. They had, all four of them, had horrible nightmares. And when they began describing the dreams, they discovered that they had all dreamed that they came to a strange town and had made their way to a house in the square. The front door of the house had a trellis with peculiar markings on it. Nick went inside and was grabbed by a group of people, intent on killing him. His friends were right behind him, and they all got into the fray. They dragged him outside. And that's when Nick woke up. As they were remarking on the fact that they'd shared the same dreadful nightmare, they arrived at a village—and there, on the village square, was the house with the trellis."

Emily gasped, but for once she didn't interrupt.

"Nick slammed his foot on the gas pedal, and they drove on into the night, much too terrified to stop until the village was well behind them."

"That's a fascinating story," said Lavinia. "Creepy, really. I'll have to include that in the material I send to my producer."

"It's interesting because it illustrates two points about the paranormal. Not only were the four men telepathic among one another, but they also had a precognitive experience."

"I can't say I liked it much," said Paul. "What do you think, Ginger?" He turned to his daughter, giving her an affectionate smile.

"It's super," she said, helping herself to another chocolate croissant. "Wish I had those sorts of dreams. All I have is Humphrey."

"Do you know this Humphrey?" asked Lavinia.

"In a way, I suppose," Emily replied.

"'Where Emily lies, likes a ruckus,'" Paul said, patting his daughter's hand.

"Would you like more to eat, darling?" Lady Chamberlain said to Emily. "You look hungry, and you're too thin, sweetie."

"I never eat much for breakfast," said Emily, who'd already eaten more than anyone else.

"Humphrey is a poltergeist who sometimes makes a mess in the sitting room," Lady Chamberlain explained to Lavinia.

"Not always. Mostly when Emily arrives. I know Paul thinks Emily does it herself. But there is no way Emily would have taken the fish out of the fish tank. She loves living creatures. The fish died, poor things, all two hundred of them. It was Emily who discovered their poor little bodies. We knew at once it had been Humphrey. Humphrey's been around here for about two years," Lady Chamberlain said.

"Anyone for a game of croquet?" Paul asked, glancing from Emily to Lavinia. "It's too nice a day to be sitting indoors talking about bad dreams and evil spirits."

"Me, Dad," Emily said, getting up and kissing her grandmother's plump cheek. "And Lavinia said she'd go out with me. Do they play croquet in the States? I can't imagine they'd want to."

Lavinia followed Paul and Emily out the back way into the garden. The croquet wickets were already set up on the vast expanse of green grass. It was a perfect summer's day, warm and sunny. Lavinia hoped it would be just that—as ordinary and normal as possible.

Emily grabbed a mallet. "I'd like to go to New York. Will you take me? School's nearly finished, and I've a few engagements booked already, mainly with Dad, but I'd much rather go to New York with you. Who wants to go to Turkey?"

"Turkey is cheaper," Paul said. "I can afford the Turkish pound but not the dollar."

"I'd rather go to New York with Lavinia, Dad," said Emily. She stared with open admiration at Lavinia's starched white jacket with rolled-up cuffs and her white cotton pants. Emily thought Lavinia was the chicest-looking adult she had seen in donkey's years.

"Well, I'll have to go too, then." Paul smiled. "On the Concorde? We'll let Lavinia buy the tickets."

He turned to Lavinia. She had a faraway look in her eyes that he had come to recognize preceded her fantasy about those bloody people who lived in the nineteenth century. Paul had begun to feel almost jealous of them, and the ludicrousness of it made him want to yell with frustration.

He knew she cared about him, perhaps more than she was willing to show. But whatever the reasons for her initial reluctance to let down her guard with him emotionally, she was now so obsessed with people who might have existed but were certainly long dead and buried, that she seemed at times to have forgotten him entirely.

Paul was accustomed to a rather different reaction from women. Normally he might have shrugged his shoulders and decided "So be it," leaving Lavinia to her visions of bleeding ghosts. But he felt more than a passing affection for Lavinia. And his ego was injured by the fact that she seemed to prefer spirits to flesh and blood—his flesh and blood.

Damn! She was not just another one of the women he enjoyed wooing and bedding. She had spunk and a good mind, lots of style and a sympathetic manner that could win anyone over. Look how quickly and easily Emily had responded to her. And Emily rarely approved of his lady friends, holding on to—as he knew she did—the hope that he and his ex-wife might still be reconciled.

Fat chance of that. That chap who'd stolen away his wife had done Paul a favor. Caroline was a nice enough sort of person, but rather dull, too unquestioning. Once he'd got over his hurt and anger, he'd realized how conventional she was. As a young man just out of university, he had wanted—needed, probably— someone of her stolidity. But once he'd grown up a bit, felt more confident about himself, he had wondered how anyone could go through life always seeking and expressing the predictable. No wonder she had fallen for someone else. He was sure she had sensed his restlessness. He and Caroline were now quite civil to each other, almost friends, although he had no sympathy for her husband.

He picked up his croquet mallet and smacked a ball at random. The ball went spinning across the grass and disappeared into the shrubbery.

"What do you think you're doing, Dad?" Emily asked. "He thinks he's playing baseball," she said to Lavinia.

Lavinia seemed to be gazing into the horizon.

"Lavinia," Emily repeated.

"Yes?" Lavinia looked up at the girl. She had had a brief flash of Sara and Christian on the grass behind his Brighton house. The day was warm and sunny, the sky absolutely clear.

"I really like your outfit," Emily said. "Is that how they dress in New York?"

"This is how I dress," Lavinia said, smiling and brushing her hand through her curly blond hair.

"I like your short hair, too," said Emily. "Are your ears pierced?"

"Yes, but I usually wear dull earrings, nothing as exciting as yours."

"Right," said Paul, standing some distance away. "Are we playing, or having a sewing bee?"

He looked at the two of them, engrossed in their conversation about clothes. There must be a way to get through to Lavinia, to make her understand how fond he was of her. He could, he supposed, simply sit her down and tell her: "Lavinia, I find you fascinating and charming, and I'd love to..."

But that was part of the problem. He didn't know what the end of that statement was. To court her? *Did* people court each other anymore? To bed her? Yes, certainly he wanted that, but he didn't think it would do to say so bluntly, not even to a liberated woman from New York. To marry her? He hardly knew Lavinia. And would never get to know her if she continued to drift off into trances and speak in strange voices.

He was almost beginning to be taken in by this nonsense. Paul had for a long time prided himself on being a rationalist. More recently, he had come to trust his sensory perceptions as well. But having grown up surrounded by his mother's dotty friends, as he called them, he had rejected any hint of a belief in the supernatural. And yet, it did fascinate him, although he was loathe to admit it.

Now here was Lavinia, apparently sane and clever, looking at him with her beautiful blue eyes and silently saying to him, "Don't you believe me? Don't you believe that other-world beings are communicating with me?" He did want to believe her, was almost prepared to, but then who would be left to keep her grounded in reality? Certainly not his mother or Dr. Hare or her friend Mrs. Patel-Ram. And if she continued to live in the past, then he had no hope of knowing her better in the present.

Had he made matters worse by introducing Lavinia to his mother? He whacked the ground with his mallet. Perhaps he should return to London and get on with his life, leaving Lavinia to work things out by herself. His interior decorator friend had rung him the other day, inviting him to dinner at her flat. She was amusing and attentive, good company.

But she was not Lavinia.

"Girls!" he shouted, his frustration more evident than he'd intended. "Don't you want to play?"

Lavinia and Emily picked up their mallets, and Lavinia took aim at a ball. She looked across the lawn to line up the wicket. When she looked down again at the ball, she was Sara, standing on the grass behind the house in Brighton, a croquet mallet in her hand.

"Are you tired from last night?" Christian asked with concern. She had been in such a deep slumber Christian had been unable to awaken her to take her home.

Now she seemed fine as soon as she had awakened on Katherine's bed. "Why am I undressed?" she had said to Christian but hadn't even waited for him to answer before she jumped out of bed and hurriedly put on her clothes. She had even chatted for several minutes with Katherine about some of her own beliefs before they left.

But she had been nervous the whole morning. Now she looked almost ill.

"I don't feel well," Sara admitted. She felt ill at ease, more than ill, and had been asking herself all morning what she was doing here. The sight of Christian, tall and handsome, every inch the fashionable aristocrat in his white trousers and loose-fitting shirt from Italy, increased her discomfort.

Yes, Christian's friends accepted her, but did she accept them? Katherine Campbell was a bizarre woman, one who intrigued her, undoubtedly. Sara had found her warm and interesting, even exciting. But now Sara felt that she was out of her depth, and she was ashamed at her behavior, too.

A mass, indeed. It was nothing more than a black mass, devil worship, and she wanted no part of it. Why had Christian thought she would like such people? she wondered, but she was too shy to inquire. She loved Christian more than ever, but she worried that he might be in some way taken in by Katherine. She herself had been taken in. The woman had some great and curious power.

"I feel very warm," Sara said, "that's all. But it's a lovely day, Christian."

"It's those clothes," Christian said, pointing to her walking-dress, a skirt of gold-colored sateen, kilted in front, with a pale blue tunic that caught in a bow at the back. She also wore black stockings, patent leather pumps and a sailor hat.

"Why don't you take them off? No one is here."

She looked at him to see if he were teasing, but he was completely serious.

"I can't do that, Christian," she said. "What if someone were to come by?"

"No one will come. No one knows we are here."

"Christian, what happened to us last night? When I opened my eyes you were standing in front of me with Katherine and neither she nor I had any clothes on. I seem to remember dancing—and other people dancing, as well. But why had I taken off my clothes? I feel as if I should be terribly ashamed, and yet I'm not."

"I am sorry about last night, Sara, but you're right not to feel ashamed. Nothing terrible happened."

"Something dreadful happened, Christian," Sara said, staring at him in confusion. "We worshipped the devil, disguised in the person of Katherine Campbell. I have sinned greatly." She began to weep, the tears flowing freely down her cheeks.

Christian gathered her in his arms, cradling her head against his chest.

"It's my fault," he said, desperately trying to assuage her guilt.

"No, I am responsible for what I do," she said, still sobbing. "I may be an ignorant woman in many respects, but I am not so ignorant as to blame you. But you must know what we are doing."

"My darling," he said. "I can't bear to see you so distressed. Please don't blame yourself. It was I who brought you to Katherine Campbell's house."

He stroked her hair, caressing the back of her neck and the top of her back, wet with tiny, clinging drops of perspiration.

Sara's sobs subsided as her body began to respond to his touch. She nestled closer to him. He could feel her quick breath on his neck and cheek.

"I love you so," Christian whispered, moving his hand around and tracing her collarbone under her tunic. Then he deftly unbuttoned the blue bodice and slid his hand under her chemise, cupping his fingers around her breast. Sara clung to him tightly, fully aware of how aroused he was. He pinched her nipple lightly between his fingers, then drew her face up to his and kissed her passionately.

"Sara, my beautiful Sara," he said.

Sara was as excited as he. The sun beat down. She felt as if she were drowning in a flood of love.

Without another word, they threw off their clothes and fell to the ground, kissing and fondling each other. They made love in the open air, gasping and crying out with desire and delight. When at last both of them had been satisfied, they lay in the noonday sun, their limbs entangled.

Sara thought again about Katherine Campbell and wondered whether she would see her again.

Christian seemed to read her thoughts.

"I don't want you to worry about what happened last night."

"Will we go back there?" Sara asked.

"Would you like to?"

"I'm not sure. I don't think so, although the lecture was interesting."

Christian batted away a bee that buzzed by them.

"Then what disturbed you?" He wondered how much of the evening's events she remembered.

"She spoke in that strange voice and what she said was so ugly. . . . " Sara shuddered. She felt sick, almost nauseated. She'd felt this way once or twice before recently but didn't want to worry Christian. He'd insist on leaving Brighton to find a doctor in London and she didn't want to ruin their stolen weekend. Besides, she was probably simply distressed by Katherine Campbell's odd behavior.

Sara sat up and looked around for her clothes, scattered about them on the grass. They had torn at each other like wild animals, and yet she felt no shame.

"Come," she said, holding out her hand to Christian. "I would like something cold to drink."

They were halfway to the house when they heard the pounding of horse's hooves.

"Oh, no, someone is coming," Sara cried, covering herself with her bundle of clothing.

She and Christian raced toward the house. Just as Christian pushed open the door, an enormous gray mare came into sight, Katherine Campbell astride it.

Christian slammed the door, but not before she had waved at them and called out a greeting.

"What does she want?" Sara said to him, her face flushed.

"To convert us," Christian said.

"Don't answer the door."

"But she saw us. She knows we are at home."

"She saw us like this?"

"She's accustomed to nakedness." Christian smiled.

"She interests you, doesn't she?" Sara said, not meeting his gaze.

"Certainly. But only as a person, not as a woman. I met her before I met you, dear Sara. I could have *had* her then, but I didn't want her."

"She wants you."

"No," Christian said. "I think it's you she wants."

"I?"

"She wants your soul, my darling."

"Are you enjoying this, Lavinia?" Paul asked. "Your heart doesn't seem to be in the game."

"Let's stop then, Dad," Emily called out. "Isn't there anything more exciting we can do? This is a bore."

Lavinia put down the mallet.

"I'm sorry. I really am. I must be tired."

"Let's go in and have a lemonade. There's a pitcher in the fridge," Emily said.

The three trooped into the house and made their way to the kitchen, where the cook was preparing lunch.

They drank the lemonade on a porch just off the music room. Emily suggested that they go upstairs and chat while Lavinia changed her clothes.

"That's a fine idea," Paul said. "And I'll see you later. I've an opinion I must work on. I've got the brief upstairs."

Emily followed Lavinia to the guest room. Just as she was about to walk into the room, Emily glanced down the hall.

"Oh, no," she said. "Someone's there."

Lavinia turned to see what Emily was staring at. Christian stood at the end of the hall, wearing a black dress coat with a heavily embroidered white waistcoat. In his black trousers and patent leather boots he looked regal and elegant, as if he were on his way to a grand party.

"Who is it?" Emily whispered in terror, clutching Lavinia's arm.

Christian walked towards them.

"It's a ghost!" Emily screamed. "I can see right through him. "He saw me, he saw me," she screamed, running down the stairs. "Daddy, Daddy, I saw a ghost!"

Emily could not convince her father she had seen the ghost. At first he was amused by how eager she was to imitate Lavinia. But then he became annoyed. She insisted that she *had* seen a very elegantly dressed man—had seen right through the man.

"He must be a ghost," she screamed at him.

"That's quite enough, Emily," Paul said firmly. "A good performance, I must say, but no need for histrionics."

Lavinia stood by quietly, determined not to mix in. She believed that the girl had seen Christian. The description certainly fit. But she felt guilty about the fright Emily had had. And Paul had told her that Emily often made up fanciful tales. It was no wonder he refused to believe her this time.

"Really, dear, you might try to keep an open mind about this," Lady Chamberlain admonished him. "Obviously the major has moved in with us."

She seemed rather pleased by the idea.

Paul shrugged his shoulders and set his mouth stubbornly.

The rest of the weekend was not a great success. The three women excluded him from their fun. He watched as they set off on a Sunday picnic without so much as asking him along.

"Why didn't you invite me?" he said when they returned several hours later, laughing and refreshed from a swim in the pond. He was bored and resentful.

"Why, we thought you had work to do, darling," his mother replied, dismissing any further discussion of the matter.

Lavinia had the grace to look guilty. Emily glared at him, her expression exactly mirroring his own.

Shortly before Emily was to leave to return to her boarding school, they all gathered for tea. Emily informed her father that he was narrow-minded.

"Children should be seen and not heard," he said amicably.

"Like ghosts?" Emily tittered.

"Don't be rude, darling," Lady Chamberlain admonished.

Lavinia looked at her buttered scone. There was even Devon cream on the table, but she was not hungry. Her stomach had ached all morning, and now she felt slightly nauseated. Thinking about her physical discomfort reminded her that when she had last encountered herself as Sara Standard she had felt sick, too.

"You're getting that look in your eye," Paul said, staring at her. "Please, don't. Don't go away, Lavinia."

Lavinia laughed.

"I'm not going anywhere," she said, "don't worry... unless it's back to London with you. Hey, I've got plenty of work to do."

"You're going to New York with me," Emily said, "you promised."

"I promised?" Lavinia said incredulously. "I promised? When?"

"You promised," Emily said, "and I am holding you to your promise. You're not one of those Indian givers, are you? Isn't that an expression you use in the States?"

"I never did promise, you rascal," Lavinia smiled, "but I'd love you to visit me in New York. I'd show you the town. The Statue of Liberty, St. Patrick's Cathedral, Fifth Avenue, the Pan Am Building, the diamond center, the Village. You'll love the Village. There are so many charming places. And there's an electricity in the air."

"I want to see rock musicians," Emily said, "and meet some mediums."

She glanced at her father for a reaction but got none.

"One day you'll come visit me in New York," Lavinia said. "I just know you will."

Emily jumped up from the table.

"Gran, it's been lovely," she said, "and wasn't I well behaved?" She smiled teasingly, then looked at Lavinia.

"I'm too shy to kiss you," she said, "but I'm thinking it over."

Then she changed her mind and leaned over to kiss Lavinia.

"That ghost was good-looking," Emily whispered. "Be careful."

And with those words she turned and went upstairs to fetch her bag.

Shortly after a schoolmate's mother picked Emily up, Paul and Lavinia started back to London.

Paul had hoped that on the way back Lavinia would offer some explanation about the supposed ghost in the hallway. The possibility that Emily might have been telling the truth made him extremely uncomfortable. But Lavinia did not want to talk ghosts. She was distracted, so he didn't press her.

In fact Lavinia could hear the sound of a penny-whistle beneath Christian's window. And as he bent to kiss her, she felt a soft breeze on her face.

"Sara," he said, his lips upon hers.

"I wish the London fashion would permit women to go about with bare legs," he said, stroking her bare knee and thigh.

"Like Sappho," Sara said.

"You've been peeking into my books," Christian said. "Who taught you to read? I know you did not go to school in Devon. So who was it, then?"

"We only read the Bible at first," Sara said, sounding almost frightened. She suddenly remembered the large, looming figure of the village priest.

He had read her the erotic portions of the Bible. As he taught her to read, he forced her to commit to memory long passages that excited him. She had been eleven and she knew they were sinning but she had to go on. It was an exchange; her favors for his reading instruction. Sara wished him dead. But he did not die, and their strange relationship continued until she was sixteen. She had tried numerous times to ignore and reject him. But she was in his power, and she knew it. He blackmailed her. He threatened to tell her parents not only that she could read but that she had magical power to make strange things happen. Then she would be disgraced forever.

She kept the fact that she could read a secret from everyone. She didn't want to be ridiculed or thought different from the others, although she knew she was.

She was tempted to tell her two cousins, the ones she liked, but they were deeply religious and she worried that they might turn against her.

And then one sunny afternoon, walking across a field, she saw the priest riding his horse. He was trotting toward her briskly, and she knew what he wanted.

She wished that God would strike him dead.

The blue sky clouded over, and the day became dark. Rain began to pour. Thunder and lightning were all around her. She started running in the opposite direction, away from the priest. Then she stopped and turned, watching in horror as the priest was struck by lightning and dropped to the ground.

Later the village doctor confirmed that he had been struck dead by lightning. Several farmers said they had seen Sara running away just as the priest had fallen. The village doctor dismissed their foolish attempts to draw a connection. She had not caused the lightning to strike, after all.

But she had been known to have strange powers. As the rumors spread that Sara Standard was some sort of embodiment of evil, the doctor began to wonder whether, in fact, she might have been responsible. No one openly accused her of killing the priest, but people avoided her, ascribing to her satanic powers. She must keep to herself, the doctor told her family. He was not usually an unkind man, but he felt it necessary in order to protect her if not himself and the others.

Her parents were glad of an excuse to abuse her. Her mother forced her to eat alone. Her father put up a makeshift tent where she had to sleep. She was an outcast. She would have gone away on her own but she did not know where to go. Her cousins were too poor to take her in. Besides, they feared that people would turn on them and destroy what little they had. And then Rob had come along and rescued her.

Lavinia looked out the window. They were already at Charing Cross. She had been lost in the past for the last hour. Paul had fallen asleep while reading the newspaper, which was spread out on his lap. She shook him gently to wake him up.

"We're here," she said.

He looked so sweet and vulnerable as he opened his eyes and

straightened out his jacket. Lavinia felt a pang of tenderness. Poor Paul! She had ignored him almost the entire weekend. And he was so considerate of her. She wondered whether he was becoming impatient with her preoccupation with Christian and Sara. She couldn't seem to free herself of them long enough to concentrate on her feelings about Paul. And he was certainly one of the kindest, most dependable men she'd met in quite some time.

They shared a taxi back to Belgrave Road.

"How about a drink?" Lavinia offered.

She opened a bottle of Blanc de Blanc and took two glasses out to the terrace.

"You know, Paul," she said, "you remind me of Alain, my college sweetheart. He was a very bright, charming Frenchman."

"Hmm, sounds encouraging. I don't mind being compared to someone bright and charming. Someone you once liked."

"Well," Lavinia said, blushing slightly, "I like you, too."

"Only you're so distracted."

"Yes, I am. And I'm sorry about that."

"I suppose you've had many beaus, then?"

"No, not really." She poured more wine into his glass. "Are you being nosy?"

"Certainly." He smiled disarmingly, then asked, "Have you ever been in love?"

"I thought I was in love with Alain. Now I realize it was more like puppy love. I've been involved several times since then, but the relationships never seemed to work out." The wine made her bold. "In fact," she confessed, "my most recent involvement was a disaster. Both the man and my behavior toward him. It put me off men for quite a while."

So that was it, thought Paul. Her cautious attitude toward him.

"How about you?" Lavinia asked.

"I loved my wife—or thought I did. Perhaps I loved the idea of who she was," he said slowly. "I had a strong taste for moderation back then. She left me for another man, but"—he raised his hand as if to stave off any expression of sympathy—"I'm honestly rather grateful to the two of them now."

Lavinia smiled.

"No, seriously. She's a nice woman, we're friendly enough, but I've had loads more fun with my life—once I got over the initial shock, of course. It's been hardest on the children, I suppose." He shook his head, thinking about his son's behavior and his daughter's show of toughness.

"Were you married long?" Lavinia was pleased that he was at last opening up to her about his marriage. She had wondered about his ex-wife, especially after meeting Emily, who was so delightful and adorable.

"Eleven years. I suppose that's long, compared to many couples these days. Sometimes it's hard for me to believe we lived together all that time, seems like another world. Another me, almost. But I have the kids to remind me that Caroline and I shared a life together."

Lavinia did some mental arithmetic. If he was forty years old, Paul had been divorced for six or seven years, probably. She wondered why he hadn't gotten involved with anyone else during that time—or perhaps he had.

"I know what you're thinking," Paul said.

"Oh? Do you?" She laughed. "Is this a case of precognitive thinking?"

Paul laughed heartily. "You're the medium. You tell me."

Their eyes met for a long instant. This was the first time they had been able to joke about what Lavinia had been going through, and she felt a rush of tenderness that she saw reflected in his eyes.

"First you tell me what I was thinking about," Lavinia challenged.

"You were wondering why I'm still single. Whether I've really gotten over Caroline—and if I have, why I've not taken up with somebody else."

Lavinia raised her glass. "A toast to perceptive men who read the minds of curious women."

Paul nodded his head in acknowledgment. "Well," he said, "at first I was too angry. And too afraid that the next woman would throw me over as well. Then I was having too much fun being courted by attractive single ladies. I'd not dated much before, and I rather took to the role of eligible bachelor about

London." He grinned sheepishly, as if to beg her indulgence for his lack of modesty.

"And now?" she prompted him. Far from being put off by his frankness, she was pleased that he was, at last, opening up to her.

"And lately I've been discovering what it is I want in a woman. I've been thinking more and more about the possibility of a permanent relationship."

Lavinia poured herself more wine to hide her confusion. What was he saying? Was he implying that he was seriously interested in her? Or that she was the *kind* of woman he was looking for? Or could he mean that he was involved with someone other than Lavinia? The latter possibility was very troubling—much more so than she would have expected.

Paul stared at her, not saying a word. She returned his gaze. A mounting tension filled the empty space between them. Lavinia's hand trembled slightly, spilling some wine on her skirt. She jumped up to find a napkin, pretending to be worried about the stain.

Paul didn't move, sat staring as she chattered nervously about how many clothes she had ruined because she was such a slob.

"I'll be right back," she said. "I just want to wash this before it sets." She fled to the kitchen, embarrassed by how she was babbling, as if she were an adolescent out on a date for the first time.

What *was* the matter with her? It was not as if she were a virgin or didn't find Paul attractive. But something was holding her back, keeping her from responding to his unspoken message. She felt the excitement between them, knew they were both thinking about sex. But she was suddenly shocked to realize that when she imagined being kissed and held and loved, it was Christian, not Paul, who was kissing her.

Paul was a sexy man, no doubt about that, but she yearned for Christian. Yearned for him as if she had fallen in love with him.

"Terrific!" she said, turning off the kitchen faucet. *Am I going mad? I want to get it on with a spirit who appears when it suits him. And in the next room sits a wonderful man who is dying to make love to me this very minute.* Well, she couldn't hide in the kitchen all afternoon, trying to make sense of her feelings.

Paul was leaning against the terrace railing, looking at the late afternoon sky. "Everything all right?" he asked.

"Just a bit of a headache. Too much wine, I guess." Lavinia joined him at the railing, almost touching him, wanting to test her responses.

"Shall I get you some aspirins?"

"No, I'll be okay." She reached out to touch his sleeve, to tell him not to bother, then quickly drew back her hand. Their eyes met again.

"Well, it's getting late, and you look tired. I think I'll go upstairs," Paul said.

She was racked with ambivalence. She wanted Paul to stay, but she wanted so much to see Christian, to be with him, to hear him speak to her. To her, Lavinia, not to Sara. But she feared the encounter as much as she feared for Christian and Sara. She knew, far better than they did, how difficult the future would be for them. She worried for them—knowing, in some vague, hazy way, the final outcome.

She walked Paul to the door, wishing he would stay, glad he was going.

"Will you have dinner with me tomorrow evening?" he said.

"I'd love to," Lavinia replied. She reached up to kiss him goodbye on the cheek and suddenly his arms were around her and he was holding her, hugging her tightly. Then he pushed her slightly away and put his hands on her shoulders.

"I'm not as patient as you might think I am, Lavinia," he said. His mouth met hers, his tongue searching for her tongue.

She stopped worrying, stopped thinking, surrendered herself to him. Her breath quickened and she fumbled to undo his belt buckle, wanting him now very badly.

He unzipped her skirt and it fell in a heap to the floor. He kissed her neck, her earlobes, her eyelids, slid his hand under her sweater to unfasten her bra. Lavinia stepped back a moment to pull off her sweater and shivered, as if a draft had just blown across the room. Paul's hands stroked her belly and moved downward, gently probing beneath the waistband of her underpants. She was ready for him.

The draft hit her bare back again, the air so chilly that goosebumps suddenly covered her arms.

Lavinia pulled away from Paul. "No!" she cried.

"What is it?"

Lavinia could not utter one word. Christian stood directly in back of him. He was holding a gun, aiming it at Paul.

"No!" she shrieked. Paul turned to see what was terrifying her but saw nothing. Before he could say a word, Christian smashed the gun barrel on Paul's head. Paul fell to the floor.

"Oh my God!" Lavinia cried. "What have you done? Why?"

She knelt down next to him. He lay still for several moments, then slowly opened his eyes.

"He was attacking you," Christian said calmly.

"No, he wasn't," Lavinia said. "He wasn't doing anything I didn't want him to do."

"He cannot see me," Christian said. "Only you can see me at this moment."

Christian towered above her, looking almost menacing in his old-fashioned riding gear. For the first time Lavinia feared that he might do her harm—not imagined harm but actual harm—as he had Paul.

"Look what you've done, Christian," she said. "Please, never do anything like this again. You attacked a good, kind man."

She stood up and looked him squarely in the eye, realizing that she did not know Christian well and could not yet trust his motives. In fact, she did not yet know what his motives were. Her voice shook slightly when she spoke.

"If you ever want my help, and I suspect you do, then never do anything to hurt Paul or me."

"Forgive me," Christian said, and then he disappeared. Lavinia stared after his image. It worried her that he might have another side, one that was aggressive and harmful. He could appear whenever *he* wished. Even as she slept. She had, of course, thought about the fact that he could come to her at any time. But she had never before considered the possibility that he might do evil, might harm her.

Paul was coming around. He looked dazed, but his eyes were open and he was staring at her with perplexity.

"You hit me," Paul stammered.

"Poor Paul," she said, bending to help him up. "Are you all right?"

"You hit me on the head with something," Paul said.

"No, I didn't," Lavinia said, "believe me."

Lavinia quickly stepped into her skirt, drew it up and fastened it, then pulled her sweater over her head. The moment was obviously lost.

"We were standing here," Paul said uncertainly. "I kissed you. You kissed me back, remember?"

He rubbed his head and looked disturbed.

"I can't really explain what happened," Lavinia said, not wishing to lie but not wishing to tell the truth either. He wouldn't believe her. He never did when she talked about Christian.

"Does your head ache? Do you want to lie on the couch?"

"Yes, my head aches, but I think I'll go up to my flat." He smiled wanly. "Is that your usual reaction when a man tries to make love to you?"

He sounded more perplexed than angry.

"No, of course not. I don't know what came over me," Lavinia said.

"You mean I shouldn't have kissed you?"

"No, I mean..." Her voice trailed off. If Paul didn't believe in ghosts, he certainly wouldn't believe that it was Christian who had bashed him on the head.

"I don't understand how I suddenly could have passed out. I don't have seizures." His voice rose in indignation.

"It wasn't a seizure," Lavinia insisted. "The ghost hit you."

Paul stared at her unhappily. Had she finally gone round the bend?

"I'd better go," he said. "Good-night." He left, rubbing his head.

Lavinia stifled an impulse to call him back and explain in

detail what had happened. He wouldn't believe her, she thought sadly. She knew that she was changing, almost becoming another person, a more rebellious person. At school she had always been teacher's pet. She had always been polite and obedient to Aunt Jane. She had never been a troublemaker or someone who would raise controversial issues in class discussions.

And here she was involved with a ghost. She didn't know whether to laugh or cry.

"I want to talk to Christian," she said aloud. Would he reappear. There was no response. He did not materialize, nor did she hear any footsteps upstairs. Did this mean she had to go into a trance each time she wanted to communicate with him? A trance projected her back into the nineteenth century, and by now she could enter a trance within seconds. But what she wanted most was to have Christian materialize in the here and now, so that she could talk to him not as Sara but as Lavinia.

"Christian!" she shouted. There was no response.

And she found herself laughing at the absurdity of the situation.

Who would believe any of this back in New York? Her friends would all think she was crazy. They would probably advise her to see a psychiatrist. She considered the idea that a belief in the unprovable was still as unacceptable to the vast majority of people as it had been a hundred years ago. Even though modern physics had posited the idea that the world was finite and that universes other than our own existed, most people could not make the leap forward to a belief in the supernatural.

Lavinia had no trouble approaching the question of whether or not ghosts—specifically, Christian Wheatley-Croft—existed as an intellectual exercise. She had much more trouble, however, handling the emotional implications of being some other woman, loving a dead man. Was she supposed to learn something about herself this way?

The implications were extremely depressing. Christian only existed outside of his body, which was just about the strangest thought she ever had about a man. And what the hell did it mean?

She thought for a moment about writing to Aunt Jane and explaining what had been happening to her. Aunt Jane was excellent at giving advice. No, she decided, she couldn't. Although Aunt Jane was sympathetic to the idea of the occult, she might look askance at the idea that Lavinia was in love with a ghost.

In love with a ghost? If someone had told her she would fall in love with a ghost, she would have laughed herself silly.

Left as usual without any answers, she went upstairs to have a bath. And then she wanted to spend some time working on her weekly cassette to send to her boss.

Antony Gold was an imaginative, well-respected television producer whose talent for thinking up new ideas was known throughout the industry. It had been his idea to do a series on the paranormal, and he hired Lavinia, convinced she would do a first-rate job. She had no intention of disappointing him. She liked and respected him, and furthermore he had hired her after she had been out of work for over a year. If he liked her work, he might hire her on a full-time basis, perhaps even as an assistant or associate producer.

The problem was that she was having increasing difficulty keeping her thoughts on her work. She felt impelled to get to the heart of the matter with Christian and Sara. And then there was Katherine Campbell. She could not shut her out. Katherine was a vital part of their story, and Lavinia was convinced she had caused conflict between them.

Lavinia ached to find a way to control their situation. It was very disturbing to know things that *they* did not yet realize. But there was nothing she could do, because in the past she *was* Sara and she could only do what Sara would do. She could only go along, swept up as she was in their story, waiting to discover Sara's destiny, looking on from a distance of a hundred years, yet at the same time there with Christian. Perhaps she was going mad.

And even as she wondered whether this was so, how she might extricate herself from the path her mind had taken, an image of Katherine appeared, and she felt unable to resist it.

Katherine was wearing a high-necked, hip-length jacket and a pair of brown leather trousers and ankle boots, the riding habit currently in vogue among the freethinking society ladies. her long hair was tucked up under her riding hat. Her cheeks were rosy from the ride, and there was a wild look in her tartar eyes.

She smiled as she pounded on Christian's door.

"Christian! Christian! Open the door!"

There was no response.

Inside the house Sara was squirming into her clothes, abashed at the thought that Katherine had seen them cavorting outside naked.

Christian had already pulled on his croquet costume and was watching her with a smile on his face.

"This is not amusing in the least," Sara said. "You promised that no one knew we were here."

"It's only Katherine. Shall we let her in?"

"*Only* Katherine? No, certainly not!"

"Whatever you say, my darling," Christian said.

"Do you wish to see her?" Sara asked. She wished to please him even if it meant facing Katherine's knowing look.

"I'd rather she not conclude that we're too ashamed to see her. Katherine is no doubt amused that we chose to take off our clothes. But she'll be angry if we ignore her."

"Do you fear her?" asked Sara.

"No, of course not," Christian replied, but at the same moment he was unlatching the door and calling, "Yes, all right, Katherine, do be patient."

Christian wondered whether he was doing the right thing. Katherine was powerful. Her charm would seduce Sara, if she were given enough time. He would get his way, finally, but would there be any repercussions that he could not control?

Katherine stopped pounding and gazed up at the house, which she had long admired. She had often wondered why Christian had never married. She knew he had been involved with several women, and that he was not celibate. During the London season she had dug up as much information as she could because she desired him for herself. He was a man who was considered to be an outsider, a rebel of sorts.

He had left his commission in India, and it was rumored he had an incurable disease. Katherine had heard of the disease, sometimes called hemophilia. She had asked the white witch about it, who told her hemophilia was an inherited disease that prevented the blood from clotting normally. But she did not suppose that was what made him a rebel. Perhaps he was destined to be different.

He had gone to America and had even written a book about his adventures there. He had met psychics, people who could cross time and communicate with spirits. But they had nothing to do with what interested her, which was the devil.

Her friend Scott Bartlett was going to read the manuscript and assess it for Christian. Bartlett was a fine publisher and he would know whether or not it had any merit. She planned to put in a good word for Christian, not because she cared about his writing but because she wanted to possess him, to have power over him.

Sara stood in her way. But this was a simple matter. With a little manipulation, she would get what she wanted. Sara might even become her ally.

Katherine was very aware that Sara Standard had never met a woman like Katherine, and that Sara was fascinated by her. And Katherine would use that fascination if she had to.

And who was Sara? Christian seemed to be in love with her. He wanted to protect her. But where had he found her? She was a working-class woman. That much was obvious. Yet she seemed educated.

Katherine preferred working-class people to aristocrats. They were much easier to control. They were more naive, less dishonest.

At last Christian opened the door, and Katherine was struck again by his fine looks, his black hair that contrasted with his green eyes. He had a face full of character, with crow's feet around his eyes and creases on either side of his mouth, which gave him the look of a man who had lived. She wondered if that were true. She had heard stories about his escapades in India and wondered if any of them were true.

"Well," Christian said, pushing the door open wide, "why are you standing there staring at me? Did you come here for a reason?"

Katherine smiled confidently at him.

"I came to say good afternoon and to find out whether your lady was all right. She seemed ill last night. And then there was that unfortunate event..."

She smiled ironically.

"I am very well, thank you," Sara said, appearing at Christian's side.

"I thought you might have gone back to London," Katherine said, pretending she had not seen the two of them on the grass.

Christian knew full well that she had spotted them and wondered why she was choosing to be polite.

"Would you care to come in? We were just about to have some tea," Christian said.

"Yes, thank you," Katherine said in her crisp Scots accent. She followed him into the kitchen.

"Does this mean you were coming round to see Christian?" Sara said, feeling somehow bolder.

Katherine looked at her and laughed, ignoring the question.

"I have never been in this kitchen," Katherine pronounced, glancing around. "It's rather splendid, but so is the house. . . . "

"And do you love it?" Sara said, trying to keep up the light-hearted chatter, wanting to blot out her jealousy of this tall, elegant woman.

"Ah, yes, I suppose you could use that word, if you must. . . . But you seem very much at home here in the kitchen, Sara. You must love it, too."

Sara wondered whether Katherine knew she was a servant. Was she making a veiled reference to her position in life?

Katherine could know only if Christian had told her, and Christian would not have betrayed her.

"I would like you ladies to take tea in the sitting room, and I shall bring it in to you when it's ready," said Christian.

"Oh, no, of course not, I will bring tea. You and Katherine go into the sitting room," Sara said quickly.

The idea that Christian would wait upon her in front of Katherine was unacceptable. Sara had been brought up to wait on men, and only recently and reluctantly had she allowed Christian to bring her tea in bed.

"I insist," Christian said.

Sara gave in immediately, seeing from the expression on his face that for some reason it was important to him that he bring the tea.

She and Katherine walked into the sitting room and Katherine removed her riding hat.

"You've not been here before?" Sara asked.

"I said no, I hadn't," Katherine said in a vexed tone. "I have never been invited to the major's. I barely know him from London. Last night was the first time we have ever spent time together." She laughed. "But I am being rude."

"No," Sara said politely, admiring the woman's outspoken honesty. There was something untamed and wild about Katherine. She wished *she* could be less timid.

"How did you get involved with black masses?" Sara said, surprised again by her boldness.

Katherine looked pleased.

"This is a story that would take a year to tell. Do you have a year to spend with me?" she said flirtatiously.

"Perhaps."

Katherine chatted on, avoiding the question. She talked about the people who had been at the lecture, those who had left and those who had stayed behind. Then she compared living in Brighton to living in London. She talked at length about her childhood in Aberdeen, where she had been born into one of the leading families.

"My mother was a musician, and my father disappeared when I was nine. Every night we had music. But first we had a party. Sometimes the music came first, and then the party. My mother was a witch."

"A witch?"

"Oh, yes. She taught me everything. She could see into the future. She knew I would go to London. And she said I would have a house on the sea. She knew the exact time and date of my marriage."

"You are married, then?"

"Oh, no," Katherine said. "It is not yet time. But soon." She smiled slyly. "My mother could see into the past, too. Hundreds of years ago. She had lived before. And we often had the same dream."

"What do you mean? That you had the same ambitions?"

"We used to have the identical dream. In the morning we

would compare them. Mother wrote hers down. Perhaps one day I will publish them in a book. After her death."

"And do you visit her often?"

"No," Katherine said, her face clouding over. "Ten years ago she fell ill. She cannot speak. We do not know if she can hear. She lies there, day after day. We are waiting for her to die."

"I am so very sorry," Sara said.

"That is when I stopped believing in God, when my mother's brain stopped functioning in the usual way."

Sara did not know what to say. No wonder Katherine was so odd, she thought. She wished she knew how to express her sympathy but hesitated, not certain how Katherine would respond to her gestures of comfort.

Christian came in, carrying the tea tray. Sara jumped up to help him, relieved to be able to busy herself pouring the tea.

She would have been astonished to know that Katherine had invented nearly every word of her story.

The truth was that her parents were not at all rich. Her father had not disappeared, and her mother was healthy. Her parents lived together in a simple house in Aberdeen. Her father had owned a sweets shop and had retired after an accident in which he lost the use of his right arm.

Katherine had rejected her family, moved to London and become engaged to a gentleman whose father had paid her a large sum of money to be rid of her. The money had bought the rambling house in Brighton, which she had renovated. And she had also been able to buy a small house in London, which she had sold for a handsome profit.

She now lived with a distant cousin, a widow, who liked to have someone share the house with her from time to time. None of Katherine's upper-class friends knew exactly where she lived in London. She invented elaborate excuses to keep her secret. The excuses were accepted, and because Katherine was such an entertaining person, she was repeatedly invited to the homes of the rich, where she made converts to her devil worship and to her Brother and Sisters of the Free Spirit masses.

"Are you coming to my church tonight?" Katherine asked. "I came in person to invite the two of you."

"I don't think so," Christian said. "I think we must get back to London."

"But I am inviting you in person," Katherine said, glancing at Sara. "We need you. If you object to the latter part of the mass, you can leave before we go on to it. I will not be offended."

Sara's innocent blue eyes sought Christian's. That moment he felt he had betrayed her, and he wondered whether, with her power to see things other people did not see, she knew this.

"I need you to be my friend," Katherine said to Sara. "Will you be my friend? Perhaps you can help me."

Help her? What could Katherine mean?

"What would you need my help with?"

Katherine shrugged uncertainly.

"I don't know. I sense you can help me. I sense that we are bonded together. I cannot explain it but maybe Isobel can."

"Isobel? You mean the voice that came through you when you were in a trance?" Sara asked.

"Yes," Katherine said, her eyes darting to Christian. She knew Christian wanted to return to her house. He did not seem very interested in her mass, so he must therefore be interested in her.

"I think it will be all right, my darling," Christian said. "Maybe you *can* help Katherine in some way. She may have something to teach you, too."

"Teach me?"

"There are other ways of believing or not believing," Christian said, "not just the Roman Catholic Church."

"Of course," Sara agreed.

"I rejected the conventional church many years ago when I was a child," Katherine said.

"How sad," Sara said seriously.

Katherine laughed. "Do I look sad?"

Sara stared at her. No, she did not look sad. If anyone were sad, it was she, whose faith in the Church and God were keeping her from marrying the man she loved.

Katherine sipped her tea and smiled.

"I would so like to have you both there tonight," she said.

Christian looked at Sara.

"So, my darling, shall we go?"

Sara slowly nodded.

"We will go to the lecture, and leave afterward. I must get back to London this night, Christian."

Katherine glanced from Sara to Christian. They were two handsome people, and she was attracted to both of them. She would enjoy Sara's innocence, but she would enjoy Christian's sophistication much more.

Chapter 7

PAUL BROKE THEIR DINNER DATE THE FOLLOWING DAY. He called at one o'clock and asked Lavinia how she was feeling, then said, "I'm stuck with a case that I have to argue on Wednesday. The fellow who usually helps me out with research is on holidays, so I've got to do it all myself. I'm afraid dinner is off."

"No problem," Lavinia said. His excuse sounded genuine enough, but she sensed that he was as troubled as she about what had happened. "Is your head okay?"

"Yes, yes, absolutely," he assured her. "Look, I'll talk to you later in the week, all right?" For the moment Paul preferred to ignore the episode. He needed some time to make sense of it, and he had to get back to work. He was also angry with Lavinia for interrupting their lovemaking and for lashing out at him, although she claimed she hadn't. Reluctant was one thing, but he would never have suspected she'd be so bloody uptight. She had wanted him. He had felt it.

"Right," Lavinia said, but Paul had already hung up.

She was both disappointed and relieved that he had canceled. She knew she'd have to face him sooner or later, but she preferred later. Whether or not it was deliberate, they avoided each other all week. Lavinia was out most days at the library, searching for further information about Christian and his family. She read whatever she could find on the Wheatley-Crofts. There was not all that much, unfortunately.

They were just one of the many upper-class Victorian families who had distinguished themselves in the British Army. It was Christian's brother who had been the socially prominent member of the family, the one who had earned all the accolades for having served in India. But for his murder, Christian might not even have been mentioned in the *Who's Who* for that decade.

But Lavinia spent so much time checking indexes and cross-references in the biographies and histories of the period that she neglected to complete and mail her weekly cassette to Antony Gold. She wrote to her producer that she was behind on the tape because she'd had so many interviews the week before, but she promised to send him two tapes next week.

She was beginning to be aware that her interest in her assignment was waning. Christian and Sara's romance was suddenly so much more compelling. She worried over this all week. She had to get the work done. It wouldn't take Antony long to figure out that she was falling behind. He had a very good nose for smelling out members of his staff who were slacking off. Lavinia could imagine the telegram: "You're fired Stop Antony Gold."

She woke up Sunday morning and promised herself that to-morrow she would devote the entire day to researching the documentary. She would put Christian on hold until she had caught up with herself. And today—today was a perfect London summer Sunday, and she and Paul were going on a picnic.

He had phoned the previous morning, apologized for having disappeared and proposed an outing to Battersea Park.

"I'd love to," Lavinia said, meaning it. "Let me pack our lunch. You can bring a blanket and wine. Make it white."

She had been just on her way out to meet another friend of Mrs. Patel-Ram's, so they quickly agreed to rendezvous at twelve-thirty.

As they strolled across the Albert Bridge and headed toward the park, Paul entertained her with a description of the bewigged judge who had heard his case on Wednesday.

"'Quite right, Mr. Chamberlain,' the chap kept saying, even when I was presenting, for argument's sake, my opponent's point of view. He was harrumphing from the bench like a bloody bullfrog. But I won the case, so I suppose I shouldn't complain."

Lavinia hooted with laughter. It was good to see her laughing, he thought. There had been an awkward few moments when she opened her door as they both remembered their impassioned embrace that had come to such a strange, abrupt ending. But the sunlight streaming into the hallway had banished the shadows left over from the week before, and they had greeted each other without any strain.

Now the breeze was playing with her blond curls and her eyes seemed to reflect the sun glinting off the river. In her peach-colored cotton blouse and peach and gray striped culottes, she managed to look both sophisticated and adorable. And very sexy. But today Paul was determined to wait until Lavinia took the initiative. He still hadn't figured out what had happened last week. She had said she had not hit him. But somebody *had*— and that left only the ghost. And he still wasn't prepared to accept that option.

The park was crowded with couples as well as men and women alone, sunbathing on their blankets or reading. Children were playing ball and jump rope on the grass, and dogs raced to and fro, in pursuit of the sticks that went soaring through the air above them.

Paul and Lavinia walked down one of the paths until they found a quiet area. Paul surveyed the spot. "Perfect," he declared. "Lots of sun, some trees close by if we want shade and not too many children in the immediate vicinity."

"What do you have against kids?" asked Lavinia in mock horror.

Paul unfolded the blanket and spread it carefully on the ground. "Nothing. In fact, I'm quite fond of one or two of them." He anchored the blanket corners with his shoes and a couple of rocks he had hunted up. "But today I want you all to myself."

He plopped himself down on the blanket and smiled like a small boy let out of school, his expression one of absolute innocence and contentment. Lavinia decided that his words were not meant as a warning to her to stay away from the subject of Christian.

"We should open this before it loses its chill," Paul said, taking a corkscrew out of his jacket pocket to uncork the Pinot Grigio. The slim green bottle still glistened with moisture. "What's for lunch? I'm starving."

"It's a good thing you are." Lavinia removed the cover from the picnic basket. "I think I may have gotten carried away."

Paul peered in and raised his eyebrows. "I'm never one to complain about that."

Lavinia glanced at him briefly. Again his words seemed both weighted and ambiguous. *Relax,* she told herself. *He has no intention of giving me a hard time about what happened.*

"Today we are serving," Lavinia declared in an attempt at a French accent, "an egg and chutney appetizer, roast chicken, liver paté, fresh cucumber and tomato salad, asparagus vinaigrette, potato salad, French bread, Brie and Stilton cheeses and sweet biscuits. And, oh yes, fresh pears for dessert." She finished arranging the containers on the blanket and looked over at Paul. "Do you think that will do?" she asked in her normal voice.

"Rather nicely, I should say." He grinned broadly. "Now pass me a glass and a plate, and let's get started. I must say, I like the way you Americans do a picnic."

"It was nothing." She snapped her fingers and giggled. "Only took me all yesterday afternoon to put this together, but it looks fantastic, doesn't it?"

"Mmm, fantastic," he agreed, spreading some paté on a piece of bread.

As they ate they made up stories about the other people picnicking on the lawn. The afternoon grew warmer. Lavinia felt more relaxed than she had in days—since the day she had first seen Christian's shadow against the living room wall. She finished a pear and stretched out on her back.

"Tell me more about these people you think you see from the past," Paul said.

Lavinia shielded her eyes with her hand and squinted at Paul "Are you really interested? I would love to talk to you about it— and about what happened last week."

"Look, Lavinia, I've watched you get more and more mixed up about all of this. I've heard those voices coming out of your mouth while you were in a trance. I can't say that I believe in ghosts, but I *am* your friend. I care very much about what happens to you. Besides, I don't want that Christian fellow bopping me on the head the next time I try to kiss you." He smiled and lay down next to her, propping his arm up on his elbow.

"Thank you, Paul."

"Do you think about them all the time?"

Lavinia nodded. Lately, whenever she thought of Christian and Sara, she was gripped by a vague, fearful premonition. Something dreadful was going to happen, and there was nothing she could do to stop it.

"Can you evoke them now?"

"Yes. It's June 11, 1885. Katherine is preparing for the evening's events."

"Katherine?"

"The Satanist."

Lavinia was transported to Brighton, to Katherine Campbell's house. Katherine stood naked in the large bathroom, anointing herself with the oil she had bought from the white witch, a midwife who lived in London. The pungent, earthy odor of the oil filled the room. Katherine's smooth skin glistened.

Katherine adored her own body. The sensual delight she experienced when she touched herself made her feel ominpotent. She wished she could deliver her lectures naked, the only true natural state. But she knew this would drive away some of the guests before she had the chance to manipulate them beyond their limits and barriers.

The summer days seemed to pass too quickly, thought Katherine, admiring herself in the mirror. Sara and Christian had returned to Brighton only twice since the first night they had come to her house. She expected to see them this weekend.

She had been successful with Sara, she believed. She already wielded some degree of power over her. Sara would gradually give up her senseless religion and cross over into the faith of the Brothers and Sisters of the Free Spirit. Was this what Christian wanted? Katherine was still unsure, but she would know in time. She already knew he had an ulterior motive, because he was so obviously unwilling to accept the Brothers and Sisters of the Free Spirit for himself and had nevertheless exposed Sara to the group.

Christian had removed his clothes the last time he and Sara visited her, but he had not shed his defenses. He was not willing to worship the devil.

Although Christian had permitted Sara to disrobe and join the other women in their dancing, Katherine had sensed that he found the experience revolting. He had never allowed the other men and women to stroke or caress Sara. She was not ready, he claimed. While the others danced and shouted and made love, paying homage to Satan, Christian and Sara always seemed to be elsewhere, out of the room or even gone from the house.

Katherine knew Sara was a married woman and wondered whether that accounted for her holding back. Sara had confessed to Katherine that she had lied to her husband ever since meeting Christian.

As Katherine smoothed the oil up and down her voluptuous thighs, she knew that she would soon be seeing Sara, sooner than she had expected. She was therefore not at all surprised when a short time later she heard a gentle knock at her bedroom door.

"Who is it?" she called.

"Sara Standard," said a hesitant voice.

"Come in."

Sara opened the door and was only slightly surprised to find Katherine naked. But she had come to expect anything from Katherine and certainly she had seen her nude before. Trying to appear worldly, she did not even acknowledge Katherine's state of undress.

"I thought you would come," Katherine said, smiling a warm welcome. "How beautiful you look, but you must be very warm in this weather. You are welcome to shed those heavy clothes, dear Sara."

Sara smiled nervously but made no move to undress.

"May I sit down?" she asked. "There is something..." Her voice trailed off and tears come to her eyes.

"What is wrong?"

"It is terrible," Sara said. "I can barely think of the right words..." She began to weep uncontrollably.

"He's left you?" Katherine said, touching her thigh to feel whether the oil had dried.

"Has the major left you?" Katherine asked again. Her heart was pounding. With Sara out of the way, she had every reason to believe Christian would come to her. Katherine knew he desired her, but she wanted him to be devoted to her, the way he seemed to be to Sara. In fact, Katherine wanted him to *love* her.

"No, no," Sara said, attempting to wipe her tears away. "I think I am going to have a baby," she said, turning her large, blue eyes on a startled Katherine.

"You said you couldn't," Katherine said. "How is this possible?"

"I don't know, but I have all the signs. I must see someone, but I can't go to any doctor I know in London because he would tell my husband."

"You mean you're going to have Christian's baby?"

"I'm not sure," Sara said, her face a study in misery.

"I don't understand," Katherine said, trying to control her impatience.

"I don't know," Sara said, whimpering. "I had to make love with Rob a few times. He suspected me of infidelity. I had to prove that I still cared for him, so he would leave me alone. He had been following me. But I don't think he suspects me any longer. He thinks I am in Devonshire with my cousins on these weekends, and when I come back and am kind to him, and loving, he leaves me alone. I *had* to make love to him."

"Yes, yes, of course," Katherine said brusquely. "But what do you want to do?"

"You must promise me something, Katherine, else you will lose me forever." Sara stared defiantly at Katherine. "You will not tell Christian."

"All right. But why not?"

"Because I intend to get rid of this baby. I feel sick all the time."

Katherine burst into laughter.

"That is normal, you silly fool. Women feel sick when they are pregnant. Besides, if it is Christian's, would you deprive him of his child?"

"Oh, no," Sara cried. "I know he would love our child and

173

accept it even if I were not divorced, even if we had to live in sin. He has told me many times he doesn't care what other people think."

"Then what is the trouble?" Katherine said, trying to conceal her jealousy.

"I'm not certain if it is his. It could be my husband's."

"But you never got with child before. Why now? Why with your husband?"

"I was sick a few months ago. I had stopped my monthly. But then I thought I miscarried. It was no doubt Christian's. I did not tell him. But we thought it best not to make love for a while. Then Rob forced me and my monthly did not come again."

She began to weep anew. Katherine cradled her in her arms and rocked back and forth. Katherine marveled at the nurturing, motherly quality she was able to project despite the fact that she half despised this pathetic woman and coveted her man.

"And then we began to make love again," Sara said, staring up into Katherine's dark eyes. "The sickness came back. It's the timing that makes me believe it is Rob's. And it is possible that if you want a baby badly enough, it comes, even with the wrong man."

"You thought you were barren."

"Yes," Sara cried again. "I wish I were. Do you know someone who can help me?"

Katherine knew that the white witch who had given her the oil was a midwife who dealt with such matters. She could send Sara to her to get rid of the baby, but she would have to warn the white witch not to divulge any details about Katherine's black magic.

"Please, you know a midwife, don't you?" Sara implored.

Katherine held her to her bosom, delighted to have such power over her. From the first evening when she had seen Sara, she had been excited by her. She wanted to kiss her and stroke her soft skin.

"I will help you," Katherine said. "I will send you to a friend of mine, a midwife. How far along are you?"

"I don't know exactly. It could be six weeks or a few months.

If it is Christian's baby, it would have happened when we first met, perhaps three months ago. But if it's Rob's, as I think it must be, then it is more recent."

"I will send you to my friend in London, but, my dear," Katherine said, pushing Sara away, "you must be calm for this evening. There are festivities. And you must participate. And since you are already pregnant, you may do what you like with whomever you like."

Sara blushed and turned her eyes away.

"I love you, Sara," Katherine said abruptly, taking Sara's hands and kissing her fingertips. Perhaps tonight Sara would give herself to someone else, and if she did, Christian would certainly do the same.

Lavinia opened her eyes. The sun was still warm, but she felt surrounded by an ugly, frightening presence. Paul looked worried.

Lavinia clutched his arm. "Sara isn't well. She's sick and can hardly get out of bed. And Christian has no idea what's wrong with her. She's moaning because she's in pain. And she's bleeding."

"Lavinia, we should get home. You've drunk a lot of wine and ..."

Lavinia didn't hear him. She was seeing Nettie Shaw, the midwife, a short, stout woman with an open, friendly face, who had recently returned from a nursing stint in the Sudan.

Nettie had formerly been a friend of Florence Nightingale, but their friendship had ended because they disagreed about the need for antiseptic procedures, especially for maternity cases. Miss Nightingale believed that if doctors used carbolic acid to help them keep clean, they would become lazy and careless. Miss Shaw found this so utterly absurd that she would no longer even speak to Florence Nightingale.

Nettie Shaw had seen with her own eyes how the patient mortality rate had dropped when antiseptic techniques were used.

175

And she was no longer prepared to put her faith in the Lord to heal the sick. After what she had been through in Egypt, nursing the British troops, she no longer believed in traditional Christianity or the Holy Communion.

She was not surprised when Sara Standard called upon her. Katherine had already written to her explaining some of the situation. Nurse Shaw had met Katherine Campbell through their mutual interest in women's rights. She was not aware in the beginning that Katherine was actively engaged in devil worship, although she had heard rumors.

Neither did she think abortion was a sin. She saw the necessity for it in some cases, particularly for working-class women with too little money and too many children. But Nurse Shaw would not help a woman lose her baby unless she felt that the woman was at risk and that she would be saving a life by destroying the fetus. Money could not persuade her. She had enough of her own.

Sara liked Nettie Shaw as soon as she stepped into her sitting room in Islington. The older woman seemed sympathetic and open-minded, and Sara was able to tell her what she thought had happened as far as her pregnancy was concerned. Katherine had said Nurse Shaw was a white witch, a witch who worked for the good. Sara assumed it was just a matter of planning when she could get another weekend away in order to undergo an abortion. Katherine had even promised to go with her and that she would never breathe a word to Christian, who knew nothing of Sara's true condition.

But when she had finished telling her story, the nurse looked at her and said, "The instinct of maternity is an essential part of your character. You will be miserable if you deny it."

Sara was stunned at Nurse Shaw's response to her detailed account of her relationship to Rob, her love for Christian, her difficulty in being able to leave her husband for the man she loved and the conflict over the baby that was growing inside her.

"You mean you will not help me?" Sara said, tears welling in her eyes.

"Oh, yes, I will help you. But I cannot in all good conscience do what you came here for. I think it would be a terrible mistake. You must go and think over what I am about to tell you. Come back tomorrow, or whenever you have had a chance to give the matter enough thought."

"Tomorrow?" Sara said. "I cannot. I shouldn't be here now. I had to get special permission from Lord Evans. I won't be free to come back for another week."

Nurse Shaw stood up and beckoned Sara to follow her into the consulting room.

"Come, my girl, I will examine you. Let us see about this baby."

She had Sara lie down on a couch covered with a heavy carpet and a pristine white cloth. Then she pressed and poked Sara's abdomen. After she had finished examining her, she told Sara to sit up and asked her numerous questions about her condition and how she felt, writing down her answers on a long piece of paper.

Finally she smiled and said, "And how is Katherine Campbell?"

"I think she is well," Sara said nervously.

"Do you see her often?"

"No."

"You must give her my regards the next time you see her. Did she mention anything about the oil I gave her for backache?"

"No."

"Oh, perhaps you are not that intimate?"

"No, we are not that intimate," Sara repeated, wondering anxiously about the outcome of the examination.

"You know, my dear, you are far enough along in this pregnancy to know that this is not your husband's child," said Nurse Shaw in a kindly voice. "You said you were only with him recently, correct? But it will be all right. It is the child of the man you love, with whom you will spend the rest of your life."

"What do you mean?" Sara asked, startled at the assertion. "I am married and have not even sought a divorce. It is against my religion. And it is very difficult in any case. It costs a great deal of money."

"Ah, but the man you love *has* a great deal of money and he will facilitate the matter for you. But you must let him. Do not run away from your destiny."

"How could you possibly know that I will spend the rest of my life with him? Can you see into the future? Are you a seer?"

Nurse Shaw laughed.

"Not a seer, but a white witch, my dear girl. But go now and return to me in a week. Everything will work out so that you and the man you love will be together."

Sara left, feeling dejected. She had accomplished nothing. She would have to find someone else to help her get rid of the baby. How could Nurse Shaw know it was Christian's? How could she be so certain? What if Sara kept the baby and it looked like Rob? She would be more closely bound to Rob. Christian would hate the baby and hate her. She would lose him.

She walked rapidly along the street toward Westminster, trying to avoid as much as possible the poorer neighborhoods. The London slums depressed her far more than their equivalent in the country. She had grown up in poor but clean surroundings, whereas in London the lower classes lived in squalor—in decaying houses with damp mud floors and unmended roofs. Open sewers in the backs of buildings were cleared only once or twice a year. For the London poor there was no escape from the stench.

As Sara quickly passed by one of the rookeries, a large old house converted into one- and two-room warrens, she thought, *there but for the grace of God go I.*

When she returned, exhausted, to St. Vincent's Square, she was greeted by Rob's scowling face.

"And what did the doctor say?" Rob demanded. "Did he tell you why you are not well?"

"Yes," Sara lied, feeling sorry for him. He must know she did not love him. Did that make him feel lonely and sad?

"It's nothing much," she said, "a bit of a cold, nothing like influenza. It will pass."

"And where is the medicine?" Rob asked suspiciously. "And why aren't you wearing your fancy dress to visit the doctor, pray?"

"No medicine," Sara said, "and there was no point in wearing my finery when I had to traipse all over the city."

"All over the city? The doctor is less than a mile away."

Sara blushed, caught in her lie.

"I feel so ill today, it seemed like ten miles," she said. "I must change into my uniform for dinner." She went upstairs to put an end to the questions.

Rob stared after her. He was determined to find out what was going on. He knew she was lying. She spent so much time away from the house, every moment she could steal, and he knew she was not visiting her relatives. She had met a man. Why else would a woman so often not be at home?

Rob wanted a wife who was cheerful and pleased to do whatever was required of her, who was willing to accept his ideas as her own. Sara's wild ideas and fantasies made him angry. The fact that she would never provide children for him deepened the rift between them. If he had known she was barren, he never would have married her. He had rescued her from her village, from her family who hated her. And what had he got in return?

At first she had seemed to want to have sexual relations with him. In fact, she actually seemed to enjoy sex, the way a bought woman did. He found that he did not like this about her. He would have preferred that she be a normal woman whose reluctance needed to be overcome by a real man. Even though she was barren, he continued to demand his rights as her husband. At one point she had refused him; then for some months she had turned her back on him completely. When he insisted, she fought with him, actually drawing blood one day by scratching his face with her fingernails. He had grabbed her hands and cut all of her nails. But her protests made him feel as if he were begging, so he stopped coming to her.

Eventually, he felt overwhelmed by his needs. Furious that she no longer obliged him, he renewed his demands for sex, and she acquiesed. She did not seem to like it very much anymore, but he did not care. He got what he wanted.

Rob glared at Sara, who was hurrying up the stairs. He noticed that she had gained weight. When he married her, he had been attracted to her partly because she was so slender. He used to feel so large and masculine next to her. But today she looked much fatter. Or was it the bustle? Was she gaining weight in order to tell him that she no longer cared whether or not she appealed to him?

Lavinia and Paul walked slowly back to Belgrave Road as she described some of the incidents that she had been witness to.

"My word, you're begining to sound like an encyclopedia of Victoriana," Paul said. "Almost as if you really had lived in the nineteenth century."

She laughed wryly. "That's precisely what I've been trying to get across to you, Paul, but you haven't wanted to believe me. The real problem is that I haven't been able to concentrate on my work. I'm feeling a little nervous that I've spent so much time thinking about Christian and haven't followed up some very good leads for the documentary. I wish there was someone I could talk to about this."

Why couldn't she talk to him? Paul wondered.

The hurt expression on his face revealed his question.

"I mean," she said hastily, "someone with some professional training. A doctor, maybe. Although I don't know how a doctor could help me."

"We could call Dr. Hare, I suppose," Paul said uncertainly. "He *is* a doctor, but he also knows about the occult. What do you think? Should I give him a ring?"

"Oh, I suppose. I don't know." Lavinia tugged at her curls. "I don't know what to think anymore. Sometimes I feel like I'm losing my mind." She took out her key and smiled. "I'm not going to ask you in, Paul, but I do want you to know that this afternoon was a wonderful distraction. If you reach Dr. Hare, let me know. I'm going to be home all evening, trying to get some work done, finally." She grimaced, then smiled. "Everything will be okay, right?"

"Right," said Paul, determined to reach Dr. Hare as soon as possible. Lavinia was trying to make light of her anxiety, but she wasn't doing a very good job of hiding her worries.

Her flat was quiet except for the dog barking across the courtyard. She watered the plants on the downstairs terrace and then sat outside, trying to sort out her thoughts.

After a while she went to her desk and glanced through the notes she needed to organize and type up. She was engrossed in reading one of the ghost stories that she had collected when she heard a voice.

"The problem with these stories is that none of these people, none, know why these ghosts are haunting. All they have is a vague explanation."

Christian was standing before her. His face looked haggard and unshaven, and his eyes seemed to sink into his head.

"I know now how you are helping me," he said. "You are living for us. And I thank you. You are good."

Lavinia trembled. She so badly wanted to touch him and to be held by him.

"Yes," she said, "I am living for you. I will set you free. But I need to know more. I have so many... questions."

"What questions?"

"Well..." Lavinia hesitated. "The ring with the red stone. Where does it come from?"

Christian's voice began to fade to a whisper. She knew he would not stay much longer.

"She left it behind," he said.

"What do you mean?"

"It is difficult for me." The lines in his cheeks deepened. He groaned, and then he disappeared.

Lavinia searched through the notebooks on her desk. She flipped to the page she was looking for:

> The mode of appearance and disappearance of apparitions also varies. The ghost is usually either seen while looking round, as a human being might be, or it seems to come in at the door. Sometimes it forms gradually out of what at first seems a cloudlike appearance. I do not think there are any cases of its appearing suddenly in a spot that the percipient was actually looking at and perceived to be vacant before. However, it can disappear

suddenly in this way sometimes, and sometimes, if the percipient looks away for a moment, it is gone. It can vanish in a cloudlike manner sometimes, retaining its form but gradually becoming more and more transparent until it is gone. Frequently, it disappears through a door, either with or without apparently opening it, or goes into a room where there is no other exit, and where it is not found.

Lavinia read the paragraph twice, wondering whether she had included this material in any of her cassettes to Antony Gold. The passage came from *Proceedings*, written by a Mrs. Sidgwick for the Society of Psychical Research in London in 1885.

Christian must have known Mrs. Sidgwick. In 1885, the Society for Psychical Research was getting attention. Eminent people who had become involved in ghost hunting were trying to provide scientific explanations for what some of them called the phantasms of the living.

Lavinia remembered that a man named Myers had even tried to describe a ghost in quite a different way from the usual interpretation. He said that "instead of describing a ghost as a dead person permitted to communicate with the living, let us define it as a manifestation of persistent personal energy—or as an indication that some kind of force is being exercised after death that is in some way connected with a person perviously known on earth."

Lavinia continued reading her notes, totally absorbed for the first time in a week. When she glanced up, she saw that it was nearly dark outside. She switched on the light and glanced at her watch. It was almost ten o'clock. Christian's appearance had propelled her back to her work, as if *he* wanted to help *her*, rather than the reverse. She had managed to read about a hundred pages without being aware of the time.

Maybe she did not need to bother Dr. Hare after all. But she still felt nervous, as though disaster lurked close by. Whether the danger was in the present or in 1885 she did not know, but something inside her was telling her to beware.

She was begining to feel like Alice in Wonderland. Alice's story had terrified her when Aunt Jane first read it to her and had frightened her all through her childhood, although she insisted on reading it over and over. It was rather like pressing a tooth that ached.

She felt like Alice in that the landscape kept changing without warning. Lavinia could fall down a hole at any time, it seemed. Like Alice, who kept changing, shrinking and then growing without warning, Lavinia too was in a sense out of control. Despite her resolution just to "let it happen," she was frightened about the unknown.

She still remembered one section of *Alice in Wonderland*:

> "Why about you," Tweedledee exclaimed, clapping his hands triumphantly, "and if I left off dreaming about you, where do you suppose you'd be?" "Where I am now, of course," said Alice. "Not you," Tweedledee retorted contemptuously, "you'd be nowhere. Why, you're only a sort of a thing in dream!"

Was she only a sort of a thing in Christian's dream? Or was he only a thing in her dream?

Lavinia was puzzling over this question when the buzzer from the front door of the building rang.

Who on earth could that be? she wondered. Paul? Surely not Dr. Hare. It was already past ten. Why would he have come over at this hour—unless Paul had made it seem as if she were on the verge of a nervous breakdown. How embarrassing!

She went downstairs and pressed the button that unlocked the building door, then peered out her door at the landing. No one was there. She buzzed again, but still no one appeared. Perhaps it was for somebody else, she decided. As she was about to go upstairs to run a bath, the doorbell rang again. This time she decided to go downstairs and let the person in herself.

But when she opened the front door, nobody was there. She glanced down the street to the right and left. Belgrave Road, usually heavily trafficked, was oddly empty.

And then she heard a baby crying.

Glancing down, she noticed a tiny crib made of straw. The

cries grew louder and more piteous. Lavinia quickly knelt down and drew back a tiny scrap of pink blanket.

She screamed when she saw what was inside. The infant's tiny face was blackened and scarred. The eyes stared vacantly, unseeing. The infant's thin arms hung limply over the side of the crib.

"My God!" whispered Lavinia. She was frozen with horror, one hand still holding the pink blanket, the other pressed against her mouth to stifle her scream.

What should I do? she asked herself. Somehow she couldn't bear to leave the baby alone, although she knew there was nothing she could do to help the poor creature. Nor could she bring herself to pick the straw crib up in her arms. . . . Paul! She would buzz him and ask him to come down and help her figure out what to do with the body.

As soon as she heard his voice, distorted by the intercom, she began to sob.

"Yes? Yes, who's there?" he demanded.

"Paul. . ." She couldn't say anything more than that before she began to sob again, huge racking sobs that shook her body.

"Lavinia, is that you? What's the matter? I'll be right there. . . ."

Paul rushed downstairs and threw open the door to the building. His arms were around her as she wept.

"Lavinia, tell me, what's wrong? Please, I beg you to tell me." He stroked her hair and wiped the tears from her cheeks.

Finally she stopped crying and pointed toward the bottom of the steps. "Look at it, Paul, it's so awful."

"What, Lavinia? Tell me what you see."

"The baby. In the crib. Who could have done such a horrible thing?"

Paul waited until her breathing had returned to normal. Then he said very quietly, "Lavinia, I don't see anything."

She jerked her head up and her eyes widened. "But it was there. I swear it! With its tiny arms and its face. . ."

She stood up and took several steps, searching the stairway for the crib. "Somebody must have taken it away. But I would have seen them. . . Paul. . ." She gazed at him, pleading for an explanation.

"Lavinia," he said gently, "perhaps you were having a bad dream and got confused...."

"No! I hadn't even gone to sleep yet. Somebody rang my bell and when I came downstairs nobody was there, but then I saw that little crib..." She ran her hand through her hair. "I don't know," she whispered. "Maybe you're right." But she knew he wasn't.

"If you don't mind, I'd like to call Dr. Hare and ask him to come over this evening to talk with you. I spoke to him earlier and told him you were having a bit of a hard time with all of this."

Lavinia felt utterly enervated. "It's very late," she said listlessly.

"Come, let's go up to my apartment. I think you could use a stiff shot of something."

His arm securely around her shoulder, Paul led her upstairs, phoned Dr. Hare and poured her a generous glass of whiskey.

"With an ice cube, just the way you Americans like it," he said. She smiled weakly. If he was still making jokes, perhaps he didn't think she was completely mad.

"Dr. Hare will be over shortly. He'd just gotten in, so don't feel that you've pulled him out of bed."

Paul described in great detail the plot of a complicated adventure movie that he had seen recently. She was grateful that he was trying to distract her, and she nodded and smiled whenever it seemed appropriate. But all she could think of was, *Somebody hurt the baby. Why? Who could have done such a thing?*

When the buzzer sounded, Lavinia felt a sudden stab of terror. Was it the same person who had rung her buzzer earlier?

"That must be Dr. Hare," said Paul, noticing how stricken Lavinia looked.

When he went to the door to let the doctor in, Lavinia chided herself. "There is an answer for all of this," she told herself. "I am not going crazy, even if I am seeing ghosts."

"Good evening, my dear," Dr. Hare said, a touch too heartily. "I understand from Paul that you're feeling a bit undone by the seances. Now, why don't you tell me what's gotten you into such a state."

Lavinia summarized as calmly as she could the evening's events, but when she began to describe the grotesquely disfigured infant, she could hardly restrain herself form weeping.

"I know what you're both thinking," she said. "That I've really lost it. That now I'm not just seeing ghosts but I'm also having hallucinations. Right?" Her tone was both a challenge and a plea for reassurance.

"Not at all," Dr. Hare said. "I know you will be skeptical, Paul, but if we accept the premise—and I do—that Lavinia sees and talks to the ghost of Christian, that you can indeed visit the past and relive the ghost's story because you were actually his mistress, then we can extend our thinking even further. We can assume that what you saw has some connection with Christian and Sara's story."

Paul protested.

"I'm sorry," said Dr. Hare, "but I do believe that if we are patient, this will all become perfectly clear."

"Oh, my God, Sara is going to lose her baby." Lavinia's eyes were round with horror.

"But we don't know that, Lavinia. That may not be the case at all. It would be a grave mistake to attempt to anticipate the facts."

"The facts?" Paul demanded. He couldn't contain his anger any longer. He must have been mad himself to have called Dr. Hare. He was no objective medical man. The man was as bonkers about ghosts as his mother. Paul was on the verge of exploding into a tirade brought on by his frustrations with Lavinia's preoccupation, but she cut him short.

"Paul," she said, her tone now more matter-of-fact, "the doorbell *did* ring. You do believe me, don't you? Or perhaps you don't?"

He stared wordlessly at her. He wanted to believe her, but even more he wanted not even to have to think about these bloody people, these ghosts or whatever they were.

"Please tell me the truth. Don't just say something to make me feel better."

"The truth? I am trying very hard to believe you saw what you say you did." He rubbed his forehead. "Lavinia, this is rather difficult. I don't put much store in the spirit world."

"Didn't you say this Katherine woman was a witch?" interrupted Dr. Hale.

"Yes," Lavinia nodded.

"Well, then, perhaps she's playing some sort of trick on you." Lavinia considered the possibility. Once such a suggestion would have struck her as thoroughly absurd, but now—tonight—it seemed perfectly logical. "Katherine frightens me," she said.

"Understandably," Dr. Hare said.

Paul frowned. "You do see," he said to Lavinia, "why I find this all so implausible."

Dr. Hare cleared his throat. "My boy, there have always been witches and ghosts, you know. And your very own daughter saw the ghost."

"Emily is always seeing things. She's as batty as my mother." He realized the implication of his statement.

"I'm sorry, Lavinia. I didn't mean to suggest anything about you..."

Lavinia felt tired and vulnerable. She desperately wanted to be left alone—by Paul and Dr. Hare and, most of all, by Christian and Sara and whomever else was drifting in and out of her life.

"Maybe I should go back to New York... but what if Christian is there in my apartment at home? Now that we've discovered each other..."

"I think," said Dr. Hare, "that you will have to relive the past in order to free yourself of Christian by helping him put things to right."

"If only Christian could tell me in the present what really happened. Then I could help, him, couldn't I?"

"But he may not know himself," said Dr. Hare.

"So then I've no choice but to relive their story to the end. And that means I'll know what happened to that poor, charred..." The thought made her too ill to speak.

At that moment the buzzer for the front door of the building sounded loudly.

"Oh, no!" cried Lavinia.

"It's just the buzzer," Paul said, hurrying over to the intercom system. Whoever was down there was buzzing insistently, as if he were in a tremendous hurry.

"Don't answer," whispered Lavinia.

"Don't be silly . . . I'm sorry, Lavinia. I didn't mean to be rude. But you're quite safe. Nothing can happen to you with Dr. Hare and me here."

"Yes?" he called into the intercom. "Yes? Who's there?" He heard a man's muffled voice but could make no sense of the words. Then he understood that the man was saying something about Miss Cross's flat.

"I'll ring you in," shouted Paul. He looked at Lavinia. "Just relax, Lavinia. Someone is coming up. I think he said he was looking for you, but if he's willing to talk to me, he couldn't be Christian or that Katherine person."

A moment later there was a knock at the door. A young man holding an envelope stood in the hallway.

"I'm looking for Miss Cross," he said in an East End London accent. "I've got this telegram from overseas, and she doesn't seem to be about. I don't like to leave it lying in her mailbox . . ."

"Right," Paul said. "Miss Cross is here, so I'll give it to her. Thanks very much for your persistence."

He signed for the telegram and tipped the messenger.

"Well, that was nothing terrible, was it?" he said, smiling at Lavinia.

She looked at the envelope suspiciously.

"I don't know. Telegrams are usually bad news."

Worried that something awful had happened to Aunt Jane, she ripped it open and read it aloud.

"Arriving Wednesday with crew. Antony Gold."

"Who's Antony Gold?" asked Paul.

"My boss," Lavinia said faintly, sinking back into the cushions of the sofa. But he wasn't supposed to be in London for at least another month. She was nowhere near ready for him. She still owed him lots of work and hadn't yet interviewed several of the people she had mentioned to him in her letter. Plus she had promised to scout some locations. She briefly thought of trying to persuade him to delay his trip, then realized she would be overstepping the bounds of her position. Antony Gold! Could her life possibly get any more complicated?

"Lavinia, would you like a sleeping pill?" asked Dr. Hare.

"No, thank you. If Paul is willing to make me a cup of tea, I think that will do the trick and then I'll go to sleep."

"Coming right up," said Paul. "And how about another whiskey?"

"Great idea." Suddenly she felt more in control of the situation. Perhaps it was the fact of Antony's imminent arrival. He was such a part of her New York professional life, her life before Christian.

Dr. Hare rose to leave. "Well, I'll be going then. Odd how it all works out. Rather than you going to New York, New York is coming to you," he said pompously. "Good-night."

He let himself out, leaving Paul and Lavinia to puzzle over the significance, if any, of his parting words.

Chapter 8

SARA CONCEALED HER ILLNESS FROM CHRISTIAN, GIVING him only a vague description of what she called chronic symptoms, but when he suggested she see his doctor she refused. He knew the problem had something to do with the fact that her menstrual cycle had become irregular, but he was unable to learn little more than that.

Christian insisted that she rest in order to restore her energy, and resigned himself to seeing her less frequently until her health improved. Despite his concern for her, he believed she would soon be well enough and that they would be together. In fact, although he hadn't yet told her, he hoped that she would be able to accompany him to his house in Venice at the end of the month. He had begun to think of the trip as their honeymoon, even if they weren't about to be married. Christian's fantasy—and fondest hope—was that Sara would agree to begin divorce proceedings before they left for Venice. They would then be free to marry a year later. Still, Sara hadn't yet come to terms with the idea of divorce, and Christian was realistic enough to know that his expectations would have to wait a bit longer to be fulfilled. Christian would have been satisfied if she simply decided to leave Rob, even if she didn't feel ready to go through with the divorce. The important thing was that she travel with him to Venice, which he knew she would love. He didn't give a damn whether society accepted them as a couple or not. He was prepared to take her anywhere, travel with her, live with her whether or not they were married. Besides, it was just a matter of time.

It had been five days since he had seen her, and he felt restless, impatient. He yearned for her, to see her lovely face and her innocent, beautiful eyes. Soon they would be together, he kept reminding himself. Soon his house on the Grand Canal would be filled with her happy, loving presence.

While he waited for Sara to recover, he prepared for his departure by going through the papers in his library on Belgrave Road. Sorting out his letters and other memorabilia from the years he had served in India, he reflected on how much he had learned about himself and his fellow man in the years he had lived in Simla.

The memories of the fresh air of the Himalayan foothills, the steep terrain, the narrow streets, the crowds of people, the women in their colorful saris, were still very vivid. And, of course, there was his friend, Akhbar Ramabal, a young man who had studied in England and France and who had married an Italian woman from Venice.

Most of the British who served in India under the Raj lived in small communities, quite apart from the Indians. They sent their children to English schools, ate bacon, eggs and porridge for breakfast just as they did at home and ignored the Indian native culture as if it did not exist. They tried to be equally unaware of the squalor in which too many Indians lived. The English had their own social events and celebrations to which Indians were not invited unless it was absolutely necessary.

Christian was one of the few Englishmen to recognize that India had its own ancient and magnificent culture. Too open-minded to accept the notion that the Indians were a lazy, inferior race, he became increasingly alienated from his fellow English officers, whose greed and hypocrisy appalled him.

But he found it equally difficult to make friends among the educated Indians, the *babus*, who too often in the past had been hurt and disappointed by the English to trust him. Eventually, however, Christian gained the confidence of Akhbar Ramabal, whose expertise with language and dialects and whose knowledge of Eastern and Western music Christian greatly admired. Akhbar had showed Christian the artifacts and customs of India, and he had opened Christian's mind to ideas he had never dreamed about before. His friendship with the highly cultured, educated Indian man had profoundly altered his view of the world. In India, his eyes had been opened to life—and to death.

And it was Akhbar, through his wife, Francesca, who had introduced Christian to Venetian society. Because of his close relationship with them, he had come to love the city and had eventually bought a house there. And soon he would be greeting them at his house, introducing them to Sara. They no doubt would be delighted to show Sara the many beautiful sights of the city. If only the days would pass more quickly until the four of them could stroll the canals and piazzas together.

Sorting through his papers distracted Christian from the fact that he was not seeing Sara. He had been warned that Rob suspected she had a lover, so he hesitated to ride by the house or casually pay a visit. Besides, Lord Evans had embarked on a long ocean voyage to Australia to avoid the English summer, so Christian had had no excuse to catch a glimpse of her.

He barely left the house on Belgrave Road, except to stroll the streets of Pimlico. Some of his friends and acquaintances were still in town, but he was desperately lonely for Sara. He forbade himself to think of her sweet face, her soft smile, her warm, willing body. But the image nevertheless tormented him.

One afternoon, tempted to walk over to St. Vincent's Square on the off-chance that he might catch a glimpse of her through a window, he forced himself to retrace his steps to Belgrave Road. He felt tired and edgy and, indeed, had not slept soundly in several nights. He poured himself a glass of port and wandered out to the terrace, where he amused himself imagining how Sara would love his Venice house. She had never been out of England, had never even thought she would journey abroad. Those were dreams for other people, she had told him, dreams for rich people who were free to do as they pleased. But he could make her dreams come true.

His valet interrupted his thoughts.

"A young woman to see you, sir," he said.

"I'll come down, Charles," Christian replied, trying to act calm.

Sara! She must be feeling better.

He hurried down the two flights of stairs to the front of the house. It was not Sara but Katherine Campbell, who greeted him with a smile on her face, her slanted eyes looking at him with obvious delight.

"Well, whatever are you doing here?" Christian said. Disappointed though he was, he was nevertheless pleased to see her. He needed some female companionship. Perhaps she would dine with him and discuss how to persuade Sara from her wavering but still conventional beliefs.

"I have come because you wanted me to," Katherine said mischievously. "I was at home with my cousin and I felt you calling me, you see. And I knew you would be alone."

"Ah," Christian said, admiring her tall, elegant figure, "how did you know that?"

Katherine laughed and followed him up the steps to the sitting room.

"Sara told me."

"You saw her, then?"

"Only in my dream," she replied saucily, sitting on the sofa.

"Let me fetch you a glass of something," Christian suggested. "Or do you prefer tea?"

"Port would do nicely, Christian."

Katherine had cut her long, black hair. She had braided and coiled what was left around the crown of her head, and Christian imagined reaching over to pull out the pins that held the braid in place.

She seemed to be warm. Her face was flushed, and she was fanning herself with a large ostrich-feather fan. Her summer dress was cut so low that each time she waved the fan Christian could see the swell of her breasts.

"Why don't we sit on the terrace," Christian suggested.

"Yes, that would be refreshing," said Katherine. Her artful smile seemed to indicate that she knew she was making him uncomfortable.

They watched the sun set, leaving behind a bright red glow in the sky.

"There is no sun like the sun in Venice," Christian remarked.

"Yes," Katherine agreed. "I do hope you get your wish and are able to take Sara with you." Her tone seemed to imply that she doubted Sara would go.

"What do you mean?"

Katherine had implied several times that something was wrong with Sara, but she claimed not to know what it was. He had pressed her for more information, but she had been unusually discreet.

"I do not think she will go, that's all," Katherine said. "Call it my intuition or what you wish. You know I have the ability to second-guess, to perceive what others do not. It is not simply circumstances that has brought me to the devil and to the Brothers and the Sisters. It is my character to see into the future. In that way Sara and I have much in common."

"And what do you see about your future?" Christian asked, wanting not to discuss Sara. He did not like the way Katherine spoke about her—as if she were keeping something from him. He believed that he and Sara had no secrets from each other.

"My future? I don't know about *my* future. When I try to envision it I see nothing." Her tone was unusually serious.

She began to pace up and down the terrace, now and then glancing at the darkened sky as if the stars that were rapidly appearing might solve the mystery of her future.

"Nothing?"

"Well . . . it's uncertain. Perhaps I don't have a future."

She stared at Christian across the terrace. The intensity of her gaze drew him to her.

"I would like to help you," he said, a look of concern in his eyes. He was glad to have his thoughts removed from Sara for a moment.

"You could help me," Katherine said in a husky voice and reached out to touch his arm. "Do you really wish to help me?"

"Yes, certainly." He felt as if she were casting a spell over him. He could smell her perfume, an unfamiliar foreign scent, like some exotic oil from the Orient.

Clasping her hands around his neck, she pulled him forward and gently kissed his lips.

"I need you, Christian, I need you so badly."

He was intoxicated by her. Forgetting his vow of fidelity to Sara and his mistrust of Katherine Campbell, he allowed her to work her seductive wiles on him.

As he bent to kiss her eager, open mouth, Sara Standard knelt before Nettie Shaw, begging the woman to help her dispose of the child growing within her.

"I am convinced this is unwise, child," Nurse Shaw finally said to Sara, who had been weeping for the better part of an hour. "But I have compassion for you. Take this medicine. When you begin to bleed heavily then I will use one of my implements to scrape your uterus."

Sara drew little comfort from the midwife's words. Had she any other choice but to do this ghastly thing? She did not want Rob's baby, and after many calculations and recalculations, she was convinced it was his. If he so much as suspected for an instant that she was pregnant, he would never set her free. She would be his prisoner for the rest of her life.

She took the small vial of medicine and made her way back to Lord Evans's house. At least she would be alone. Rob had gone out to the pub to drink with several of the other servants. Since Lord Evans had departed for Australia, they did as they pleased.

Sara had overheard them gossiping about her. Rob had told some of them about her mysterious powers, had even implied that she could injure or kill by fixing her thoughts on her victim. Sara could not even bear to speak of the accusation. She was no witch! She had no harmful intent! She *could* see into the future. And it seemed that her childhood had come back to haunt her, once again.

Sara worried as she climbed the steps to the room she shared with Rob. Was it her destiny to bear the child? Had she become pregnant for some reason she did not yet understand? And if that were so, what was the reason? And what of Christian's feelings? Would she lose him? Why could she not see the answers to *these* questions?

She lay across the bed and closed her eyes. Just as she thought she might sleep, she felt a panic so intense she sat bolt upright. Something terrible was happening on Belgrave Road. She knew it.

Sara bolted down the steps and out the front door, running toward Belgrave Road. When she reached Vauxhall Bridge Road, she could see the fire engines racing up the street, causing pandemonium as people and broughams tried to maneuver out of their path.

As she hurried in the direction of the fire engines, she prayed that the fire was not at Christian's. The mere possibility sent a cold prickle up her back. She was terrified of fires, as were most Londoners.

Sara was breathing heavily by the time she turned the corner of Belgrave Road. To her horror she saw the police and firemen in front of Christian's house. Flames shot up through his roof, and thick black smoke curled through the shattered windows. The entire block of houses on his side of Belgrave Road had caught fire.

People were running in all directions and the police had put up a barricade so that no one could enter the street. Sara swooned. A man standing on the pavement caught her as she was about to fall to the ground.

"Shall I escort you home?" he asked.

She looked up into the unfamiliar face of a gentleman.

"No, thank you, sir, I shall be all right. But I know someone in that house and I must try to help him," she said, pointing across the street.

"I think that house caught fire first," the man said sadly. "The eastern wind stirred the fire and spread it down the entire road. I fear for the people inside."

Sara leaned heavily against the man for fear she might actually faint this time.

"You had better sit down," he said. "There is nothing you can do to help whatever poor souls are caught inside."

"I shall be all right," she said, taking a deep breath.

After several moments she let go of his arm and ran forward, trying to dodge under the barricade. A policeman grabbed her.

"You can't go this way, madam," he shouted angrily. "Can't you see what's going on?"

Sara struggled for a moment with the policeman and then gave up. She could see that the firemen were doing whatever they could to put out the fire at Christian's house and to contain it so that it didn't spread further down the street. The sounds of sirens rushing to the scene from other parts of London could be heard amid the cries and screams of victims of the fire and their families.

Christian's beautiful, five-story house, so artfully designed and built by the master builder Thomas Cubitt, was falling apart like a house of cards. With the heat on her face, Sara felt as if she were watching her life burning up in front of her.

The fire devoured the windows and the wooden columns at the front of the house. The lead roof melted like the roof of a doll's house. Sara could hear the sound of cracking, and then a thundering explosion raged in her ears. The smell of burning timber and molten lead filled her nostrils.

Coughing and sputtering, unable to tear her eyes away from the inferno, she began to pray out loud, her voice drowned out by the clanging fire bells and the roar of the fire itself. The screams of people hanging out of the windows of the surrounding houses reverberated around her. The sky glowed red, and the billows of smoke rose up toward the stars. She had the feeling that Satan himself hovered nearby, gloating at this hell on earth.

Rob had thought of nothing else but his mission since discovering that it was Major Wheatly-Croft who was Sara's lover. The shock of the discovery had been so great that it had taken several days for the truth to sink in. Rob had believed for some time that she was seeing some other man, but he had assumed that it was someone he knew, perhaps one of the chaps who looked after Lord Evans's horses or drove Lord Evans about in his brougham. Rob had never entertained that startling notion that it might be a gentleman.

He was determined to punish the two of them. Sara's disloyalty, her infidelity, made him feel humiliated beyond description. She had rejected him, and another man knew it. He despised her for her betrayal. Hadn't he, after all, saved her from a lifetime of isolation in the rural slum in which he found her? He knew that the other villagers had feared and disliked her. Was this how she showed her gratitude?

It had been bad enough that he had had to come to terms with her barrenness and her unwillingness to be a proper wife. She had opposed him and fought with him even more about what he believed in. He hated her freethinking opinions, which angered him so that finally he had had to beat her. Her nonsensical utterings made his blood boil. He blamed her for the failure of their marriage, but she was his, and he would never let her go.

Rather than confronting Sara with the knowledge of her deceit, Rob had decided to take the matter into his own hands and deal with it the way *he* wished. And there it would end.

He had spent the evening drinking glass after glass of ale at the Lord Gladstone Pub. Then he bade the publican good-night and stumbled toward Belgrave Road, a pile of faggots concealed in a bag tucked under his left arm. In his right hand he carried the paraffin lamp that he had taken from Lord Evans's house.

He knew the major's house must have a cellar kitchen that adjoined a storage space under the pavement. He would get in and out of the house by the steps the tradesmen used when they made deliveries.

It would be easy enough to set the house ablaze. The gas-fed chandeliers would spread the fire. The house might even have electricity.

Rob thought about what must have passed between the major and his wife. How many times had they met? And where? No doubt in the major's bedroom. And how many times had they made love, had she taken her marriage vows in vain? Sara was an adulteress, and she would burn in hell. No wonder she had not been well. She was suffering from natural feelings of guilt about the treacherous thing she was doing. She deserved to be ill. She deserved to die as much as the major. But killing her love and letting *her* live was a much more cruel punishment.

Rob would be able to enjoy her grief. How he wished he could drag the major's charred remains from his house and present him to her on one of the major's silver plates. He wished her to suffer as she had made him suffer.

Although he was drunk, Rob was apprehensive enough to look out for whomever might be in the kitchen at that hour of the night. He had brought with him a small hammer and a sharp knife in case he should encounter a kitchen maid or one of the cooks. He was prepared to kill anyone who tried to stop him.

But to his relief, the kitchen was empty. Rob had never killed another human being and did not relish the thought of a face-to-face encounter in which he would have to use the weapons he had brought with him. Killing the major was an entirely different matter. That was an eye for an eye, he believed. What he was about to do was acceptable in the eyes of the Almighty.

He brushed the coal dust from his face and set about his business, spreading the faggots on one side of the kitchen, close to the electrified kitchen range with its spacious ovens. He glanced briefly around the kitchen, taking in its opulence and chortling to himself as he dashed paraffin over the faggots. The pots and pans, fish kettles, baking trays, mixing bowls, the bread-slicing machine, the knife-cleaner, the coffee roaster—these might be the only items to survive Rob's holocaust. But the devil and the rest of his house would be demolished.

As he was about to strike the first match, he heard footsteps. Someone was coming down the stairs. For an instant he did not know what to do. He stood rooted to the spot. But then his thoughts cleared, and the fear disappeared. He flattened himself against the back of the door, well hidden in the gloomy kitchen, and waited for the person to appear. His hand sweated against the handle of the knife in his pocket, and he kept his other hand free in case he would need to grapple with the person.

To his astonishment, a half-naked woman walked into the kitchen. She wore a perfume with a smell so pungent that he felt himself becoming aroused. The woman went to the cupboard and took out some biscuits. She was so intent on what she was doing that she did not see him.

Perhaps she would do whatever she had to do quickly and leave. He did not want to kill her, but he would have to if she looked around and saw him.

He watched nervously as she arranged biscuits and cheese on a large plate. Where were the servants? he wondered. Was she a servant? Hardly likely. No servant wandered about a household in silken undergarments. He stared at her through the dark. She was very tall with tousled dark hair, and she looked as if she had just climbed out of bed. And whose bed?

She must be a harlot, he thought, as his eyes lingered on her heavy, firm thighs.

"I know someone is here with me," Katherine said suddenly.

She turned around, her eyes adjusting to the dim light of the kitchen. Rob trembled with dread and desire as he saw her large breasts beneath a thin chemise.

"I know you are there," she said. "Who are you and what do you want?"

Rob did not reply. He moved forward, one hand holding the knife behind his back.

"You've entered this house illicitly," Katherine said, "and now you may go. If you leave immediately, I shall not report you, but if you dally, I'll have the police here in a trice."

Rob thought the whore smiled as he reached out and grabbed her by the hair to pull her forward. Caught completely off guard, Katherine began to struggle. She was strong and she had the advantage of height, but Rob was incensed beyond reason and his rage gave him the strength he needed to subdue her. He threw her to the kitchen floor and began to viciously rip away her undergarments. In moments, she was completely naked and at his mercy. His small, mean eyes came at her like a snake's.

First he bit her on the cheek, drawing blood. She thrashed and screamed, her hands clawing at the air, but he had the upper hand. He sank his teeth into her cheek and breasts and belly, drawing blood. Then he raped her, pressing her hard against the cold floor.

And afterward he stabbed her until blood spurted against his face and clothing. He got up, sure she was dead, but when he looked down at her he saw that she was still alive. Her dark, tartar eyes stared at him with hatred. A strange smile curled her lips, and she got easily to her feet.

How could this be? He had stabbed her repeatedly.

Rob backed up, reaching again for the knife. He grasped it tightly as she advanced toward him, her naked breasts taunting him for what he had done to her.

She grabbed the knife, and they wrestled over it until it dropped to the floor. Rob grabbed the hammer and smashed it down upon her head. She fell to the floor, stunned. He didn't waste any more time. He took out the paraffin and rapidly spread it over the pile of faggots and around the kitchen. At one end of the room a coal fire was burning brightly, and he threw some of the paraffin on a small table near the fire. Then he lit the pile of faggots and ran from the room, escaping through the coal hole that led to the street.

As he reached St. George's Square, he turned and saw the smoke spurting through the downstairs windows. A grin of satisfaction on his face, he kept running.

He felt triumphant. He had accomplished his mission. The major's house would burn to the ground, along with those on the rest of the street. The houses of the high and mighty would be destroyed in the inferno.

Rob did not give a single thought to the woman he had murdered. He slowed his pace only when he was too exhausted to continue running. Finally he slowed to a halting gait, stopping now and then to catch his breath. He wanted to celebrate his act of vengeance, so he went into the next pub he passed and ordered three pints of ale, gulping them down thirstily. Then, already drunk, he ordered a whiskey, which he swallowed in one gulp. No sooner had he put down the glass than he was sick all over the bar.

The barman grabbed him by the shoulders and threw him out into the street.

"We don't serve trash in here," he shouted and spat directly into Rob's face.

Enraged, Rob stumbled back into the pub, whereupon the

barman punched him in the face. Blood poured from his nostrils, but this did not stop him. He swung at the barman, and two customers jumped him and joined the barman in flinging him back onto the pavement. A carriage narrowly missed running him over.

For a moment he fancied he saw the major inside the brougham. Then he passed out, overcome by all the alcohol he had drunk.

When he awoke, several policemen stood over him, scowls on their faces. They dragged him roughly to his feet and marched him briskly to the police station, a few hundred yards away.

His hands chained together behind him and a leg iron locked on one leg, he was pushed into a cell.

"The Old Bailey," Lavinia said. "Rob was tried at the Old Bailey. He was found guilty and hanged."

Paul was staring at her, a cup of tea in his hand.

"I must have gone into a trance. I didn't even realize it was happening, though," she said, confused about how much time had passed since Dr. Hare had left Paul's apartment.

"I was out of the room for just a few minutes," said Paul, offering her the tea. "Did you see the ghost again?"

She sipped the strong, whiskey-flavored tea. "No, not exactly. But I was there, I saw what was happening to Sara and to Rob." She could almost smell the flames and smoke that had engulfed this very house where she was now calmly sipping tea.

"It's almost as if you have to hurry up and get to the end of the story. To find out what happened to your ghost before your producer arrives," said Paul thoughtfully.

She smiled at his choice of words. "Your ghost," he'd said. Was Christian hers? Or Sara's? Or were she and Sara one and the same? Paul was right. She didn't want these images lingering in her mind when Antony arrived. She wanted to get on with what she considered to be her *real* life.

Paul sat down on the armchair next to the sofa.

"I know this may sound very odd," he said hesitantly, "but the manner in which you talk about Christian, the way you describe him . . ." He stopped and cleared his throat.

"Yes," Lavinia prompted. He was having a difficult time expressing his thought.

"It's almost as if you were . . . that you had . . . that you're in love with the chap." A tinge of red stole across his face.

He was blushing! thought Lavinia. Poor Paul. He was so obviously uncomfortable.

"He seems so real to you, and you're rather obsessed with him, aren't you?"

"Yes, I suppose I am," she said slowly. "If you're wondering, Paul, whether he turnes me on, as we say in New York . . ."

She looked at him questioningly.

"Yes, not that it's any business of mine."

"Well, it is, because you've been nice enough to listen to me carry on. The answer is I do desire him. I know that's ridiculous, but I feel sexually drawn to him."

Paul opened his mouth to say something but stopped before the words were out. He could put up a fight against a human rival, but a ghost was another matter. Was he simply to accept that the story had to play itself out before Lavinia could be herself again—herself and not Sara Standard or whomever she had herself confused with? And would she then be the woman he had been attracted to when she had first arrived in London, which seemed like such a very long time ago? Or would she be forever marked by this experience, so that for the rest of her life she would be hearing voices and seeing spirits and falling into trances? He wasn't sure he cared to know the answer.

"I only know," Lavinia continued, "that I can give him up when I set him free."

Now she saw the ring with the red stone. It lay on the stone floor among the charred remains of Christian's kitchen. Katherine Campbell's burned body had been removed for burial, and no one noticed the ring until Christian, poking through the debris, discovered it. He slipped it into his pocket and forgot it.

Christian had not been at home when the fire began. The servants, who had been upstairs in their rooms, had smelled the smoke and managed to escape before the fire had spread very far. But no one had known Katherine Campbell was in the kitchen.

As soon as he and Katherine had satisfied their passion in frenzied lovemaking, so wild that they might have been two animals coupling, Christian had felt a guilt so intense that he fell to his knees and prayed. He prayed to the God in whom his faith had wavered for some years, begging to be forgiven for his sin of betraying Sara.

Katherine laughed at him. "I know you despise me, Christian, but one day you will feel much more fondly about me," she said.

She leapt from the bed and pulled him toward her, kissing him violently on the mouth so that shudders of desire shot through him once more. But he pushed her away roughly, threw on his clothes and almost ran from the house, hoping the night air would clear his head of the images of Katherine and himself. He was thankful he had sent the servants to their quarters earlier so that he could have quiet while he worked in his library. Certainly they would have heard Katherine's bizarre animal noises. It was as if he were making love to an uncontrollable beast, he had thought at the time, and he had been both repulsed and fascinated by her behavior.

Christian strode away from the house, deliberately heading in the opposite direction from Lord Evans's house. He passed a drunken man who was swearing loudly as he lurched down the street. But for his obscene curses, Christian would have paid no attention to him. Later, recalling the events of the night, he remembered the man. He had seen him before—Sara's husband, Rob the gardner.

Others also had seen Rob. A doctor, walking his cocker spaniels, had noticed him entering the coal cellar, and two women had seen him running away just as the fire broke out. They had described him to the police, who immediately went in pursuit of the man they took to be the arsonist.

Almost at the very moment that a policeman was slamming

shut the door to Rob's cell, Christian was approaching Belgrave Road. He had walked several miles, until he felt calmer, and had hailed a passing taxi to return home. He wanted Katherine Campbell out of his home as soon as possible. And he would make sure she understood that there would never be a recurrence of what had happened.

He jerked forward in the seat as the driver of the brougham abruptly reined in the horses.

"Beg pardon, sir," said the man, "but I can't go any further. Police have got a barricade here at the end of the street. Seems to be some trouble further down the road."

Christian was suddenly aware of sirens and people screaming. He quickly paid the driver and jumped out of the carriage. The air was thick with smoke. Glancing toward his house, he caught sight of the huge, leaping flames. But by the time he had pushed his way through the curious crowds, little was left of his home but the stone foundation and some of the bricks.

"My servants!" he shouted, trying to get the firemen to hear him above the din.

"They got away, sir," a policeman informed him. "The butler says they are all accounted for."

Katherine! Had she left the house before the fire spread? Nobody would have known she was there. But he knew that neither the firemen nor the policemen could answer his question, and he was forced to stand by, helpless, until the flames had subsided.

They found her body soon afterward, and Christian was almost physically ill with remorse. He was certainly to blame, he told himself. Although he knew that she was not a good woman—perhaps even, if one were to believe in such things, one who had an unholy alliance with the devil—she surely did not deserve such a fate. But in the back of his mind a small, rebellious voice wondered whether her death by fire had been a horrible, unfortunate accident or whether it had been her fate.

And with her death had died their secret—two secrets, actually. The fact that they had had sexual relations, and the fact that he had used Katherine Campbell to try to wrest Sara away from the Church. That he felt some relief about this only increased his heavy burden of guilt. He felt that he had to confess the truth to Sara and perhaps expiate his sins.

A police sergeant tapped him on the shoulder.

"Major Wheatley-Croft? I got some information about the fire."

Christian tore his eyes away from the rubble of his house.

"Yes, Sergeant?"

"We think we've caught the bloke what started it. 'E fits the description we got from some of your neighbors of a fellow they seen lurkin' about just before the fire broke out. 'E's a nasty piece of work, drunk so bad 'e can 'ardly stand up straight. Says 'e works for Lord Evans. We threw him into jail for the night. . . ."

"I beg your pardon, Sergeant. Did you say he works for Lord Evans? Do you know his name?"

"'E says it's Rob, sir; Rob Standard."

The hour was late and Christian was exhausted. But after he had made sure that all his servants had a place to stay for the night, he hurried to Lord Evans's house in St. Vincent's Square. A sleepy servant opened the door.

"Major Wheatley-Croft, Lord Evans has not yet returned."

"I'm here to see Sara Standard. Show me to her room, please," Christian said brusquely.

The servant looked shocked and was about to protest, but Christian started up the stairs in the direction of where he knew the servants' quarters must be.

"I'm going, you fool, whether or not you show me the way. So spare us both much trouble, else I'll be waking all the servants, knocking on doors to find Sara."

"Very good, sir," the man replied. This would make a fine story to tell in the downstairs kitchen come morning. He had no doubt about what the major wanted with Sara Standard, who held herself so above the rest of the staff.

Christian knocked gently on Sara's door but got no answer. He pushed the door. Sara lay under several blankets, shivering with cold, although the room was almost too warm. She looked pale as wax and wretchedly ill.

"Sara, my love," he said, kneeling by the bed, "why didn't you send word to me?"

"Christian?" she whispered.

Her eyes and face were swollen from crying.

"I thought you had died," she murmured as he kissed her cheeks, still stained with tears.

The servant stood in the doorway, gaping at this unlikely sight.

"Get out of here," ordered Christian. The man disappeared.

Sara looked as if all the life had been drained from her.

"Sara, has the doctor been to see you?"

"May God forgive me," she moaned, sobbing quietly.

"You have done nothing," Christian said, trying to soothe her.

She struggled to sit up. "Christian, you must leave here. Rob will be back soon, and he has already threatened to kill me."

"I have something to tell you, my dear." He hoped the shock would do her no harm. But he felt she had to know, and that he must be the one to tell her. He held her against him and put his arms around her shoulders. Then he told her that Rob had been spotted entering the back way of his house shortly before the fire had broken out and that the police had arrested him.

Sara buried her head in his chest and wept until no tears were left. Putting his hand to her forehead to stroke her face, he immediately realized she had a high fever. At that moment, Sara clutched her abdomen and screamed with pain. She was bleeding again, and the cramps she had suffered after swallowing the midwife's medicine were becoming more frequent and more intense.

Christian rushed to the top of the stairway and summoned the servant who had let him into the house.

"Run and get Dr. Cox at eleven Maudsley Street," he said. "And bring him back here quickly. The woman is very ill."

Dr. Cox arrived breathless, fully expecting to find Major Wheatley-Croft stretched out in Lord Evans's parlor, bleeding. He was astonished, therefore, to find the major in the servant's quarters with his arms around a woman who appeared to be in false labor.

After carefully examining Sara, he called Christian back into her room and said, "She will be fine, but she must be kept calm and stay in bed for at least a week." He handed Christian a bottle. "This will help her sleep tonight." Then he turned to Sara and said sternly, "I don't know what you took, but I warn you I won't be able to help you if you try a second time to destroy the baby."

"The baby?" asked Christian. What could the man mean?

Dr. Cox picked up his black bag of medicines and glanced at Christian. "She's four months pregnant, Major. Good evening."

Lavinia blinked her eyes. "I must have dozed off," she said, fingering the mohair blanket that was tucked around her.

"You drank half a cup of tea and fell asleep in the middle of a sentence," said Paul. "I didn't have the heart to wake you."

He didn't add that he had enjoyed watching her sleep. She looked so young and untroubled, and he had been in the midst of a fantasy of the two of them in a green meadow filled with flowers, their arms around each other. Earlier, after they had returned from their picnic, he had decided he was wasting his time, hoping to be more than friends with Lavinia. He had made a vow to call up one or two of his girlfriends and spend some time with them, to get Lavinia out of his mind. But, he had realized as she napped, he was too intrigued with her to make good on his promise.

She folded the blanket, stretched her arms and yawned.

"Time for bed," she said. "Thanks for the tea and everything else."

"Will you be all right? You could sleep here, if you like. You can have my bed and I'll take the couch." *Or we can share my bed*, he added mentally. If only she weren't so besotted with this Christian fellow. But he was willing to wait—at least a little while longer.

"No, I'll be fine, I can feel it. I'm so tired I'll be lucky if I stay awake walking down the stairs." She kissed him lightly, and said, "Thanks again, Paul," and walked wearily out the door.

"Ring me tomorrow," Paul called after her.

Lavinia's last thoughts before she fell asleep were about the phone calls. "Call Paul," she reminded herself. And then she thought, *And Mrs. Patel-Ram. I must speak to Mrs. Patel-Ram.* She struggled for a moment to think why it was so important that she talk to Mrs. Patel-Ram, but was sound asleep before she had the answer.

Chapter 9

LAVINIA DREAMED ABOUT SARA, WHOSE AMBIVALENCE about the baby increased with each passing day. She and Christian were living in a beautifully decorated, spacious suite at the Cadogan Arms while Christian supervised the rebuilding of his house. In fact, Sara had discovered, the house belonged to Christian's brother, a colonel in the army, serving in India. But Colonel Wheatley-Croft and his family were very happy in Delhi, so for all practical purposes the house belonged to Christian.

"But you told me it was *your* house," Sara had said when he first mentioned that his brother was the actual owner.

"Well, it is mine in the sense that I live here," Christian replied.

"What you possess you own. Is that what you mean?" she said, teasing him. "And does that include me as well, Christian?"

"Absolutely, my love. You are very much mine," he answered with a happy smile.

Sara was becoming better acquainted with her lover, now that their time together was not restricted by Rob or by her duties as a servant. She was learning how possessive he was, but this character trait amused her. It was his insecurity, she felt, that fed this quality, and his vulnerability only further endeared him to her.

And now that he knew she was pregnant, she did not have to pretend she was ill. Christian was ecstatic, never for a moment questioning, as Sara did, whether he or Rob was the baby's father.

He had no reason to believe that she had had relations with her husband once she had become his lover. Now could Sara bring herself to tell Christian that the baby might be Rob's.

At times she even prayed she would miscarry, dreading as she did the birth of a child who resembled her husband. Surely Christian would realize this, and she would lose him forever. Dr. Cox, who at Christian's insistence visited her regularly at the Cadogan Arms, assured them that the pregnancy was progressing normally. "A healthy baby, no doubt of that," he told Sara, misinterpreting her anxiety.

Perhaps the baby would look like her, Sara comforted herself, hugging her expanding belly. It would not matter who the father was. It was *her* child, and she and Christian would love it dearly, providing it with the security and affection that Sara had missed in her childhood. But then her worry would return, and she would lie awake at night with Christian fast asleep beside her, wondering about the fate of her child and herself.

"Think only happy thoughts," Dr. Cox reminded her with each visit.

But this was a difficult time. Christian had not told her about his experience with Katherine Campbell, nor did she know that Katherine had died in the fire. Thanks to a favor owed him by a high-ranking police officer who had served under him in India, Christian had prevailed upon the police to suppress the truth about Katherine's death. Another story was invented, so that a week or so after the fire, Sara got word that Katherine had died in a traffic accident. It was many days before Sara was able to accept the fact that she would never again see the strange and fascinating woman.

Rob's trial loomed ahead. She and Christian planned to leave for Venice as soon as the trial ended, so that they would be away from England when Rob was hanged. It seemed to be a foregone conclusion that Rob was guilty, and his crime preyed on Sara's conscience. She felt she shared the blame for the fire, her behavior having driven him to this act of revenge. Each afternoon, after Christian had kissed her goodbye and gone off to yet another meeting about his house, she sat alone, reviewing her sins and wondering how she could ever be happy when she had caused such suffering to both Rob and Christian.

One day Christian returned unexpectedly early and found her crying. "But it was his destiny," Christian protested, having insisted that Sara explain her tears. "The man was bent on destruction. The means, the instrument, is unimportant. And it is your destiny to be my wife and have my child."

Her destiny. Christian had discussed with her the idea, which he had learned from Akhbar, that the choices people make are often irrelevant, for their future is predetermined by a force over which they have no control. And it was her destiny to go to Venice with Christian.

Christian brought her books about Italy and Venice. She devoured the descriptions of Renaissance sculpture and painting, of the distinctive Venetian architecture, of Venetian culture—so different from anything she had known in England.

The comfort and opulence of the Cadogan Arms paled in comparison with the wealth and exotica she would encounter in Venice, Christian promised her.

"You will fall in love with Venice, but you must not fall in love with Akhbar," warned Christian.

"Is he attracted to pregnant women?" Sara smiled.

"Any man would be attracted to you," Christian said, stroking her protruding belly. "When will we feel life? Has Dr. Cox told you?"

"He says it should be soon," Sara replied, wondering as always about his reaction to a baby born with Rob's eyes and mouth.

Rob's trial had begun. It was being held at the Old Bailey *in camera*—behind closed doors—again thanks to Christian's well-placed connections. Christian attended each day, his eyes fixed on Rob, who sat impassively, his face a mask. But the testimony by the witnesses seemed irrefutable and on the fourth day, as rain beat on the windows of the courtroom, Rob broke down and confessed.

"It was him that made me do it," he shouted, pointing to Christian. "He stole my wife, that whoring bitch. May you both burn in hell alongside me."

Two burly policemen hustled him, still screaming, out of the room, and the judge banded his gavel to declare the trial over. The verdict was clear.

Christian brought the news home to Sara, who ate no dinner that night and sat silently, staring into the distance and sighing from time to time, until Christian forced her to drink some sherry and put her to bed.

The next day, hoping to distract her, he bought her a book about Casanova, full of colorful pictures.

"When we, the English, were expanding our empire, the Venetians were making love, and Casanova embodies eighteenth-century Venice," he said.

Sara was fascinated by the story of the brazen adventurer who was so adept at skullduggery. In the seventeen hundreds, after Venice had lost its overseas outposts, its citizens turned to revelry and pleasure as their chief distraction. Venice was like one grand festival where noblemen could live like kings even if they had little money. Many a family had income that came to tens of millions of florions, eighty or more servants, and ten gondolas tied to the watergate.

The Venetians, it seemed to Sara, were the most self-indulgent people she had ever heard of. She laughed long and loud when she read about one Caterina Querini, who merely smiled and continued dancing with the king of Denmark as they stepped around and over the pearls that had fallen from her neck. The Venetians were far more interested in gambling and pleasures of the flesh than in religion. One Venetian ditty read:

> A little trip to Mass,
> A little hand at cards, to pass
> After-luncheon hours until
> A little woman, later still.

Would she fit in there? she wondered. Would she feel comfortable and accepted among those women who, with their dyed red-gold hair and innate sense of style, were said to be among the most beautiful and sensual in the world?

Another afternoon Christian brought her a book of lithographs of Venice. One was of the elegant, beautifully dressed men and women eating and drinking and gossiping at the Caffe Florian, the famous café on the Piazza San Marco. But Sara's attention was caught by the massive basilica that dominated the piazza. On the next page was a picture of the statue of the archangel Gabriel. Here was the other side of Venice, with its many churches and religious icons. Would she be damned forever for the tragedy she had set in motion? Or would she find comfort and salvation in the city that was both sophisticated and spiritual?

"When will we be leaving?" she asked Christian.

"Soon . . . it is a long journey. And before too long you won't be able to travel." Christian searched her face for a hint of excitement or pleasure.

"Are you happy to be going to Venice? Or have you agreed simply to please me?" he asked.

"Will your friends like me, Christian? Will they know about me . . . and about Rob?"

"It's been many years since I've cared what people think. I choose my friends for who they are, not what they might think about me. But there is no need for them to know about the unhappy past."

He kissed her lips and, suddenly aflame with passion, moved his hands down to her breasts, swollen and enlarged by the pregnancy. She was even more beautiful than she had been when they first met at the beginning of the summer. But she seemed different, distracted, less willing to share with him her thoughts and feelings. He conjectured that she was holding back something important, but he trusted her to share the thought with him when she was ready. Wasn't he, after all, still harboring his secret about Katherine Campbell? He intended to tell her, but not now, not while they were still in London.

"In Venice," he murmured, moving his mouth between her breasts and stroking her dark brown nipples with his tongue. "In Venice we will be happy."

He lifted his head to kiss her mouth and saw tears in her eyes.

"My darling Sara," he said tenderly, "I promise you. In Venice we will start anew—you and I and our precious child."

She pressed herself closer to him and her lips met his, but even as they embraced passionately, Christian sensed that her mind was elsewhere.

Lavinia awoke in the middle of the night and glanced at her clock. Four A.M. She was starving, and her stomach was growling. She switched on the lamp by the bed and got up, remembering that she hadn't eaten anything since the picnic lunch, hours before. This won't do, she told herself sternly. Got to keep up my strength now that Antony is on the way.

The contents of the refrigerator were uninspiring. She would have to make do with scrambled eggs and toasted pita bread. Plugging in the electric kettle, she measured two tablespoons of Cadbury's drinking chocolate into Mary's café au lait cup. Paul would probably disapprove of hot chocolate instead of tea at this hour, but ever since she had been a little girl and Aunt Jane had made it for her when she couldn't sleep, hot chocolate had been her favorite cure for insomnia.

She wished she had some peanut butter, another of her favorite foods from childhood, to spread on the pita. She'd have to look for it at the grocery. Too bad she hadn't had more notice about the television crew arriving. She could have asked Antony to bring a jar of Skippy with him.

Her post-midnight snack tasted delicious in the way that ordinary foods often do when consumed at unordinary hours or in unusual circumstances. *How nice,* thought Lavinia, *to be dwelling on the mundane.* What would it be like to have Antony and the other crew members here in London, perhaps even in her apartment, while Christian and Sara were still flitting through her mind? While Christian was still appearing whenever it suited him in her living room and bedroom?

She laughed aloud, imagining the look on Antony's face were she to inform him that she had taken her assignment so seriously that she was actually seeing ghosts. The producer was a very matter-of-fact, down-to-earth person. Just because he was putting together a show about the supernatural didn't mean he had to believe any of it, he had told her when he'd hired her.

And now here she was, obsessed with a man who had died in the previous century—more interested, if she was perfectly honest with herself, in sleeping with him than with her twentieth-century upstairs neighbor. What puzzled her was whether her feelings for him were the same as Sara's, or whether she was attracted to him as Lavinia, totally separate from Sara Standard. What was the dividing line between herself and Sara, especially in relation to Christian?

Oddly enough, she realized that she was more curious than troubled by these questions. What disturbed her was the premonition that whatever lay ahead for Sara and Christian, the story that was slowly being revealed to her would end horribly.

And she would have to live through it for Christian. She would have to suffer for him. But she supposed this meant that at last he would be released to the world of the dead, where he belonged. Where he wanted to be. And she would lose him. And she wanted him so! The intensity of her desire was getting stronger as she learned more about him. She was not satisfied to have him kiss and caress her in the body of Sara Standard. She wanted Christian to make love to her, Lavinia Cross.

She pushed away her empty plate and took a last sip of hot chocolate. "Christian," she said aloud, "please materialize for me. I need you. I must see you now."

He was immediately there in front of her, looking out of place in Mary's modern kitchen, dressed as he was in his single-breasted tweed lounge suit. On his head he wore a high-crowned bowler hat.

"I know I am becoming more and more a part of your present," Christian said softly.

Lavinia sprang out of her chair, startled as much by her ability to make him appear as by the fact that here he stood, just a few feet away from her.

"Do you know who I am?" she asked.

"Of course, Lavinia. You are a reincarnation of my wife, Sara."
He began to weep, holding his hands in front of his face to hide his tears. After several moments, he calmed himself and said, "I do not wish to be here. I am terribly unhappy in this place."

Lavinia ached for him. She reached out to take his hand, but her fingers touched only air.

"I want to join my wife, and I cannot," Christian continued.

"Why not?"

"Because there was a deception, and the truth has never been told. I must have the truth told."

"Is that why you came to me?"

"I love you," Christian said abruptly. "I did many wrong things in my life, but I thought I had paid for them. The end was unfair.

It took everything in her power not to kiss his troubled face. She yearned to put her arms tightly around him and hold him close to her.

He must have read her thoughts because he smiled kindly and said, "I cannot do what you want, but you can do what I want."

"I know," Lavinia said, determined not to cry. "You will always be only in my mind."

"And in your heart. What is in the mind is in the heart, Akhbar used to tell me. But a ghost has only one desire, and that is to be released from imprisonment."

"But you have a heart—and I am a part of your life."

He nodded gravely. "Yes, we are linked inextricably. But you are alive, and I am not. I cannot exist in this life, because I have not been able to give up my previous one. Do you understand? If I were released, I might perhaps be reborn."

"In another body?"

He nodded again.

He was one of the most handsome, most desirable men she had ever seen. She didn't like to think of Christian's soul in another's body. She wanted him as he was now. Except, she knew he wasn't . . . She sighed, angry with frustration. The hopelessness of the situation gave her courage.

"I would give anything to make love to you," she said.

Having admitted her desire, she pressed on. "Why *can't* we make it possible?" she demanded. "You exist, in some form or another. You are real to me. You can come and go. Why can't you let me touch you and love you?"

"I cannot, Lavinia," he said, shaking his head sadly.

"Put out your hand and try to touch me," she said.

She felt nothing, although she could see his hand reaching for her cheek.

"Your skin is so soft, like Sara's," he said wistfully.

Lavinia was astonished. "But how can you feel my skin? When I touch you, my hand goes right through you."

She stared at him, baffled, then—excited by the realization—said, "But if you can touch and feel me, you can make love to me."

"It would mean nothing to you." His tone was flat and without emotion.

"I love you. And I want you, Christian."

"We cannot be together that way, Lavinia. Don't you see?"

"See what?" she cried.

"I am afraid for you," said Christian. He disappeared through the kitchen wall.

"Don't go." But she was talking to an empty room.

"Christian, Christian, please come back!" she called urgently. She was alone. He wasn't coming back.

She sat down at the table and began to sob, her tears splashing down her cheeks. The grief seemed to fill her up completely, leaving room for no other emotion. She wanted Christian, and he would not be hers. And with that thought, the tears stopped. She was being so selfish. The poor man was stuck in this hellish limbo, and she seemed to be the only person who could help him. And here she sat, crying because she couldn't make love with a ghost.

She fished a tissue out of the pocket of her bathrobe and blew her nose, then put the dishes in the sink to soak until morning.

As she walked upstairs, exhausted from the turbulent emotions she was feeling, she spoke to Christian, certain he would hear her, wherever he was.

"I will help you, Christian, I promise. No matter what it takes. You and Sara will be reunited."

She was asleep as soon as her head touched the pillow. But her sleep was filled with dreams.

There was her mother, whose long, brown hair was pinned on top of her head as if she were a Victorian lady. There was her father, smiling and talking happily. There was Aunt Jane. She was giving a party in her apartment in New York. Lavinia knew some of the many guests. Paul sat in a corner talking to the mad Hungarian. Emily was on the other side of the room, her red hair done in stiff, mousse-coated spikes, her eyes outlined with kohl. She was laughing and telling a story to her grandmother. Mrs. Patel-Ram stood surrounded by a small group of men. She wore a magnificent turquoise sari, gold thread running through it. The men were listening attentively to her story but didn't seem to notice when she abruptly turned into Sara, radiant in a Venetian ball gown. Lavinia was leaning against the wall of Aunt Jane's apartment, the wall where the reproduction of Van Gogh's sunflowers hung. Lavinia wanted to shout that Mrs. Patel-Ram had disappeared, but when she opened her mouth no words came out.

Thrashing around in the bed, she woke herself up. Someone was in the room with her. She sat up and caught a glint of gold. With only the moonlight to illuminate the darkened room, she could barely make out the outline of a woman.

She reached forward and her hand touched soft, silky fabric. "Mrs. Patel-Ram? It is you, isn't it?"

There was no response. Lavinia leaned closer. Mrs. Patel-Ram was gazing at her from the foot of the bed, a strange smile on her face as if to say, "Yes, this is the last time we will see each other, but that is all right."

Lavinia stared back at her until Mrs. Patel-Ram faded away. Was she still dreaming or had she seen an apparition? Why had Mrs. Patel-Ram appeared? Lavinia remembered the story about the Nepalese princess who had been improperly attended to at her death and who had visited Mrs. Patel-Ram by night. But surely there was no parallel here. Mrs. Patel-Ram was healthy and very much alive—at least, she had been the last time they had spoken some days ago. Lavinia resolved to call her first thing in the morning.

The early morning songbirds were beginning to chirp as Lavinia once again drifted off to sleep. Their twittering was the only sound to be heard in the peaceful green meadow, dotted with buttercups and narcissus, where Lavinia and Christian strolled hand in hand. The sun shone directly overhead in a cloudless blue sky, and a gentle breeze delicately ruffled the surface of a turquoise blue pond where swans swam lazily.

A butterfly swooped down and alit upon Christian's outstretched hand before flying off in the direction of the pond. Christian turned to Lavinia and looked into her eyes with such longing and love that her breath quickened and her lips parted to meet his. He lifted her off the ground into his strong, muscular arms and pressed her so close to him that she felt almost a part of his body. And then he lowered her gently and they were ripping away each other's clothes, his shirt and pants, her cotton blouse and summer skirt, their underwear all in a heap among the flowers and green grass. Christian pulled her down to the ground and grasped both her breasts in his hands as his tongue traced a path from her nipples down across her belly to the cleft between her thighs.

"Christian, Christian," she moaned, her voice joining the cries of the meadowlarks and sparrows. She pulled his head up to hers and pushed herself up to capture him inside her. But it was Paul who was thrusting deep into her, and it was Paul whose tongue and lips caressed hers. And it was Paul whose name she called, waking herself just as she was on the verge of fulfilling her desire.

The sun was pouring into the bedroom, and the cover was all in a heap at the foot of the bed, where she must have kicked it as she was thrashing about in her sleep. Lavinia looked around the room, expecting to see the people who had visited her dreams.

So many strange dreams... And then she blushed, suddenly and vividly remembering the image of herself, naked in Christian's arms, reaching out—for Paul. She had dreamed of making love with Paul. Or had it been Christian?

The lovemaking had felt so real she could almost believe it had actually taken place. But of course it couldn't have.... If it had been Christian with whom she had lain in the meadow, could he have . . . ? The thought was too disturbing and confusing to pursue.

And Mrs. Patel-Ram. She had been at Aunt Jane's party, but then she hadn't been there anymore. But she had appeared to Lavinia in the night . . . or had that been another dream? She had to call her as soon as she had breakfast. Lavinia checked her clock and was amazed to find it was already past ten. *Oh, no,* she thought, jumping out of bed to shower and dress. *And I have so much to do today.*

Still groggy from her frequently disturbed sleep, Lavinia hurried downstairs to make herself coffee so that she could face the day with a clear head. And discovered that she had used up all the milk for her four A.M. cup of hot chocolate. Dumb! she thought, annoyed. Well, the morning was already a bust, so she might as well go have her coffee at the corner café, and then she would drop in on Mrs. Patel-Ram rather than call her. She grabbed the pages of the last interviews she had transcribed so that she might edit them as she drank her coffee.

Paul was walking briskly down the stairs, whistling cheerfully, just as she locked her front door.

"Good morning," he said, grinning broadly.

"Good morning," she replied, feeling oddly shy and embarrassed.

Don't be silly, she told herself, trying to look Paul straight in the eye. *He doesn't know about my dream.*

"You look ever more beautiful than usual this morning," Paul said, holding open the front door of their building.

"Why, thank you," Lavinia said, her voice almost cracking with nervousness. In fact, she was feeling very sexy and vibrant despite a curious sense of distraction, of having a mission left unfulfilled.

"I didn't sleep very well after everything that went on last night, so I gave myself a late morning," Paul said. "And I was just coming to ask you to have coffee with me at the corner. Are you in a hurry to get wherever you're going?"

"Actually," laughed Lavinia, "I was just headed that way myself."

"Excellent. I trust you slept well—no intrusive ghosts?"

"Some very strange dreams, that's all." She couldn't bring herself to tell him about her predawn encounter with Christian, nor her vision of Mrs. Patel-Ram.

She stopped walking. "Paul, I have the oddest feeling. I was going to visit my friend Mrs. Patel-Ram after I'd had breakfast, but I just now got this sense of... I just want to call her and say I'll be by." They walked to the telephone booth at the end of the street.

But the line was busy. Lavinia waited several minutes and tried again. Still busy.

"I know this is rude of me, but I think I'll pass on the coffee. I don't know why, but I need to go see her right now."

"What's the matter?" he said, annoyed because she was being so flighty. "Surely it can wait another hour. You can try her again from the call box at the café."

"No, I have to go right now." She spoke more forcefully than she had intended. "I'm sorry, I didn't mean to shout at you. I can't explain this sense I have... I'll see you later," she called, turning in the direction of Mrs. Patel-Ram's apartment.

"Wait a minute, I'm coming with you." Paul strode briskly beside her, easily keeping up with her hurried steps.

"Don't be silly. You have to get to work. I'm fine, honestly."

"I've no doubt of that," Paul said. "But after what we've been through together, I'm loath to be left out when you get one of your feelings."

"What do you mean, 'after what we've been through'?"

For one unsettling moment, Lavinia wondered whether in fact they had made love this morning. It certainly had felt real—and extraordinarily wonderful.

"Your ghosts and the seances—and that business with the disappearing baby last evening. I don't know how you've managed to do it, Lavinia, but you've pulled me into this mess." He smiled goodhumoredly.

"Thanks for sticking by me," she said, briefly squeezing his hand.

"Well, you needn't let go of my hand as if it were on fire. I rather enjoy walking down the street holding hands with a lovely woman." He took her hand and held it firmly as the traffic light changed and they crossed the street.

As they passed Vauxhall Bridge Road, Lavinia glanced around for Christian. She half expected to see him galloping by, dressed as he had been that first afternoon, in his army uniform. And what would she do if he did appear? Wave and call out a greeting? Not that it would surprise Paul, who by now seemed to approach the idea of Christian with far less than his usual skepticism. What a dear man Paul was. What would it be like to sleep with him? Would he be as skilled and ardent a lover in real life as he had been in her dream? The prospect of finding out sent a shiver of desire through her.

Paul looked down at her questioningly and wrapped his hand more firmly around hers. An electricity flowed between them that she remembered from the night he had kissed her and tried to make love to her. The night Christian had interrupted them. But last night Paul had taken Christian's place. What did this all mean?

"When is that producer fellow arriving?" Paul asked.

"Late Wednesday afternoon, don't remind me. I have a pile of work to do before Antony gets here. The guy means business. I'll have to introduce the two of you."

"I'd like that. How long do you suppose he'll be here?"

"I don't know, he didn't say. Until we get the scenes shot and wrapped, I suppose. Maybe a month, maybe less."

"And what about you, Lavinia? Does that mean your work will be done here?"

"Well, it will be once we've gotten all the footage and interviewed the people whose stories we'll be featuring. I'll probably stay on for a few weeks to clear up some details and to have a little vacation." She pointed to the right. "It's just down this way on Carlisle Mansions."

"That will be right around the time I'll be going to Turkey," said Paul.

They walked in silence for a couple of minutes, and then Paul asked, "Lavinia, have you given any thought at all to you and me?"

"What do you mean?"

224

"I'm sure it's no surprise that I'm very fond of you and that I find you extremely attractive. Quite the most interesting, attractive woman I've met in some time." He pulled her close to him and bent his mouth toward hers to kiss her.

"Paul," she said, struggling to get out of his grasp, "you pick the worst times to get romantic. I *told* you I'm in a rush to see Mrs. Patel-Ram, and I thought you took me seriously. I care about you, Paul, I really do, but you don't seem to understand that at the moment I have other things on my mind."

"My apologies," he said coldly.

"Look, you don't have to come with me. I'm sure..."

"Quite right, Lavinia," he said, but he walked along with her, not taking her hand again.

Why was he coming along? he asked himself. He didn't believe Lavinia needed him for protection. He knew she was perfectly capable of taking care of herself. He wanted to spend as much time as possible with her, he realized. And her adventures, as improbable as they were, were so damned interesting. None of his other woman friends had conversations with eighteenth-century British army officers or went spying on female Satanists who got themselves stabbed and raped and burned to death. And on Belgrave Road, no less.

But her accusations about his ill-timed romantic overture stung. The other women he was intimate with never spurned his kisses. He wondered whether she appreciated the fact that he was taking time away from *his* work this morning to be with her. And then he chuckled to himself, imagining her indignation were he to say such a thing.

"Who asked you to?" she would probably tell him in her forthright American way.

Who indeed? He felt a bit of an idiot, his ego bruised by her rejection. And he nevertheless felt compelled to continue on with her. Wouldn't do for him to let on that his pride had been damaged.

Rain was beginning to fall, not a light summer shower but a more serious downpour that had people opening up their umbrellas and pulling their jackets up around their necks. Paul of course had brought his umbrella; he seldom left the house without one unless the sky hadn't even a wisp of a cloud. And he had expected a good rain today after yesterday's glorious sunshine.

He pushed it open and held it high above them, inviting Lavinia to join him underneath it.

"I forgot to bring one," she said sheepishly, huddling close to him as they walked.

"Well, of course. You're from New York. What do Americans know about rain?" he said lightly, glad to have their conversation diverted from the earlier unpleasantness. He was still angry at her for having pushed him away, and he sensed that she, too, was still annoyed. But the rain was washing away the bad feeling, at least temporarily.

"What do you expect you'll find at Mrs. Patel-Ram's?" he asked as they rounded the corner to her block.

Lavinia sighed with exasperation. "Okay, I know what you're going to say, but you asked. I had a dream about her last night— except I don't think it was a dream. I think she was there with me, in my bedroom. She just stood there, not saying a word, looking at me with a very strong expression on her face. And then she disappeared, faded away into thin air."

"Like Christian."

"Yes, exactly."

"Lavinia," he said, trying to be as polite as possible, "don't you think it might be possible . . . you said it was a dream . . . I mean, it's one thing for ghosts to fade in and out, but Mrs. Patel-Ram . . . ?"

"Paul, I knew you wouldn't believe me. But it wasn't a dream," Lavinia said stubbornly. "I touched her sari—I felt the fabric. That was real."

"I don't suppose you've had me appearing in your bedroom at night, have you?" he said jocularly.

If only he knew! "Sure," she said defensively, "it's all a big joke, isn't it? Here we are. This is her building."

She glanced up at Mrs. Patel-Ram's first-floor window expecting to see her looking out, but the drapes were closed.

"Look, you really don't have to bother coming up with me. I appreciate your support but I know how you feel about all of this, and Mrs. Patel-Ram believes very sincerely in spirits and ghosts. I don't want you saying something to offend her."

Paul snapped shut the umbrella. "My dear woman, whatever else I may be, I am *not* rude. My mother brought me up to be a very proper, well-behaved Englishman." He tried to keep his tone light, not to reveal how offended he was. "Now, then, shall we go pay a visit to Mrs. Patel-Ram?"

Lavinia ran up the stairs and rang the doorbell. There was no response. She rang again, and this time they heard the buzzer that unlocked the front door of the building. Mrs. Patel-Ram's door opened when they were still halfway down the hall. A man stood in the doorway.

"Marcus, how nice to see you!" cried Lavinia. "I came to call on your mother."

"Lavinia, come in." His voice was oddly strained and hoarse.

"This is my friend, Paul Chamberlain. Marcus Patel-Ram. Marcus and I met several years ago. Mary gave him my name when he came to New York."

Lavinia sniffed the air as she walked into the apartment.

"Are you burning sandalwood incense?" The apartment was strangely still. "Is your mother at home, Marcus?"

"She's gone," said Marcus quietly.

"Gone? Doing errands, you mean?"

"She died last night," he said blinking his eyes rapidly as if fighting back tears. "I'm just back from Italy and we were up rather late talking, until one-thirty or two, it must have been. She was fine, full of stories and plans. In fact," he said, turning to Paul, "she mentioned having just met a Lady Chamberlain. Your mother?"

Paul nodded.

"She said they had made a date to visit a medium that your mother was very enthusiastic about. We said good-night, and since it was so late I slept in the spare room rather than going back to my flat. I knocked on her door at about nine o'clock. My mother never slept past six-thirty, you know. But I thought that since we'd been up so late..." His voice broke.

Lavinia sat down, faint with shock. If only she had had a chance to say goodbye to the older woman...but she *had* said goodbye.

"I rang the doctor and he came over directly, but it was too late. Her heart, he said it was."

"Is there anything we can do?" Paul asked Marcus.

"Yes," said Lavinia, trying not to break into tears. "Please, Marcus, if we can help you in any way... your mother was a very special person to me." She swallowed a sob.

"No, but thank you." He shook his head. "She's already been taken to the crematorium. .... God, this is so sudden, I can hardly think."

Lavinia got up and put her arm around him. "What about the funeral? Would you like me to help you notify your friends and family?"

"She left instructions that she didn't want a funeral. Just some sort of memorial service, but not immediately... in a month. Of course, you'll come?" he asked Lavinia.

"Of course."

"Oh, and she left you some of her things. There was a note in her top drawer with instructions. Excuse me a moment."

He returned with a large box, which he set on the table in front of the couch.

"What is it?" Lavinia asked. She was touched more than she could express that the woman had left her something.

"I don't know. She wanted you to open it."

The box was filled with five or six exquisite pieces of delicately carved Indian jewelry, two finely embroidered, brightly colored silk saris, one of which had gold thread shot through it, a pair of black patent leather shoes decorated with perky bows, and a small notebook.

Lavinia opened the notebook to the first page. "Dear Lavinia," it read in Mrs. Patel-Ram's old-fashioned handwriting, "I have always enjoyed and admired you very much. You may think I am gone, but I know we will meet again. I have left you some mementos to remind you of me until we next meet. I hope you will enjoy my drawings and poetry as well as the bracelets and my saris. And when you wear the shoes you will always be in love. Mrs. Patel-Ram."

"She was very proud of these shoes," said Marcus. "She only

wore them once or twice. She bought them in Italy. She was part Italian, you know."

"But how did she know they would fit me?" said Lavinia, astonished that in fact the shoes were a perfect fit for her size-seven feet.

Marcus simply shrugged and smiled. "My mother knew many things."

"Marcus," said Lavinia, getting up to leave, "we shouldn't take more of your time now. But let me give you my number, and please call if I can help out, even if you just want to talk. I will miss your mother very much. I wish I'd seen more of her since I've been in London."

"My mother would say that you felt each other's presence even if you didn't actually meet face to face," he said, giving her a hug. "Look how you happened to come by today, as if she had summoned you here personally. And I'll ring you in a few days to let you know about the service."

The rain had let up, although the sky was still gloomy and the air was damp and chill. Paul took the box under one arm and held her with the other. They walked slowly, Lavinia lost deep in thought. She was oblivious to the people passing by, the London traffic, not looking up until the sun broke through the overcast. "Where are we going?" she said.

"Some tea or coffee might be nice, I thought. I know of a quiet restaurant near here that serves lovely homemade soup."

"Good idea," she said, happy to have his company. The spire of Westminster Cathedral soared in the distance, high above the tops of the other, less lofty buildings. Lavinia thought about Sara, about her own ambivalence toward organized religion and spirituality, and about Mrs. Patel-Ram, who was not conventionally religious but spiritual in the truest sense. And about Venice . . . where Sara had arrived, her mind still troubled by her worries about the baby.

Christian's house on the Grand Canal, the social register of Venetian nobility, was far grander and more elaborate than either his house on Belgrave Road or in Brighton.

They arrived at Christian's palace, as he called it, at sunset in a high-prowed, shiny black, thickly carpeted gondola. The brilliant red sun disappearing behind a bright red cloud made Sara gasp in disbelief. The six-storied palace seemed to be illuminated. She had never expected a house of such magnitude, and at first she thought Christian had made arrangements for them at one of Venice's famous hotels. Several servants sprang instantly out of the mist to remove their trunks and help them from the gondola.

The front doors to the Byzantine-style palace opened onto the water, where several boats were moored to tall, sturdy posts.

"Those boats belong to me," Christian said, ushering her into the entrance hall on the ground floor.

Together they mounted the massive staircase that led to an enormous central living room running the length of the second floor of the house. A balcony at one end overlooked the canal, and the windows and alcoves on each side also had views of the water.

"Let me show you around, Sara, just a brief look because I see you are tired. The house is huge, and you will explore it all yourself sooner or later."

As tired as she was, Sara's excitement and wonder grew as Christian showed her the bedrooms, large and small, the book-lined library, the music room with its grand piano and harp, and the game room. A retinue of servants followed them from room to room, chatting amongst themselves in a language she did not understand but which she took to be Italian. Whenever she looked at them, they smiled warmly and stopped speaking until she glanced away.

Flowers ornamented every room so that the air was sweet and fragrant. Christian briefly showed her the other floors, the many rooms containing marble and stone sculptures, and Christian's collection of Rajput miniatures from India. At last he brought her to the master bedroom where Sara, by now exhausted, gratefully curled up on the bed like a sleepy kitten.

Christian fetched her water in a crystal decanter. "This is delicious drinking water, just as good as any wine, perhaps better. It comes by pipe from artesian wells at Trebaseleghe, on the mainland. You will enjoy it. Drink, my darling."

"You are right," she said, smiling.

"Are you hungry? Twelve servants are waiting to bring you something to eat. They know you are with child and they are very happy to serve you."

"I am not hungry, not at all," Sara said laughing. "You have been feeding me all day. I will be like a large goose soon."

"Yes, I hope so," Christian said. "Venice is the right place for a baby," he said. "You could not be in a better place. Venetians worship children and old people. The strongest man and the lowest criminal are tender to babies."

"I am pleased to be here, Christian," Sara said, pushing her long hair to one side, closing her eyes. "I am so sleepy."

She awoke an hour later, wondering where she was. And then she remembered. She was in Venice.

She climbed out of bed and opened the window louvers and looked out. Below her she could see the moon's reflection in the water of the canal. She smelled the fragrant air, the aroma of food being cooked somewhere in the palace, and she felt as happy as a child at play. Standing before the open window, gazing down at the water, she wished that time could stand still.

After a while she went into the bathroom and turned on the brass taps to fill the marble tub. She bathed, then dressed for dinner in her finest French silk dress, which she had copied from a drawing of an Italian-style gown. She knew she looked well. Her color was good, her eyes clear. She combed her hair high on her head and gathered it in back with glittering blue combs. She looped sapphire earrings through her earlobes, then went to find Christian.

He was nowhere to be seen, but five servants, three men and two women, immediately greeted her with wide smiles and winsome dark eyes. A table of hors d'oeuvres had been laid out in the dining room.

She could not understand their words but she gathered from their gestures that they were urging her to taste the delicacies. Sara willingly helped herself to a heaping plate of the tempting foods, none of which she recognized. A beautiful, dark-haired young woman poured her a glass of red wine in a delicate, crystal goblet. Sara suddenly thought of how not long ago she had been a servant girl in the house of Lord Evans. She thanked the girl in English, trying to convey with her eyes what her tongue could not, and the servant curtsied and kissed Sara's hand.

"Oh, you probably think I'm nobility," Sara said quickly, "but I'm not. I don't even deserve any of this." Tears came to her eyes. The girl merely stared, not understanding a word.

Sara smiled and brushed away the tears. Having decided to keep her baby—no matter what the infant looked like—no matter what ambivalence she felt, she was suddenly acutely aware of her vulnerability. She could no longer dream of competing with men, an independent woman in their world. Where was the woman she used to be, the one she had dreamed of becoming?

She did not want to surrender herself completely to Christian, nor even to motherhood. She wanted to remain herself and also be what Christian wished. She slowly sipped the heady wine, vowing not to become overly submissive or dependent.

Christian hurried into the room, breathless and apologetic. "I'm sorry I've been so long. I've just been making sure all is in order. You look rested. Venice agrees with you, I can see that already. Tomorrow I shall take you out for all the world to see."

"I feel rested and energetic now," Sara said happily.

"Well, then, we shall go out this very evening. After we have dined I shall take you for a tour of Venice by night. And by morning all of Venice will have heard of Sara Standard."

Sara was almost too excited to taste the noodles cooked with ripe red tomatoes and large black olives, drenched in garlic and oil.

"Venice is a snoopy, gossipy city, my darling, not discreet like London. Venetians wish to know everything about everyone. They have an insatiable curiosity. I shall introduce you as my wife, as you shall indeed be soon."

"As you like," Sara said, ignoring her qualms about calling herself Christian's wife while Rob still lived.

"I shall take you to the cafés to meet my friends, especially Francesca and Akhbar, who are, after all, responsible for my buying this palace. I will tell them the truth, that we are not yet married. But when we have a proper, traditional, Venetian wedding, they will be our attendants!"

"That sounds wonderful," Sara said. "I feel as if I am having a wonderful adventure."

"As indeed you are," Christian said, delighted by her enthusiasm.

After they dined, one of Christian's private gondolas took them to the Campanile of St. Marks, to the Rialto and then on to the Piazza. Sara was eager to see the ducal palace, which was in the process of being restored. They walked along the upper colonnades and leaned upon the balustrades, where they looked across Saint Mark and felt the cool breeze blowing in from the Adriatic Sea.

As they absorbed the beauty of the Venetian night, Christian put his arm around her and said, "Did you know that the Venetians believe an unborn baby is affected by the things his mother sees around her, which is why they paint the ceilings with angels?"

"How lovely," Sara said, "but let us not dwell on babies this evening. Let us be entirely silly and irresponsible and drink and stay up all night."

"Excellent," declared Christian. "This night is for the two of us only."

Sara stared up at the moon, perfectly round and high in the night sky. "I should like to see the haunted house I read about, the Casa degli Spiriti," she said, giggling with anticipation.

"You've been doing research." Christian smiled. "It was well that I brought you those books."

"Yes," she said. "It's even more beautiful than the books described it. I think I will fall in love with Venice as I have with you."

"Indeed, yes," Christian agreed, looking down at the water, thinking that Venice seemed to float on the lagoon. This was a city that defied the laws of nature, a place with water where ground should be.

"Yes, a dream world," Christian said, "unreal."

"There is so much to see, so much to know."

"You will see it all. You will know it all. We can stay as long as you like. . . . But now let us visit the cafés and search for Akhbar and Francesca. I have already sent a note round to their palace, which is not far away." He scrutinized Sara. "You really are not too tired?"

"No, I want to stay up the whole night, just as I said. I want to see the sun rise and go round to that smelly fish market and watch them bring the fish in."

"And so you shall," Christian said, taking her arm. "Sara, we shall probably meet as many English people tonight as Italians."

"English? I want to meet the Venetians."

"There's a long history between the English and the Venetians. There is a house nearby with a plaque on which are engraved Lord Byron's words. He said, 'Open my heart and you will see/ Graven inside of it, Italy.' He spent much time here. The English have made Venice a second home since the fifteenth century."

"And now it is your second home, my love, and mine," Sara said with a happy smile.

The first café they visited was alive with laughter, music and the din of conversation. Sara was immediately caught up in the festive atmosphere. Christian introduced her to a dizzying number of people, men and women, all of whom seemed to know him well. They greeted him with warm embraces and kisses. Even the men kissed him, which struck Sara as the height of sophistication.

Between sips of a delicious liqueur that smelled of licorice and attempts to communicate with Christian's friends who did not speak English very well, she scrutinized the women. Most of them were tall and fair with heavy-lidded eyes. They looked almost like overdressed dolls, so sumptuously attired and bejewelled were they.

The second café was hidden away behind the Basilica and looked from the outside like a typical Venetian house. But behind the Gothic façade was as lively a café as Sara could ever imagine. A group of musicians strolled from table to table, serenading the patrons, who for the most part ignored them. They were far too busy drinking wine and chatting with each other.

Christian introduced Sara to a tall, dark-eyed, handsome Venetian who kissed her hand and stared so directly into her eyes that he seemed to be inviting her to make love with him in this very café. His amorous attentions unnerved her and she dropped her eyes. She had much to learn in Venice, she decided.

"Akhbar will be arriving with Francesca next month," said the man, whose name was Tomaso.

"I'd hoped they would already be here," said Christian, "but may I rely on that news, Tomaso?"

"No." Tomaso grinned. "You can rely on nothing in Venice."

They stayed at this second café until a patch of light showed through the window. It was nearly dawn, and Sara wished to leave. There were still more sights she wanted to see and the sunrise was not the least of them.

She shivered in the gray mist and wrapped her fur cape around her shoulders for protection. Christian hugged her, holding her against himself to warm her.

"Let us walk briskly," he suggested, "and in ten minutes you will be warm."

"Oh, do people walk in Venice? I thought everyone traveled by water, by gondola."

Christian laughed.

"People do walk in Venice. There are even pretty green parks where the children play. And there are some fascinating streets, too, so let us walk a little."

Sara smiled up at him, admiring his beard, which he had recently grown. It was streaked with blond and red tints that made his eyes seem very green and contrasted handsomely with his black hair.

"Venice is really very small," Christian said. "We could walk to many places. Of course, one often ends up in a cul-de-sac. There are miserable hovels here, too, you know. You are seeing the rich but there are poor people as well."

"Of course," Sara said, "more poor people than rich, just as it is everywhere. We are living in a fairyland, but I know that poverty is all around us."

"Let us live this fairytale a while longer," Christian said, "for one day we might wake from this dream and find it gone forever."

Sara stopped and stared at him.

"Why do you say that? You put terror into my heart."

"I am sorry. Pay no attention," he said contritely.

They walked silently as the mist began to lift. The sky was growing lighter. Soon it would be dawn.

"I do want to see the haunted house," Sara said suddenly. "May we? Please? This seems the perfect time."

"Wouldn't you rather have a filling breakfast in a café in the Piazza?"

"Yes, indeed, but later. I'm not hungry just yet."

"I cannot refuse you anything," Christian said, "but if I take you to this house, you must promise me one thing."

"Yes, anything."

"You must promise to marry me soon as possible."

"But Rob . . . ?" Sara whispered.

"Yes, Sara. I know you find any mention of Rob quite odious. But it will be over soon."

"How will you now?"

"I will know," Christian said. "I will get word from London." Sara stood on tiptoe to kiss him.

"I love you, Christian. I want nothing more than to be your wife."

"And to have my baby," he added.

"Yes," she murmured, looking away into the mist.

"Good," Christian said, "and now I must find my gondolier." They walked along, arm in arm.

"I have forgotten where the haunted house is," Sara said.

"I know the location. It's on the northeastern side of Venice. It looks across the northern lagoon, near a church called Madonna dell'Orto. Do you know the story of the ghosts?"

"No, only that it's supposed to be haunted. Tell me about it, please."

"The story goes that a married couple and a friend lived in the house together. The friend fell in love with the wife, and all three of them were unhappy. Then the lover became ill and died, and then the wife also became ill, and she died. But before the poor women died she made her servant promise to watch over her. At midnight the dead lover came into the room, and when the servant saw him her blood ran to water. He dressed his dead lady and the three of them descended into the cellar of the house, whereupon the servant fainted. It's an odd little story, and that is where it ends. Venetians having a way of never finishing anything."

Christian signaled to his waiting gondolier, who helped them into the boat and headed for the Casa degli Spiriti.

"An interesting story and, yes, rather unfinished. But I like it," Sara said.

They arrived at the house just before dawn. It was tightly shuttered except for a window on the second floor where the green shutter was missing, as if the wind had whipped it away.

"Ugly, isn't it?" Christian said.

"No, I think it looks suitably ghostly," Sara said. She could see the vestiges of its former beauty, although it looked as if it were on the verge of crumbling and sinking into the lagoon.

Christian looked up at the window with the missing shutter. Did he see a woman up there?

"Maybe this house is truly haunted," he murmured, staring at the window. He glanced around at Sara, who was staring fixedly at the window.

"I see someone," she said, "a woman with black hair."

"Paulo," Christian asked the gondolier, "do you see anyone in that upstairs window?"

The man merely shrugged. "In Venice anything is possible."

"I think we ought to leave," Christian said, trying to tear his eyes away from the window.

"No, let's wait a little," Sara said.

"No," Christian insisted, giving instructions to the gondolier to proceed.

The gondola sped across the dark lagoon. As a pale sun rose above the horizon, slowly dispelling the mist, Christian felt a deep melancholy come over his spirit. The wan spectral face at the window of the Casa degli Spiriti had been Katherine Campbell.

Sara touched his hand.

"Do not be disheartened," she said. "I share your sadness that she died so suddenly. It was an untimely death. But she is remembered."

Christian was silent. Knowing the true circumstances of Katherine's death, there was little he could say. He had no intention of ever telling Sara what had really happened.

And yet as the mist began to clear, the sun rising like a blinding gold disc in the multicolored sky, he had another thought. One day he would have to tell her the truth, and in the telling redeem himself.

Chapter 10

THE CUSTOM IN VENICE WAS THAT WIDOWS WERE MARried on Saturday. Although Christian was not Roman Catholic, he received a special dispensation to be married in the Catholic Church. The wedding took place at the Basilica of St. Mark. Sara wore the widow's black veil and the widow's dress of black lace with a long train that trailed behind her, carried by two children, daughters of Christian's friends. Tomaso was the best man, as Akhbar had not yet arrived in Venice.

The ceremony was simple. They knelt together at the crimson-covered altar and the priest read them their wedding vows. Afterward they and their guests, a mix of Venetian and English aristocrats and bohemians, crossed the lagoon in their gondolas to feast at Christian's palace on an enormous, elegant breakfast prepared by his chefs. The guests stayed all day, enjoying the constantly replenished food and the abundant wine. In the early evening the last of them left, except for Tomaso, who remained to drink a last brandy imported from France.

The three of them sat on the balcony that overlooked the Canal.

"The traffic is heavy tonight," Tomaso commented as he sipped from the snifter. "Soon there will be a regatta. That is wonderful, Sara."

He glanced sideways at Sara, whom he considered to be the most beautiful Englishwoman he had seen, although she was not

239

quite as sensuous as the Venetian women, whose red-gold hair streamed down their backs and whose dark eyes spoke of secrets no Englishwoman could ever possibly know.

Sara smiled. The day had been perfect. The idea of a regatta, with all its attendant pagentry, crossing right below her windows appealed to her.

"Tonight?"

Tomaso laughed.

"No, later in the summer."

Sara stood up, the long, lace dress brushing against her hand-made patent leather shoes. Tomaso immediately got to his feet and gripped her arm.

"I thought you might topple over."

"Not likely," Sara said, tossing her head. "I am as steady on my feet as a mule."

The three of them laughed.

"Well, I shall leave you Venetian lovebirds alone to coo to each other, but I must confess to you my jealousy."

"You must take a wife," Sara said.

"I have a wife," Tomaso said, "and I despise her."

"I am sorry," Sara said, embarrassed by her mistake.

"He's not," Christian smiled, ringing for the servant to show Tomaso out.

"Ah," Tomaso sighed, "to be in love again..."

He kissed Sara's hands, looking deeply into her eyes, and bade them goodnight.

Christian and Sara yawned, almost in unison.

"To bed?" suggested Christian. Sara nodded her head sleepily.

They slept naked in each other's arms on the first night of their marriage. In the morning, when Sara woke, she felt lighthearted and happy. Christian was still sleeping, but she crept out of bed and went to the window, pulling back the blue curtains and pushing open the shutters. The day was bright and cloudless— a wonderful start, she felt, for her new life as Christian's wife.

She gazed lovingly at Christian, who opened his eyes and smiled affectionately.

"I have a feeling," she said, "something special will happen to us today. I think Akhbar and Francesca may arrive.

Sara was right. Akhbar and Francesca appeared after lunch to join them for coffee. Francesca was a tiny, blue-eyed Venetian with high cheekbones and masses of dark hair, which she wore piled carelessly on top of her head. Although she could afford the best money could buy, she was not fashionably dressed. Akhbar was a slim, handsome, dark-skinned man with large eyes the color of maple syrup. Sara had worried that they might not like her, that they would look at her critically and find her wanting. But they welcomed her gladly and openly. She knew that they would become good friends to her.

In fact, everyone she had met in Venice, all the people who loved and respected Christian, seemed to feel the same about her. Never before had she been in such a loving, accepting atmosphere. There as nothing of the strangeness she had felt with Katherine Campbell and her friends. There was no depravity, nothing sinister. If the devil were in Venice, he was far removed from Christian's palace on the Grand Canal.

Akhbar was eager to hear about Christian's book, his visit to America and their shared interest in the occult. They quickly resolved that they would get a small group together to talk about the occult. They knew many people in Venice who were interested in the subject. Perhaps they might even have a seance, suggested Akhbar.

"I think Sara is a medium of some kind," Christian said, "and perhaps one evening she will give us a demonstration."

"I don't know if I should," Sara said. "Would it be wise?"

"Because of the baby?" Christian said.

"Baby?" Akhbar and Francesca exclaimed. Akhbar got up and put his hand on Sara's stomach. She blushed at the intimacy of the gesture. But when she looked into his eyes she saw he meant nothing sexual by it.

"How joyous," he said. "A baby. When is it due?"

"In February, I think," Sara said, "but it's difficult to calculate exactly."

"Of course it is difficult," Akhbar said.

"No one ever knows the precise date, do they?" Francesca

chimed in, smiling. "What difference does it make, anyway, whether it's February or January or March? So long as it is a healthy, normal, fat baby. And if it isn't fat we will feed it with our Venetian cuisine which, as all the world knows, is the finest. Far better than anything in India."

Akhbar immediately took issue with his wife, and they argued amiably, to Sara and Christian's amusement, the rest of the afternoon.

In the evening the four dined in an elegant, crystal-chandeliered restaurant in San Trovaso, under the innocent eyes of marble nymphs and leering satyrs. Six waiters served the meal, each course delivered with great pomp. Sara hardly had room for the various puddings, ices and chocolates that were proffered for dessert.

Afterward they took the steamboat up the Grand Canal. The steamboat had only recently appeared in Venice—to the great alarm and consternation of the gondoliers, who saw the invention as an enemy. The two couples debated whether they should hear music or go to the theater. Since Sara wished to hear as much Italian as she could, they decided on a play.

"I am learning this lovely language,' she said, "and I intend to be able to speak it to my baby."

"Our baby, you mean," Christian said, stroking her arm.

"Yes," she said, relieved that she was accepting the baby. She no longer considered trying to get rid of it, and she prayed to God that there would be no physical resemblance to Rob.

"And what shall be the name of this baby? I like the name Antonio."

"Antonio, yes," Francesca said. "This is my father's name."

"Emily?" suggested Christian.

"Ah," sighed Francesca, "so English. So very charming. Emily."

"Yes, I think it is a fine English name," Christian said, "although we may prefer something more exotic."

"Perhaps Sara will wish to name the child for someone in her family," said Akhbar. "Your mother or father?"

Sara shook her head. She and Christian had agreed that they

would tell Akhbar and Francesca the truth about Sara's previous marriage and background, but they had not yet done so. But Sara was certain of one thing—she had no wish to remember her parents by naming a child for them. She and Christian had a new future and, despite the pain and tragedy that had befallen them, she looked forward to a long and happy life with him.

"Yes," Francesca said, "what of your family? Will they visit in Venice after the baby is born?" She was pleased that her dear friend Christian had made such a good match for himself. She could see how his eyes sparkled and glowed whenever he looked at Sara.

As the steamboat moved slowly up the canal, Christian, with Sara's approval, explained to his friends the circumstances under which they had met. Although he was forthright about Rob and the fire, and mentioned the untimely death of Katherine Campbell, he downplayed her influence on them, saying merely that she had been well known in England for her interest in the spirits and Satanism, and they had been, for a time, a part of her circle.

"How terrible for you both," said Francesca sympathetically. She took Sara's hand in hers and said, "But how wonderful that you should fulfill your true destiny and find Christian. My wish is that you will know the same happiness Akhbar and I do." Her eyes lit up. "You know," she said, "we are similar to you in that we are also an unusual, unlikely couple. And our lives are much more interesting and richer for our differences."

"Yes, indeed, Sara," laughed Akhbar. "When I rescued your husband from the ignorant English, I knew he was destined for something far beyond an army career in India."

"But do you have a doctor here in Venice?" asked Francesca.

"No," said Sara, "not yet. I've been well since we arrived."

Francesca waved her hand impatiently. "Of course you've been well. You're in Venice. But I will send my doctor to you in the morning. Christian has waited far too long to take even the slightest chance."

Sara felt a stab of remorse when she thought of how she had tried to kill the baby. She had worked so hard to hide from Christian even the knowledge that she was pregnant. And yet he had never once reproached her for that, although he must have gathered, from Dr. Cox's warning to her that dreadful night, that something had been amiss.

"You are very kind," Sara said, "both of you. I am grateful to have found such good friends."

"Fate," said Akhbar, "fate brought us all together."

"And is it fate that is bringing us to the theater?" teased Francesca.

"Indeed," said Christian, "fate and this sturdy contraption that has our gondoliers all in an uproar."

Their laughter could be heard down the length of the Canal as the four friends enjoyed the company, the Venetian night sky and the anticipation of an entertaining evening at one of Venice's fine theaters.

This was the first of many evenings that Sara and Christian spent with Francesca and Akhbar. Sometimes they would dine in an elegant restaurant, then enjoy a concert of music by Mozart or Handel or Beethoven. Often they visited the cafés, stopping at one table after another to chat with their friends and gossip about the latest talk of the city. Or they might simply pass the evening in one or the other of their homes, drinking wine and talking lightheartedly until the hour grew late and their talk became more serious as they turned to religious and political issues.

During the day, Francesca and Akhbar, or sometimes only Francesca, explored the streets and alleys with Sara, so that soon Sara came to feel as if she had lived there for a very long time. She grew to love the smells of Venice: the cloves and peppers and garlic, the fish at the market, the aromatic flowers that surrounded so many of the buildings. And always the scent of the sea. The baroque and gothic buildings became as familiar to her as the buildings she had passed each day in London as she went about her errands.

And she thought less and less about Rob or poor Katherine Campbell, and more about her baby—what they would name it, whether it would be a boy or a girl, the wonderful life they would give their child.

Christian was thrilled that Sara had so quickly acclimated herself to his beloved adopted city. He could see how healthy and robust she was. The doctor reassured him that all was in order. Although it hardly seemed possible, he loved her more each new morning. He felt he might burst with happiness when he lay next to her in bed, watching her as she slept, the sun glinting through the shutters, casting a thin beam of light across her face.

Akhbar was right. Sara was his destiny. And whatever had happened between them and Katherine was in the past. It no longer mattered. There was no need to destroy the perfect happiness he shared with Sara by burdening her with the knowledge of his mad surrender to the woman he knew was as evil as the devil himself.

No one need ever know—no one but himself. And punishment would be that he had to carry that knowledge with him forever.

Sara and Christian had arrived in the heat of the summer, and by the end of September Sara felt very much at home in Venice. Even her Italian tutor, a gentleman from the College for Foreigners near the Lido, said she had an excellent ear for the accent. She learned the language by studying and listening carefully and by practicing on the servants, who grinned and applauded even her mistakes. She had to beg them to correct her. In a short time she was able to speak to all of Christian's Venetian friends in their own language.

But by the end of October Sara no longer enjoyed staying up late, talking about Venetian society, the poverty in India, precognition, dreams or any of the many topics Christian delighted in exploring with Akhbar and Francesca. After the late evening meal she preferred to go right to bed.

The baby had been kicking inside her, and often she would wake at night feeling that she might be rocked from the bed because of the baby's violent movements. Sometimes she would wake Christian, who would put his hand on her stomach to feel the movements.

"This is very good," he would invariably say, and then fall back asleep in her arms.

Sara continued to be fascinated with Venice. She found the pearly gray lagoon more enchanting with each passing day. The fiery sunsets behind the hills, the vast expanse of water, the brilliant blue skies filled her with happiness. She could not imagine anything more idyllic.

It was not just the place, however. The people, too, seemed to reflect the beauty that surrounded them. The Venetian women looked so happy as they sat outside, sewing or stringing beads. They smiled and chattered, sitting on the steps or in the cafés doing their exquisite lace-work, which Sara greatly admired.

The days were cooler now. The summer sun had faded and the sky was a little less blue. But the continuous pageantry on the Canal, the color and the luxury of her everyday life, and the fact that Christian spent so much time with her occupied her thoroughly.

Sara would have been perfectly content except for her lingering anxiety about the forthcoming baby. She took to going regularly to church to pray that all would be well. She needed a miracle.

Venice abounded in churches, and Sara visited many of them. Most of the churches were very old. Many were brightly colored on the outside and lavishly decorated inside with frescoes, the walls aglow with brilliant paintings. In many of the churches, bands provided music, which at first seemed irreverent to Sara until she became accustomed to the practice.

Eventually she found she was most comfortable at St. Mark's, named for the patron saint of Venice. She prayed regularly in the Basilica, which had been the Doge's private chapel. In retrospect she was deeply ashamed of the wild evenings at Katherine Campbell's home in Brighton, and she wanted to burn the memory out of her mind and spirit. She had come very close to abandoning God—and Christian had encouraged her in that patch.

She barely allowed herself to think about it, but now and again she found herself dwelling on those nights when she undressed and allowed men to stroke and kiss her, and almost to be intimate with her. She did not want to mar her relationship with Christian and therefore she never attempted to discuss that period with him. She knew that he must think about it as she did, although he too ignored the subject, as if those nights had never happened.

And then, abruptly, it was winter. A strange melancholy air settled into place. The canals were no longer pearly gray, azure and blue. They became mud-colored and dismal-looking. A raw wind and a somber fog penetrated all the rooms of Christian's palace so that a fire burned night and day. The rain came in torrents, making it almost impossible for Sara to leave the house. When she did go out, leaning heavily on Christian's arm, the fog was so thick that they could not see even three feet ahead of them.

Many of Christian's friends left for the winter, including Akhbar and Francesca, who bade them a sad farewell and set off for India. Although they did not intend to return until the following summer, they vowed to keep in touch.

Even the pigeons in the Piazza seemed to shiver. People no longer sat outside the cafés. There were no children playing in the streets, and the fish and vegetable markets were nearly empty of customers.

Mist seemed to wrap itself around everything. Sara felt weighted down by desolation as Christmas approached. She was now well into her pregnancy, and there was no choice but to stay in Venice.

She forced herself to get up early and go to Mass each day, returning to wake Christian and to take breakfast with him, snuggled up in their large bed. He did not like her going out alone in the weather nor did he like the idea that she had gone back to her religion. But he held his tongue, recognizing that she found prayer a comfort. He respected her freedom to do as she liked even if he felt it was pointless.

"How dreadful is the winter," Sara remarked one morning in January when the teeming rain obscured the canal in front of the house. She had not dared to go to church this morning and felt trapped inside the palace. She prayed for the rain to end, for a little sunshine to peep through the gray mists that surrounded them.

"Yes, and it's not any better when it snows here," Christian commented, sipping his coffee. He had been reading most of the morning, having discovered an interesting book on seventh-century Italy.

"No, snow does not suit Venice. But I suppose that, like London, there isn't much snow."

"Oh, you must see Boston in the winter," Christian said, glancing up at Sara, who looked like a figure from a Renaissance painting in her maternity gown.

"Will I ever see Boston?" Sara said, a sudden feeling of panic clutching at her.

"What is it, my darling?" said Christian, springing out of his chair to hold her.

"I don't know," Sara said, "I am suddenly filled with a terrible sense of doom."

Christian bent and kissed her on both cheeks and then upon her pale lips.

"I will take you to Boston, of course. We will go next year with our child. You will like the Americans very much. We will meet all the psychics I have written about. And we will visit New York. New York has a dreadful winter, too, but we will be there in spring, when it's charming."

He held her at arm's length for a moment.

"Do not be sad, Sara. We are together. We have so much ahead of us."

Sara stared at him. She did not feel there was much time ahead of them but rather that they had too little time left to be together.

"Hold me," she said, and he held her tightly in his arms.

They remained indoors for the rest of the day, playing cards in the afternoon for imaginary high stakes. Sara giggled and pouted when she lost five million lire. Then they played chess. Christian had taught her to play and she was becoming quite skilled at the game.

Around five the mist began to clear and a pink haze filled the winter sky, the last light of the setting sun.

A servant brought them tea with chocolate and sweet cakes in the library.

"What a shame the Carnival is no longer celebrated," Christian said. "It must have been extraordinary."

"Yes," Sara said, "but was it not just an excuse for the most terrible lasciviousness? Were not most of the women who participated more or less whores?"

Christian shrugged. "I cannot make this judgment. Why should you?"

Sara blushed.

"Perhaps I am a whore, too," she said suddenly, wondering where this thought had come from.

"What?"

Christian frowned and put down his cup of strong black tea.

"I don't know why I said that," Sara said. "Forgive me."

"You are my wife," Christian said, "and no Wheatley-Croft marries a whore. Do you understand?"

His voice was soft, but she thought she saw a hardness in his eyes that she had never seen before. A shiver went through her.

"I think you need some more cake," Christian said, and smiled as he offered her another piece.

"No, I couldn't," she said. "I'm full. But I think I might nap before dinner."

"A splendid idea, and I shall attend you, my lady," said Christian, getting up to accompany her to the bedroom.

A fire roared in the fireplace, making the room warm and cozy. Christian slowly undressed her and they made love until the sky was black. Then they fell asleep to the sound of the rain beating against the windows.

Christian woke first, aware of a strange movement in the room. Except for the fire, which had burned down to a low flame, there was no light in the room, and yet he could quite clearly see a woman standing at the foot of the bed. She was tall and slender with long, wild hair.

Then she disappeared, simply vanished before his eyes, leaving him with a churning sensation in his gut. And then he realized he was bleeding.

He quickly got out of bed and ran into the bathroom, where a candelabra illuminated the room and he could see more clearly. Blood was streaming out of his mouth. His arms and hands were bathed in blood. Pouring some mineral water into a glass, he drank it down rapidly. For a moment the bleeding seemed to stop. But he realized he was still bleeding from the nose. He held a cloth against his nose and, careful not to rouse Sara, crept out of the bedroom in search of one of the servants. He found one at once.

"Go quickly," Christian said to the shocked man, "and fetch the doctor. And don't tell a soul what is happening. I don't want to worry my wife."

While he waited, he tried to stop the bleeding. He had bled several times in India and had had to be hospitalized. The doctors there had warned him this could happen again and that he must take care. But so far as he knew, he had done nothing to bring on the attack.

The doctor arrived at last and lay him down in the sitting room, where he carefully examined him. As he was puzzling over what might have caused the bleeding, it stopped.

"Your healing presence did it," Christian said, trying to make light of the episode although he felt weak and worried.

After waiting an hour to make sure the bleeding did not recur, the doctor left, promising to return the next day, ostensibly for a social visit. He vowed secrecy. Sara must not know what had happened that evening.

Christian crept back into the bedroom and inspected the bed-sheets. There was no sign of blood on them. But the bathroom was a dreadful, frightening sight, and Christian hurriedly scrubbed the basin and floor to clean away the stains. Then he woke Sara. It was past their dinner hour and she would be hungry.

"I had a strange dream," she said, getting out of bed, her naked, pregnant body as beautiful as a sonnet. She wrapped herself in her velvet dressing gown.

"I dreamt that Katherine Campbell did not die. She was in the house on Belgrave Road . . . in the bedroom with me. She was telling me about her childhood, which was rather ugly. She began to weep and rant and then she took off her clothes and she had no skin. It was horrible. She looked like death."

"Ghastly," Christian said, hugging her tightly. "You must not have such thoughts."

Sara shuddered, remembering Katherine's horrible appearance. "What could it mean, Christian?"

"I cannot imagine," he said, "but you must not think about it. Katherine Campbell has no part in our life today. We must keep you better amused so that you do not have such melancholy dreams. Now come, the chef has prepared a special fish for you—

he swears that it will make the baby fat and healthy even before it is born."

Sara jumped up, shutting out the image of Katherine. "Then I must hurry," she said, and kissed him lightly on the lips.

Christian smiled but his spirit was troubled. Despite his reassuring words to Sara, Katherine *was* still a part of their lives. She had appeared to both of them, and he wondered whether he was foolish to ignore what he understood to be a warning.

On a freezing cold February morning, long before the pale sun rose in the pearly gray sky, Sara began to have labor pains. Christian sent a servant to fetch the doctor and the midwife, and he sat beside her as her labor progressed. Her piteous screams carried to every floor of the palace. Christian suffered with her; his face was drawn and his hand numb from gripping hers. The servants covered their ears, and those who could, fled the palace, unwilling to eavesdrop on their beloved mistress's agony.

As her shrieks grew shriller, Christian wept, feeling helpless to ease his wife's torment. The doctor urged him to leave the room, insisting that Christian could do nothing but hinder the delivery. And the midwife stood by, shaking her head and muttering about "this crazy Englishman" who didn't understand that a man had no place in his wife's labor room.

But Christian stubbornly declared that he would not—could not—leave Sara, and at last the doctor conceded. Sara seemed unaware of who was present, but the doctor feared for Christian's health, so adamant was he that he stay.

For five hours Sara wailed and screamed and begged that they put an end to her misery. "Push," urged the midwife, motioning Christian to wipe Sara's brow. If he must be present, let him be useful, she thought. The doctor alternated between supervising the midwife's progress and reassuring Christian that Sara was as healthy a prepartum mother as he had ever seen and that the delivery was proceeding normally.

"Better than normal, in fact," he said jocularly, noting how dilated Sara was. But Christian was not comforted. Sara was in pain. Beyond that, nothing mattered.

How had he ever let her get with child, he berated himself. How could he have been so selfish? Christian scowled, blaming himself for his lack of caution. And the midwife again ordered Sara to "push harder, *cara*, one last time." And with a fearsome bellow, Sara delivered a squalling baby girl.

The infant weighed seven pounds and her tiny head was covered with a mass of silky black hair. Even at one hour old, she was the image of her father, Christian. Although her eyes were blue, the doctor explained that all newborns had blue eyes and predicted hers would turn to green in due course.

The midwife bathed the baby and wrapped her in a soft cotton swaddling blanket, then carefully placed her in Sara's arms. Exhausted as she was, Sara fell instantly in love with her daughter. She sighed with relief, noting the baby's resemblance to Christian, and felt that her heart might burst with joy.

"What shall we name her?" whispered Christian, his eyes moist with tears of happiness. Never had he expected such blessings.

"Emily." Sara smiled. "A fine English name for our fine English daughter."

"Emily it is," pronounced Christian. Emily opened her eyes and blinked, as if agreeing with their choice.

The doctor's prediction came true. By the time Emily was six weeks old, her eyes had changed from blue to deep green, just like Christian's. Her thick black hair further emphasized her resemblance to her proud and doting father.

Sara and Christian vied for the right to take care of Emily. But they also bowed to English and Italian custom and hired a nanny, an Italian woman named Teresa who spoke not a word of English. During the dreary months of February and March, as winter lingered in Venice, Sara and Teresa formed a closed friendship. Teresa looked after Emily as if she were her own baby, and Sara trusted her as she would a sister.

Sara felt she must be the happiest woman in Venice. But her tranquility was disturbed by Christian's suggestion that they return to London. Sara's attempts to dissuade him were in vain; he had made his decision, although he tried to present the idea as a matter for both of them to resolve. The fact of the matter was that the house on Belgrave Road was close to being finished, and Christian felt it was his duty to his older brother to oversee the finishing touches.

"Think of wheeling Emily's carriage through the streets of Westminister. She will make us the envy of the neighborhood," he said, trying to coax Sara into agreeing.

Sara dreaded returning to all the unhappy memories that London held for her. Nevertheless, she spent the month of April preparing for the return trip, saying goodbye to her new friends and revisiting one last time the many places she had come to love in Venice.

By May they, along with the devoted Teresa, were back in London and settled into the new house on Belgrave Road. Although they had been gone less than a year, it seemed to Sara that they had been gone for a much longer time. Indeed, her whole life had changed. She had left London as Christian's mistress. She returned as his wife and the mother of his child.

At three months Emily was a roly-poly baby, all smiles and dimples. She was good-natured and intelligent, and Sara often wondered whether her daughter had inherited her psychic gifts. Gazing into Emily's dreamy green eyes, Sara decided that yes, she showed signs of these special abilities. And Sara was determined to cultivate her gifts, never deny them. Her child would be raised under far different circumstances than she had been.

Despite her success among Venetian society, Sara had no great desire to conquer its English counterpart. She doubted whether London nobility would be as accepting of her as the Italians, especially since there was more likelihood that they would question her place among them. Many of them of course knew exactly who she was, having been served by her when they were guests of Lord Evans. She missed the freedom and tolerance of Venice more than she could have imagined and looked forward to returning there, as Christian had promised, toward the end of the summer.

For now she occupied herself by spending time with Emily and Teresa, taking long walks in Hyde Park or on the banks of the Thames. Teresa was more a companion to her than a servant.

She and Sara spoke only Italian to each other, as Sara was eager for Emily to be fluent in the language. But Teresa was quickly picking up English from the other servants in the household. She played no small part in getting them to accept Sara as their mistress, snapping at them whenever any of them dared refer to her background.

Sara's secondary preoccupation was with redecorating the house. With Christian's approval, she chose simple wooden furniture and oriental rugs in rich but muted colors. She scoured the tiny art stores in search of drawings and paintings that reminded her of Venice and the exotic lands that lay beyond the mouth of the Adriatic Sea.

Surveying the front sitting room, she was reminded of the sparsely decorated rooms in Katherine Campbell's house at Brighton. From the very beginning, Sara had admired the interior design of Katherine's home. In retrospect, it seemed the only thing worthy of admiration. How had she been so taken in by the woman, she wondered, shuddering with horror when she recalled confessing to Katherine her doubts about the baby's paternity.

But that was all behind her. Katherine was dead, and the baby was certainly Christian's. And whatever had happened in Brighton, whatever Katherine's interest had been in her and Christian, was of no account. What mattered was that Christian loved her, that both he and Emily were healthy and that, if anyone dared question her right to call herself mistress of the house on Belgrave Road, they did so very quietly and in private.

Chapter 11

ANTONY GOLD AND THE THREE OTHER MEMBERS OF the television crew arrived at Lavinia's flat straight from Heathrow Airport. Lavinia greeted them enthusiastically, her nervous exhaustion masquerading as excitement. She had gotten very little sleep since Sunday night and she was still preoccupied with the news of Mrs. Patel-Ram's death.

After she had eaten a lunch of thick vegetable soup, homemade black bread and strong coffee with Paul on Monday, she had hurried back to her apartment. Determined to get through as many interviews as possible before Antony showed up on Wednesday, she transcribed tapes until one story seemed to blur into the next. But she had managed to get through almost all of the material she owed him. She was pleased with what she had managed to do, under the circumstances.

Antony was accompanied by Marion Brown, his production assistant, who doubled as his lover when his wife was not around; his favorite cameraman, Jack Douglas, and his technical director, Roscoe Helm. Antony was a slender, middle-aged man whose articulate manner often intimidated people. He was fast and efficient, and gave the impression that he always knew what he was doing. Lavinia greatly respected him. She was thrilled when he congratulated her on a superb research job almost as soon as she walked into the apartment.

"How about some wine?" she suggested, her cheeks flushed with the unexpected praise from her boss. She brought out a bottle of Pinot Grigio and joined her friends on the downstairs terrace. Jack was giving himself a tour of the flat. He found it very interesting from a visual point of view, and was already shooting the interior and the garden beyond the terrace with his 16mm camera.

Lavinia was about to offer the crew some cheese and crackers when her doorbell rang. Paul had seen a taxi pull up in front of the building and had surmised from their accents and gear that the Americans had arrived.

"Come on in," said Lavinia. "We were just about to propose a toast to the success of our film."

"And to your promotion," said Antony. He lifted his glass. "To my new executive producer, Lavinia Cross."

Lavinia was so stunned that she was momentarily speechless. But Paul introduced himself and shook hands with Antony, Marion, Roscoe and Jack, adding how pleased he was to meet Lavinia's colleagues.

"She's gotten to be quite an expert on the subject of ghosts," he remarked. "She even has a cynic like me on the verge of becoming a believer."

Lavinia tugged nervously at her curls, hoping he wouldn't say anything about her very personal involvement with the subject. But he knew enough not to say anything more and poured himself a glass of wine.

As always, Antony took center stage.

"I have it all planned out," he said, wasting no time in getting down to business. A couple of other crew members are standing by here in London, and I have your list of the places in and around London that I want to shoot. I'd like to set up an interview with that librarian you talked to at the Society for Psychical Research at Adam and Eve Mews. The name is fabulous. They'll love it at home. I want to do a couple of ghost walks like the ones you outlined for me, Lavinia, and that old lady, the one with the double name, sounds like she'd be dynamite."

"Mrs. Patel-Ram..." Lavinia said.

"Yeah, the one who saw the princess."

"I'm afraid you're too late, Antony."

"What do you mean, 'too late'? Did somebody else get to her first?"

Lavinia cleared her throat nervously. "Actually, she died several days ago."

"Damn! Too bad. She would have been terrific. Well, how about Lady Chamberlain? Think we could talk her into letting us come down and do a shoot? Maybe we could get her to hold a seance."

"My mother loves an audience. I'm sure she would be delighted," said Paul.

"Oh, is that how you found her, Lavinia? Through Paul, here?" Antony briefly wondered whether Paul was Lavinia's new boyfriend. She wasn't Antony's type, but she was a good-looking woman. He wasn't opposed to her having some fun while she was over here.

Lavinia nodded.

"Nice guy," Marion murmured, looking longingly after Paul.

"Hmmm," Lavinia agreed, "a very sweet man."

"This apartment is great," Jack said. "I'd love to take it back to New York. Actually there's something about it that reminds me of Greenwich Village, although it's very Victorian."

"I'm about to crash," said Roscoe. "I'm exhausted."

"That's what you get for burning the candle at both ends," Antony said. "He drank the whole way across the Atlantic," he explained to lavinia.

"I'm pooped, too," Marion said, yawning. "This wine is putting me to sleep."

"Why don't you people head on back to the hotel," Antony said. "I'll be there later. I have some things to discuss with Lavinia."

Marion picked up her suitcase and hand luggage.

"I wish I could give you a hand, but I've got all my stuff," Jack said, grabbing his equipment. "Lavinia, may I come back tomorrow and take some more footage from the terrace? I want the back of the building. I like those Georgian windows, or whatever they are. Okay?"

Lavinia smiled. "Make yourself at home," she said. She glanced from one to the other. "It's nice to see some Americans."

"They're all over London, kid," Antony said. "Where've you been?"

"I guess the library, mostly," Lavinia said, hoping Christian wouldn't decide to put in an appearance any time soon.

"Well, now, you've got other work to do," Antony said, "and so do we. I want to go over some things with Lavinia. I'll see the rest of you later."

"See you tomorrow, Lavinia," said Marion, following the two men out the door.

Seeing that the rest of the crew was leaving, Paul took the moment to excuse himself, telling Lavinia he would call her later. Once alone, Antony was anxious to get down to business.

"I think our special is going to be quite exciting," Antony said. "The network is behind it all the way. I may go on to Scotland from here. The Scottish material has been interesting. Of course, in the U.K., London and its environs are the main point of interest for the ghost segment. But we're so close to Scotland, we can just take the train. It would be a shame to miss out on anything."

He took his notes out of his briefcase.

"I think it's important to have a few minutes on the old established ghosts in London, even if they are well known. Americans don't know that much about them. I think the audience will want to see some of those London theaters that are supposed to be haunted. Then there's that Oscar Wilde thing."

"Thing?"

"Oh, you know, at the St. James. You had it on one of the cassettes. The bit about that seance in 1923 when he supposedly got through to some people with automatic writing. And how about Dylan Thomas—being seen at the Bush Theatre?"

"Shepherd's Bush Green, I think," Lavinia said. "Yes, we can go there."

"Lavinia, I noticed that several times you mentioned a ghost named Christian, but you never gave me any material on him."

"I don't remember that," she said nervously.

"I have it right here," said Antony, rummaging through his

briefcase. It stuck in my mind because it sounded as if you were saying you had *seen* a ghost."

"I don't recall anything like that," Lavinia said, thinking that at least that was true. She didn't remember having reported to Antony that she had met Christian.

"Well," Antony said, "I figured something was off. I know how stable you are."

"Thank you," Lavinia said, "but let me assure you that all the people I interviewed here are sane and rational. It isn't a matter of stability at all."

"Oh, don't be ridiculous, Lavinia. It's all craziness but it makes a damned good special. There's a big audience out there for the paranormal. The ratings should be high."

"No, really, Antony," she persisted. "These people aren't imagining things or making any of it up. Their experiences have been verified."

"Verified?" He looked at her sharply. "How the hell can ghosts be verified? Lavinia, you haven't been taken in by all of this?"

"What about the ghosts who have been seen by more than one person? How do you account for them?"

"Like I said—craziness. It happens all the time."

"Look, Antony, I'm not going to defend the people I've interviewed. If you're a skeptic, you'll probably remain one. Unless..."

"Unless what?"

"Unless and until you encounter a ghost yourself. If anything changes a skeptic into a believer, it's a direct, personal experience."

"Have you had one of those personal experiences yourself, Lavinia? That guy Paul said something about you making a believer out of him." Antony leaned forward in the chair to hold her gaze. "You're not hiding something from me, are you?"

"No," Lavinia said, wondering what he would think if he knew the truth.

"Good," said Antony decisively. He stood up and patted her on the shoulder. "I wouldn't want you to lose your objectivity. I have work to do back at the hotel. Let's set up that shoot with Lady Chamberlain as soon as possible."

"Right," Lavinia said, showing him to the door.

He kissed her cheek. "Hey, you look terrific, kid. London suits you. Must be the air or something." He raised his eyebrows suggestively to emphasize the last word. "I'll call you in a few hours."

He ran down the stairs and out the front door without even saying goodbye.

Typical Antony, she thought, sinking down onto her couch. Blow into town and blow me away. Well, at least Christian is making himself scarce. I don't know whether I could handle him and Antony in the room at the same time.

A knock at the door disturbed her reverie.

"I was on my way out when I saw your boss leaving," said Paul. "How did your meeting go?"

"It was okay," she said wearily, though she wished she could feel more enthusiatic about the unexpected promotion.

"What's the matter?" asked Paul. "You look a bit undone."

"Culture shock." She laughed. "No, it's more than that. I'm thrilled that Antony named me executive producer. It's exactly the opportunity I've been waiting for. But that means I have to worry about the budget, coordinating the staff, vetting the material and making sure everybody stays happy."

Paul snapped his fingers. "That's nothing for a woman of your talents and intelligence."

"No, seriously, Paul," she said. "You know what I've been like lately, so distracted by Christian and Sara. I've barely been functioning as a researcher."

"But you said yourself at lunch the other day that you felt so close to solving the mystery. Perhaps these more demanding responsibilities are just what you need to snap you back to reality."

She grimaced at his choice of words. "Is that how you see it?"

"Well, I simply meant..."

"Forget it. I'm tired and overreacting."

"What's first on the agenda?"

"I should probably call your mother and see how she feels about having a television crew tear her house apart. Do you think she'll agree to hold a seance so that the cameras can record it for the entertainment of millions of American viewers?"

"My mother?" Paul widened his eyes for emphasis. "I can't think of anything she would like better. Why don't you ring her straightaway and then we can decide where I'm taking you for dinner."

"Oh, I can't," she protested, getting up to use the phone in the kitchen. "I have lots of work to do, and Antony said he would be calling me and besides, I'm..."

"Exhausted," Paul finished her sentence. "That's precisely the point. You have to eat. And you need to relax for a bit or you certainly won't be much good as executive producer. And I'm the perfect person for you to relax with."

She smiled and raised her hands to signal her surrender.

"Give my love to Mum," he said, pleased that he had talked her into joining him.

He knew she was feeling frazzled, but she looked beautiful. Her hair was mussed—a sure sign that she was nervous and had been playing with her curls. Her blond mop reminded him of Little Orphan Annie.

Except that Lavinia was not a poor little orphan girl. And today she looked even sexier than usual. Her lavender dress emphasized the purple tint of her eyes. Paul fantasized about slowly unbuttoning the front of her dress, pulling down the top and burying his head between her breasts.

"You were right," Lavinia said, returning from the kitchen. "She said she'd be delighted... Paul?"

"Sorry. What did you say?"

"You looked just now as if you were a million miles away," Lavinia said.

"Not at all. I was right here. Lavinia," he said impulsively, "will you come to the Lake Country or Cornwall with me for a few days after the show is done?"

"I don't now..."

"We could bring my children with us, if you'd like. Though I'd much rather have you all to myself. Or you could come to Turkey with us. Emily would be delighted."

Emily. She thought of baby Emily, cooing innocently, smiling back at her father, both of them so unprepared for the inevitable tragedy.

"I can't make any plans now. There's still too much to be resolved."

"Please promise me you won't rush back to New York."

She knew what he was asking, but she just couldn't tell him what he wanted to hear. Not yet, anyway.

Changing the subject, she said, "Your mother wants to invite Dr. Hare and Marcus Patel-Ram to a seance on Sunday. Marcus called to tell her about his mother's death, and she wants to meet him. And of course she'd like you there. You will come, won't you?"

"I wouldn't miss it for the world. Will you participate as the medium?"

"And be seen by millions of people? Absolutely not. No thanks. Besides, I don't want Antony to know anything about what's been happening to me since I came to London. If he knew about my going into trances or contacting people on the spirit plane, he'd fire me on the spot."

"I thought Americans were so broadminded. And he seemed a likeable bloke."

"Yes. He's a damned good producer, but a little calculating. You saw how he didn't bat an eye when I told him that Mrs. Patel-Ram had died."

"Your secret is safe with me. Now what do you fancy for dinner?"

"I haven't a clue. You decide."

Paul thought a moment, then said, "I've a suggestion. We already have some wine, so why don't I go buy a pizza?"

He pointed to Mary's antique brass candlesticks. "We can even provide our own atmosphere. A romantic candlelight dinner."

"Sounds great," said Lavinia, suddenly very hungry. "I want lots of mushrooms, green peppers and garlic, with double cheese."

"Stick the wine in the refrigerator. I'll be back in about twenty minutes," Paul said, privately resolving to have them hold the garlic, just in case the evening took the turn he hoped for.

Lavinia poked her head out the door just as he was leaving

the building. "Get a large," she called. "Just in case Christian shows up."

"Very funny," he laughed. But hurrying toward Victoria Street, he thought, *I wish that bloody bastard would disappear. I can't compete with a ghost.*

Chapter 12

LAVINIA AND PAUL DROVE DOWN TO KENT IN THE VAN that Antony had rented for his crew, including the English technicans he had hired in London. The afternoon was wet and cloudy. "Perfect for a seance," said Marion, shivering from the damp.

Marcus Patel-Ram arrived just as the van pulled up in front of Lady Chamberlain's home. Lavinia made the introductions while Antony surveyed Lady Chamberlain's estate.

"Whew!" he whistled. "Quite a spread. Lavinia, you've done all right for yourself with Paul."

Glancing around to see whether Paul had heard his comment, she said, "We're friends, Antony, nothing more."

"Sure, kid," he grinned. "'Friends.'" He winked broadly.

Lavinia was annoyed but held her tongue. The truth was that she and Paul *were* just friends, although clearly he would have preferred that it be otherwise. As for herself... she had been tempted to say yes to the trip to the Lake Country. But she had to get back to New York. That was where she belonged... didn't she?

"Do come in," Lady Chamberlain said, opening the big front door herself. "I'm so eager to meet all of you. This way," she said, pointing the technicians, who were loaded down with their equipment, in the direction of the seance room. "Dr. Hare will show you the way—won't you, my dear?"

"Shall we have drinks first in the library?" she suggested after she met and shook hands with everyone. "I'm afraid we're having one of our traditionally chilly English summer days, but I have a good fire burning in there."

As the lighting people set up the lights so that the seance room began to resemble a television studio, the sound technicians worked at stringing an overhead mike in the middle of the room. The rest of the guests trooped into the library and gratefully accepted Lady Chamberlain's offer of sherry and whiskey.

"I'd suggest gin and tonics," she said to Antony, "but the weather doesn't seem quite right for it."

Antony laughed, taking in her outfit. He loved her long, white Victorian gown, white flowers woven through her hair, and the silver bracelets that dangled from her arms. She could have been a visitor from a previous century. Fantastic, he thought. This woman has a real sense of drama. He couldn't wait to see how the rest of the afternoon shaped up.

Lavinia sipped her sherry as she chatted with Marcus.

"I see you're wearing my mother's shoes," he noted. "Are you in love?"

"Not that I know of," Lavinia said lightly.

"Ah, I would have guessed otherwise." He smiled and looked meaningfully at Paul.

"Lavinia, could I interrupt for a moment?" said Lady Chamberlain.

"Excuse me, Marcus," Lavinia said.

"Certainly," he nodded, his eye on Marion.

"I've just been telling Mr. Gold how even as a child I knew I had been born to the occult," explained Lady Chamberlain. Turning to Antony, she said, "But I suppose you know that you have a person of exceptional medium ability right here."

Lavinia barely stifled the impulse to reach out and put her hand over Lady Chamberlain's mouth to hold back the words. But it was too late. She had forgotten to warn her about saying anything to Antony.

"Is that right? Have you sensed this with your own psychic powers?" asked Antony, assuming his professional role as a producer-reporter.

Lady Chamberlain laughed. "Not at all. That's now how I use my powers. It's Lavinia I'm talking about, of course."

"Lavinia?" Antony raised his eyebrows and turned to Lavinia. "I had no idea she had this . . . gift."

Lavinia swallowed hard. He was looking at her as if she were an exhibit in a freak show.

"You mean to say you did not know what a wonderful medium your dear Lavinia is? Not even a suspicion? Ah, of course, it has been fairly recent. But I always believe that the powers are there from birth, although some of us only become aware of them later in life. It is a gift from God, don't you think?"

"I'm not sure, Lady Chamberlain," Antony said, still gazing speculatively at Lavinia, who hadn't said a word.

Suddenly aware of the tension, Lady Chamberlain said, "I'm sorry. Did I say something wrong?"

"No, of course not," Lavinia replied. "But it's getting late. Maybe we should move into the other room and begin the seance."

"Good idea," said Antony, "let's get things organized."

Lavinia knew he had dropped the subject only temporarily.

Jack examined the room for the best camera angles while Roscoe checked the mike and lights. Six chairs were arranged about the table.

Lady Chamberlain, Dr. Hare, Paul and Marcus sat down.

"We need more people on camera," said Antony. "Marion, you'll look good in this scene. Take a seat."

"And how about Roscoe?" suggested Lavinia. "He said he believed in ghosts and that he'd like to sit in on the seance."

Antony nodded.

"Then we're ready to start," said Lavinia.

"No, I want you in there, too," Antony said.

"I'd rather not," she said quietly.

He matched her tone so as not to disturb the others. "Since you have these special powers, Lavinia, I expect you to participate."

Lavinia could see there was no budging him. When Antony made up his mind, he could rarely be dissuaded. She brought another chair to the table and sat down, determined to stay aloof from the proceedings. Lady Chamberlain was the medium, so she could watch and not get pulled into the seance.

Antony announced that they were all set.

"Just look straight into Jack's camera when you are speaking to the audience," Antony explained. "We're ready whenever you are, Lady Chamberlain."

Lady Chamberlain cleared her throat.

"To begin, we will have some table-tipping. Table-tipping is a tried and true way of getting in touch with the spirit world. I would like everyone to put their hands palms down on the table. This helps to summon the spirits."

Lavinia glanced at Paul, who smiled reassuringly. He had overheard his mother talking to Antony and knew how apprehensive Lavinia must be feeling.

"When we ask questions, continued Lady Chamberlain, "the table will tip to the right for yes and to the left for no."

She stopped speaking. Several minutes of silence followed. Lavinia thought about editing the film. She didn't expect anything sensational to occur, but Lady Chamberlain was a medium and might be able to summon up a few voices from the past. At least enough to give American viewers a taste of a seance.

The only sounds in the room were of feet shuffling, sighs and breathing, and Roscoe coughing nervously. Lavinia felt nervous too and tried to distract herself by keeping her mind on the technical aspects of the film. She looked critically at the lights arranged around the room. Was the set overlit? Should she disturb the mood of the seance and say something to Antony?

The table moved. First to the right, then to the left. Marion giggled and rolled her eyes. The table shook discernably for several seconds and then settled back into place.

"Palms down again," ordered Lady Chamberlain, noticing that Lavinia and Marion had removed their hands from the table.

"There is someone here," Marcus said, "perhaps my mother. I've been trying to contact her since she left us."

"Yes," Lady Chamberlain said, "this is possible."

She closed her eyes. Breathing deeply, she seemed to be going into a trance. She looked neither asleep nor fully awake but somewhere in a twilight zone, Lavinia thought.

"Are you there, Mrs. Patel-Ram?" Lady Chamberlain asked.

The table tipped to the right.

"Oh, Mum," Marcus said, tears springing into his eye, "are you happy?"

The table tipped to the right again.

Antony moved closer, crouching down to see whether the table was being moved from below. But so far as he could determine, no one was moving it.

"Is that you, Mrs. Patel-Ram?" Lady Chamberlain asked again.

The table tipped to the right, then shook vigorously.

"I think there is some interference," Lady Chamberlain said. "Another spirit is trying to contact us, someone at the table. Is that right?"

The table tipped to the right.

"I am sorry, Marcus, your mother is gone now. Another person is trying to communicate."

"It could be my Aunt Bev," said Roscoe. "She died recently."

"Are you a woman?" Lady Chamberlain said.

The table tipped to the right.

"A young woman who died an untimely death?"

The table tipped to the right.

"Will you speak to us then?" Lady Chamberlain murmured, her voice becoming weak and faint.

Antony signaled the sound man to turn up the sound monitor.

"How does she know the woman died an untimely death?" he whispered to Jack.

Jack shrugged. He zoomed in for a closeup of Lady Chamberlain. "This is wild," he said.

"Are you related to someone present?" continue Lady Chamberlain.

The table tipped to the left.

"Will you speak to us?"

The table tipped to the right. Marion gasped and the table jerked violently.

"Please try to be quiet," Dr. Hare said, "and let her get on with it."

"Will you speak to us?" Lady Chamberlain repeated. She began to speak in a strange voice. The first few words were gibberish, but then a very loud, distinct "no" could be heard.

"No, no," the voice said again.

"Who are you?" asked Lady Chamberlain.

"My name is Katherine," the voice said in an unmistakable Scots accent.

"Jesus, it's creepy," Marion said.

"Shh," warned Dr. Hare.

"That's my sister's name," Marion persisted, her voice trembling. "She died when I was little."

"Are you related to some person present?" Lady Chamberlain said again.

"No," the voice replied emphatically.

Lady Chamberlain suddenly opened her eyes and looked around the table.

"I feel interference," she said. "Someone at the table is interfering. Did you hear any voices? Was someone from the spirit world trying to talk?"

"A woman named Katherine spoke through you," said Dr. Hare. "A communicator or a control, perhaps?"

"It doesn't matter," Lady Chamberlain said, "but I sense interference."

She looked around the table, searching each of their faces until she came to Lavinia.

"Lavinia, dear, I sense that the interference is coming from you."

Lavinia didn't know what Lady Chamberlain meant. She couldn't feel herself consciously trying to disrupt the seance.

"You are the source," Lady Chamberlain said, staring at her. Then, just as abruptly, she closed her eyes and returned to her trance.

"I have a cousin named Katherine," Dr. Hare said, "and she's half Scots. But so far as I know she is still with us."

"Are you Dr. Hare's cousin?" Lady Chamberlain asked.

"No."

Antony inspected the table again. Was the shaking some kind of a trick? The table seemed to be rising upward as well. Marion was clutching her hands to her bosom, looking as if she were about to pass out. He hoped she could keep her cool and not ruin the footage. Otherwise they would have to reshoot the segment.

To Antony's astonishment, the table was indeed about two inches off the floor. The table began making sounds as if *it* wanted to speak. What the hell was going on? How could a table make noise?

Roscoe removed his hands from the table. "Man, this is incredible," he said, looking down at the table, which seemed to be floating in space.

"Who are you?" Lady Chamberlain demanded.

The table settled back to the floor with a resounding crash.

Marion jumped from her chair, her eyes filled with terror.

"Cut!" Antony called.

Jack stopped shooting.

"What are you doing, Marion?" he said. "Sit down. This is good stuff we're getting."

"I'm not going to sit here any longer," she said. "I don't like this at all. It's scary, and I don't want to be part of it. Something awful is going to happen."

"Chicken," Roscoe said, smiling.

"It isn't funny," Marion insisted.

"All right," Antony said, "sit over here. But let's get back to the shooting before we lose everything."

Lady Chamberlain was still speaking, her voice barely audible. She seemed to be talking to someone invisible, or else someone was talking through her.

Suddenly Lavinia recognized Katherine Campbell's voice. Yes! It was she.

"What do you want?" Lavinia asked.

"You," the voice replied, speaking through Lady Chamberlain.

"Why?" Lavinia said nervously.

"You took Christian from me. Your husband killed me. You are to blame. If I could, I would bring you here to hell."

Lavinia trembled.

"Are you in hell?" Lavinia asked. "Then you've been vindicated."

Paul came over to Lavinia's side. "Do you want to go on with this?" he whispered. The pained expression on her face worried him. And what would Antony make of this strange dialogue?

But she did not seem to hear him. Her eyes glazed over and she began to make strange sounds in the back of her throat. She shook her head and her eyes rolled up into the back of her head. It looked as if she were having a seizure.

"Shit!" Roscoe said. "I don't want any part of this." He got up and left the room.

By now Lady Chamberlain had opened her eyes. She smiled when she saw Lavinia in a trance.

"Let her go on," she said.

"Will she be all right?" Paul asked. He didn't give a damn about the television special as compared to Lavinia's welfare.

"Oh, yes," Lady Chamberlain said. "It will all come right, dear."

"Are you a ghost?" Lavinia asked.

"No, I'm in hell," Katherine said, emitting a cry of anguish, her words now coming out of Lavinia's mouth.

"How could Christian and Sara see you?" Lavinia asked.

She spoke very slowly, now and then her head bobbing backward. Her bizarre performance would be hot stuff for the special, thought Antony.

"I haunted them. I haunted their house, and I followed them everywhere. Yes, I was set free to go to hell. But I had my revenge?"

"What revenge?"

"I was set free," the voice repeated, and then her words were garbled.

Even Antony, normally blasé and unflappable, was shaken by how strange Lavinia looked—almost as if she were mad. But he didn't know whether she was faking this or not.

For all he knew, Lady Chamberlain might have been putting on a good act, although she obviously believed it herself. She might not realize she was a quack. This was one of the issues to be discussed in his show. But he had not expected nor did he want his researcher to be so actively involved. She was clearly unstable.

"She was let go," the voice said in a Scots accent.

"I don't understand," Lavinia said. "Who was let go?"

The table shook violently and suddenly leaned heavily to one side. Lavinia began to weep.

"Mother, let's get her out of this trance," Paul said emphatically."

"No, son, let her go on."

"I agree," Marcus said.

"Is there anyone else there?" Lady Chamberlain said.

"I am here," a man's voice answered.

Antony stared incredulously at Lavinia. He had definitely heard a male voice coming out of her mouth. Unless it had been one of the men. He looked closely at Marcus, Paul and Dr. Hare. Could one of them be a ventriloquist? He was sure this was some sort of trick, although he could see with his own eyes that Lavinia's lips were moving.

For the first time he felt that something real was happening, something out of the ordinary.

"Christian?" Lavinia said faintly.

Antony stared at her with fascination, forgetting temporarily that they were shooting a film sequence for a television special. She couldn't be faking the emotion that showed on her face.

"I want to help you," Lavinia said. Antony could not tell whether the moans that filled the room came from Lavinia or from the man whose voice had come from her mouth.

"You will free me by learning what really happened," Christian said. "And when you know, and I have the permission to return to the world of the dead, then Sara's spirit will live on in you."

"Christian, why didn't you tell me before?" Lavinia pleaded. "I could have saved you much suffering."

"I did not understand before," Christian said, "but now I do. And now I know why we are linked. You are the only one who can set me free once you know exactly what happened. Forgive me, Lavinia, for once I sinned against you."

"This is very private. We should stop her," Paul said.

"Private?" Antony all but shouted. "*Private?*" He was not about to let this idiot interfere with such great footage.

Paul put his arms around Lavinia, as if to protect her from Antony.

"Hey, what are you doing? You're ruining this footage. If you are not going to be helpful, clear out." Antony lunged at Paul and grabbed him by the neck.

"This is nuts," Jack yelled and stopped the camera. He ran over to the table and separated the two men, who were grappling like schoolboys.

"Stop! Stop!" Lady Chamberlain shouted, pulling at Antony's jacket.

Antony let go of Paul and looked around, as shocked as everyone else by his attack on Paul. Suddenly, without any warning, Jack's camera burst into flames. Smoke spread through the room, and then with a loud bang the camera exploded.

Lavinia awoke from her trance and shook her head, dazed by all the smoke and confusion. Jack and Antony ripped off their jackets and threw them over the camera to smother the flames.

"My goodness!" Lady Chamberlain exclaimed. "This *is* more than the usual excitement." She jumped up and pushed open some windows to clear the smoke from the air.

"I'm sorry," Antony said, having extinguished the fire. "This sort of thing has never happened to me before. What do you think did it, Jack?"

Jack stared at his melted camera in disbelief. "I haven't a clue," he said.

"Well, I apologize for attacking you, Paul. I don't know what got into me. I'm not the sort to resort to physical violence."

"The film's ruined," said Jack, still not able to take his eyes off the wreckage.

Paul touched Lavinia's cheek.

"Are you all right? Do you remember what happened?"

"I'm all right," she said, wondering what Antony thought about her now. "I remember what Christian said, yes."

"I'm glad it's over," Paul said.

"No, Paul, it's not over. I still don't know what happened to Christian."

"Who the hell is this Christian?" Antony shouted.

Paul ignored him. "I mean this seance, this television thing," he said. "I'm glad it's over. There's not another camera, thank God."

274

"Oh, but there is," Roscoe said, stepping forward with the Port-a-pak camera.

"What?" Paul frowned.

"I was really scared there, but after I calmed down I grabbed this camera and snuck back into the room. I started shooting and I think I got some pretty good footage."

Roscoe beamed. So did Antony. The day had not been a total waste. If what Roscoe had shot was halfway decent Antony could probably use it, or some of it, anyway. Maybe that's all he would need.

"Well, let's wrap it up, folks," he said.

He went over to Lavinia, who looked pale and wobbly. "I think you'd better rest for a couple of days, kid. I'll be in touch, okay?"

Lavinia nodded, not trusting herself to speak.

"Thank you," he said, shaking her hand. "I think your appearance on camera added a fantastic dimension. Maybe you should be an actress."

Lavinia wanted to lie down. Antony was right. She needed a rest. She attempted a wan smile but instead tears came to her eyes. Antony patted her on the shoulder.

Paul glowered. He wanted to punch this bloody Yank.

"There was a moment there when I began to believe it myself," said Antony.

Noticing her son's shimmering rage, Lady Chamberlain clapped her hands to get everyone's attention.

"Some brandy?" she asked brightly, trying to break the tension.

"Thanks, Lady Chamberlain, but we have to collect our equipment and get the van back to London so we don't get charged for another day," said Antony. "Has anybody seen Marion? I take it she's recovered by now."

It took the crew about half an hour to clean up and get the gear stowed in the van.

"Thanks again," Antony told Lady Chamberlain. "If there's any damage or breakage that we didn't notice, here's my number in London." He turned to Paul and Lavinia. "Ready?"

"Thanks just the same," Paul said, "but we've decided to stay on a while. We'll get back by ourselves."

"Okay, let's go," said Antony and gave them all a farewell salute.

Lavinia leaned against Paul's shoulder, grateful not to have to drive back with Antony. She wasn't ready to face him alone yet.

"My dear," Lady Chamberlain said, "I think you may have missed the last train. But you're welcome to stay for dinner and the night. I've already invited Dr. Hare."

"I'd offer you a lift, but I'm having dinner with some friends who live nearby," said Marcus.

"Not to worry. I've already rung for a taxi," Paul said.

"All the way to London?" asked Lavinia, her voice still tremulous. "Won't that cost a fortune?"

"For you, Lavinia, I would spend my last shilling," Paul declared, bowing low at the waist and gesturing grandly with his right arm.

Lavinia rewarded him with a bright smile.

"In that case, I'll treat you to dinner. It's the very least I can do."

Lady Chamberlain beamed but held her tongue. Marcus stared pointedly at Lavinia's hand-me-down black patent leather shoes.

"When you wear the shoes..." he murmured, but the rest of the words were drowned out by the taxi honking out front.

Lavinia fell asleep quickly that night, but she tossed and turned and woke up several times. At about five in the morning, she went downstairs and made herself some hot chocolate, hoping it would calm her nerves. It didn't. She wandered from room to room in the apartment, waiting for something to happen.

Glancing in the bedroom mirror, she decided that she was more and more resembling Sara. Although when she touched her head her hair was the same short, curly style that she had worn all summer, in the mirrored reflection her hair appeared to fall almost to her shoulders. Like Sara's.

Sara's long, blond hair was combed into a neat chignon. Around her neck she wore a strand of brilliantly shining circle-shaped diamonds. And through her pierced earlobes were looped dangling strands of heart-shaped diamonds. The set had belonged to Christian's mother, and he had presented them to Sara on May 1, her birthday.

She had thought the diamonds were excessive, too much a symbol of the aristocratic life with which she still felt uncomfortable. She did not wish to wear the jewels, although she recognized their beauty. But Christian pressed her. To him they symbolized not wealth and prestige but his love for her.

It was June. Sara and Christian had met exactly a year ago. The evening was balmy and smelled of flowers as Sara prepared for a celebration of their first meeting. She wore the diamonds to set off her ice-blue silk evening gown, which she had had made in Venice. The sparkling diamonds perfectly complemented the understated elegance of the gown.

She carefully scrutinized herself in the mirror, wishing to look her best for Christian. Something moved behind her. Turning to get a closer look, she was shocked to be standing face to face with what appeared to be the ghost of Katherine Campbell, shrouded in a long, white cape.

"Katherine!" she gasped. The face above the collar of the cape was wild, the eyes black, the hair uncombed and tangled. Her expression was one of frenzied hatred.

"I am Katherine Campbell," she said. And then she disappeared, leaving Sara to wonder whether she had imagined the vision. A moment later the ghost reappeared.

"But you are dead," whispered Sara. Why had Katherine come back to this house?

"I am dead, but I have been waiting to reappear at the right moment. I was in Italy. I am here now. I am wherever Christian is."

"What do you want?" Sara asked, her heart constricting with fear.

"To tell the truth."

"What truth?" Sara looked toward the door of her bedroom, praying that Christian would suddenly appear. But he was out of the house on business and would not be home for at least another hour. She felt so vulnerable here alone. Dreadful memories, which she had kept buried for months, now assailed her. She felt as if she were about to descend into a pit from which she would never escape. She must not fall under Katherine's spell again. She had come so close the last time to denying her religion, her faith, her belief in God.

"Christian is evil," said Katherine. "He is an incubus. Your child is the devil."

"Leave us alone," Sara cried. "You are lying. *You* are the devil."

"He is a man of the devil," Katherine continued, taking no notice of Sara's words. "He is a liar and a thief. He stole my life. First he made love to me—and then he killed me."

"Made love to you?" Sara said faintly.

"He seduced me the day I died," Katherine said, her voice fading slightly.

Sara's heart beat quickly. She could not bear to hear what Katherine was saying, yet she felt impelled to listen.

"You died in a traffic accident," Sara protested weakly. Katherine's image was becoming more distinct. The cape disappeared and Sara could see her as clearly as if she were still alive. Katherine wore the same clothes as the last time Sara had seen her. Her long legs showed through the thin material of her skirt, and a thin blouse barely covered the upper part of her body.

"I died right here, in the kitchen. I was raped and stabbed. But I am a witch and cannot die by the knife." She looked like a mad woman, her eyes red and gleaming, her skin alabaster white.

"On the day this house burned to the ground he made love to me in this bedroom. In his bed, Sara. Your bed. Afterward I slept, and when I woke he was gone. I looked for him in all the rooms. He was waiting for me in the kitchen."

Sara felt she might faint, but she forced herself to hear what Katherine had to say.

"He forced me to lie on the floor. Then he stabbed me many times so that I bled profusely, but I used my powers to stop the bleeding."

"I don't believe you," Sara said, tears in her eyes. She wanted to rush out of the room, away from Katherine. But Katherine would be in the present anywhere she went.

"Why did you wait so long to come to me?" Sara asked, fighting her panic. Katherine had been at the window of the haunted house in Venice. Both she and Christian had seen her. That must have been a warning.

"I waited for the right moment, until you returned from Venice with your devil child. And now Christian is not well."

"What do you mean?" Sara cried. If this were so, why had he kept it secret from her?

"He is at the doctor this minute," Katherine said.

"I don't believe you," Sara shouted. "We tell each other everything. We love each other." She was about to declare that they had no secrets from each other, but the words froze on her lips.

"You have no secrets, then? You are a liar. But I am telling the truth. Because he could not kill me with a knife he set this house on fire. A witch can only die by burning."

"Rob set this house on fire," Sara cried hysterically. "He paid the price, too."

Katherine abruptly disappeared. Sara was alone. A strange smell, which she remembered from the past, lingered in the room. It was the smell of Katherine's oil, the oil she used to rub on her naked body.

Sara ran to the window and flung it wide open, breathing in the early evening June air.

"Christian is good," she said aloud, trying in vain to make sense of what Katherine had told her. It couldn't be true. . . . But as she went to the nursery to kiss Emily good-night, a remnant of doubt remained in her mind. Why was Katherine here, in their house, if what she said was false?

Emily was smiling and gurgling at Teresa when Sara entered the nursery. She waved her plump little hands and laughed with pleasure when Sara tickled her. Sara picked up her daughter and held her close, cuddling and kissing her. As Emily grew tired, Sara changed her into her lace nightdress, tucked her into her crib and gave her one last kiss before going downstairs to the library to wait for Christian.

Should she confront Christian with Katherine's accusations? she wondered. And was he really ill? She felt almost sick herself with worry. Katherine's every word and movement threatened revenge. If she truly believed that Christian had done what she claimed, she would no doubt return to hurt him. Sara must protect him. But how?

At last Christian returned home. She was tempted to tell him immediately of Katherine's visit but could not yet bring herself to say the words. She would wait until later, when they were together in bed.

"Shall we go, my dear?" he said, offering her his arm and looking very fit and handsome in his evening clothes.

She smiled as she accepted his compliments.

"Thank you, Sara, for wearing the diamonds. No other woman could ever wear them so beautifully," he told her.

Their carriage was waiting to take them to Christian's private club for dinner. Nestled close to him in the back seat, Sara was glad she had decided to postpone speaking to him of Katherine. If Katherine had in fact told the truth, the very foundation of her relationship with Christian would be shaken. She would never stop loving him, but her trust in him would be shattered. She wanted one more wonderful evening with him before discovering whether he had committed any of the crimes Katherine had enumerated.

Christian seemed not to notice her distracted mood during dinner. He laughed and teased her as he always did and insisted that she describe to him everything she had done since he had left her after lunch.

"And tell me exactly what Emily did when you put her to bed," he said.

His eyes shone with love as she described Emily's tiny fists wiggling in the air. Surely this was not a man who could have committed rape or murder. Surely Katherine had lied.

Later, after they had given the sleeping Emily a good-night kiss, they made love in their large double bed. Afterward, lying in Christian's arms, Sara wondered whether Katherine would appear before the two of them to rant and rave. She knew that she had to tell Christian about Katherine's intrusive visit.

She felt him stiffen as she described exactly what had happened. His face paled and he stared at her sorrowfully.

Finally he spoke. "Yes, I was at the doctor today, but she is lying about her murder. . . ." He began to weep so that Sara's cheeks were soon wet with his tears.

"I wanted to tell you for such a long time, but I did not want to hurt you. I hoped you would understand, but perhaps I did not give you enough credit for your ability to forgive me. I love you so much, my darling," he said. "I wanted nothing to come between us. Then Emily was born, and life was so wonderful. I did not want to ruin your happiness or mine. And I thought my terrible secret had died with Katherine Campbell."

"She says you are evil, Christian, that you are an incubus and Emily is the devil's child," whispered Sara.

Christian wiped away his tears. "I am neither evil nor a devil. But I did something terribly wrong."

"Tell me," implored Sara, her arms around him. "I love you, Christian. And the force of our love will get rid of her."

"I had sexual relations with her," Christian admitted, hardly able to look directly at Sara. "It was the day of the fire, when you were so ill. Sara, will you ever be able to forgive me?"

"Christian, it is far worse than a matter of my forgiveness. I feel sure she means to harm us, especially you, because she was murdered. Christian, you must tell me the truth. Did you kill her?"

"I could never kill another human being. You must believe me or my life is meaningless."

"I believe you."

"Can you forgive me for having her?"

"But why does she say you murdered her?" Sara asked, not yet ready to face his betrayal of her.

"After we made love, I went out, just as she said. I hated myself for what I had done, for having succumbed to temptation and betraying my love for you. I had to be away from her, from my shame. When I returned, the house was blazing, already half destroyed. I didn't go into the house. I couldn't get anywhere near it. I never saw her again. Later, after the ashes had cooled, her body was found in the kitchen. She had been stabbed. We deduced that Rob had murdered her before he set the house on fire.

"How awful."

"Please say you forgive me," begged Christian.

"I love you, Christian," she said gently, "and I do want to forgive you, but I cannot immediately forget."

She blew out the candle that had been burning by their bed.

"We must sleep now. Tomorrow is another day and we can talk more then. We must find a way to free ourselves of her."

Christian had an appointment early the next morning with his solicitor to discuss business matters. After he left, promising to return as soon as possible so that they could talk further about Katherine, Sara went to her desk in her sitting room to answer some correspondence. Just as she was sealing her letter, Katherine appeared.

Sara stood up, determined to challenge her words.

"What do you want?" she demanded.

"I want your husband," said Katherine, and vanished.

Lavinia was seated at her desk on the landing without any recollection of having left the bedroom. She looked toward the foot of the stairs, half expecting Christian to appear. Instead the telephone rang, and she ran downstairs to the kitchen to answer it.

"Hello, Lavinia," said Antony. "Feeling better today?"

"Yes, thanks, much."

"Good." He got down to business. "We looked at the film Roscoe got in the Port-a-pak and some of it is very good. I'd like you to come over to the hotel. There's something we have to talk about. How soon can you get here?"

"In about half an hour," Lavinia said, wondering what Antony had in mind.

"Great," he said. "See you soon."

Lavinia stuffed her tape recorder and notebooks into her canvas bag, quickly combed her hair and hurried out of the building to hail a taxi.

She worried all the way to Antony's hotel, convinced that he was about to fire her. So much for my chance to be an executive producer, she thought grimly. After this, I'll have trouble finding work as a researcher. By the time she knocked on his door she was almost sick with anxiety.

But Antony greeted her cordially and offered her coffee and croissants. After a few minutes of small talk and gossip about people they knew in the industry, Antony cleared his throat.

Here it comes, Lavinia thought.

"I'm really sorry about this, kid, but I don't think you should be working on the show anymore." He handed her an envelope.

"What's this?" she said, determined not to cry in front of him.

"I don't know," he said uncomfortably. "Call it a bonus for good work or severance pay or whatever you like."

Lavinia tore open the envelope. Inside was a check for a thousand dollars.

"You think I'm crazy, don't you?"

"I'll give you a good reference, I promise. And I told the others that I want them to keep their mouths shut about what happened."

"Why did you bother, Antony? You have it all on film. Half of America will soon see me communicating with the spirit world. What's the big deal? You said you liked my work."

"No big deal, Lavinia, really. But you're too involved. I can't have you talking to ghosts everywhere we go. You'll never get your work done." He laughed, hoping she would join in.

"I may be too involved, but you better think about being more tolerant or you're going to have a hard time putting together a program." Lavinia was surprised by her nerve. She usually kept her mouth shut instead of defending herself.

"Give me a break, Lavinia. Figure it this way. You just got a paid vacation."

She didn't bother replying except to say, "Goodbye, Antony," before she slammed the door behind her. And then the tears came. She sobbed in the taxi all the way back to Belgrave Road, sniffling so audibly that the driver finally turned around and offered her a tissue. She had lost her job, lost her shot at climbing the television ladder. Despite Antony's promises, she knew how quickly word would get around about the seance. She would be branded a weirdo, at the very least. Would Antony really give her a good recommendation? And would it help or would she be blacklisted?

She walked into the apartment and thought about calling Paul to tell him what happened. She could use some sympathetic words. But she knew what he would say: "How dreadful, Lavinia, but now you can come traveling with me."

And still there was Christian. Perhaps if she left, went off with Paul or returned to New York, she would be free of him. She remembered his words—that to redeem him, she must know the truth. But why?

The question nagged at her as she sat on the terrace, drinking tea. The neighbor's dog barked, as always, but Lavinia didn't hear him, she was so absorbed in puzzling over Christian's quandary. Better to think about his past than my dubious future, she decided, wondering whether she should call British Airways to ask about flights. And then it hit her. Perhaps Sara had never known the truth about the circumstances of Christian's death. If, somehow, she were to find out what happened, Christian would be set free. And since she had lived a previous existence as Sara, she had to be the one to find out how he died.

She had no choice but to stay, she realized. And having made that decision, she suddenly felt very free and unencumbered to pursue Christian's story to the end. She felt sleepy and decided to lay down on Mary's bed. The moment she closed her eyes, she saw Sara outside the house on Belgrave Road. She was pushing Emily in her pram. Then she saw Emily asleep in her crib, and Teresa and Sara were walking down an unfamiliar street. They stopped in front of what appeared to be a Catholic church and went inside.

The image of the church faded and was replaced by Katherine Campbell in Christian's library, her eyes like those of a wild, tortured animal, starting at him with such hatred that Lavinia felt she must cry out and warn him. But she kept silent and watched as Katherine seemed to float around him. Pointing an accusing finger at him, she rose into the air so that she dwarfed him.

"Bleed," she said in a strange, hoarse voice. "Bleed," she rasped.

"You are Satan!" cried Christian, striking out at her. But his hand passed right through her body.

Blood began to seep from his nose, his mouth and ears. Then it was flowing more quickly, gushing from his body like a volcanic eruption. He collapsed on the floor, fainting, dying, drowning in his own blood. At the moment of his death, Katherine Campbell's ghost disappeared. The room was utterly dark and still.

Some hours later, Sara and Teresa returned home with the priest who had heard Sara's story and had agreed to help exorcise Katherine.

"Christian," she called. There was no answer. A horrifying premonition seized her. She ran into the library, urging Theresa and the priest to hurry.

By the light from the hallway she could see something in a heap on the floor. "My God," she gasped. And then the room was lit and her terror was realized.

She knelt on the floor next to Christian's body and cradled him in her arms, her tears washing the blood from his face. "My beloved," she murmured. "My precious Christian. I forgive you. I will love you forever."

Time passed. Lavinia saw Sara lay a wreath on a tombstone in the middle of a peaceful, shaded cemetery. And then Sara was standing on the balcony of the palace on the Grand Canal. Emily and Teresa were by her side. And in her hands Sara held a bouquet of summer flowers as she smiled in the softly glowing Venetian morning light.

The front doorbell rang. Lavinia slowly emerged from the trance, feeling dizzy and disoriented. She ached for Sara's loss but finally, now, Sara knew the truth. She had forgiven Christian, thus freeing him. The two of them could be reunited.

She opened the door. "It's over, Paul," she said excitedly. "Christian wasn't shot. Katherine Campbell murdered him. The reference books have it all wrong."

Paul took her hand and led her into the living room, sitting her down next to him on the couch. "Now Christian's spirit can join Sara's, is that right?" he asked.

"Yes, exactly. He and Sara and Emily are together."

She closed her eyes, then opened them a moment later.

"He's gone. I can feel it."

She seemed almost to be glowing with happiness.

Paul leaned over and kissed her, then put his arm around her shoulders and pulled her close to him. She responded, passionately returning his kiss.

After several minutes, they drew apart and held hands, each waiting for the other to speak.

Lavinia finally broke the silence.

"Antony fired me, Paul. He said I'd gotten too emotionally involved with the project."

"That's awful, Lavinia," he said, kissing her again. "Now you can come traveling with me."

Lavinia smiled. "How did I know you'd say that?"

Paul's eyes twinkled mischievously.

"You're a psychic, aren't you?" he said.